D1562628

THE NIGHT IN QUESTION

THE NIGHT IN QUESTION

AN AGATHAS MYSTERY

KATHLEEN GLASGOW
& LIZ LAWSON

DELACORTE PRESS

This is a work of fiction. Names, characters, places, and incidents either are the product of the authors' imagination or are used fictitiously. Any resemblance to actual persons, living or dead, events, or locales is entirely coincidental.

Text copyright © 2023 by Kathleen Glasgow and Elizabeth Lawson
Jacket art copyright © 2023 by Spiros Halaris; balcony and girl images used under license from Shutterstock.com
Map art copyright © 2022 by Mike Hall

All rights reserved. Published in the United States by Delacorte Press,
an imprint of Random House Children's Books, a division of Penguin Random House LLC, New York.

Delacorte Press is a registered trademark and the colophon
is a trademark of Penguin Random House LLC.

Visit us on the Web! GetUnderlined.com

Educators and librarians, for a variety of teaching tools,
visit us at RHTeachersLibrarians.com

Library of Congress Cataloging-in-Publication Data
Names: Glasgow, Kathleen, author. | Lawson, Liz, author.
Title: The night in question : an Agathas mystery / Kathleen Glasgow & Liz Lawson.
Description: First edition. | New York : Delacorte Press, [2023] | Audience: Ages 14+. |
Summary: When Iris and Alice's high school dance at the infamous Levy Castle, the site of starlet Mona Moody's unsolved death in the 1940s, is interrupted by a violent assault, they pull out their murder boards and get back to work.
Identifiers: LCCN 2022050998 (print) | LCCN 2022050999 (ebook) | ISBN 978-0-593-64583-3 (hardcover) | ISBN 978-0-593-64585-7 (ebook) | ISBN 978-0-593-70536-0 (int'l ed.)
Subjects: CYAC: High schools—Fiction. | Schools—Fiction. | Dance—Fiction. |
Mystery and detective stories. | LCGFT: Detective and mystery fiction. | Novels.
Classification: LCC PZ7.1.G587 Ni 2023 (print) | LCC PZ7.1.G587 (ebook) | DDC [Fic]—dc23

The text of this book is set in 12-point Spectrum MT.
Interior design by Ken Crossland

Printed in the United States of America
10 9 8 7 6 5 4 3 2 1
First Edition

Random House Children's Books supports the First Amendment and celebrates the right to read.

Penguin Random House LLC supports copyright. Copyright fuels creativity, encourages diverse voices, promotes free speech, and creates a vibrant culture. Thank you for buying an authorized edition of this book and for complying with copyright laws by not reproducing, scanning, or distributing any part in any form without permission. You are supporting writers and allowing Penguin Random House to publish books for every reader.

To all besties, everywhere:
never stop searching for the truth

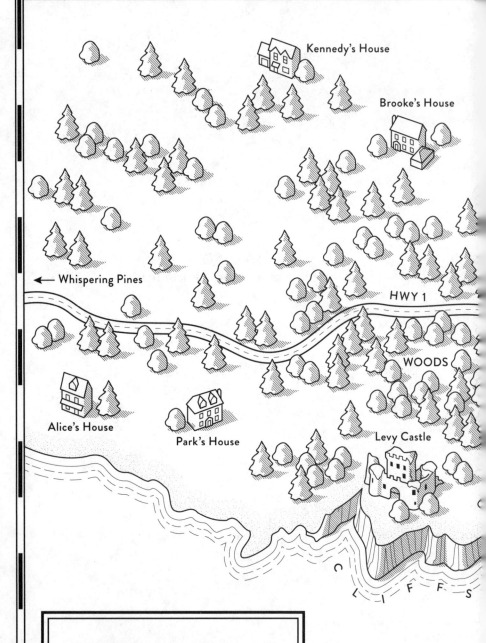

Kennedy's House

Brooke's House

← Whispering Pines

HWY 1

WOODS

Alice's House

Park's House

Levy Castle

C L I F F S

CASTLE COVE

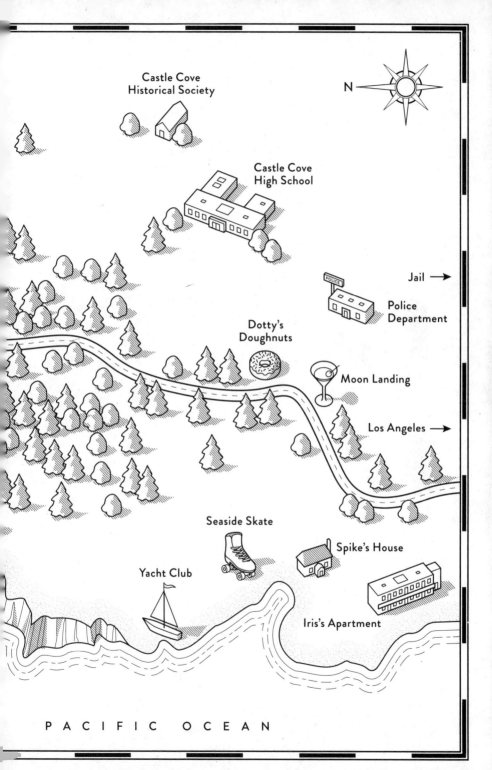

THE NIGHT IN QUESTION

CHAPTER ONE

ALICE OGILVIE
FEBRUARY 11
9:02 P.M.

"I'm not often bored," I assured her.
"Life's not long enough for that."
—AGATHA CHRISTIE,
MURDER IN MESOPOTAMIA

BROOKE DONOVAN IS STARING at me from across the room.

She's wearing the dress we picked out in LA freshman year, when her mom drove us down there to go shopping for prom. The two of us were the only freshmen invited that year, much to the chagrin of our mutual friend, Rebecca Kennedy.

She looks good, Brooke, fresh and happy, smiling and carefree.

I crumple a cocktail napkin into a tight little ball in my hand. Whoever decided to hang a giant portrait of her in here should be stabbed.

Tearing my eyes away from Brooke's picture, I survey the ballroom. It's filled with my classmates from Castle Cove High School, all in various stages of celebration, all here for the annual Sadie Hawkins dance. To my left, a group of guys from the basketball team huddle together in a circle, not-so-slyly passing a

1

silver flask between them. To my right, couples are dry humping on the dance floor.

I frown.

We're at Levy Castle, for god's sake. Some respect should be shown to its past. The site of elegant balls for almost a hundred years, a place where Old Hollywood used to come and play. Charles W. Levy would be rolling over in his grave if he knew what this room is being used for now.

As Brooke's best friend, I grew up listening to all sorts of tales about Brooke's great-grandfather. He spent millions of dollars building Levy Castle. It's five stories and sixty thousand square feet of opulence. And with eighteen bedrooms, three pools, two kitchens, and secret passages extending throughout, it basically put the tiny town of Castle Cove on the map. It was also where the film star Mona Moody lived for a few short years, until her untimely death on Castle grounds at the age of twenty.

Mona Moody, with her platinum blond hair, baby-blue eyes, and the husky, sexy voice that made her famous. After several years starring in popcorn flicks, she was all set to break out in her first serious film as the titular role in *Jane Eyre,* but tragically fell off the Castle's side balcony just before filming started.

According to the internet, she and Charles Levy had a brief but super intense love affair, and he was so broken up by her death that eventually his own life collapsed around him: he lost everything he'd worked so hard for over the years when he was arrested for embezzlement and spent the rest of his days in prison.

Ever since I was little, I've been fascinated by Mona Moody's life and death, and tonight is my chance to sneak upstairs to see her private quarters.

I turn to try to find Iris, when raised voices pull my attention to the massive DJ booth Rebecca Kennedy's dad had built for the dance. According to Kennedy, it's the only way DJ Porcini would agree to play tonight.

I pop up on my toes for a better look, and I'm entirely unsurprised to spot the very same Kennedy arguing with my other former friend Helen Park. They're both wearing this season's Natasha Matte off-the-shoulder satin gown in blue, the only difference being the obnoxiously expensive necklace around Kennedy's neck.

I let out a sigh. This won't end well. Ever since Brooke died last fall, the two of them can't seem to hold it together to save their lives. Clearly, they forgot to consult with each other about what they were going to wear tonight. Which is, like, Dance Etiquette 101.

Through the crowd, I spot Ashley Henderson. She's watching them, probably trying to figure out a way to interject herself into the drama. She thrives on this stuff; says it's good for her craft, since she desperately wants to be an actress. Mostly, though, I think she's just nosy. I never really meshed with Henderson, so it's a relief not to have to pretend to be friends with her anymore. Which goes for all of my former friends, if I'm being perfectly honest.

"What's going on up there?" Iris says, sidling up to me. "Want one?" She holds out a plastic cup of sparkling apple cider and I take it, noticing Spike at her back.

Iris is wearing a 1950s vintage prom dress, a black blazer, and Chuck Taylors. I adore the dress, but the blazer and shoes . . . they're cool and all, but not exactly right for a formal dance. I inhale a calming breath, reminding myself I'm not that person anymore. The one who judges everyone by the labels on their clothing. I've *evolved.*

"Park and Kennedy are at it again," I say, taking a tiny sip from my cup.

Cole Fielding materializes in front of me. "What's going on up there?" he asks, echoing Iris. From somewhere outside the Castle, there's a loud crack of thunder.

Spike immediately glances at Iris, who's whispering into Cole's ear. Spike's face falls.

"Park and Kennedy," I repeat loudly. "They are arguing, yet again."

"Brooke's murd . . . er . . ." Spike's eyes dart to my face as he realizes what he's saying. "Without Brooke around, they've really fallen apart, huh?" he finishes.

I shrug. Kennedy tried to pull me back into their little circle after Iris and I figured out who was responsible for Brooke's death, but I wasn't interested. I have no desire to be involved in mundane high school drama, and I have Iris. That's enough. For now, at least.

"Do you think they're fighting over—" Spike starts, but a familiar voice interrupts him and my stomach, my most traitorous of organs, does a little dance.

"Blini with caviar?"

I turn.

"Hello, Raf."

"Hello, Alice." He smiles.

"Hey, Raf," Iris says, taking one of the blinis off the tray and examining it. "Um, what the hell is this thing?"

He shrugs. "Hell if I know. I just bring out what they tell me; I don't ask questions." He squints down at his tray. "I think it's like . . . weird little eggs or something?"

I sigh. "It's basically a pancake with caviar." I take one and pop it in my mouth. "They're delicious."

Iris nibbles off a corner. "Oh, that *is* good," she says, and nudges Cole. "Grab one." Cole does as instructed, and as soon as Iris turns away, he wraps it in his cocktail napkin and stuffs it into his back pocket.

"How's work going?" Iris asks Raf. Since Raf helped Iris and me out with Brooke's case last year, we've all become . . . well, I guess the best word for it is *friends.* It's odd: I've never been friends with a boy before, not really, so I'm not sure what to do about it or how to act with him, although Iris doesn't seem to have that same issue. They chat all the time, or at least that's what it seems like to me. Not that I care.

What I do care about, maybe a little more than I should, is that he has a *girlfriend* now, who just so happens to be Cole's older sister. She works for Splendid Spread Catering part-time, and (according to Iris's intel) got Raf this gig so he could make some extra cash for college since the Castle Cove Police Department barely pays their interns.

He smirks. "Fine. I'm pretty much invisible to most of the kids here. Which works for me. Really don't need to get recognized from my high school days, you know?"

"Okay, break it up," someone—a teacher?—yells over by Porcini's booth. I sigh again. I suppose I should go help calm those two down. It's what Brooke would have wanted, after all.

"Be right back," I say, and push past Reed Gerber and Mason Jefferson to make my way through the crowd.

When I reach the front of the throng I end up next to Henderson and my ex-boyfriend, Steve Anderson, who are watching the scene. Henderson's mouth is curled up into a grin, but when she spots me, she quickly rearranges it into a frown. She's so transparent it's laughable.

Steve, on the other hand, looks petrified. "Alice," he says when he notices me. "You've gotta do something. They're at it again."

I haven't seen him in two months. After Iris and I figured out who'd really killed Brooke and got him out of jail, all the media attention went to his head, and he dropped out of school and moved down to LA to try to make it in the entertainment industry. He's only back tonight to catch up with some of his old friends. I bet he's regretting it now.

"Fine," I say, irritated that it's the first thing he's said to me all night. I step forward at the same moment Park leaps at Kennedy. She grabs a clump of Kennedy's hair and yanks her head back, hard.

"Ow!" Kennedy screeches, trying to twist out of Park's grasp. "Get off me, you brat."

Ms. Hollister, one of the teachers chaperoning the dance, hovers on the other side of Park and Kennedy wearing a horrified expression. Ever since the stuff came out about Coach and all his lady friends, Hollister and a few other teachers have been going above and beyond the call of duty, kissing Principal Brown's ass.

A hand clutches my arm. Iris.

"I'll help you, Alice."

I look over at Park and Kennedy, now wrestling on the floor. "I'd like that very much."

And together, we make our way toward my ex-friends—the Mains.

CHAPTER TWO

IRIS ADAMS
FEBRUARY 11
9:14 P.M.

All a girl wants is to put on a pretty dress and dance
for a few hours. Is that too much to ask?
—MONA MOODY, *MATCHED SET*, 1947

ALICE AND I MANAGE to extricate Park and Kennedy, though not without difficulty. Park is quite flexible and keeps slipping from my grasp, though I'm finally able to subdue her by wrapping her in a bear hug just as Alice is able to yank Kennedy backward.

The instant the fight stops, a disappointed "Aww, no, they were gonna kiss!" rises up from the crowd. Of course, it's from the boys because it's typical (and boring) that when girls fight, all guys can do is stand there hoping at any moment it's going to turn *sexy.*

Alice smooths her hair and glares at Park and Kennedy. Kennedy is inspecting her nails.

"Jesus, Park, I spent fifteen hundred dollars on this," Kennedy pouts. "What's your problem, anyway?"

Park is huffing, trying to scoop her disheveled hair out of her face and straighten the neckline of her dress. She's wearing a lacy pink strapless bra with tiny embroidered hearts, which I find oddly endearing.

"I specifically told you I was going to wear this dress! I sent you pics! And you *copied* me, anyway! God, sometimes I wish you'd just shrivel up and die," Park says.

Kennedy rolls her eyes and plays to the crowd. Phones are back up and filming. She'll be on a hundred stories in about three minutes. This is her moment. "Sounds like a *you* issue to me, babe. Jealous much?"

Park lunges at Kennedy again, almost catching Kennedy's necklace in her fingers. It's an extremely expensive-looking thing with teardrop-shaped jewels. But Kennedy cackles and ducks away. Then Park storms off.

Alice shakes her head and looks at me, her eyes drifting from my seafoam-green gown down to my sneakers.

"Gorgeous girl, gorgeous gown, and yet . . . a blazer and sneakers," she says, sighing.

I finger the lapels of the black velvet blazer. I just like to feel protected. And I was already nervous about other things concerning this dance, like Cole Fielding. I'd casually asked him if he was going to the Sadie Hawkins dance, definitely stressing the fact that it was a *group* thing. Ever since Brooke, and the investigation, and, you know, me accidentally accusing him of murder, we've been hanging out. Very *casually*. Roller-skating once or twice during his breaks at Seaside Skate. Maybe a coffee together at Dotty's Doughnuts. Texting sometimes. None of which I've told Alice about, because her feelings toward Cole are well-known. She sees me sometimes chatting with him at school and that's enough to get me some pointed looks. My mom doesn't know anything but the barest details, either, because she'd flip out, especially if she knew about me riding on the back of his motorcycle along Highway 1. I don't know how to explain to anyone, even Alice, what's happening inside me. Like something's been knocked loose. I can't stop thinking of Brooke's body at the bottom of the cliff. I can still feel my father's fist on my face. The whole time on the back of Cole's motorcycle, I felt . . . free. Like nothing could touch me.

Brooke is dead, but she's still here. The Thing is locked up, but for how long?

The only other place where I feel like nothing can touch me is when I'm reading one of the many Agatha Christie novels I've borrowed from Alice, in a vain attempt to catch up with her knowledge of the Queen of Mystery, losing myself in the spirals of deceit and deception. Or when Raf and I are talking about the Remy Jackson case, painstakingly reading the poorly put together case files about his cousin, who was found in a dumpster in downtown Castle Cove, wrapped in a trash bag secured with duct tape. I'd like to see how Miss Marple would tackle *that*.

Alice isn't happy about me hanging out with Raf, either. I can't tell if she's jealous or just . . . doesn't want to get that close to a death case again, after Brooke. The Mona Moody thing she's skirting around . . . it's a mystery, for sure, but one that maybe Alice likes because it's so far in the past, it can't really touch her. Who knows? As long as I live, I'll probably never fully understand Alice Ogilvie.

She snaps her fingers at me. "Helloooo?"

"Sorry," I say. "Brain fog."

I take a deep breath to get my bearings, look around the mammoth Levy Castle ballroom.

9

I love this, actually. I didn't think I would. The dance. But everyone looks beautiful, even me and my ragtag friends the Zoners: Neil in his suit with the patched elbows, Zora in a shiny gold lamé tux. I feel like we look fancy, and grown-up, even Spike, gazing at the chandelier glistening above us, mesmerized by what seems like a thousand twinkling lights. Usually, we're on the edges of things at school, keeping to ourselves, but tonight, we're a part of the whole.

Spike seems different tonight, more mature somehow, dressed in his powder-blue suit with a paisley tie. His hair's grown out a bit. He's been checking in on me regularly since last fall, texting me at night to make sure I get some sleep, and not calling me out for lying when I answer "Yep."

I shake myself away from the tingling in my stomach. Spike? *Stop,* Iris. There are entirely too many hormonal things happening to me lately. I force myself to look anywhere but at Spike.

The inside of Levy Castle, with its golden walls and polished marble staircase, is like something from a dream. That chandelier above us? A placard on the wall says it weighs almost 1,700 pounds and has 9,500 crystals. Above the grand, Spanish-tiled staircase to the second floor, a glossy banner hangs: *The Films of Mona Moody: A Retrospective, March 29–30, 2023.* All around the downstairs, hung carefully on the walls for tourists, are movie stills from Mona Moody films and placards with tidbits of information about the Castle when it was built: six suits of armor from Spain; a private zoo on the grounds for Levy's daughter, Lilian, that included llamas and lemurs.

Shouts and laughter from the corner of the room distract me. The selfie booth has become a madhouse of photobombing, our classmates jumping in and out of each other's frames, displaying some choice hand gestures and what looks like a lot of booty patting.

Alice suddenly frowns, staring at something in the distance.

I follow her sight line.

I know we did the right thing. I know it's good that we found out who murdered Brooke Donovan, even though all hell broke loose.

But having Brooke stare down at us from the huge portrait in the middle of the room makes my heart sink.

"It's gauche," Alice says. "And it's creepy. I know the Castle can do what it wants, and they want to honor her with a permanent portrait. But it . . . feels weird."

It's been four months since Brooke died. Alice doesn't talk much about her, but I know she's hurting. I'm trying to let her have some space. Lately, she's been throwing herself into odd projects, like learning how to pick locks. While I think all that is valid and interesting, I'm a little worried she's not spending enough time on other things, like school. She hasn't even started the ancestry project in McAllister's class and it's due in two weeks.

"I might," she says now, very smoothly, "look around. Just while I'm here. Mona stuff, you know?"

In 1949, Mona Moody was found dead at the age of twenty on the lawn of Levy Castle. From my casual internet sleuthing, old articles say her death resulted from a prolonged bout with tuberculosis; weakened, she lost her balance, tumbling off the second-floor balcony. But if you spend some time digging, there are whispers that maybe it wasn't an accident. After all, she was young and beautiful, with creamy skin and a sparkling smile— a film star in the making. She was also Charles Levy's younger girlfriend, and people love to gossip. He was powerful and wealthy and, as my former babysitter Ricky Randall once told me, "The closets of the rich are positively ringing with skeleton bones." But she's a lawyer, and it's her job to consider all angles.

"Alice," I remind her. "This is supposed to be a dance. You know, something *fun.*"

She fixes her ice-blue eyes on me. "It will be fun. Plus, you'll be busy," she says, nudging me. "With *that.*"

I follow her eyes.

Cole Fielding is standing by the fountain (I still can't believe there is an actual fountain inside this mansion), hands in his pockets, looking at me.

"I don't approve," Alice murmurs. "But you know that."

From the corner of my eye, I see Spike. Our eyes meet. He smiles and flicks his hand toward the crowd of dancers. The song is a bop. Is he asking me to . . .

Just then, one of the Stitch Bitches, Tabitha Berrington, sidles up to him and slips her arm through his, tugging him toward the dance floor. He gives me a last glance as he disappears into the writhing bodies.

Why . . . does my stomach drop a little?

I look back at Cole. He tilts his head to the side, like *Let's get outta here,* and I can't help it. I just can't. My whole body lightens at the sight of his smile, his tousled hair.

But there is also the tiniest part of me that wants to do what Alice is doing, what I know she's about to do. Snoop around for Mona Moody stuff. I don't know what we'd find; there can't be much here, but . . . you never know.

"Alice," I say as she turns to walk away. "Wait—"

But she's already gone, disappeared somewhere into the vast gold beauty of the Castle.

CHAPTER THREE

ALICE
FEBRUARY 11
9:21 P.M.

When I want to get anywhere, I usually do.
—AGATHA CHRISTIE,
THE SECRET OF CHIMNEYS

ORNATELY FRAMED PAINTINGS OF half-naked women line the walls on either side of me as I make my way down a hallway toward the back rooms of the first floor. According to Castle lore, Charles W. Levy had them flown in from Italy. They should probably be in a museum, but, as I've learned, when people have more money than god, they tend to just think about themselves.

I keep walking, past the cavernous Dining Hall, where an intricate tapestry, handwoven by sixteenth-century Spanish monks, runs the length of two walls, then past the Dayspring Room, where Levy breakfasted every morning at seven a.m. without fail, no matter what sort of raucous party he'd thrown the night before. Next to it is the Billiards Room, which is spacious enough to hold three full-length pool tables.

I've been through most of these rooms before, with Brooke. Back in the mid-1950s, the Castle transitioned into the hands of the California government, but they allowed Brooke's grandmother, Lilian Levy, to retain some control. For reasons I don't quite understand, she was always very hands-off, but when Brooke and her mom, Victoria, moved to town, Victoria wanted to learn more about her family's history, so she joined the Castle's board of directors. She occasionally brought Brooke and me along when she had meetings, so we got to explore the first floor in private.

I round the corner and finally reach my destination. The South Library. Brooke and I used to play hide-and-seek in this room. There are tons of amazing hiding spots in here, behind heavy drapery, under old settees. Just like the other rooms in the Castle, this one is huge, with an arched ceiling and floor-to-ceiling bookcases that require ladders to get to the top shelves.

One day when we were playing, I couldn't find Brooke anywhere. Just as I was starting to worry, a tiny bubble of laughter burst out from one of the bookshelves.

While looking for a spot to hide, Brooke had discovered a secret room behind the bookcase, accessed by pulling a specific book down. Behind it was a narrow winding staircase. Naturally, we freaked out. What's cooler than a hidden passage? Pretty much nothing, if you ask me.

Before we could see where the staircase went, we were interrupted by Victoria, wearing a panicked expression on her face. She told us that the upper floors of the Castle were off-limits and under no circumstances were we allowed up there.

So, we never went. Brooke was far too much of a rule-follower and I could never persuade her. But she's not here to stop me anymore.

It's dark in the library. Outside, the sky is covered by thick clouds and rain pounds against the windowpanes, a real winter-time coastal California storm. I tap on my phone's flashlight and head over to the bookshelf that hides the secret passage Brooke found all those years ago.

This is so Agatha Christie: a secret passage, a hidden staircase, sneaking around in the dark with a storm raging outside. A shiver of pleasure runs through me.

At the bookshelf, I run my flashlight along the row of old books until I find it.

Agatha Christie's *The Secret of Chimneys.* A choice of literature I didn't understand when I was little, but now wholeheartedly approve of. Anyone who's read any Christie at all knows that in *Chimneys* there's an important clue hidden inside a secret passage.

I tug the book toward me and voilà: the corner of the bookcase cracks apart.

My heart leaps.

Oh my god. I did it. I have to tell Iris. She should be here with me.

I text her. *I opened the secret passage I told u about!! Come meet me.*

I wait several long seconds for her to respond, but there's nothing.

Rude. What, is she too busy with Cole?

Whatever. Her loss. I can do this myself.

I tuck my phone into the top of my dress and tug at the panel with both hands. After a moment, the gap widens just enough that I can fit through it and I slip into the dark beyond.

In front of me is a narrow staircase that winds up and up and up. I'm halfway to the top when a loud scuffling sound from below makes me freeze. I grab my phone and shine the light down toward it, but I can't see much of anything through the thick black.

I'd never admit it out loud, but this is actually a little creepier than I had anticipated. Maybe I should have made Iris come with me.

Speaking of . . . I check my phone, but she still hasn't responded.

I continue to the top of the staircase and stop. Instead of an exit, my light illuminates a wall. I should have known the secret passage wouldn't simply exit into another room; I should have thought of that before I started climbing. Still, this can't just be a staircase to nowhere. I pat around on the wall in front of me until my fingers land on a tiny round button.

I press it and wait for a door to open or a light to come on, but nothing happens. I poke at the thing harder, but still nothing. Finally, out of sheer frustration, I smash it with the palm of my hand, hard enough to leave a mark.

There's a loud groan as the wall in front of me splits in two, revealing a space too small for me to fit through.

I push at one side, trying with all my might to widen the gap. There's no way I'm going back down these stairs, especially given the noises below me, which sounded suspiciously ratlike. Finally, after several more strenuous pushes, I manage to slip through the opening.

I'm enveloped by the smell of cedar. The dim light of my phone catches glittering golds and reds and blues. It takes me a few moments before I realize I'm surrounded by ball gowns. I run a finger along the fabrics—satin and silk and crepe. So many dresses. I want to pull them off their hangers and try them on one by one—and why shouldn't I? They've clearly been hanging unused in this closet for decades, which is, in my opinion, literally a crime.

I shed my own dress and pull a floor-length, emerald-green velvet dress from its hanger, slipping it onto my body and zipping it up the back.

There.

Perfect.

Now I just need a mirror—and I bet there's one on the other side of the closet door.

CHAPTER FOUR

IRIS
FEBRUARY 1 1
9:26 P.M.

Good golly, boys are complicated.
You practically need an owner's manual!
—MONA MOODY, *DOUBLE TROUBLE*, 1946

IT'S EASY ENOUGH FOR me and Cole to saunter past Ms. Gilpin, the new guidance counselor. She's on door duty, and if you leave, you aren't supposed to be able to come back in. But this is a school of rich kids who could not care less about the nervous woman at the door whispering, "Rules, rules. You can't . . . no, stop."

Kids are loping in and out of the ornate double doors of the Castle. Their parents have helicopters and yachts and masseuses who *live in their homes.* Cole and I are dressed up as fancy as we can; how is she to know who we are or where we come from? She sags against the wall as we pass by.

I feel sorry for her, really. No one goes to see her. It must be hard to replace a murderer.

Outside, it's raining, not as hard as before, the grass slippery under our feet. Cole loops his arm in mine. It feels old-timey and . . . romantic? Am I blushing? Maybe.

There's a weird rumble above us and I look up.

The sky is very dark, the clouds moving fast. I heard thunder earlier, but this seems ominous. A chill runs down my spine.

"Cole," I say nervously, just as the sky splits with a threatening sound.

"Oh shit," he says. "Run."

We take off.

We round the Castle, music vibrating from the inside. On this side of the Castle, the palm trees, willows, and wisteria are clustered together around a large swath of dense shrubbery. I think I remember reading that Levy had built a maze on the property. It might be fun to find it and go in if it wasn't raining so hard. My hair and clothes are sticking to me. Petals from the carnation corsage my mother bought me are fluttering to the ground. I unpin the corsage from my lapel and stick it in my blazer pocket; I've never gotten a corsage before. I want to save what I can.

"There," he says, pointing.

High up in a thick oak is a . . . treehouse, complete with windows and a door. There's a widow's walk around it. Nailed to the tree is a wooden ladder.

We make a break for it and I scoot up the ladder. The rungs are springy, but I don't have time to worry about that. Rain is lashing my face and I just want to get somewhere dry.

The wood of the widow's walk is suspiciously soft under my feet. Will we fall through? I touch the outside of the treehouse before carefully opening the door and stepping inside. It's not fancy. It wasn't built by expert carpenters. The nailing is janky, the hardware rusted and askew. This was built by someone who wanted to build a treehouse, was determined to build a treehouse for their child, maybe the one thing they did themselves, rather than hiring it out. I have a brief pang of something I can't name. . . . Charles Levy genuinely loved Lilian. He surrounded her with the finest things his money could buy, yet he built his daughter a treehouse all by himself.

I feel for my phone in the pocket of my velvet blazer. Behind me, Cole shakes out his wet hair. Alice has texted about some passageway, but I skip over that quickly. I'm sure she'll send a million more.

I'm in your treehouse, I type.

Lilian Levy answers immediately. We text every few days now, ever since everything went down in the fall. Sometimes I think she imagines me as what it would be like if her granddaughter Brooke were still alive: she asks me about school, what my plans are, my (cough) imaginary love life. She's an extremely wealthy and intelligent woman running a worldwide cosmetics empire and yet . . . she's still interested in talking to me. I thought it would end once she paid me the reward money for us finding out who murdered Brooke, but it didn't. It's kind of nice.

What an interesting wrinkle. I imagine it involves romance of some sort. If you have time between blushes and youthful longing, perhaps you'll find my secret hiding space.

I haven't told Alice I'm still in contact with Lilian. She's so weird about me hanging out with Raf and Cole, I don't want to add to the fire. She can get prickly.

Secret hiding space? I text back.

Poke around. I'm sure you'll find it. In between whatever nefarious business you're up to. I slide my phone back in my pocket.

Cole turns on the flashlight on his phone. The floorboards creak under him. Vines and leaves are growing through the slats in the wood. There are thin cracks in the windowpanes. He whistles. "This is pretty old," he says. "Maybe we shouldn't be up here? Dangerous?"

"Where else are we going to go?" I say. "Might as well wait out the storm."

The music from the Castle ballroom filters faintly around the treehouse. Cole's face is soft in the half dark. I'm shivering in my wet clothes.

"Kind of nice up here," Cole murmurs. "With just us. Alice really hates me, doesn't she? And Spike. What did I ever do to *him*?"

He gives me a sheepish smile. I want to tell him that Alice is probably being protective of me, and Spike, well, it's a bit more complicated with Spike, and frankly, I'm confused about that as well. I really don't know who I am lately.

"Well," I say. "They aren't here. So, we don't have to think about them."

He turns off his phone flashlight. In the pearly light of the moon through the window, he looks handsome and soft. "Iris, it *is* a dance. You want to dance?"

My heart flips. I nod. Can he hear how hard my heart is beating? I've never even danced with a boy. He starts to put his arms around me. Time seems to stand still.

And then my phone buzzes from the pocket of my jacket, startling us both.

Cole drops his arms. "You need to get that?" he asks.

"No," I say.

He slides his arms around my waist.

Just as I relax, an ear-piercing scream erupts above the dreamy music, causing both of us to jump. We drop our arms and whirl away from each other.

"What the hell," Cole says, and as he does so, a floorboard snaps beneath him. He swears, and trips, snagging his jacket on an errant nail on the wall.

His face reddens and he swears again. "Goddammit. Fuck."

Something in his voice sends tendrils of fear up my spine. It's just a jacket, a rip, a tear, but he's so angry, almost . . . in tears. His face solidifies into something I've never seen on him before. He jerks his arm in my direction.

The Thing, the Thing, the Thing.

I dash out the door and down the ladder. I have to get away from him. My body is cold and hot all at once. He raised his hand. There was a scream. My phone is buzzing nonstop in my pocket as I run blindly through the storm, slipping and wobbling on the wet lawn, back to the Castle.

Where is Alice, Alice, Alice.

EMERGENCY ALERT SYSTEM
FEBRUARY 11
9:32 P.M.

 The National Weather Service has issued a SEVERE WEATHER THREAT for Manzanita County until 3:00 a.m. Flood warning in effect for Castle Cove, Blossom, and neighboring towns, with potential risk of mudslide along the coast. Avoid travel and shelter in place.

CHAPTER FIVE

ALICE
FEBRUARY 11
9:36 P.M.

It has just happened that I have found myself
in the vicinity of murder rather more often
than would seem normal.
—AGATHA CHRISTIE, *NEMESIS*

I'M NOT ALONE. THERE'S a person standing across the room from me, backlit by soft moonlight.

When I shine my flashlight in their face, they start screaming.

It's freaking Helen Park. What the hell is Park doing up here, alone in this room? And why is she screaming?

I squeeze my eyes shut and then open them again, but she's still there. Park, screaming. I catch a glint of something gold clutched in her hand, and I step closer, direct my light toward it. It looks like . . .

I blink.

It looks like a knife.

Park, in the study, with a knife. Park, in the study, with a knife, screaming bloody murder. Good lord, that noise is hurting my head. I can't think straight.

"Park!" I bark, but she ignores me, her attention directed toward the floor beyond her feet, hidden from my sight by a very large desk. Jesus Christ. *"Park!"* I say, louder this time.

I cross the room as fast as my billowing gown will allow and grab her elbow. "Park! Shut up!"

She gives no indication that she hears me, the knife clenched in her outstretched hand. I realize it's covered in red.

That's when I notice the other thing, the thing on the ground in front of her, which I hadn't been able to see.

Is that . . . a *person*?

Park's scream pitches louder, something I would not have guessed was humanly possible just a moment ago.

"Park, shut *up*!" She ignores me again, and I can't take it anymore; I grab her by the shoulders and shake her, hard.

The scream dies in her throat and she blinks as her gaze lands on my face, like she's only just registering that I'm standing in front of her.

"Alice?" she asks. Then she looks down at the thing in her hand and her face goes white. Her fingers unclench, the knife clattering to the carpet next to the lump on the ground. It lands, skittering a few inches away from us, and I realize it's not a knife at all—it's a gold letter opener with a very sharp tip.

"Park. Are you okay? What the hell is going on?" I shine my flashlight on the person lying on the ground and my heart skips a beat.

"Oh my god. Is that . . . *Kennedy*?" I ask, even though there is no doubt in my mind that it is, indeed, Kennedy. Kennedy on the floor, red oozing from her chest, hair matted with blood. Blood *everywhere.* I stumble back a few steps, away from her.

My brain is not computing: Park with a sharp, stabby object in her hand; Kennedy unmoving on the ground, red seeping onto the front of her dress.

Their fight earlier in the ballroom, Park leaping at Kennedy . . . Kennedy, the classic asshole victim, like something straight out of one of Agatha Christie's novels.

It finally snaps together in my brain. And I call myself a detective. Hercule Poirot would not be impressed.

"What did you *do*?" I say, my mouth falling open in horror.

"I d-didn't——" she stammers, stumbling backward away from me. I grab her arm to try to make her stay, make her answer me, but she wrenches out of my grasp and takes off out the door.

Crap. Kennedy is clearly in need of serious medical assistance, but if I let Park get away, who knows if I'll ever see her again. Her dad is both extremely protective of his family and extremely successful in his business ventures. More likely than not, Park is on her way to call him right now. He'll probably show up and whisk her away to another country on his private jet. One with no extradition laws.

I pull up my Favorites list on my phone and hit the second name.

"Alice?" says a breathy voice. "Where are you? I heard——"

"A scream?" I finish for Iris. "I'm here. In the room it came from. Kennedy is . . . I don't know. Bleeding. A lot. Park was in here. Holding a . . . basically a knife. I don't know if she did something stupid or what, but she just took off. I have to go after her."

Now that I have her on the line, I head out into the hallway. Park is almost to the other end, skirt in hand, black hair falling loose from its updo.

I break into a run.

"What?" Iris yells into my ear.

"I don't have time to explain," I pant. "Can you come up here? Someone needs to help Kennedy—*ow!*" My feet are already killing me. These heels aren't made for this sort of physical activity. Maybe Iris is on to something with her Converse.

"Where are you?" Iris asks.

The hallway is unfamiliar. I've never been up here before. "I don't know. Somewhere on the second floor. I came up here through a secret staircase in the library and—" I stop, gasping, feet on fire, and make an executive decision. Fashion be damned. I rip off my shoes and break into a much more comfortable barefoot run.

"Second floor. Okay." Iris mutters something I don't catch.

"What?"

"Nothing, nothing. We're on our way. Did you call nine-one-one?"

Shoot. Right. Nine-one-one. I forgot in my panic over Park.

"No. Can you?" Park rounds the corner up ahead, disappearing from sight, and I let out a scream. "She's getting away!"

"I'll do it. We'll be there soon," Iris says.

"Cool." I hang up. At the end of the hallway, I follow Park's path to the right, but screech to a stop in front of a staircase with steps leading both up and down. Which way would she have gone? If she's trying to make a break for it, she must have headed down.

I take off down the stairs, breathing a sigh of relief to have gravity on my side. I'm flying down them so fast, in fact, that I don't notice a person at the bottom of the stairs, standing directly in my path. Not until my nose is buried halfway into his armpit, and his hands are on my shoulders.

CHAPTER SIX

IRIS
FEBRUARY 1 1
9:44 P.M.

Henry, I think we're in a lot of trouble.
—MONA MOODY,
THE HOUSE AT THE END OF THE STREET, 1946

I'M RUNNING, TRYING ALL the doors on the second floor, opening them to find classmates in varying stages of undress (gross)
or clustered in circles smoking weed, my heart beating like a wild
bird in my chest, Cole at my heels. I tripped on the way up the
grand staircase from the first floor and my knee hurts like hell.

"Iris, *what* is happening?" Cole's voice is frightened.

"I don't . . ." My god, how many rooms *are* there in this freaking place? "Alice . . . Kennedy is hurt. Oh god. We have to call
nine-one-one. Kennedy is, like, really hurt. I don't know. Jesus."

Bedroom, bedroom, Trophy Room (Trophy Room?? Are
those . . . antelope heads on the walls? Barbaric!) . . . and then . . .

It's dark in this one, just moonlight through the wall of windows at the back, trees waving in the wind and rain. I feel for a
light switch. The room blossoms brightly.

"Oh my god." I suck in my breath.

A body, a beautiful gown, and a hell of a lot of blood.

Kennedy.

Weakly, Cole says, "My phone's dead."

I hand him mine.

Cole's voice is shaking as he talks to 911. "It's . . . wow, she's really hurt. You have to come. Now. I don't know. Levy Castle, second floor somewhere. There's a *what*?"

It's like time stops as I walk to Kennedy, my heart and throat pounding. So much blood. Her eyes closed. A gurgling sound from her throat. She's alive.

I sink to my knees next to her. My hands are trembling. I don't know what to do. I tear off my blazer, put it under her head. Isn't that what you're supposed to do? Elevate the head? But her head is covered in blood. Her body is bloody. Blood all over the expensive carpet.

Cole kneels next to me. "They said it'll take a while. The rain. There's a mudslide. I don't . . . oh my god. Iris."

"Your jacket," I say hesitantly. "Take it off. Cover her. I don't know. Cole, I don't know what to do. What do you mean, a *mudslide*? No one's *coming*?"

He wipes at Kennedy with his jacket, gives up, finally places it across her. We stare at each other.

"Cole," I say, "Alice said she saw Park in here, with Kennedy. And that Park . . ."

Cole snaps his fingers. "Wait." He punches at my phone, holds it to his ear.

"I need you. Now. Upstairs. Something bad happened. Somebody's bleeding really bad, Candy. There's so much blood. I don't know! Like sixth door down the hall, left side. Door's open."

He nods at me. His voice shakes. "My sister. She's coming.

She's here, working catering. It's her other job. To pay for school. She'll know what to do. She'll . . ."

He trails off. That's right. I remember. Cole's sister, Candy, aka Raf's girlfriend. She's training to be a dental hygienist.

I press two fingers on Kennedy's throat. Beneath my fingers, a steady, slow beat. That's good.

"We have to stop the bleeding," I say.

"How? Where? There's so much. . . ."

Cole turns away from me and retches.

From the corner of my eye, I spot something. Glints of gold glistening through blood. A knife? I reach for it, then stop myself, leaning closer. It's not a knife. It's an old-fashioned letter opener. And it's bloody.

Alice said Park was in here with Kennedy. Did Park . . . ?

"Kennedy," I whisper. "Just hold on."

A sound, soft, clogged, from her throat. Her closed eyes twitch. That must be good, right?

There's a rush of movement behind us, and suddenly there's Mr. Flick, Spike's dad, and Spike, and Candy, Cole's sister, clutching a first-aid kit, pushing me out of the way. Mr. Flick gets down on his knees, pushing hair from Kennedy's eyes, opening her eyelid with his fingers.

"What happened?" Candy asks, all business. She's checking Kennedy's pulse. "Good god."

"I don't—"

"Did you call nine-one-one?" yells Mr. Flick. His voice hurts my ears.

"Is that Kennedy?" Spike whispers. "Oh my god."

"I called," Cole says hoarsely. "But they said . . . they said . . ."

Just then, phones begin bleeping.

Spike's face turns white and he holds out his phone. "Emergency alert. The storm. There's a mudslide. No trav—"

"No one's coming," I say.

Mr. Flick throws down his phone. "Dear god," he mutters. Then he lets loose with a string of expletives.

Candy is pulling bandages, gauze, anything she can from the first-aid kit. "This is beyond what we have here," she says quietly. "I have four years of lifeguard training and I've learned some things in school about blood loss and wounds, but . . . I don't know where to start. I need towels. I think I need tape. Duct tape might work, I think? I don't know." Mr. Flick is gently feeling around the top of Kennedy's head with one hand.

"Her pupils are blown," he says. "This isn't just . . . There's head trauma, I think. I can't . . . That's . . ."

Head trauma? So she wasn't just stabbed?

Candy is feeling around Kennedy's stomach. I think she's searching for the wounds there.

The wounds.

I look again at the bloodied letter opener. Wounds. Park. The fight earlier. It doesn't make sense. Did Park attack Kennedy over a stupid outfit? Her words from the fight downstairs echo in my head. *"God, sometimes I wish you'd just shrivel up and die."*

I look around. We're in some sort of study. Long antique mahogany desk, huge floor-to-ceiling fireplace against one wall, an expensive and elegant piano, a bank of windows, old portraits of musty-looking people on the walls, a bookshelf on another wall, and there, next to the fireplace, a door thrown open and what looks like a cache of old ball gowns in the room beyond. Where *are* we? Where is *Alice*? Did she find Park?

It's just then that I realize drawers in the desk have been

pulled open, papers are scattered all over the floor. The desktop is littered with pens and pencils, their holders knocked over. I scan the room again. A painting on the wall hangs askew. Books from the bookshelf appear to have been thrown to the floor. Three bankers' boxes, their tops torn open and things scattered on the carpet.

Someone was here. Someone was looking for something.

From the corner of my eye, I see Spike walking slowly to the letter opener, his hand reaching down, down . . .

"Stop!" I scream.

Everyone freezes.

"Don't touch it," I say firmly. "We have to keep everything intact for whenever the . . . police get here, I guess."

I falter. Everyone is staring at me.

"Spike," I say. "Go down to the kitchen, get more towels and anything you can find, tape, whatever. We have to try to stop this bleeding somehow."

"Got it," he says, rushing out the door to the hallway.

Everyone is still looking at me. Minutes ago, I was in a rickety treehouse, in a pretty dress, dancing with a boy while rain fell outside, and now I'm stuck in a room, a mudslide suffocating Castle Cove beyond this elegant castle, a bloodied girl on the carpet in front of me, and everything in this room is pointing to whoever's responsible.

"We have to protect any evidence," I tell them. I gesture to the letter opener. "That's a *weapon*. It has fingerprints. This entire room is now a crime scene. Don't touch anything."

ANNOUNCEMENT OVER
LEVY CASTLE SPEAKER SYSTEM
9:52 P.M.

Attention CCHS students. Please be aware that the
National Weather Service has issued an alert about a
mudslide that has blocked Highway 1. No one can enter
or leave Castle property at this time. Please remain
inside, away from windows, and do not—I repeat—do
not attempt to go outside. . . . [mumbling] What?
No, Astor, you cannot ask your father to send in
his helicopter to get you. [mumbling] Well, first
of all, it's far too dangerous, the authorities
have instructed everyone to shelter in place. Even
emergency vehicles have been—Astor Jansen, that is
enough. [mumbling, throat clears] Excuse me, where
was I? Yes, everyone please remain inside, and make
yourselves as comfortable as possible. We might be
here for a while.

CHAPTER SEVEN

ALICE
FEBRUARY 11
9:57 P.M.

They have a genius, young ladies, for getting into
various kinds of trouble and difficulty.
—AGATHA CHRISTIE, *THIRD GIRL*

"ALICE, ARE YOU OKAY?" asks Raf, steadying me with his hands. "Where are you going? Were you just . . ." He glances up the staircase and then back to me. "Were you just . . . running?"

"Have you seen Park?" I ask, gasping for breath, trying to ignore the warmth of his palms against my shoulders. Behind him in a large foyer stands a small clump of my classmates holding red Solo cups and watching the two of us curiously.

"Park?" Raf's brow creases.

"Helen Park? She's in my grade. About yea high." I hold up a hand at the height of my chin. "She has straight black hair that's all over the place right now because she was running—"

"I know who Helen Park is," Raf interrupts. He steps back from me, hands falling to his sides. "Haven't seen her. Why?"

"You looking for Park?" calls one of the kids in the foyer.

"Yes, have you seen her?" I say.

"We saw her run by a minute ago. Came down the stairs right before you, then disappeared down that way." He points to the flight of stairs leading down into the basement of the Castle.

"Thanks," Raf says.

"Thanks," I echo. I'm about to take off when Raf grabs my elbow.

"Alice, what the hell is going on?"

I glance at the kids, then lean toward him, dropping my voice to a whisper. "Kennedy . . . er, Rebecca Kennedy?" I search his face for recognition, and he nods. "So I decided to go upstairs, through this secret passage . . . never mind, that doesn't matter right now . . . the point is, I went into a room and there was this *person* in there, Raf, holding a freaking sharp object, and that person was Helen Park . . . and there was this other person on the ground, bleeding, and *that* person was Rebecca Kennedy, and then Park ran out of the room and I chased her and now she's gone down to the basement, and I have to go get her because I think she did something bad and—"

Raf holds up his hands. "Okay, whoa. Are you saying Kennedy's upstairs, bleeding? We have to call nine-one—"

"Iris is taking care of that," I say, and pull out of his grasp. "I gotta go." I dart away from him, taking the stairs down two-by-two and find myself in a pitch-black room that smells of mildew. The flashlight on my phone barely cuts through the thick black. I'm about to search for a light switch when something heavy slams into my back.

"*Oof.*" The air is knocked from my lungs. I spin around, shining my light into . . . Raf's eyes. He followed me. "Raf, what the hell?"

"Sorry, I didn't expect you to stop on the bottom step."

"Why did you follow me?"

"Um, to help you?" he says, like it's the most obvious thing in the world.

"I can handle it," I tell him, then add, "but you could find the light switch."

He shuffles away and a second later the lights blink on, black spots dancing in my vision as my eyes struggle to adjust to the sudden bright. We're in what appears to be a storage space—it's filled with large cardboard boxes, wooden crates, and a statue of a giant pink elephant in the corner. Charles Levy really had questionable taste. Movement beyond the elephant catches my eye.

"Park!" I scream to Raf. "Behind the elephant!"

"Got her," he says, his mouth set in a grim line as he takes off in her direction. He's fast; I'd forgotten that when he played basketball at Castle Cove High, he was one of the best players on the team.

Park leaps up from behind the statue and takes off away from him. They disappear behind a bunch of shipping crates.

Before I can follow them, they reemerge, Raf hot on Park's tail. He corners her between two crates.

"Park, just stop for a minute," I hear him say. "I'm sure there's a perfectly reasonable explanation for—"

Before he can finish the sentence, Park darts past him, running straight at me. I reach out to grab her, but she snakes away and disappears through a door next to the bottom of the stairs. Shit. I spin around to follow her, and as I reach the doorway, a scream of frustration rings out from inside.

Park is standing in the center of a small room with a low, curved ceiling. She's breathing hard, wearing a panicked expression.

And Raf and I are blocking the only way out of the room.

"Helen, just talk to us," Raf says. "We have people helping Kennedy, and we want to help you. What happened up there?"

She clamps her mouth shut, folding her arms tight against her body, and shakes her head back and forth emphatically.

"We can't help you, if you won't talk to us," Raf says.

"My dad always tells me that if I get in trouble, not to say a word until I speak to our lawyers," she says.

Raf cuts his eyes to me, and I shrug. He sighs. "God, to live a life where you have not just one lawyer, but lawyers. What now, Ogilvie?"

"Well, she can't be trusted to stay in one place, and she refuses to talk, so I think we only have one option, really."

I pull the door closed, shutting Park inside the tiny room.

CHAPTER EIGHT

IRIS

FEBRUARY 11

10:11 P.M.

I've no idea what's happened, but I do know
whatever it is, it's very, very, very bad.
—MONA MOODY, *THE GIRLS IN 3B*, 1947

EVERYWHERE, I SEE POTENTIAL evidence: Strands of hair on the carpet, clinging to the corner of the mahogany desk. They could be Kennedy's or they could be from whoever attacked her, perhaps Park? The open desk drawers. The letter opener. The papers. They could hold fingerprints. I know we should leave it all to the police, but I'm a little worried other people might get in here and mess up potential evidence. There's already a crowd of kids amassed at the front of the room. They've untucked their formal shirts, taken off their heels. Some of them look a little . . . drunk? Oh god. They might have snuck stuff in, but there was probably liquor in the kitchen area. This night is turning out to be pure chaos.

Mr. Flick looks like he's going to be sick.

Candy is methodically trying to tamp Kennedy's bleeding stomach with the kitchen towels Spike brought back. They have bandages and torn-up towels folded into squares on her head wounds, duct-taped unceremoniously to her scalp to keep them in place.

"Is she gonna die?" a kid in the crowd shouts. "You can't let her die!"

"This isn't *Grey's Anatomy*," Mr. Flick yells back. "I'm not Izzie Stevens on a ferry using a hand drill to open someone's skull!"

"*Grey's* what, now?" someone in the crowd murmurs.

"God, you're old, Flick," someone chuckles.

"Do you think it was Park, Iris? I mean, really?" Spike says quietly, giving me a searching look.

"Spike," I say calmly. "I'm not jumping to any conclusions."

"Helen Park might have done this?" It's Zora, breaking through the crowd to stare at me sternly. "I think we can all remember what happened the last time someone was falsely accused of murder in Castle Cove, yes? Maybe we should be more careful this time. Neil!"

Neil squeezes out from the crowd. "Here," he says breathlessly. "Aww, no, Kennedy. I just tutored her to a B in Spanish. Pobre chica."

Zora scans the room. Our eyes meet. I nod. She and Neil need to be put into action. I reach down into the giant Tupperware full of latex gloves, towels, and first-aid supplies Spike lugged up from the kitchen and toss some gloves across the desk to Zora, who flicks a pair to Neil and then snaps on her own.

"Neil," she says. "Let's go. This room might not be the only room with evidence. It's a mess in here. We need to check the other rooms on this floor and see if they were disturbed as well."

"Right," I say. "But don't take or touch anything. Just look and note what you see that might seem suspicious."

"Got it." Neil pulls on the pair of gloves and he and Zora wedge themselves through the crowd and out into the hallway.

Cole looks over at me, my phone to his ear. "They say at least thirty—"

"You tell them to do something right now!" Candy suddenly shouts at him. "There's got to be a medevac helicopter, something, anything, or this girl is going to die. I do not want her to die."

The room quiets, and then a teary sound emerges from the crowd. Ashley Henderson pushes her way through. Her hair is mussed and her dress is wrinkled.

"Rebecca," she cries. She slams down on the ground next to Kennedy, dropping her purse, which makes a heavy clunk on the carpet. Girl certainly packs for a dance, I guess. "Oh my god. What happened?" she wails.

She pats Kennedy's blood-spattered arm. She's wearing glamorous pink opera gloves. There are splotches of mud on the hem of her dress and her hair is damp.

"Henderson, why are you so wet?" I ask.

"I was outside enjoying a beverage, and then it started pouring. I had to wait in the gazebo before I could make a run for it back here. Not that it's any of your business, Abby."

"Iris," I say coldly. "And you can take that attitu—"

Spike interrupts me. "Someone attacked Kenn—Rebecca," he tells Ashley.

Ashley narrows her eyes. "Attacked? By *who*?"

I hesitate before answering, but then I do. "Alice found Park in here. Then Park ran."

Ashley stops patting Kennedy's arm and scrunches her face. "*What* are you even talking about? *Park*? Over the *dress*?"

Cole holds out my phone to me. I take it and hold it to my ear. The operator sounds weary. "Sit tight. Helicopter and police on the way. Let me talk to the person assisting the injured, please."

I move around the desk and put the phone on speaker and set it next to Mr. Flick. Thank god someone's coming.

"Spike," I say. "Text Alice help is on the way. And tell her not to do anything irrational."

He pulls out his phone. "Will do."

Henderson is sniffling. I start to put a hand on her damp shoulder, maybe to comfort her, although that seems like a weird thing to do to a person who pantsed me freshman year in PE, but then again, these are weird times, when Spike suddenly says, "What happened to *your* dress, Iris?"

I look down. Beneath Kennedy's blood, there's a large gash in my dress, and mud, and grass splatters.

I went down the ladder of the treehouse so quickly, I don't even remember falling, but I must have.

"Iris." It's Cole, whispering, pulling me away from Kennedy, Candy, Mr. Flick, and Ashley. "Iris, I'm sorry. I don't understand what I did. . . . Please, I'm sorry I got so angry."

My heart flutters. He looks nice and gentle now, like always, but back there in the treehouse, he was different. "I—"

"Wait." Spike moves around the other side of the desk to stand by me and Cole. "Did you *hurt* her? I'll—"

Spike's face is filled with anger. This is exactly what I, and we, *don't* need right now.

I fit myself between them.

Just then, the sea of kids parts and paramedics in rain gear, clutching a gurney wrapped in plastic, rush in. They start shouting questions at Mr. Flick and Candy and surround Kennedy, pushing us out of the way. They fit her neck and head with a brace and cushion and count, lifting her onto the gurney at *three*. Things drift from beneath her body as they lift her. A flattened pink corsage and torn-up . . . pieces of paper. I gather them up and peer closer. The paper is stained pink from Kennedy's blood. I can make out some writing, but before I can figure out what it says, a familiar, disgruntled voice rings out from the doorway, and without thinking, I close my fist around the torn paper pieces.

KWB, CHANNEL 10

Breaking News

February 11

10:12 p.m.

Ben Perez: We're sorry to interrupt your programming, but we have a live report from Tessa Hopkins, on the scene of the mudslides that have completely blocked off portions of Highway One. Tessa, over to you. Wow, it's a wet one, isn't it?

Tessa Hopkins: Well, Ben, as you can see, conditions are dangerous and volatile out here. The storm is expected to lessen in the next hour or so and crews are working hard to clear the road. Everyone stay safe and shelter in place until this can get cleaned up. But in addition to this, there's another emergency brewing.

Ben Perez: What can you tell us, Tessa? Ooh, careful, are those tree branches blowing behind you?

Tessa Hopkins: Unfortunately, yes. Ben, a situation is developing at Levy Castle. According to several tweets by students, who are at the property for their annual Sadie Hawkins dance, a student has been attacked and is in critical condition. We aren't releasing the name of the student, as family hasn't been notified, but the situation is apparently dire.

Ben Perez: Attacked? Do you have any more information than that, Tessa?

Tessa Hopkins: Ben, I do not. I've asked the students tweeting to contact me with any information about what's unfolding. I can say, though, that coming right on the heels of the Brooke Donovan case, this is deeply disturbing. Castle Cove Police are working closely with emergency services to get help as soon as possible to the Castle. A staff member of the school is apparently providing medical assistance to the student. Teachers are also trying to keep the other students safe and accounted for.

Ben Perez: That sounds like a volatile environment, Tessa. An apparent assault and kids locked down for what could be several hours.

Tessa Hopkins: Yes, Ben. It's a situation that could get out of control very quickly.

CHAPTER NINE

ALICE
FEBRUARY 11
10:13 P.M.

> "What do you expect Cust to tell you?"
> Hercule Poirot smiled. "A lie," he said.
> "And by it, I shall know the truth!"
> —AGATHA CHRISTIE, *THE A.B.C. MURDERS*

WITH MY EAR PRESSED up against the door, I can hear the low murmur of Park's voice, presumably talking to someone on her phone. Knowing her, her dad is on the other end of the line, which is not ideal. Park's dad is not someone to be trifled with.

I catch a few mumbled words—"trapped me . . . didn't *do*"—and some muffled sobs. After a few minutes, her voice stops, and there's a brief moment of silence before a sudden bang on the door makes me snatch my head away. I rub my ear.

"My dad says you're going to pay for this!" Park shouts.

Raf flinches. "I'm not sure keeping her in there is a good idea, Alice. It's false imprisonment. Not exactly on the up-and-up."

I shrug. "Do you have a better idea? If we let her out, she's just going to take off again. It's not like she can go anywhere, but I don't feel like spending the rest of my night chasing her through the Castle, do you?" My phone buzzes and a slew of texts from Spike appears, one on top of the next.

Paramedics took Kennedy.
Mudslide being cleared.
Cops going to be here any second.
Did you find Park??

A pause, and then: *Iris says do not do anything IRRATIONAL, Alice.*

Irrational? I would never. I'm in the middle of composing a response when another violent thump against the door startles me, and my phone clatters to the ground.

"Let! Me! *Out!*"

Raf runs a hand through his thick black hair. "Alice, we really cannot keep her in there." He's looking at me like he thinks I'm being totally unreasonable, which is just rude. It's not like he's come up with a better plan.

"What would you suggest, then?" I say.

"I'd suggest we try to talk to her."

"I tried that! She refused. No matter how much I wish I could, you know I can't force her to talk. That would *really* be illegal."

He shakes his head. "I'm not suggesting you torture her to get information, Ogilvie. We aren't Cold War spies. I'm just saying, if you try to talk to her in a calm environment, she might be more willing to speak."

He has a point. "Fine. But we can't let her leave that room. I know her. She'll take off, and my legs are tired. If she's on the lam when the cops get down here, I'll never live it down. I think we should tie her up. Then I can question her face to face without worrying."

"Excuse me? *Tie* her up?" Raf says. "Alice, absolutely not—"

"Yes! With, I don't know, rope or something." I look around the room. "What about this?" I walk over to one of the large shipping containers and peel off a long piece of packing tape from its side.

"That is a terrible idea."

"Do you have a better one? If you do, I'm all ears." I make a face at him, the tape half off the box. God, he's bossy.

"Yes. I think we should talk to her. Calmly. Without tying her up."

"She'll run away!" I walk back to him, clutching the piece of tape.

He sighs. "What about this? You go in and talk to her. I'll guard the door and text Iris and the rest of them to let them know where we are. If Park tries to run, I'll stop her. Simple."

I consider his approach. "All right. Fine," I say, sticking the tape to the wall next to me, just in case we need it later. "We'll do it your way." I open the door and walk inside.

Park is crouched on her haunches in the far corner of the room. She scowls at the sight of us, leaping to her feet and holding out her phone like a weapon.

A blue suede couch sits in the center of the room, and in front of it is one of those boxy TVs from a thousand years ago. Beyond that is a small kitchenette with open shelving, lined with hundreds of cans of food. And, built into the back wall, is a set of bunk beds.

"Merde. What the hell is this place?" I ask.

"I'd guess a fallout shelter," Raf says. "Probably built in the early 1950s because of the escalating tension between the United States and the Soviet Union."

Park interrupts us. "My dad knows what you did, Alice. He's going to be here as soon as he can, and you better bet you're going to be in some deep shit when he—"

"Tell us what happened up there." I cut her off.

"Um, *why* would I do that?" she says. "You know I could just run out of here and—"

Raf sighs behind me. "Please don't. I really don't want to have to stop you."

Park's mouth tugs down. "Fine. I'll stay. But I'm not saying anything without my lawyers present." She folds her arms against her body.

"Park, you were up there standing over Kennedy with that letter opener. You need to tell someone what happened," I say, trying to keep my voice calm. She shakes her head, pressing her lips together tightly.

"Come with me." I walk over to the couch and take a seat, and a moment later Park follows. She settles on the farthest cushion possible away from me.

"I'm recording this." I unlock my phone, open the voice memo app, and press record, and set it between us on the couch.

"Where did you go after your altercation with Kennedy on the dance floor?"

Park presses her lips together.

"Park. When I found you standing over Kennedy, you were literally holding a bloody letter opener. Everyone saw you guys arguing earlier. None of this looks good. If you're innocent, what were you doing in there?"

"I didn't—" She slaps a hand against her mouth.

I sigh. "Come on."

She shakes her head forcefully. "Not without my lawyers present."

"Alice?" a distant voice calls.

My heart skips a beat. I only have a little time left with her alone.

Raf walks to the doorway and calls out, "Down here! We're in the basement!"

"Park, please tell me——" Before I can finish, there's a commotion outside the room and Spike and Iris appear in the doorway, flanked by police officers.

"Hello, Alice," says an unfortunately familiar voice from the middle of the throng. Out steps none other than my least favorite detective of all time.

"Detective Thompson," I say, not trying in the slightest to hide my displeasure.

CHAPTER TEN

IRIS
FEBRUARY 11
10:35 P.M.

I've wanted to be an actress since I was a very little
girl. Who wouldn't want to pretend to be someone
else, even if only for a little while?
—MONA MOODY, INTERVIEW, *MOVIELAND,* 1948

DETECTIVE THOMPSON PURSES HIS mouth and surveys the
scene in the strange basement room we're in. Alice is sitting on
a blue couch—wearing a ball gown that is *not* the dress she came
to the dance in—where Park is sitting with her arms wrapped
around herself. And Raf is off to the side, a sheepish expression
on his face.

"Alice Ogilvie." Detective Thompson rubs his eyes as though
he's suddenly tired. "I have no idea what you think you're doing,
but if history is any guide, I'm betting you've broken several laws
already."

"You're mistaken, Detective Thompson. I'm simply making
sure a possible suspect in an assault doesn't—"

Thompson holds up a hand. "Can it, Ogilvie. I don't have time
for your shenanigans. I've got a girl being airlifted to a hospital, a

hundred kids running wild upstairs, and the last thing I need is interference from you, and *that* one—"

He points to me and I glare at him.

"—upstairs thinking she's on some sort of TV show and messing with possible evidence."

"I was *trying* to keep everything secure," I point out.

"Zip it," Thompson tells me. "Do you want me to haul you in on tampering with a crime scene? I'd be more than happy—"

"The mudslide," Raf interjects. "We weren't sure when you would get here. We were just trying to help."

Thompson gives him a long look. "Don't you work for me? What are you doing here? Why are you wearing that jacket?"

Raf starts to answer, but Alice interrupts. "Excuse me, Detective Thompson. Let me recap for you. There was a fight earlier at the dance between Helen Park, who is right here, and Rebecca Kennedy, who is on her way to the hospital. I came upon Helen in the study upstairs, holding a bloody letter opener, Rebecca Kennedy at her feet and bleeding profusely. Helen ran. I'm not concluding anything, because that would be unwise, but I simply wanted to ask Helen some questions about how she came to be standing over a wounded person, while holding what appeared to be the assault weapon *in her hand.*"

Alice looks proud. On the couch, Park is still as a stone.

I look around. This room is weird. Are we in a fallout shelter? Everything in here is ancient and looks like it's from the fifties. I scan the rows of canned food on the shelves. *They* can't still be good. There's probably oodles of bacteria lurking inside those cans of green beans and cubed ham. Why didn't anyone get rid of this stuff?

"I think I'll make the decisions about who to interrogate, Alice. You," he gestures to Park. "Come with me. We're done down here."

"*Thank* you," Park says, rising from the couch slowly. She turns to Alice and sneers. "Hah. And my dad is going to sue your ass off for false imprisonment."

"Oh, hold up, missy," Thompson says to Park. "I'm not *done* with you, not by a long shot. I'm just taking you somewhere else for a little talk."

"*Missy?*" I say. "That's a little condescending."

Thompson swivels his head to me. "I'm sorry, did I offend your feminist sensibilities, Iris? I have half a mind to slap a fine on you for contaminating a possible crime scene."

"I *told* you, I didn't touch anything," I say through gritted teeth. But my still-latex-gloved fingers twitch nervously against the pieces of ripped paper I shoved in my blazer pocket upstairs when he wasn't looking. I can't tell him about this; I don't want to go to *jail.* It's probably nothing.

Spike barks out a laugh. "Missy? Feminist sensibilities? Whoa, lord, man. You are positively *archaic.*"

Raf covers his mouth to muffle his laughter.

"Enough!" Detective Thompson shouts, holding up his hands. "The experts are here now and the *children* will go upstairs, where they will wait to be interviewed. The roads should be available to general traffic in about an hour and you will be free to leave. But in the meantime, everyone, and I do mean *everyone,* will go upstairs and *stay* there. Now, take her out."

He nods and two police officers standing by the doorway beckon to Park.

Park tosses her hair and swans by Alice, not-so-gently knocking into her.

"Oh, no, you did *not* just do that," Alice says to her.

"Detective Thompson," I plead. I can't help myself. "There are tons of kids upstairs. Everyone is a potential witness or a possible suspect. Are you really letting everyone leave in an hour? That's hardly enough time to—"

"Iris Adams," he says, leaning so close to my face I can see every pore on his rather dry, flaky nose. "One more word and you'll spend the night in that pretty dress in a very dirty jail cell. Do you understand? One. More. Word."

Before I can think of a snappy retort, my phone buzzes.

Iris, what's going on? Are you all right?

I sigh. *Yes, Mom. I'm fine. Can't talk.*

What's happening there? I keep hearing awful things. Did someone get hurt?

Complicated. Police here. Got 2 go. Will text later.

I want you to come home.

Going to Alice's remember?

I want you—

I drop my hand to my side and ignore her. Beside me, Alice's mouth is set in a firm line and her eyes are steely.

TEXT CONVERSATION BETWEEN
ASHLEY HENDERSON AND HELEN PARK
FEBRUARY 11
11:59 P.M.

AH: what tf is happening back there? I'm at the hospital. Went with paramedics. It's a madhouse here

HP: That freak Ogilvie thinks I hurt Kennedy. The cops asked me a bunch of questions.

AH: She's in surgery. That band geek's dad says she has brain swelling

AH: Are the cops done? What did they ask u

HP: I DIDN'T DO IT

HP: I walked into that stupid room and she was on the floor! I saw something shiny on the ground so I picked it up

HP: I didn't know what was happening!!! You believe me right??

HP: Everyone's going to think I did it because of the fight

AH: Well

HP: I did NOT DO ANYTHING TO HER

HP: Is she going to be ok

HP: Henderson?

HP: You there

AH: I don't know. I'm kind of worried

AH: It's hard to figure out what they're saying

AH: I thought I heard somebody say a coma

HP: ohhh no

HP: I didn't do it!! You know that, right? I would never do that.

HP: Henderson??? You know that right????

CHAPTER ELEVEN

ALICE
FEBRUARY 12
1:38 A.M.

Only cats and witches walk in the dark.
—AGATHA CHRISTIE,
THE MOVING FINGER

"GOOD LORD, NEXT TIME we get trapped in a castle during a torrential rainstorm, let's do it somewhere with better roads," I say to Iris as we pull into my driveway at long last. "Or at least, *more* roads. That traffic was horrendous." Getting out of the Castle's parking lot and back down Highway 1 took approximately forever, even though it's less than a mile drive.

I stop my car at the top of the driveway and stretch before unbuckling my belt, relieved to finally be home. Iris is silent next to me.

"Tired?" I ask.

"Huh?" She blinks at me like she'd forgotten I was there. "Oh, no. Mostly just thinking. I have a weird feeling about all of this."

"Park?"

"Park," she confirms. "It looks really bad for her, and you know Thompson. How he operates. You told him she was holding the letter opener and standing over Kennedy and then there's their fight, which was filmed by like a hundred people. All of that spells trouble for her."

"You think she's innocent?"

"Not sure. But we have to be careful. Remember what happened with Coach last year."

I let out a displeased sound. "It's not like Coach was totally innocent. . . ."

"But he didn't kill Brooke, you know? We need to learn from that mistake, I think."

I sigh. "Fine. We can discuss. But inside, okay? Brenda's texted me about sixty-four times in the last hour asking if everything is okay, so I need to make an in-person appearance."

Outside the car, I hear the rush of unusually heavy late-night traffic back out on Highway 1 as everyone heads home from the Castle. Somewhere far in the distance, the wail of a siren cuts through the night. A shiver runs down my spine. I wonder if the cops arrested Park, if what I'm hearing is them taking her to the jail.

Iris is right. We have to think about this.

I'm about to say as much when there's a rustling sound from the row of trees closest to the cliffs. My heart jumps. What the hell was that?

I glance at Iris to make sure I'm not hearing things. She's frozen next to me, eyes trained on the tree line.

"Did you hear that?" she whispers.

"Yes," I whisper back. "That was . . ."

"Loud." She finishes. "Should we check . . . ?"

I shake my head. "It was probably just a squirrel."

"Yeah."

"A really big, loud squirrel."

Iris nods. "So, we should—"

We both sprint to the front door. While I'm fumbling with the keys, there's another, smaller sound behind us.

"Hurry up," Iris hisses.

"I'm trying—" I finally get my key into the lock and I'm about to shove the door open when movement catches in the corner of my eye.

I burst out a laugh.

"What?" Iris asks.

"That noise—did you see where it's coming from?"

"No?" She raises an eyebrow in question.

"Look over there."

"Is that . . . a cat?" Iris peers through the dark. "Oh my god, Alice, look at it! It's so tiny!"

A small kitten crawls up onto the grass between the driveway and the house.

"Yes," I say. "It's very . . . small."

"Let's bring it inside? It looks lost."

"*Ew,* no thank you." I swing open the front door. "I'm sure it has a perfectly nice life out here."

Iris looks back at the cat, hesitating for a second before following me inside.

"Alice?" Brenda's disembodied voice floats into the foyer. "Is that you?"

"Yes!" I call back.

She appears from the dining room wearing her pajamas, a mug of tea in hand. "Alice. Iris. Oh, thank god. You wouldn't believe the reports that were coming out of the Castle—they're saying that someone was stabbed, but they didn't say who and I was so worried." She puts her mug down on the front hall table and wraps me into a big bear hug. I'm slightly mortified, but there's no denying one of Brenda's hugs, so after a moment I sink into it.

"I'm so glad you're okay. And you, too, Iris," she says into my hair. My throat tightens. I pull away from her, clearing it a few times before speaking.

"See? I'm fine." I do a little curtsey, but Brenda is staring at Iris in horror.

"Dios mío, Iris," Brenda gasps. "Is that *blood*? What happened to you?"

Crap, I hadn't even noticed the blood on Iris's dress; I should have made her change in the car.

Iris glances down at it. "Well, it's kind of complicated. . . ."

"It's not her blood!" I jump in.

"Well, whose blood is it, then?" Brenda narrows her eyes at me. "Alice, that's not the dress you were wearing when you left the house earlier tonight. What happened? Did you get yourself involved in another situation—"

I fake a big yawn. "Brenda, I love you, but can we please do the whole *I'm so worried about you, stop sticking your nose in places it doesn't belong* thing tomorrow? I promise, that's not Iris's blood. We're here, in one piece. It's the middle of the night, and I'm *so* tired." I yawn again, this time, for real.

She purses her lips and, to my great relief, nods.

"Okayloveyougoodnight," I say. Skirt gathered in one hand, I run up the stairs before she changes her mind, Iris at my heels.

In my room, I throw myself across the bed. I'm exhausted. "Well . . . tonight was different," I mutter into my pillow.

I feel Iris sit down next to me. "Not that different, unfortunately," she says.

"True," I say, flopping over to my back and staring up at the ceiling for a long moment before I pull myself up to sit. "That was crazy. And Park never talked. I don't know what to do."

"Lemme see if there's any news," Iris says. She takes her phone out of her blazer pocket and a few small pieces of paper flutter down to the mattress.

"You dropped some trash." I point to the pieces.

Iris scoops them up. "No! Not trash," she says. "When they lifted Kennedy onto the gurney, I spotted these in the place where she'd been lying, stuck in all that blood. I wonder if they . . ."

She spreads the pieces out onto my comforter and starts examining them. "Look! These fit together!" She holds up two fragments with scribbling on them and then places them next to each other on the bed.

I poke through the paper. "These match!" I say, scooting over to make room on the bed. We hurriedly match the rest of the pieces together, forming part of a small piece of paper.

"Are there any more?" I ask, and Iris shakes her head.

She reads what we have. "Some of them must be missing. We have the word *Meet* . . . look at those *e*'s, how they're written like backward threes . . . and this part says *nine-thirty*. Maybe that's the time they planned to meet?" She looks at me. "That would make sense, given the timing of how things went down tonight. Then there's a chunk missing, but . . . here's, I think, the word *Study*?"

"Do you think someone sent this note to Kennedy telling her to meet them in Levy's study? Good lord. Does this mean—" I look at Iris with wide eyes.

"Could be from the person who attacked Kennedy, but maybe not. Could be from anyone who was in that room at any time for any reason. But why did someone tear it up? And when? We should—" She jumps off my bed.

"Where are your yearbooks?" Iris says.

I make a face. "Um, is now really the time for a trip down memory lane?"

She shakes her head. "No—did Park sign your yearbook last year?"

"Yeah, and? I— Oh!" It finally dawns on me what she's saying. "We can compare handwriting."

"Yeeees," she says. "Took you a minute."

"It's been a long night." I rub my eyes. "They're over there." I point to the big bookshelf that runs the length of one wall. It's filled with my entire collection of Agatha Christie books, including her short stories, and a bunch of other mystery novels I've gotten into over the past few months.

"Yearbooks are bottom shelf."

Iris finds what she's looking for and brings it back over to the bed. She starts flipping through it. "Where would Park have written?"

"Check the front." That's where we always signed our names: me and Brooke, Kennedy and Park and Henderson.

Iris flips to the front. "Henderson . . . Kennedy . . . Steve . . . here it is!" Her finger lands on a scribble. *"Ogilvie, ur 1 crazy beyatch,"* she reads, and wrinkles her nose. "Lovely sentiment."

"Park's not exactly a poet."

Iris points to the pieced-together note. "So those ε's, how they're written in caps, a sloppy sort of cursive?"

"Yeah?"

"And see how Park wrote hers, here?" Iris points to the inscription. "They're different."

I look back and forth between the letters. "You really think this is enough to prove that someone else did it? I'm not saying I disagree, I just . . ."

"I think," Iris says, "that this is a good place to start. You know Park. Does she seem like the type of person who could stab someone?"

I consider this and then shake my head. "I can't see her stabbing someone, no. Drugging them? Sure. But I don't think she has the balls to hurt someone if she has to see their face. Though, then again, sometimes the quiet ones surprise you. You've read *And Then There Were None,* right?"

Iris nods.

"Think about Vera Claythorne, the tutor. How she seems so sweet and innocent at first, but then you find out—"

"True . . . ," Iris muses.

"Plus, Park ran. Why would you run if you were innocent?"

"Well, you found her holding the letter opener. I think it's entirely possible that she panicked and ran out of fear, not because she's guilty." She picks up her phone. "What did Agatha Christie once write? Lemme find it . . . oh yes. *'But I know human nature, my friend, and I tell you that, suddenly confronted with the possibility of being tried for murder, the most innocent person will lose his head and do the most absurd things.'*

"Do you understand what I'm trying to say?" she asks, watching me closely.

I turn it over in my head. My brain feels like it's been dipped in molasses, but what she's getting at clicks after a long moment. I nod.

"Yes," I say. "Park might have run not because she was guilty, but because she was scared. It makes sense. But you *know*

Thompson and his cronies aren't going to see it that way. Park's in deep shit." I yawn and glance at the clock on my phone. It's nearing three a.m.

"I'm too tired to think. All that running through the Castle . . ." I yawn again. I want to stay awake, want to work on this more, but I can barely think straight. "I need to crash for a few hours so I can tackle this with a fresh mind." I fall back on my bed and burrow under the covers without waiting for a reply. Seconds later, I fall into a deep sleep.

CHAPTER TWELVE

IRIS

FEBRUARY 12

3:45 A.M.

*My head is positively spinning, Henry! One thing is
for sure, we can't trust anyone.*
—MONA MOODY, *THE HOUSE AT THE END
OF THE STREET*, 1946

I'M SURPRISED ALICE WAS able to fall asleep so easily, and yet I'm
not surprised. Alice is good at turning things off. Or at least she
seems to be. Not me.

I'm lying next to her in her enormous bed, staring at the
glamorous dress she stole from the Castle, draped over a plush
chair. Was it Mona Moody's? Did Alice put on the dress of a dead
woman and not blink an eye? Next to it, my own velvet jacket,
crusted in blood from being stuffed under Kennedy's head.

Alice's house is quiet. So different than my apartment would
be, where people are moving throughout the building at all
hours. Getting ready for night shifts, coming home from work.
Televisions droning. Dogs whining to go out.

I check my phone. I'd called my mom during the car ride to
Alice's from the Castle. She was relieved to hear my voice and
relented about me going to Alice's for the night.

I thought Cole might text, but there's nothing. I guess I could text him, but what would I say? *Sorry I freaked out. You got so angry I thought you were going to hit me, like my dad would have done.* I know he knows about what my dad did to me last fall; he saw my face the day we caught Westmacott, the day I thought, for an hour or so, that Cole might have been Brooke's murderer. But we've never talked about it.

I wish I could stop thinking about the Thing. I wish he'd evaporate from my brain, stop making me scared of sudden noises, even sudden silences. It was too freaky when Alice and I heard that noise outside earlier. I know he's in jail, but I also know he'll get out soon. It's like I can never fully relax. I'm always waiting.

I sigh, staring at my phone, practically willing it to light up.

And then it does. But it's not Cole calling. It's Lilian.

It's Lilian Levy. I get off the bed and move to a far corner of Alice's room so as not to wake her.

"Hi," I say softly.

Lilian's voice is at once familiar: soothing, calm, almost bemused. "Can you girls even have one night of peace? I'm beginning to think you're both as cursed as the Castle."

"So, you heard."

"Of course I heard. I'm worried about you! I've kept myself up hoping you were all right! And that poor girl. The PR manager for the Castle has been wailing in my ear all night, too. I must have spoken to him fourteen times already. Beautiful movie star who perished at the Castle? Now, *that's* a mystery that draws people in. Local girl stabbed? Not wonderful for the optics, my dear."

"It might be one of Brooke's old friends who did it. We aren't sure."

"I'm all ears. Do tell."

I sigh. This is going to sound nuts. "Alice came up through a secret staircase passageway thingy into the study and found them. She was trying on a gown in like a cedar closet?"

"Oh, yes," Lilian breathes. "Probably one of Mona's. Her belongings became the property of the Castle during the embezzlement proceedings. They trot them out sometimes for exhibitions. And the secret staircase! There are so many secrets in the Castle. Mrs. Pinsky—she worked in the kitchen—used to delight in adventuring with me to discover them. She was quite young and had no children of her own—I don't think she could—and oh, I adored her. After Mona died and I was sent away, I think she and her husband left the Castle. I never saw her ag—"

"Anyway," I interrupt, before she can keep going down memory lane. "Alice found them, Park and Kennedy. Kennedy was unconscious on the floor and Park was standing over her holding a bloody letter opener. Then Park ran away. As you can probably guess, Alice and I are very interested in this whole thing now."

There's a pause.

"Kennedy? As in, Rebecca Kennedy?" Lilian's voice is crisp. "They haven't used her name in the media yet."

"No."

"Interesting."

"Why?" I'm running my fingers along Alice's collection of books. So many mysteries, and now we have another one of our own. But authors are lucky: they know how things will end before they even begin, right? Real life is another matter.

"The Kennedy family has been twisting Castle Cove into knots for years and years. Perhaps now a chicken has come home to roost."

Chicken? "What do you mean?"

"I must go. I'm simply exhausted now. I'm a rambling old woman who's been up all night, don't mind me. One last thing, though."

"Yeah?"

"Be careful. You and Ms. Ogilvie have made many enemies in Castle Cove, some who you might not even be aware of."

Then she clicks off.

I shudder. Enemies? We solved Lilian's granddaughter's murder last fall, for crying out loud. Isn't that a good thing?

Well, there is Coach and that whole *us accidentally getting him arrested for Brooke's murder and at the same time revealing he* might *have been involved in the death of his* first *wife*, so yeah, he probably hates us. That's valid. My mom says he comes into the bar sometimes and just sits quietly drinking and not talking to anyone. I wonder what he's doing with his life now that he doesn't work at the school anymore and everyone in town is pretty convinced he's responsible for at least *one* murder. He might be rich, but his life is ruined.

I think of the sound outside earlier. What if it wasn't just a kitten?

I look over at Alice on the bed. Sleeping, Alice's face is perfect and beautiful. Peaceful. It's a shame I'm going to have to wake her up, tell her we need to go back to the Castle on the ruse of picking up her dress and dropping off Mona's so we can poke around. But when? It's a crime scene now, right? It's got to be closed. There's so much to work out. Obviously, Kennedy wasn't just stabbed, she was hit on the head with something. But *what*? And *why*? The room was torn apart; someone was looking for something. And how *is* Kennedy? There are so many questions swirling in my brain.

Park's writing isn't the same as on the ripped paper pieces, but the note could be from *anybody*. Who was Kennedy at the dance with? A corsage fell from beneath her as she was lifted onto the gurney. Did the police take it? Was it hers? Who gave it to her? Would their fingerprints be on the stem? Somewhere? This is going to require Raf and his sneakiness at the police station. We need to know, just to be *sure*, that the police are working all the angles. And why would Lilian say that weird thing about the Kennedy family and chickens coming home to roost and Castle Cove? My brain is reeling.

I walk over to Alice's mammoth bed.

"Alice!" I shout. "Alice, get up. Get up now."

She blinks blearily from under a sheath of glossy hair. "Rude, Iris. I am trying to *sleep*," she mumbles.

"You can sleep when you're dead," I tell her as my eyes settle on a whiteboard sitting in the corner of her massive room. She must have moved it in from the conservatory, where we did our work for the Brooke Donovan case. Across it she's scribbled *Mona Moody, Charles Levy, real mystery or senseless tragedy?* And a bunch of dates—what looks like a rough timeline. She's been busy on her own, apparently, thinking about Mona Moody, which is certainly something that piques my interest, but right now we have more immediate things to ponder.

I reach down and flip the whiteboard over to the fresh side so I don't ruin Alice's Mona Moody investigative work, and pick up a black marker.

"Iris," Alice says. "Are you . . . drawing a *chicken*?"

"Yes," I say. "Listen to me, Alice. We have a note that may or may not be from the person who attacked Kennedy. I just had a very cryptic conversation with Lilian. And we have Park standing over Kennedy's body with a letter opener in hand, with you, Alice Ogilvie, as the only witness. That means your word could put her in jail. And we should make freaking sure this time around that we don't make mistakes. So yes, I'm drawing a chicken, because one might have escaped the coop, and things are going to get a little crazy."

KWB, CHANNEL 10

Breaking News

February 12

6:00 a.m.

Ben Perez: As dawn breaks on Castle Cove, the town is still in the midst of recovering from the storm last night.

Valerie Metz: It was a dark and stormy night in more ways than one, Ben. Road crews were out before midnight, clearing the mudslide that blocked Highway One, and half the town is still without electricity. Yet, the most disturbing thing to occur was not weather-related at all, but an incidence of violence against a Castle Cove High School student. We have an update on that situation.

Ben Perez: That's right, Valerie. Since it involves minors, we're not releasing the names of the parties at this time, but we *can* say that one was medevaced from the Levy Castle to Mercy General. They underwent surgery and are currently in a medically induced coma due to injuries from the alleged assault. The other party is being questioned as a person of interest.

We're told this person is another student at Castle Cove High School.

Valerie Metz: The kids are not all right, Ben.

Ben Perez: You can say that again, Valerie.

TEXT CONVERSATION BETWEEN
ALICE OGILVIE AND RAFAEL RAMIREZ
FEBRUARY 12
3:32 P.M.

AO: Any updates?

RR: Hello to you too Alice

AO: Good lord. HI. Any updates?

RR: I guess you havent turned on the news recently have you?

AO: No

RR: Well it looks like youre sending someone else to jail. Again

AO: Excuse me?

RR: The cops have formally charged Park . . . and I hate to tell you this but youre the sole witness that puts her in that room holding the murder weapon

AO: Theyre charging her already?

RR: Yeah but she'll be out on bail by tomorrow
morning. Her lawyers dont mess around

RR: It doesn't look good for her. You placed her at
the scene with the weapon. The cops found pieces of a
note that implicate her. Theyre talking about it like
it's a slam dunk.

AO: Pieces of a note? What did it say?

RR: You know I cant tell you that

AO: Well WE have good reason to suspect that someone
who is not Park lured Kennedy up to that room

RR: What do you mean you have reason to suspect?

RR: Whats the reason?

RR: Alice if you know something you have to tell the
cops. Like immediately

AO: I have to go

CHAPTER THIRTEEN

ALICE

FEBRUARY 13

6:39 A.M.

No innocent person ever has an alibi.

—AGATHA CHRISTIE,

THE BODY IN THE LIBRARY

I'M ALMOST FINISHED GETTING dressed Monday morning when my phone buzzes with a text from Iris.

Still good to meet in the Pit before class?

Yesterday, Iris worked at the Moon Landing and I spent the morning mostly in my room, thinking about what had happened the night before and how we might best help Park. Around midday, Brenda knocked on my door and told me there were detectives downstairs who wanted to speak to me about that night. I found Thompson and his partner waiting in our formal living room.

They asked me, yet again, whether I'd found Park in that room with the letter opener in her hand. Obviously, I had to reply yes, and they didn't listen to anything I said after that, even when I told them Agatha Christie once said that "real evidence is usually vague and unsatisfactory."

In fact, they laughed when I brought Christie up.

Clearly, they see an easy answer and are trying to wrap up the case posthaste, without considering other potential assailants.

Which is where Iris and I come in.

See you there, I respond to Iris.

I'm lost in thought as I make my way to the kitchen, compiling a mental list of all the things we need to talk about, and don't notice the voices coming from there until I'm halfway through the dining room.

Great. My mother must be home. She's been saying she was going to show up one of these days, and I guess she made good on the threat. Maybe I can just slip out of here and head to school before—

"Alice, is that you?" Brenda calls, ruining my escape.

I sigh. "Yes." I head into the kitchen, mentally preparing myself for my mother.

But when I reach the entryway, I realize I woefully underestimated the situation at hand. Sure enough, Brenda and my mother are sitting there . . . and so is my father.

My mom's white-blond hair is perfectly coiffed, her makeup tastefully understated, her Jil Sander cashmere turtleneck expensively minimalist. She has that sort of ageless beauty that only good genes, expensive skincare products, and a world-class surgeon can buy.

My dad's face is half-obscured by the *Wall Street Journal,* his salt-and-pepper hair poking up from the top of the paper. He's one of the few people left in the world who still prefers to read a hard copy of his morning news. When he sees me, he lowers the paper and pushes his eyeglasses up his nose.

"Morning, Alice," says Brenda the Traitor. She could have at least texted me to let me know this was happening in our kitchen. I glare at her and she gives a tiny shrug of apology.

"Alice," my mother says, standing and moving toward me with outstretched arms. When she reaches me, she pats my shoulders, air kissing my cheeks. No hug. Of course not.

My father rises part of the way off his stool, hand raised in greeting, but I make no move toward him and he sinks back down.

"Hello, Alice. Nice to see you."

I force the corners of my mouth up. "Father. Mother. What a pleasant surprise." A total lie, but then again that's pretty much what our relationship is predicated on, so.

I walk over to the cabinet above the kitchen sink, take out a to-go cup, and pour some coffee from the pot into it as they continue on with their previous conversation like I'm not even here.

Brenda sidles up next to me, taking the pot from my hand. "Are you okay?" she asks in a low voice.

It's clear whose side she's on, given I received absolutely no heads-up on this horrifying development.

"I'm *great.*"

She gives me a look. "Alice."

"Brenda," I reply, mimicking her tone.

"I'm sorry I didn't tell you they were coming; I didn't know for sure until early this morning when they arrived and you were asleep—"

I plaster on my prettiest, fakest smile. "It's fine. Now I have to get going, or I'll be late for school."

"Heading off already?" my dad says in a hearty voice as I retrace my steps out of the kitchen. It's the voice he usually reserves for strangers, which I suppose is appropriate, considering we've spoken three times in the past four months.

"Yes." I try to keep my voice as neutral as possible. They don't deserve my energy. They didn't even bother to tell me they were coming home.

"Darling, why don't you take the morning off? We'd love to catch up with you," my mother says. "I brought you a first edition of *A Caribbean Mystery,* which I found up in Vancouver last month. Plus, Brenda tells us that you've made some new friends, which I was so glad to hear after all that *terribleness* last fall—"

"You've heard of cell phones, right?" I interrupt, ignoring the comment about *A Caribbean Mystery.* Sure, on the surface it might seem nice that she bought me a first-edition Agatha Christie novel, but here's the thing: She has money. Spending it on things is easy. Showing up, in person, when I need her is what's hard, and what she doesn't do.

My mom stops talking, pressing her lips into a thin white line before she responds.

"Yes, Alice. I have."

"Well, if you were so interested in catching up with me, you could have used one." I've never talked to them like this before, but I really don't care if they're angry about it. The three of us haven't been in the same room together since last summer. My dad didn't even bother to call to see if I was okay after everything happened with Brooke. I've spent years pretending their lack of interest in me doesn't bother me, but I've just about reached the end of my rope.

My mother visibly bristles. "Alice, please. I know we've been a little out of touch recently, but—"

"Recently?" I scoff.

"Alice, watch your tone. That's your mother you're speaking to," my father says, voice sharp, reminding me that I want nothing more than to be as far from the two of them as possible.

"Never mind. I barely noticed you were gone," I say. "Anyway, I have to get to school. I'll see you later."

And with that, I walk out of the room.

I find Iris waiting as promised in the bathroom commonly known as the Pit, tucked onto a small counter under the room's only window. She's scribbling in a notebook.

She looks up and smiles as I enter. It's nice to be around someone who's pleased to see me, rather than someone who's only there because of blood ties. Our whole grade is doing a dumb project on genealogy in bio right now, and that's one of the reasons I've put it off for so long—why should I spend my time tracking down my extended family, when I already know what a disappointment my immediate family can be? The other reason is that McAllister paired me up with Ashley Henderson, like the cruel, cruel man he is.

"My parents are home," I say as I swing my bag up onto the counter.

Her eyes widen. "*Both* of them?"

"Both of them," I confirm, raising my thermos for a slug, only to find it empty. Dammit. I should have stopped at Dotty's on my way to school, but I was running late because of my parents' unexpected appearance. Which is yet another thing that's their fault.

"Are you . . . okay?" Iris asks, voice tentative.

"I'm fine." I wave a hand. "Let's get down to business."

"Alice——" she starts, but I cut her off.

"Can we not do this?" I say pointedly, and she nods. We know each other well enough at this point to know when not to push certain things—the stuff with her dad, how jumpy she's been since he got put behind bars, me with my absentee parents. Raf. Spike and Cole. It's a running list.

"Absolutely. Let's begin," she says, and scoots over so I can get into my bag.

As I rummage through it, I start to talk. "First of all, Raf told me the cops have part of a note, which I'm guessing is the other half of the one you found."

"They do?"

I finally locate my notebook and tug it free. "Yeah. He wouldn't tell me what it says, exactly, but he claims it gave them the evidence they needed to arrest Park."

"But the handwriting on the part of the note we have doesn't match Park's!"

"I know. I was thinking that we might need to get that to them somehow——"

"No way. Absolutely not," interrupts Iris. "Thompson told me the night of the dance that he'd haul me in if he found out I'd tampered with the crime scene. I can't even imagine what he'd do if he found out I stole evidence."

I think for a moment. "We could turn it in anonymously?"

Iris shakes her head. "We pieced the note together. Our

fingerprints are all over it. We'd be in so much trouble; they might even think *we* did something to Kennedy. My mom . . . she'd kill me." Her voice wavers. "I messed up, Alice." She slumps backward against the wall.

She's right. There's no way we can put that note in front of the cops now. But she looks so despondent, all I want to do is make her feel better.

"It's okay!" I pat her knee awkwardly. "There are other ways we can show the cops that they should be looking at people other than Park. Ways that won't end with you going to jail."

Iris takes a deep breath and then pushes herself up off the wall. Some color has returned to her cheeks, and I feel a small flash of pride that I managed to help her. "True. We need to figure out who else had motive and opportunity to do that to Kennedy. No one was getting into or out of the Castle during that time because of the mudslide. The suspect list would be limited to the Castle."

"A closed-circle mystery," I mutter.

"A what?" Iris asks.

"That's what it's called: when there are only a certain number of suspects because of the setting of a crime—in this case because a storm blocked access to the Castle. Like you said, the only people who could have done it were already inside. Agatha Christie used closed circles a lot—*Murder on the Orient Express* and *And Then There Were None* are two of the best-known examples, and—"

"So that helps, right?" Iris cuts in, interrupting my rundown of Christie's collected works. I suppose she's heard it before.

"Yes," I say, working it out, "except we still have to consider all our classmates, the teachers who were there, and everyone working at the Castle and the party."

"True . . . but doesn't the assault seem personal? Like, whoever did it, they stabbed *and*—judging from her head injury—hit Kennedy. That seems kind of excessive for a run-of-the-mill high school spat she might have had with one of our classmates. And then there's what Lilian said about people who have vendettas against the Kennedy family as a whole. Did someone attack Kennedy for something her family has done?"

I mull this over. "All good questions."

Iris scribbles something down in her casebook. "Okay. I guess the other question is, *Why* did Kennedy do what the note asked? Was she expecting to find someone in particular when she walked into that room? I double-checked last night, and according to the videos posted on socials, Kennedy and Park had their fight at nine-fourteen p.m., and you got upstairs at . . . what time?"

"It was nine-thirty-six p.m."

"Okay." She writes that down. "Plus, we should find out if she had a date. And, maybe before anything else, we need to try to talk to Park. Raf said she'd be out of jail today?"

"Yeah, on bail. She should be home soon." I sigh, remembering how reluctant to talk Park had been that night. "At the dance, she wouldn't tell me anything. Wouldn't even talk to me. Though, now that she knows she's in deep trouble, she might be more inclined."

"All right. That's a good start," Iris says, gathering her stuff together. "I have to run. I have a genealogy quiz in McAllister's class second period, but we can ditch out before lunch and go to Park's. Do you have a quiz in his class, too?"

"Yeah," I say with clear distaste. Right now, the thought of going to class is even more unappealing than it usually is. We have a case to solve.

Iris raises an eyebrow. "Alice, you're going to go to class, right?

You know what Principal Brown said about your attendance record. You have to go to class—"

"Yeah, yeah. I'm going." I grab my bag and follow her out of the bathroom. I don't add that when I say I'm going, I don't exactly mean to *class*.

Iris stops in the hall, hiking her backpack farther up onto her shoulders. "All right, we'll regroup before lunch?" she says. "We can head over to Park's house then?"

"Sure," I say. I wave her off and pretend to head in the opposite direction. I wait until she's disappeared around the corner, then duck into the nearest empty classroom.

I don't care what Brown or anyone else says. Sitting in geometry class, learning about right angles, isn't going to help stop people from getting murdered.

I settle down into the teacher's empty chair and take my laptop out of my bag.

**THE KENNEDYS: CASTLE COVE, CA, ROYALTY
THREE FAST FACTS YOU NEED TO KNOW**

The rich and moderately famous of Castle Cove, California, are at it again. News broke late the night of February 11 that one Rebecca Kennedy, former classmate of now-deceased American heiress Brooke Donovan (granddaughter of Levy Cosmetics founder Lilian Levy, and great-granddaughter of billionaire hotelier and movie producer Charles W. Levy), is in critical condition following an attack that took place in none other than Levy Castle.

Here are three fast facts you should know about the Kennedy family and their connection to the Levy family:

Much like her former classmate Brooke Donovan, Rebecca Kennedy comes from a family that was instrumental in the founding of Castle Cove, California, and has been there for generations.

Her family came to prominence in the mid-1950s, a rise that was inversely proportionate to the Levy family's, as Charles W. Levy was incarcerated for embezzlement around that same time.

Her father, Robert Kennedy, a real estate developer and former music producer, is heavily involved in state and local politics, and is one of the drivers of plans to develop high-end condos along much of the coastline in Central California. The plans, heralded by state officials as a positive for the surrounding local economies, are concerning to both environmentalists and small-business owners, who worry the development will serve to drive them out of business, as well as the lower-income homeowners who may soon find their dwellings demolished to make way for more high-end condos and a luxury resort.

CHAPTER FOURTEEN

IRIS
FEBRUARY 13
9:45 A.M.

There are too many clues to keep track of, Henry!
This case has gone completely cockeyed.
—MONA MOODY, *THE HOUSE AT THE END
OF THE STREET,* 1946

I SHOULD HAVE STUDIED harder for this quiz, but I was tired when I got home last night. Around me, everyone is tapping away at their iPads. McAllister likes to assign quizzes using an app that's a little wonky and sometimes you get logged out halfway through and have to get him to sign you back in. That's exactly what happens to me. I stare at the error message on the screen. Across the room, a student grunts in frustration and heads up to McAllister's desk. Good. He'll be busy for a few minutes.

Two rows over, Rebecca Kennedy's desk and chair are conspicuously empty. She's been my lab partner all year. McAllister hasn't given me a new one.

I text Raf. *News?* I decide not to mention that Alice told me about the police having other pieces of the note, or that *I* have the pieces they might need.

He answers immediately. *Castle closed. They've got some forensics and investigators out there. Park's dad got a real legend for a lawyer, by the way.*

No doubt. They practically bleed money, I answer. *Are the cops looking at anyone else besides Park? There were a lot of people in the Castle.*

> **Alice putting her in the room got Helen charged, but they're doing more interviews today. Not sure how far they've gotten, but what about Kennedy's date? Did she have one?**
>
> We're going to find out.
>
> **Did Alice tell you about the note?**

My stomach tightens. Dammit. *Yes.*

> **The police think Helen gave Rebecca that note to get her upstairs so she could attack her. That's pretty damning, especially after their fight.**

My stomach is on fire now. I don't know what to do. The handwriting on the note is *not* Park's, and this could help her, but . . .

I swallow hard. *Raf,* I type. *Please don't hate me.*

> **Whaaat?? What is it?**
>
> I have some of that note. I took it. That night. But please, you have to know, the handwriting on the pieces I have, they don't match Park's! We checked Alice's yearbook! That note's not from her

I watch as an endless succession of the "typing" dots appear and disappear.

Iris, Raf types, finally. *If it's evidence, it has to be given to the police. NOW.*

I can't. You heard Thompson, he'll put me in jail.

It could have fingerprints on it, Iris. From someone else, then, if not Helen. It's a clue.

Tears spring to my eyes. It would kill my mother if I got in trouble like this.

I can't. Alice and I are going to do what we can for Park, but I can't, I just can't.

Don't make me, Raf. Please.

Fine. I'll think on this. There might be something I can do. But now your fingerprints, and Alice's, are on it, too. Iris, I thought you were smarter about this stuff.

I bristle a little. *It was a mistake.*

I decide to change the subject.

So, the people at the Castle, I type. *Potential suspects. There were a lot. Kids, chaperones, Castle staff, cater waiters . . .*

Why one of the waiters? That means I'm a suspect, too, right? Let's not get hasty. He inserts a smiley face with a stuck-out tongue emoji.

FINE.

Don't get mad! I'm just saying!

A loud sucking sound to my left makes me look up. It's Tabitha Berrington, the Stitch Bitch who pulled Spike onto the dance floor at the Castle, slurping a cherry yogurt, even though we aren't supposed to eat in class. She's hunched over her desk and iPad. A glob of yogurt drops onto her shirt. She tries to wipe it away. Gross. Does Spike know his dance partner is such a slob?

I blink, watching as the pinkish stain smears across her shirt.

Raf, I type quickly, *there was a lot of blood on Kennedy, and in the room.*

Uh, I imagine so. Head trauma. The stab wounds.

So . . . whoever hurt her? There'd be blood on their clothes, right?

There goes my lunch, Iris. Thanks. But, yeah, most likely. Depends on the angle and the force of the object. You can't come out of that without blood on you. I don't think.

Right. So . . . blood on clothes, right?

I'm going to hazard a yes on that.

Did Park have blood on her? I can't remember. Did you notice? In the basement?

It was a little crazy. I don't remember, now that you mention it.

Can you find out? Like, would it be in the investigation notes? Did they take Park's clothes for evidence? Her shoes?

Can you hear me sighing right now, Iris?

Yup.

88

So I'm getting roped back into Alice and Iris World, am I right? You two are doing this? Again?

> We're just sussing things out, Raf.
> Obviously we have faith in the Castle
> Cove PD.

I want you to imagine the groan that's emanating from me right now, Iris, Raf types.

Fine, Alice and I will find out ourselves, I type.

I'll do it.

Also, he types, *on another note, I have some Remy Jackson stuff. There's an interview with Veronica Chavez. She owns the laundry on Guadalupe and—*

"Ms. Adams?"

It's McAllister, standing over me. The classroom is empty. I shove my phone under my hoodie.

"What a day for you," he says sarcastically. "Your first F in my class. How *ever* will you celebrate?"

My face burns as I slide my iPad into my backpack. I stand up and brush by him. Why was he standing so close to my desk? What a creep. He was one of the chaperones at the dance, too. If you don't like kids, why be a teacher in the first place? Or even chaperone a dumb dance?

On my way out of the classroom, I make a mental note to add McAllister to the list of suspects Alice and I will have to compile. Spite is a good feeling sometimes.

CHAPTER FIFTEEN

ALICE
FEBRUARY 13
11:43 A.M.

"Ah, mais c'est Anglais ça," he murmured, "everything
in black-and-white, everything clear cut and well
defined. But life, it is not like that, Mademoiselle.
There are things that are not yet, but which cast
their shadow before."

—AGATHA CHRISTIE, *THE MYSTERY OF THE BLUE TRAIN*

MY CLASSMATES STREAM BY me as I stand outside the entrance
to the cafeteria. They chat like it's just another normal day in
Castle Cove, California. Brown's half-hearted announcement
during second period was heavy on thoughts and prayers for
Kennedy, but lacking any concrete information or updates. The
general consensus around here seems to be that Park did it and we
can all get back to our regularly scheduled programming. I swear
to god some of my classmates are so oblivious, it's entirely possible that they've already forgotten what happened at the dance
altogether.

Through the throng, on the other side of the hallway, I
catch sight of Henderson standing by her locker with her phone
pressed to her ear. She's leaning against a sign advertising the

Sadie Hawkins dance, frowning like whoever's on the other end of the line is really disappointing her.

I generally try to avoid Henderson as much as humanly possible, especially these days, but I'd bet money that she knows the latest breaking news on Kennedy's health. Her dad works as a gaffer for movies down in LA, and her family has never had quite as much money as the rest of us. She's always used information as a way to make up for that gap.

I wave to her, but she doesn't notice—or pretends not to, at least—so I march over and tap her hard on the shoulder.

"*Ouch!* Hang—" she says to the person on the other end. She turns, finding me behind her. "Oh, for god's sake—I gotta go," she says, and hangs up, turning to me with nostrils flaring.

"Yes, Ogilvie? By the way, where were you in bio this morning? McAllister was pissed—you have to show up and do your work or it's going to affect my grade, too, you know."

"Who was that?" I ignore her question. It's not *my* fault that McAllister forced us to be partners for the genealogy project we're doing in his class. "Have you heard anything about Kennedy? Is she awake yet? Has she told anyone what happened?"

Henderson sniffs. "So many questions. No. According to Kennedy's little sister, Rayne—"

"I know who Rayne is," I mutter. God, Henderson is annoying.

"Yeah, well, I thought maybe you'd forgotten, since you decided hanging out with that weird Iris girl was more important than your old friends," she says. "Anyway, according to Rayne, Kennedy is in a medically induced coma to try to keep the swelling in her brain down. Plus, we already *know* what happened. Park smashed Kennedy over the head then stabbed her. Who would have thought timid little Park had it in her, right? Girl's turned out to be a real cuckoo."

I frown. "I don't think—"

"You don't think what, Alice?" She cuts me off. "Saturday night, you were the one who found her in that room, standing over the body with a *weapon* in her hand. You're changing your tune now? Remember, this is the same person who drugged Steve last semester. She practically caused Brooke's dea—"

"I'm covering all my bases," I interrupt.

"Riiiight," Henderson says. "You sound like Rayne. For a thirteen-year-old, she sure has a lot of opinions."

She turns her back to me and starts digging for something in her open locker. I'm tempted to thwap her, but force myself to refrain. I won't get anything out of her if I cause her bodily harm.

"She doesn't think Park did it?" I ask, surprised. Kennedy's little sister has been off at boarding school for the last six months, so I haven't seen her for a while. She's always been precocious, to say the least. Kennedy used to say Rayne reminded her of me, which in my opinion is a huge compliment to Rayne, but never quite sounded like one coming out of Kennedy's mouth.

"She's thirteen," Henderson says into her locker. "I wouldn't put a lot of weight on her opinion. What *I* think," she says, slamming her locker door shut and then turning around to face me, "is that just because you were right one time, about Steve, doesn't mean you were right the other time. Remember how you dragged Coach's name through the mud? You really want to go down that path again?"

I bristle. I'm about to give Henderson a piece of my mind, but before I can, Iris runs up to us, breathless, and grabs Henderson's arm.

"What the——" Henderson pulls out of her grasp with a scowl.

"Oh god, sorry, I thought you were Alice from the back," she says, looking between us in horror. "Your hair is the exact same color . . ."

"Gross." Henderson makes a rude expression. "I gotta go. See you later, Ogilvie."

"Not if I see you first," I mutter at her back as she walks away. I cannot believe McAllister is forcing me to do a school project with that . . . that total B.

Iris shudders. "I can't believe I touched her. What was that all about?"

"Nothing. Henderson's a jerk," I say, shaking off Henderson's words.

"You ready?" Iris asks.

I nod and the two of us take off out of school.

We drive up Highway 1 and I pull off toward Park's house, stopping in front of the large wrought-iron gate that blocks the entrance to her driveway. I roll down my window and press the button on the security intercom.

"Hello," comes a faint voice. "Who is calling, please?" It's Park's nanny.

"Frances, it's me. Alice Ogilvie," I answer. "I'm here to see Helen. Open up."

A long pause. "Helen is not available at the moment, Miss Ogilvie. You may want to——"

"I know she's there," I interrupt. "She's got nowhere to go. And if you don't let me in, I'll have Brenda cut you off from the Castle Cove nanny club. No more goss——"

"Go away, Alice." It's Park now, her voice wavering. "Leave me alone."

I sigh. "Park, you need our help. I know you're being charged for assault and battery. We can help. Let us in."

Silence.

Iris leans across me.

"Helen," she says firmly. "It's Iris Adams. We don't think you did it and we think we can prove that. And frankly, we're your only friends right now."

"Nice," I whisper.

There's a long pause in which we can hear Park's soft, anxious breath through the intercom.

Then, with an elegant squeak, the massive gates in front of us begin to part.

"I don't even know why I let you in here," Park says as she paces back and forth in front of the giant fireplace in her living room. "My dad would kill me—" Her cheeks redden at this turn of phrase. "I mean, be so mad at me if he finds out. Which, he will, because he knows everything that happens in this house."

Iris cuts her eyes to me, probably wondering if Park's dad is as terrifying as she makes him sound.

He is, but I keep my face composed. "We're here to help you, Park. Stop freaking out."

She turns to face me. "Um, sorry if I don't buy it, *Alice*. The last time I saw you, you had me trapped in a tiny room in that dank, nasty basement so the cops could take me in. And now, what, I'm supposed to believe you're suddenly on my side?"

"First of all, *Helen*," I say. "You were standing over Kennedy's bleeding body holding a weapon. Sometimes the most obvious answer is the correct one. Hello, have you never heard of Occam's razor?"

"I'm surprised you have," Park says rather nastily.

"You know what—" I start to get up, but Iris's hand clamps onto my arm.

"Can we stay on subject, please?" she says. "Park, you need to listen to us. Alice and I don't think you did it."

"Then why'd she tell the cops all that stuff?" Park says, her voice rising. "She did this to me!"

"I told them the truth!" I yell back. "It's not *my* fault that the truth looks so bad for you."

Park lets out a squeak and Iris gives me a dirty look.

"I think what Alice means," Iris says, "is that we know this situation is not . . . ideal, and we don't want to be the reason you go down for something you didn't do." She motions to me, and after a moment I nod. "So, again, we're here to help."

Park sinks down on the couch, head dropping into her hands. A moment goes by, then another. It's painfully quiet. I'm about to break the silence but Iris catches me and puts a finger to her lips.

After another long minute, Park finally meets our eyes. "I need to talk to my dad." She grabs her phone off the coffee table and walks out of the room.

"What is up with her dad?" Iris whispers to me, and I shrug, pretending I'm not worried. Which I'm not . . . at least not really. Sure, Park's dad is intimidating as hell, and sure, I have always tried to avoid being in the same vicinity as him as much as humanly possible, but . . . I'm sure it'll be fine. We're here to help Park, and if there's one thing that man loves, it's his daughter.

Park comes back into the room, her mouth tugging down at

the corners. "He said he'll be here in two minutes and I'm not supposed to say a word until he is."

I make an irritated noise in the back of my throat. She's acting like we're the enemy—or the *cops*—when all we're trying to do is help her. I don't want to get into another situation where someone's life is pulled apart because of something I said.

No matter what Henderson might claim, Coach wasn't totally innocent. At the end of the day, I'm pretty sure everyone would agree that it's likely his first wife's death was not exactly on the up-and-up. But I still recognize that the way things went down with him was maybe not the best.

"Park, you know we're only trying to help here. Maybe you could—" I stop at the sound of the front door opening. Her dad. Anxiety stabs at my gut.

"Dad!" Park yelps, jumping off the couch and running into the foyer. Iris and I exchange a glance, and I wipe my hands against the fabric of my pants.

"It'll be fine," I say unconvincingly.

"Right. Fine," Iris replies.

A moment later, Park returns, followed by her father. He's wearing sunglasses even though we're inside, his black hair slicked back from his face. He's not a tall man, but there's something about him that's imposing, that makes you know he's used to getting his way.

"Alice Ogilvie?"

I'm surprised he remembers my name. Even though I've spent hours at this house over the years, Park's dad has never taken much interest in her friends. I suppose she could have reminded him out in the hallway just now.

"Hi, Mr. Park," I say, standing to greet him.

"And who's this?" he says, indicating Iris.

"Iris Adams." She rises, holding a hand out for him to shake. Mr. Park looks at it with a sneer, and then turns back to me. A moment later, she drops it back down by her side.

"I hear you want to speak to my Helen about what she saw last weekend. I'm not sure what you're trying to accomplish here, but I already have a team of the best lawyers in the state on the case."

I clear my throat, reminding myself that Mr. Park is not the first intimidating man I've dealt with and he certainly will not be the last.

"That may be so, Mr. Park," I say, "but we know what they have on Park—er, Helen. We know that the cops think it's an open-and-shut case, that they have an eyewitness who puts her at the scene of the crime—"

"Yeah, *you*," Park interjects darkly.

"Yes, fine, me. But Iris and I also found evidence that makes us believe that you're actually innocent. And," I add, turning to address Mr. Park, "we brought down the person who was guilty in Brooke Donovan's case, last fall. We want to help your daughter."

CHAPTER SIXTEEN

IRIS
FEBRUARY 13
12:15 P.M.

It's an awful mess, but somehow we're going to find
our way out of it, come heck or high water.
—MONA MOODY, *THE HIDDEN TRUTH*, 1948

PARK'S DAD STUDIES US, his face impassive. He's taken off his
slick sunglasses and put on thick-rimmed black eyeglasses, the
kind that would make you look like a dork from the fifties except
for the fact that they're sleek and shiny, with just enough sharp-
ness at the corners to signal *expensive* and *important*. Obviously, the
type of glasses a person wears to say *I'm smarter and also richer than you
could ever dream of being.*

My hand, the one he wouldn't shake, tingles at my side as he
looks us over.

"What," he says smoothly, "on god's green earth do the two
of you think you could do for my daughter that my twelve-
hundred-dollar-an-hour lawyer cannot do? I'm absolutely dying
to know."

Beside me, Alice opens her mouth, but I angle my elbow into
her side before she can speak. I don't *necessarily* want to mention

the ripped note at the moment, since taking it was extremely illegal and I don't, as Thompson so rudely threatened, want to end
up in a dirty jail cell.

"It's all very Clue, isn't it?" I say to Park's dad. "Helen was
found in the study with the body, with the letter opener in her
hand. All we need now is an appearance by Colonel Mustard."

Park's father waits, no expression on his face.

I forge on. He is obviously not a joking man.

"There are two pieces of evidence against Helen right now,"
I say. "One, what I said just now, which is . . . pretty bad. Two,
she was filmed fighting with Rebecca Kennedy earlier in the
night and said, and I quote, 'I wish you'd just shrivel up and die.'
That's . . . not optimal, am I right?"

Park scowls at me and looks at her father.

"But," I say slowly, "there are three things that work in her
favor. At least, we hope. One, and please answer honestly, Park,
did your clothes have blood on them?"

Park blinks at me. She looks at her father again.

Ever so slightly, he nods at her.

"No," she says quietly. "Of course not. I didn't touch her. I *told*
you. The police took my clothes and my shoes and, like, checked
my hair and nails and stuff. My shoes, the soles, had some blood,
because I stepped in it, but not my dress, or my hair, because I
never *touched* her."

"Right," I say. "Based on my research, I think it's highly unlikely that whoever did this to Rebecca Kennedy would leave that
room without some sort of blood on their clothes, wouldn't you
agree, Alice?"

"Yes," she says promptly. "You can't just stab and thunk
someo—"

"Two," I say, cutting her off. "We have something that I can't tell you about, because it was obtained under secretive circumstances. But we think it's important and can help clear your name.

"Three," I plunge on, because Mr. Park's eyes behind his glasses are growing steelier by the minute. "It's possible that what happened to Rebecca is connected to her family's position in Castle Cove."

"As in, revenge," Alice interjects.

"Possibly," I add, quickly. "Regardless, it's very important that Helen talk to us because we want to help. We don't think she did this. It doesn't add up. The police might also decide to raise the charge to attempted murder, right? And if Rebecca dies . . . murder."

The room grows eerily silent. Park whimpers and moves closer to her dad.

"Let me tell them," she whispers to him. "Please. They did . . . they did figure out who killed Brooke. And that lawyer you hired doesn't believe me, I can tell."

Silence.

"Mr. Park," Alice says calmly. "You have nothing to lose and everything to gain by trusting us. You have fancy lawyers and probably a private investigator. But we can get information they can't."

"Daddy," Helen urges.

He nods at her.

Helen swallows. "When I went up the stairs, I *was* looking for her. And no, I didn't want to apologize, because she totally stole my look for the dance. I just wanted to fight some more, I admit it. I was a little tip—"

She cuts herself off when her father frowns at her, then continues.

"I went from door to door on the second floor, you know, looking around for her. I found kids hooking up or whatever. But the thing is, when I came to that one door? Before I opened it? I heard shouting. And then, like, I don't know, a piano?"

"Shouting?" I ask. "Was Rebecca shouting at someone?"

She shakes her head. "I didn't hear her voice. It was . . ."

Helen looks at her father and then back at us, biting her lip. "It seemed like two different people, they sounded angry, but everything was also a little muffled because the door was closed and the music coming from downstairs made everything hard to understand. And then that piano sound, it was like, I don't know, not a song, really, but like something banging on keys, but not for long. It was brief. Then it was quiet and that's when I went in."

Piano? I try to picture the study in my head. There was a piano against the wall, but why would someone be playing it?

"Two people?" Alice asks, her voice curious. "But Pa— Helen. That's . . . crazy—"

"I knew you wouldn't believe me!" she cries out.

"Wait," I say, trying to wrap my brain around this. "You heard two people shouting and you say you didn't hear one of them as Kennedy's voice, right? That there were two, and they were different? But when you came into the room, only Kennedy was there, on the floor. Helen, the only entry and exit to the study were the door off the hallway and the door Alice came through. *Two* people couldn't have gotten by you *and* Alice. Are you *sure* one of the voices wasn't Kennedy's?"

"I would know her voice; I've been listening to her yell at me for years." Tears are forming in Helen's eyes.

"I knew you wouldn't believe me," she says. "Ms. Mystal, the main lawyer, was very rude about it. She asked if they went up the fireplace chimney and then laughed at me."

Mr. Park shoots her an irritated glance. "She did? I'll speak to her about that."

"There are those windows behind the desk," Alice says slowly. "But I don't think they open. Helen, are you absolutely sure you heard *two* voices in the study and one wasn't Kennedy's?"

"Yes." Helen's voice is pleading. "I'm *not* lying."

"And what," Mr. Park says slowly, "do you think you can do with *that,* Alice and Iris, that our lawyers and the Castle Cove Police Department cannot do?"

Alice and I look at each other. It does sound a little outlandish. There's no way someone could have gotten out of that room without running into Alice or Park. It's just impossible.

The idea that one person, let alone *two,* could have evaded Park and Alice seems unlikely, but why would Helen lie about something like that, knowing how weird and improbable it would sound?

I look at Park. I scan her face and arms. No scratches. Kennedy would surely have scratched, bitten, fought in some way. Right?

I think back to the fall, when Park dosed Brooke's drink with Ambien at the Halloween party. That was sneaky and required no physical prowess. It was devious. And no one would have known if Alice and I hadn't catfished Helen and she fessed up.

Park's body is pressed against her father's side. She looks exhausted and frightened.

I might be wrong, but I'm pretty sure Helen Park, when attempting to commit a crime, prefers more under-the-radar methods than physical attacks. And most criminals tend to favor the same method over and over.

"Well," I say finally, taking a deep breath. "For one, I—we—believe her. And if that isn't the most important thing in helping her, I don't know what is. A lawyer's job isn't to believe their client's innocence. It's to win a case. Those are two different things. Which would you rather have? Helen might not go to jail with your fancy lawyers, but her name will be stained forever."

Because even though Helen Park tried to drug Brooke and inadvertently drugged Steve Anderson instead and set off an astoundingly chaotic series of events, I truly don't think she tried to murder Rebecca Kennedy over a dress at a dance.

Mr. Park lifts his chin. "An astute observation, Iris. You may have one hour with my daughter in which she'll tell you everything, in explicit detail. Do what you can with it. I'll be very curious to see where you girls go with this. I've always admired upstarts who aren't afraid of a challenge. But remember, my daughter's very life is in your hands. Don't muck it up."

And with that, he plants a kiss on Helen's head and walks out of the room.

CHAPTER SEVENTEEN

ALICE
FEBRUARY 13
1:38 P.M.

"Poirot," I said. "I have been thinking."
"An admirable exercise, my friend. Continue it."
—AGATHA CHRISTIE, *PERIL AT END HOUSE*

ZORA, NEIL, AND SPIKE are waiting, half-hidden behind a large bush, when we pull up outside the Castle Cove High School gates an hour later. We texted them as soon as we left Park's, telling them that we have information and that we needed to meet, stat, and they all agreed to ditch out on their last few classes of the day. I pop the trunk and they throw their backpacks in before tumbling into the car.

"Took you long enough to get here," Neil grumbles. "We're lucky no one saw us waiting."

"Sorry, we got stuck behind a truck," Iris says. "We got here as soon as we could."

In the rearview mirror, I see Spike elbow Neil in the side. "It's no big deal," Spike says as Neil glares at him.

"Everyone buckled?" I ask. Everyone nods, and I press the gas pedal and yank us onto the road back to my house, ignoring the shouts of protest from my passengers.

Once there, we successfully manage to avoid all grown-ups by sneaking inside through a side door, grab some snacks and head straight to the conservatory. After we settle, I pull the whiteboard into the center of the room and turn to face everyone.

Zora, Neil, and Spike are arranged on the long couch that sits in the middle of the room, all engrossed in their phones. Iris stands next to me, marker in hand.

"Ahem," I say sternly to the other three. "Could you all please put away your devices?"

"At your attention, Ogilvie," Neil says, dropping his phone to his lap. "Let's get this perp."

CHAPTER EIGHTEEN

IRIS
FEBRUARY 13
4:06 P.M.

The most important thing to remember, Megs,
is that everyone lies.
—MONA MOODY, *THE HIDDEN TRUTH*, 1948

ON THE WHITEBOARD, I write *WHAT WE KNOW* in all caps.

Everyone looks at me. I take a deep breath.

"Listen," I say. "I know it was wrong, I don't want to hear about it, but I stole evidence from the study the night Rebecca was assaulted, and I'm sorry, but that's just the way it is."

I turn back to the whiteboard and write, *THE NOTE: strange E, meet me* and then look back at the group. Neil has his chin in his hands, which means something is percolating in his brain. I decide not to ask him about it right now. He works best when you let him incubate his thoughts.

"I found bits of a ripped note that night. It kind of fell off the back of Rebecca's dress when they lifted her onto the gurney. It said—*we think*, because we had to piece it together—'*Meet me.*' Both of the *e*'s were capitalized in kind of sloppy cursive, like backward threes, but not any of the other—"

"We compared it to Helen's handwriting in my yearbook and they aren't the same," Alice says, munching a cracker.

"Did you take a picture of it?" Spike asks.

I pull up the photo on my phone and hold it out to the group. Zora leans forward.

"Interesting," she says. "Is that . . . dysgraphia? Like, sometimes you write letters in reverse or mix in lower- and uppercase."

"Really?" I say. "I didn't know that was a thing."

"If you can match that handwriting to someone's handwriting, someone who was at the Castle that night, maybe, especially with that weird lettering, it might . . ." Spike trails off.

"Be a clue," I finish.

We beam at each other.

"Noice," he murmurs, rubbing his chin with one hand.

Something is different about his face all of a sudden. His eyes look . . . bluer? Is that possible?

"Iris!" Alice snaps her fingers.

I break myself out of my Spike moment and clear my throat. "Onward," I say.

"There were a ton of people at the party," Zora says, nibbling a slice of cheese. "I mean, at least a hundred? Students, staff, caterers, kitchen people, teachers. Are we going to get handwriting samples from everybody? There might be fingerprints on the pieces you have, though not everyone has their prints on file, of course."

"I wonder where the missing pieces are," Neil says. "That would help."

I look at Alice. She nods.

"The police have them," I say. "I don't know what their parts say, but I can't give them these pieces."

Spike frowns. "Iris, you should."

Beside him, Zora shakes her head. "Absolutely not. Thompson has it out for her. You heard him the night of the dance."

Neil rubs his chin. "True. I'm not sure how we could get away with getting them the pieces, either, without raising an alarm."

"The police think the note was meant for Kennedy to lure her upstairs," Alice says. "They think Helen wrote it, obviously, plus the whole *me finding her in the study over Rebecca's body,* and voilà, she is the prime suspect right now."

"Yes," I say. "But."

I turn back to the board and write, *Two voices, piano.*

"When we talked to Helen today, she swore she heard arguing inside the study before she went in and that there were two voices and neither was Kennedy's. And she said she heard banging on the piano."

"How can she be positive one wasn't Kennedy's voice?" Spike says.

"She's pretty sure," I said. "She's been listening to that voice for years."

"Piano?" Zora asks. "Why would someone be playing a piano at a time like that?"

"Not playing," I say. "Like banging. She said it didn't last long and then everything got quiet."

Neil shakes his head. "Mmm, no. This doesn't add up. I was in that room that night. There were two doors. One was the door out to the hallway and one was that other closet door, where the dresses were, and—"

"Exactly," Alice says. "How would one person, or even two, have gotten out without running into Park or me, because I came up the hidden stairs and through the closet door."

"There were windows in the room," Spike says.

"I don't think they open, and plus, if you went through those windows, how would you close them on the outside of the Castle? There's no balcony on that side; you're dropping down to the ground," I say.

"We need to go back there," Neil says. "To the Castle. To look around."

"Right," Zora scoffs. "That place is probably crawling with security now."

"Regardless," I say, "if Park is lying about hearing two people, that's quite a lie, because, obviously, how did they get out of the room? I mean, even the cops don't believe her. She could just say she walked in and found Kennedy, but she's sticking to this story."

Spike stands up and begins pacing slowly. "I'm inclined to believe that. She *could* have said two people rushed past her, made up some descriptions to lead the cops elsewhere, et cetera. This thing she's saying is preposterous enough to be true."

I turn back to the board. *EVIDENCE,* I write. *No blood on Park's clothes, hair. No scratches on her body.*

"None?" Zora asks.

"None," Alice says. "And if you fight, stab, and hit someone superhard in the head like that, you should have some blood on you, right?"

"Park is quite small," I say. "I'm just having a hard time believing she could stab Kennedy *and* hit her in the head with . . . well, whatever Kennedy was hit in the head with without getting blood on herself or a scratch."

"Kennedy's a scrapper," Zora agrees. "She's a demon when we do soccer in PE. She would have fought."

"Okay," I say. "Onward."

On the whiteboard, I write SUSPECTS. Then I turn around and face the group.

"Well," Zora says. "I mean, everybody. There were over a hundred people at the Castle that night."

I write:

Cater-waiters
Students
Teachers
Castle staff

"We might want to narrow that down a little," Spike says. "It's a bit broad."

"Be specific," I say. "Who would want to hurt Rebecca Kennedy?"

"Everyone," Zora says. "Rich, beautiful, mean. That's a long list. Girl's not one for making nice. Maybe she pissed someone off and they hatched a plan to confront her? And it went bad? Some of the rooms Neil and I went in were kind of messed up, like someone was looking for something."

"That could have just been kids being stupid," Spike says.

"True," I say. "But all of those boxes in the study were torn open, too; we didn't get a chance to look at them. Maybe someone was looking for something specific and Kennedy walked in?"

"Robbery," Neil says quietly. "Perhaps."

"You know," Spike says slowly, looking at me, "it still could be that Park is lying. I know you think she isn't, but . . . maybe she was working with someone else, and they got out somehow and she didn't have time to before Alice came into the study."

He does make a point. Park is small, so it would be difficult for her to do what was done to Kennedy all by herself, but . . .

"But what about the fact there wasn't any blood on Park?" I point out.

"So maybe the other person did the dirty work and Park did the luring," Spike answers.

Alice and I look at each other.

"I'm just tossing it out there," Spike says. "We can't entirely rule it out, right?"

Alice nods. "Right," I say. Park seemed genuine when we talked to her, but then again . . . maybe we should listen to the conversation we recorded with her again.

Neil gets up and walks to the whiteboard. "I don't object to Spike's line of reasoning. I mean, we thought Coach and Westmacott were cool and look what we found out about *them*."

"Excuse me, *I* never thought Westmacott was cool," Alice says.

Neil takes the marker from me and stands in front of the board, thinking.

"Sorry," he says, and writes HELEN PARK under SUSPECTS.

"Gerber," Alice says suddenly, and quite loudly. "Write down Reed Gerber. Park said he was at the dance with Kennedy. Let me see . . ."

She pulls out her phone and starts scrolling. "The time frame for Kennedy's attack was twenty-two minutes, between nine-fourteen p.m. and nine-thirty-six p.m. Gerber didn't post anything on socials between nine-oh-one p.m. and eleven-fourteen p.m. Hmm. He posted a pic with a bottle of Jäger at nine p.m. and then at eleven-fourteen he was on Discord—why didn't they remove me from that damn group—and he says—"

She looks up at us. *"Shit, this shit is bad."*

"What *is* it?" Zora presses. "What did he post?"

We all look at each other.

"No," Alice says. "That's what he posted. *'Shit, this shit is bad.'*"

I raise my eyebrows. "He might mean . . . he did something he shouldn't have, then? Hmm . . ."

Spike says, "Motive? Other than being a general jerk? Were they hooking up? Did *they* fight at the dance?"

Alice shakes her head. "Unknown. But we'll have to talk to him."

I grab another marker and write under *WHAT WE KNOW: Gerber—possible motive? MIA on social during attack, posts cryptic note after attack.*

"But," Spike points out, "just because he didn't post anything doesn't mean he wasn't in the ballroom. He might just have . . . not posted."

"He's chronically online," Alice says. "We still have to talk to him."

Spike stands up and moves closer to the whiteboard. "So basically what we need now is to know who might have written that note, what Gerber was doing and what he meant with that last post, and we need to know, oh geez, I mean, like what *everybody* at the freaking dance was up to that night. Iris! That's impossible! There were too many people."

"Spike," I start, but Zora interrupts me.

"Well," she says. "Maybe my girlfriend can help. She was taking photos that night for yearbook and *Cougartown*—"

"Perfect," I say. Angelik is the editor of the school newspaper, *Cougartown,* and yes, the name is unfortunate. "If we could see the photos she took of kids in the ballroom during that time frame, we can eliminate some people."

"Excellent," Alice says. "Zora, set up a time with Angelik for tomorrow."

Zora glares at her. "I'm not your servant, Alice."

Alice rolls her eyes. "Forgive me for being brusque in the middle of an investigation, *Zora.*"

"Stop it," I tell them. "We're a freaking team. Stop bickering."

"And," Neil says pointedly, stepping aside from what he's drawn on the whiteboard, "we need to go to the Castle Cove Historical Society. I want to see the blueprints for the Castle. I mean, who knows, maybe there's a crawl space above the study. Maybe there's one below. Because if Helen isn't lying, how did two people get *out?*"

I look back at the whiteboard.

Neil has drawn a pretty impressive layout of the study, with the cedar closet and fireplace on the right side of the room, the large windows behind the mahogany desk, the door coming off the main hallway (where Park and Kennedy came into the room), and the wall on the left side of the room, with the piano and bookshelves. He's even included some of the paintings on the walls. I scribble some more things on the board and turn around.

"Very nice, Neil," Alice says. "Excellent work."

Under *WHAT WE KNOW,* we have:

> *Gerber—possible motive? MIA on social*
> *during attack, posts cryptic note after attack*
> *No blood on Park*
> *Weapon was letter opener and UNKNOWN (head injury)*
> *Note—sloppy capital E, MΕΕt me . . . 9:30 . . .*

The room is silent.
Under *SUSPECTS*:

> *Helen Park*
> *Gerber*
> *Cater-waiters*
> *Students*
> *Teachers*
> *Castle staff*
> *UNKNOWN*

"Unknown?" Spike asks. He's standing very close to me at the whiteboard. It's a little disconcerting, but also kind of comforting at the same time.

"Rebecca Kennedy's family is rich and powerful," I tell him. "You don't live like that without having enemies, so there's going to be an unknown."

"Merde," Alice murmurs.

CHAPTER NINETEEN

ALICE
FEBRUARY 14
7:22 A.M.

"One does see so much evil in a village," murmured
Miss Marple in an explanatory voice.
—AGATHA CHRISTIE, *THE BODY IN THE LIBRARY*

I FOLLOW IRIS DOWN a hallway I swear I've never seen before on the second floor of CCHS's main building. Last night before our brainstorming session ended, everyone agreed to meet here this morning before school to look at the photos Zora says Angelik took the night of the dance. We need to figure out who was in the ballroom when Kennedy was attacked.

I have literally never gotten to school this early, and the building is quiet. It's spooky, the echo of our footsteps the only noise I hear. My parents were happy, at least, when I left at the crack of dawn to grab Iris; my dad was all *go get 'em, kiddo,* like he thought he was talking to someone who's eleven and not his almost-eighteen-year-old daughter.

Halfway down the hall, Iris pushes open the door to a small room. The space is crowded with several long tables clustered in its middle. On them sit a few hulking desktop computers that look like they're from the turn of the century. Way to invest in your children, Castle Cove.

A girl with short black hair sits with her back to the door, typing furiously on a laptop. Zora is standing behind her, leaning over her shoulder to look at her screen. As we watch, the girl lets out a burst of laughter at something Zora just said. They look so happy. Something tugs in my midsection, something a little sad and a little painful, and I shrug it off, clearing my throat.

The two of them turn.

"Hey!" Iris says, making her way to them. "Angelik, thank you so much for helping us out. This is great."

"No prob," the girl says, scooting back her chair to give Iris a one-armed hug. "It's good to see you. How are you? I didn't see you the night of the dance, although from what I've heard, you were otherwise occupied—"

Iris's cheeks flame.

"—with Kennedy," finishes Angelik, and Iris exhales. I'm pretty sure she thought Angelik was talking about Cole, and I make a mental note to ask Iris about that whole situation. She hasn't mentioned it, although I suppose we've been a bit distracted by more important matters.

I drop my bag onto a table with a thud. "I'm Alice," I say. We need to speed this up if we want to get anything done before class starts. "We appreciate the help. Zora filled you in, I assume? We're interested in taking a look at any photos you took the night of the dance, particularly between—"

"Beat you!" Spike appears in the doorway. He's slightly out of breath, and I spot Neil just behind him. They jostle for a moment, attempting to fit through the doorway at the same time, and then pop through into the room.

Neil is holding a cardboard coffee box, which he sets down next to my bag, and then he pulls a sleeve of cups out of his backpack. "Coffee, anyone?"

"You are a lifesaver," Zora groans. "Coffee me, please."

"To answer your question, Alice, I have the files from that night ready to go on my computer," Angelik says, standing and picking up her laptop. She moves over to one of the long tables in the center of the room and sets it down. "Happy to help you all look through them, figure out who was where when Kennedy was hurt . . ."

I clap my hands, pleased that she's taking this seriously. "Great," I say. "Iris and I will do that with you two, and Neil and Spike can start going through everyone's social accounts, checking the pictures other people took that night."

"What if they're private?" Spike asks, and Neil snorts.

"Do you doubt me? I can get around that," he says with a wave of his hand.

"How—" Spike starts, then shakes his head. "I don't even want to know."

"No. You don't," replies Neil, pulling up a chair to the other side of the table. Spike sits next to him, and Zora, Iris, and I gather around Angelik.

"We're looking at a specific time frame," Iris says. "Photos taken between nine-fifteen, when Park ran out of the ballroom after her fight with Kennedy, and nine-forty-five-ish. Alice got upstairs at nine-thirty-six, shortly after Kennedy was attacked, so whoever did this couldn't have been in the ballroom during that period. We need to see who's missing."

"Sounds good. Ready to start?" We all nod, and Angelik clicks on a thumbnail and a photo opens on the screen. Two girls smiling next to their dates.

Iris scribbles something into her casebook, and when I glance at it, I see four names on a page titled *RULED OUT.*

Ryan Wheeler
Sydney Sinclair
Bradley Wong
Emma Billingsley

"It looks like I have . . . ten photos and two videos from that half-hour span of time." Angelik frowns. "Sorry, guys. I thought I was snapping pics left and right, but apparently I got distracted." Zora smiles.

As Angelik clicks through the files, Iris adds more names to her list.

"We're getting later and later into the night . . . this one is from nine-forty-eight . . ." Angelik twists in her chair to look at Iris. "Do you want to keep going?"

Iris shakes her head. "I have to get to class, but can you send us all of them so we can look at them later?"

"Sure. Like, the ones from that time frame, or . . . ?"

"Might as well send us everything you took that night. We can go through them all later, just in case."

"No problem."

I sigh. Iris's list only has twenty names on it, and there are about 110 people in our class, all of whom Kennedy has pissed off at one time or another.

Iris nudges me. "There were a few people in those pics I didn't recognize, caterers, mostly."

I nod and start tapping out a message on my phone as Iris reads over her list. "I'm texting Raf to see if he's around later and can make some IDs for us."

"Did you notice who *didn't* make an appearance in those photos?" Iris asks. She taps the end of her pen against her notebook.

"Who?"

"Our friend Reed Gerber. Looks like we need to pay him a little visit."

CHAPTER TWENTY

IRIS
FEBRUARY 14
12:21 P.M.

Did you miss me, Jimmy? Because I sure didn't
miss you. You're a liar, a cheat, a thief,
and a downright scoundrel.
—MONA MOODY, *BOOM SHAKALAKA!*, 1949

"HE'S IN THE CAFETERIA," Alice says as soon as I meet her outside her classroom. "Let's go."

"He's not," I say, maneuvering around kids in the hallway.

"And you know this how? That boy is an eating machine. He doesn't miss lunch," Alice says, huffing to keep up with me.

"Because. It's Tuesday. And Tuesday is the day he has athlete tutoring in the library during lunch with Tabitha Berrington, but he started batting those baby blues at her, so she basically does his homework for him now. It's a little sickening, to tell the truth."

I pull open the library door and Alice follows me.

"Well, if he charmed her into doing his work, how do you know he's here?"

Kids sitting at tables look up at us.

The librarian scowls at Alice to keep her voice down.

"Why," Alice whispers, "am I constantly being reprimanded for simply being myself?"

"I know he's here," I say, passing Tabitha at a table, where, judging by her annotations in *Pride and Prejudice,* she's patiently doing Gerber's lit homework. She looks up and narrows her eyes at Alice.

"Ew," Alice says. "Rude."

"I know he's here," I say again, turning the corner of an aisle at the far end of the library, where the books are slightly dusty from being unused. "Because he sits in my favorite section. It's where I come to chill out, and believe me, I do not like him being in my favorite section. He's ruined Tuesdays for me."

"Oh. So this is where you are when you aren't at lunch?" Alice says. "I kind of wondered."

She's right behind me, so I can't see her face, but I can hear the concern in her voice. Yes. This is where I come when I can't think straight, or I'm tired. Or when I just need to be by myself. Lots of things.

I round the corner and there's Reed Gerber, at the end of the aisle, stretched out on the floor, his giant sneakers crossed at the ankle and his basketball team hoodie over his head, napping.

Alice and I stand over him. He doesn't move.

"Please," Alice says. "Let me do the honors."

"My pleasure," I say.

Alice kicks him in the thigh.

"Hey, what the . . ." Gerber's head jerks up, the hoodie falling from his face. He rubs his thigh. "Ogilvie, what the hell? I'm trying to sleep, here."

"So nice that you've bedazzled poor Tabitha into doing all your homework for you, Gerber, but it's time for baby to wake up and face the music," I tell him. My voice has an unexpected edge. Gerber has always been kind of a bully and I've never particularly liked him.

"Do I even *know* you?" he asks me blearily, sitting up and rubbing his eyes.

"Gerber," Alice says sharply. "You were Kennedy's date to the dance. And, during that time period, you were MIA on socials and in photos. Care to explain yourself?"

Immediately, his handsome face hardens. "Whoa, whoa, whoa, now, Ogilvie, don't even—"

"Answer the question, Reed Gerber," I say. "Where were you? Did you and Kennedy have a fight?"

He looks from me to Alice. "Who do you think you are, anyway? I didn't have anything to do with what happened to her. And she wasn't my date, we just went together, like friends. With some extra added fun."

He looks at Alice knowingly and then winks at me. My stomach curdles. I kick him in the sole of his sneaker.

"What the—"

"Then you can tell us where you were during nine-fourteen p.m. and nine-thirty-six p.m., the approximate time of the assault," I say. "And after that, when you didn't bother to post on socials until after eleven p.m., isn't that right, Alice?"

"Correct," she says. "Where were you, Gerber?"

He looks very slowly from Alice to me and then back to Alice.

"What's happened to you, Ogilvie? You used to be cool, you know? Then all that Brooke stuff, and, like, I get it, girls betraying each other and all, you had to have your alone time or whatever, and you *did* do Anderson a solid by proving it wasn't him but . . . like, who *are* you now, anyway?"

"Excuse me?" she asks, but her voice wavers ever so slightly.

"Like, hanging out with this . . ." He gestures to me. "Thing. That's not you. We keep texting you and stuff. To come back to us. Bygones or whatever. You're turning into a weirdo, to be honest."

I've gotten numb to the insults from the Mains over the years, or at least I pretend to not care, but next to me, I can feel Alice's body stiffen. I wonder, *does* Alice miss her old friends sometimes?

And he called me a Thing. Something in me jars a little, remembering my dad. How he used to act. The way he'd play my mom. Make it seem like she was the problem. Turn it around on *her,* so the focus was off him, like what Gerber's doing now.

"Gerber," I say, my voice tight. "The simplest thing in the world for you to do is answer our question, and yet, you won't. You aren't even trying to make up a lie. Which makes me think you're hiding something. Why did you write a Discord post that said 'This shit is bad'?"

His face pales. "You two are not the fricking cops. I *don't* have to answer to you. You want to know what went down? Ask Park. Right, Ogilvie? You're the one who found her, after all."

He pins his electric-blue eyes on her.

"Just tell us the truth, Reed," she says, switching her voice to a kind tone. "Rebecca's really hurt. Did she fight with anyone besides Park at the dance? Was someone mad at her outside of school? Where were you? Did you see anything odd? Anything you can tell us would help. Have the police interviewed you yet? If you lied to them, that's not going to be good for you if we find out . . . something else."

For a brief moment, Gerber's face softens. My nerves tense up. Is he going to tell us something?

But just as quickly as it softened, his face goes tight.

"You're not cops. I already talked to them and I'm all clear. It's Park all the way."

"Park says there were two people in the study, Gerber. Arguing. Before she went in. Unless you can tell us otherwise, we're going to assume one of those people might be you," I say.

He shakes his head and chuckles. "Okay, True Detective. *Whatever.* Play your little game."

"What did you tell them for your alibi, Gerber?" I make my voice cold. "I think you're forgetting we have information on you."

Gerber's face crinkles. "You've got nothing," he says warily.

"Oh, I'll tell you what I have—a girl out there doing your homework for you," I say, "which is a violation of the athletic code. I can report you and you'll get kicked off all your precious teams."

"You—" He starts to stand up, his face blazing, but Alice reaches out and pushes him back down.

"Reed," she says gently. "I know a lot about you, too. Especially that one thing. Remember? That particular night?"

My ears prick up. Alice with secret information?

Reed's face blanches. "You wouldn't."

"Oh, I would. And I have pictures to prove it. That night alone would probably get you kicked out of school. Or, at the very least, extremely socially humiliated."

Reed looks back and forth from Alice to me. He looks like he might be sick.

"Okay, I'll tell you. But you can't tell anyone."

"Where were you, Gerber?" I say.

He twists his hands together. "I . . . had to go to the bathroom.

I was pretty drunk. And I couldn't find it. Got stuck in a pantry or something and I couldn't get out. I . . ."

He looks at the library carpet, his face blooming red.

"Oh god," I say, my brain filling with an image I'd rather not have in there. *Oh.* That's what he meant by the Discord comment. *This shit is bad.* He didn't mean anything with Kennedy, he meant . . .

Alice says, "What? *What?*"

I take a deep breath. "He pooped himself."

Alice makes a grossed-out sound. Reed points his finger at me.

"Do *not*. Tell. Anyone. I already told the cops. And my alibi is that new guidance counselor. She heard me pounding on the door and got someone to open it. I spent an hour in the laundry room by the kitchen wrapped in a towel with her washing my clothes. So *there.* And I will *kill*—"

"That particular secret is safe with us, Gerber, no problem," I say quickly.

He looks at Alice.

"Happy now, Ogilvie? And by the way, we're here for you, anytime you want to come back to the normals."

"No, thank you," she says politely. "I'd rather eat cat turds, followed by broken glass, and topped off with a kerosene cocktail."

She turns on her heel and marches down the aisle.

"Alice," I ask, trailing after her. "What secret information do you have on Gerber, anyway?"

She chuckles. "Never you mind, Iris. I might need that information someday."

CHAPTER TWENTY-ONE

ALICE
FEBRUARY 14
2:54 P.M.

One has to dare if one wants to get anywhere.
—AGATHA CHRISTIE, *THE MIRROR CRACK'D*
FROM SIDE TO SIDE

IRIS CHOMPS NOISILY ON a fry. We're waiting at the diner for Raf, who's ten minutes late. I'm already planning to give him a piece of my mind when he arrives; I know he's busy, but so are we.

"Iris," I snap as she sticks another fry into her mouth and chews loudly. She has her phone and casebook in front of her, ready to grill Raf whenever he finally arrives.

"What?" she says innocently. Fine, maybe she isn't doing it on purpose, but *still.*

I shake my head. "Never mind. Give me one." I steal a fry off her plate and take a bite, the warm grease coating the inside of my mouth. I have to admit, they're good.

The bell over the diner door dings, announcing Raf's arrival. He wanders over to us all casual, like he isn't totally late.

"Good lord, Raf. Where have you been?" I say, not trying to hide my irritation.

"Nice to see you, too, Ogilvie." He slides into the booth next to me. "Sorry, I'm behind schedule because Candy has to work at the club tonight, so we celebrated Valentine's Day over lunch."

I look away, trying not to think about the fact that Raf is sitting only a couple of inches from me, or about the fact that he has a girlfriend now, or about them celebrating Valentine's Day together, or about anything of that sort at all. We have a mystery to solve; I can't let myself be distracted by ridiculous things.

"Hey, Raf," Iris says. "Want a fry?"

"Do I." He reaches out and takes one and then leans forward. "Thanks. So, you all are at it again, huh? I knew you were . . . but I was hoping maybe, I don't know, this time you'd leave it to—"

"The cops?" I finish with a snort. "Yeah, sure, okay. We know how good they are at creative thinking. If we left it to the cops, Park would spend the rest of her life behind bars. Let me catch you up."

I give him a brief rundown of what we've figured out so far, bringing him up to speed through our visit with Gerber.

"Alice," Raf says when I'm finished. "You are amazingly—"

"We have photos," Iris interrupts, sliding her phone across the table to him. I cut my eyes to Raf but can't tell from his expression whether he was about to compliment or insult me.

On her phone are the files Angelik sent to us of the photos she took the night of the dance. "We're narrowing down our list of suspects. Kennedy isn't well-liked at Castle Cove High, and unfortunately that means almost everyone in our grade might have motive of one sort or another."

"Oh, I know," Raf says darkly, and I wonder briefly what Kennedy did to him.

"The editor of the school newspaper took these photos, plus we're sifting through everyone's social media accounts. We've started to rule out people who were clearly in the ballroom during the time period that the assault took place—"

"But there are some people we don't recognize—cater-waiters, mostly," I finish for her. I snatch another fry off Iris's plate, and she gives me a dirty look. I stick my tongue out and she mouths *mature* at me.

"Ah. You need me to tell you who they are?" Raf asks.

I nod. "Yes, please. Also, do you know how many people from the catering company were working the event? We need the names of everyone who was there."

He pauses, considering my words. "Okay . . . but what's the motive? Why would one of the caterers want to hurt Kennedy? It's not like they know her."

"We're not sure yet, but we have to cover all our bases. For all we know, she attended another event someone worked and got into it with one of them. Anything is possible; it's *Kennedy*," I remind him.

"Fair point."

Iris turns to Raf. "Let's start with how many people were working that night?"

He squints, thinking back. "Besides me and Candy"—at the name, my stomach turns, but I force myself to ignore it—"there was our manager, so . . . eight? No, nine. Nine other people. So, all in all, uh . . . eleven of us."

"Do you know all their names?" I ask.

"Of course," he says. "Candy, me, our manager, Evan Perez.

Then there was Shannon Sheedy, Kristin Fernandez, Jess McFarlane, Terry Eckles, Alex Schaefer, Justin Grumman . . ." He rubs his forehead with the bottom of his palm. "I'm trying to remember the last two, gimme a sec. . . ."

"Check the photos," Iris says, pushing the phone even closer to him.

He nods and grabs her phone to examine the screen. "No catering people in this one. Oh, here's Kristin." He turns the phone toward us and points to a girl with short brown hair wearing a black-and-white catering uniform. Iris crosses the name off the list she's made in her notebook.

"Sheedy's in this one, plus Eckles. They're dating, so they practically spent the whole night attached at the hip. Evan was getting so annoyed because they kept feeding each other the food—"

"Raf," I say. "Focus."

"Calm down, Ogilvie." He pokes me in the arm and my stupid stomach does a little flip.

He turns back to the phone. "Oh, here's one of the people I forgot—Kiran Patel. The other one was . . . lemme think . . . Jimmy Benone, but I haven't seen him in any photos yet. Clearly it wasn't me or Candy; I was with her during that time in the kitchen, getting some new trays ready to bring out. Actually, now that I think about it, Evan was back there that whole time, too, so you can rule him out. So who does that leave?"

Iris reads off her notebook. "Jess McFarlane, Alex Schaefer, Justin Grumman. Do you happen to remember seeing any of them in the kitchen then?"

He shakes his head, focus back on Iris's phone. "No. And I don't see them in any of these pictures, either, but they could have been out in the main room or on break."

I pull my legs up under me on the bench, bumping Raf's in the process. He clears his throat.

"Well, that was helpful. Mostly," I say.

"You're welcome, Alice." He rolls his eyes.

Iris kicks me under the table. "Thanks, Raf, we appreciate it," she says sweetly. I make a face.

Raf nods. "No problem, ladies. I gotta get going; I have a shift down at the station that starts soon."

"Speaking of," I say, grabbing his arm before he can get up and tugging him back into his seat. "Have you gotten any info about all this from them? Overheard anything? Looked at——"

He shakes his head, peeling my fingers off his forearm. "Unfortunately, not this time around. They're holding things close to the chest; I think they're trying their best to avoid . . . well, you know what happened last time."

"Well, if you do . . ."

"I know, I know. Call you."

"A text would suffice, but yes."

He stands, grabbing one last fry for the road. "It's been real, ladies. Keep out of trouble, all right?" He directs this mostly to me and I glower at his back as he heads out of the diner. He's not my mother.

Something nudges at the edge of my mind. I turn back to Iris. "What club was he talking about?"

She tilts her head. "I'm sorry, what?"

"When he first got here, Raf said something about Candy working at the club tonight. What club?"

Iris freezes for a moment, then lets out a long, loud sigh.

"Alice——"

"*What* club, Iris?"

"People need to work, you know."

"What is that supposed to mean?"

"Fine." Iris shuts her notebook with some force. "He meant Sultry Sirens."

My mouth falls open. "The *strip* club?"

"Alice, don't judge. You're better than that. That's how Candy pays for college. The catering company and Sirens. She has a job to do and so do we, so let's do it."

CHAPTER TWENTY-TWO

ALICE
FEBRUARY 14
4:45 P.M.

One may live in a big house
and yet have no comfort.
—AGATHA CHRISTIE,
THE MYSTERIOUS AFFAIR AT STYLES

AFTER WE LEAVE THE diner, I drop Iris at the Moon Landing and head home, even though I'd really much prefer to go somewhere—*anywhere*—else right now. I even considered going into the bar and hanging there, harassing Iris and chatting with her mom, who I've grown to really like over the past few months, but sometimes that place gets a little rough as the evening goes on.

Worse yet, sometimes *Coach* makes an appearance, and I can do without seeing him. The last time we ran into each other was in downtown Castle Cove, outside the skating rink, and it was extremely unpleasant. Lots of yelling on Coach's end. I'd rather avoid that happening again if at all possible.

My parents' cars are still in the driveway—my dad's obnoxious bright red Tesla that screams midlife crisis plugged into its outlet, charging like he thinks he might need to make a sudden escape.

Great. A part of me hoped that they'd simply . . . disappear by the time I got home, but clearly the universe is not on my side today and now I'm in a *mood.* First the run-in with Henderson yesterday, then the mental image of Raf celebrating Valentine's Day with his dumb girlfriend, and now . . . this.

Suddenly, the crowd at the Moon Landing—even Coach—doesn't seem so bad. I'm about to reverse back down the drive when something darts out of the bushes in front of my car. I slam on the brakes and spot the freaking cat from the night of the dance standing in the center of the driveway. Good lord. I might not particularly care for animals, but that doesn't mean I want to murder them. What the hell is that thing doing? It clearly has a death wish.

I throw my car in park and jump out. Dusk is falling and the branches of the huge redwood trees that sit on the edge of our property cast long shadows across the drive.

Something soft rubs against my legs and I jump about eight feet into the air, heart hammering, before I realize what it is: the cat, obviously, winding its way in and out of my legs, tail tickling my skin, purring up at me like it thinks we're friends or something. It has some nerve.

"Shoo," I say, waving it away. It ignores me and the purring gets louder. Ugh.

Clearly, I am not going anywhere, because even though this cat is super annoying, I'd still feel bad if I drove over it. I walk back to the car and grab my keys from inside, leaving it sitting haphazardly in the middle of the driveway.

There's another soft rub against my ankle as I grab my bag from the trunk.

"Go *home,* cat," I say again, shaking it off my leg. It doesn't take the hint. In fact, it has the audacity to follow me as I head toward the house.

It looks up at me expectantly as I unlock the front door. If it thinks it's coming inside, it has another thing coming.

"Meow?" it says, its little wet nose kissing at my calf. Which, fine, is sort of cute, I guess, if you like that sort of thing.

"What are you doing?" I say, and then realize I'm talking to a freaking cat. I need to get a grip. "I have to go now." I step into the house and start to shut the door. The cat lets out a pitiful sound, and suddenly there are tears in my eyes.

I blink them back. This cat is so rude; what does it *want* from me?

Food, probably, I realize.

"Fine, if it'll get you to leave me alone, I'll get you a snack. Hold on. I'll be right back."

I stalk into the kitchen, which thankfully is empty of other human beings, and I grab a can of tuna from the pantry and an opener from a drawer.

"Here," I say once I'm back at the front door. I shove a bowl of tuna onto the front step and the cat mews. I swear to god as I close the door, it smiles at me.

My mom catches me halfway up the stairs.

"Alice, is that you?"

I freeze, then turn around slowly. She's standing in the foyer, perfectly put together as usual. Blond hair curled just so, like she just had a blowout, wearing a pressed pair of high-waisted silk pants and a blouse I recognize as this season's Valentino.

"No, Mom, it's not me."

She ignores my comment. "Come back downstairs, please. Your father and I would like a word."

"I'm actually sort of in the middle——"

She gives me a thin smile. "I'm sorry, did that sound like a question? Because I can assure you, it was not."

I flare my nostrils but comply, heading slowly back down the stairs and following her silently into the living room.

"We're *concerned*, Alice," my mother says for the eighth time in the past five minutes, leaning forward to put her teacup on the coffee table in front of her. "You do realize we know when you skip class? Every time you decide not to attend one, we get an automatic email through your school's online portal."

"Yeah. I *know*." My arms are crossed tight against my chest. I swear the pressure of them against my midsection is the only thing stopping me from letting out an earsplitting scream.

It's so like my parents to swan in here, trying to tell me what to do after basically ignoring their parental responsibilities for, let's think, oh right—*my entire life*. Sure, my mom showed up for Christmas, but did my dad? No, of course he didn't. He begged off because he was in the middle of some giant merger thingy, and then my mom left less than two days later to fly to Atlanta for the new film she was working on, and I was left with Brenda. You'd think after Thanksgiving, when I very nearly died, they might have reassessed their priorities, but you'd be wrong. Their first priority has always been, and always will be, their work.

"I know you think that all of this"——my dad sweeps his arm grandly around the room, at the stupid Jasper Johns over the fireplace, the Chihuly glass chandelier hanging from the ceiling—— "grew on a tree, Alice, but I——*we*——worked for it. Worked *hard*. And we expect you to do the same. You're used to everything being handed to you on a silver platter, but when I was your age—"

I swear, I black out. I have heard this speech eleven billion times in my life: how my father grew up with nothing, how he graduated with an MBA from Wharton at the age of twenty-one, blah blah blah, wunderkind, snore.

"—and college," he continues, my brain focusing back on his words without my permission, "was an important part of that process. If what your principal tells us is true—that you have barely been doing your schoolwork this semester—you're going to have a hard time—"

It's like listening to a very poorly written script of what a concerned father is supposed to say. Then again, this is one of the first and only times he's acted concerned about me, so I guess he hasn't had much practice.

My mom reaches over and puts her hand on my knee for a brief moment. "We're worried," she says, the (not-so) grand finale of their *Alice, we want the best for you* speech.

"Got it. I'm sure you are," I say with a straight face, and they look at each other, probably trying to figure out whether I'm being sarcastic. I am, but that's no business of theirs. "I'll be better. Do my homework and stuff. Okay? Is that all?"

They exchange a glance. "If you can promise us that you'll be going to your classes from now on, then I suppose so," my father says. He pushes his glasses up the bridge of his nose with his index finger.

"Great," I say.

And then I stand and march out of the room.

TEXT CONVERSATION BETWEEN RAFAEL
RAMIREZ AND ALICE OGILVIE
FEBRUARY 14
7:05 P.M.

RR: Alice you there?

AO: Maybe

RR: Hey—so I talked to my supervisor from the night of the dance

AO: And?

RR: Jess McFarlane, Jimmy Benone, and Justin Grumman—they were in the back kitchen, helping with prep stuff. And Alex Schaefer was on break.

AO: Ok

RR: You okay? I thought you'd be more excited to cross names off the list

AO: Yeah. I'm fine

RR: Are you sure?

RR: I know . . . things are maybe a little weird right now, Alice, but you can always talk to me

AO: I know

KWB, CHANNEL 10

Breaking News
February 14
7:30 p.m.

Ben Perez: Good evening, Castle Cove. We're about to go live with our own Tessa Hopkins, who's at the Castle Cove Police Department for a press conference on the latest in the Rebecca Kennedy case. Tessa, what can you tell us?

Tessa Hopkins: Ben, Castle Cove was rocked last Saturday not only by a dangerous storm and mudslide, but the news that a local teen was attacked during the Sadie Hawkins dance at Levy Castle. Rebecca Kennedy was airlifted to Mercy General, where she's currently in a medically induced coma due to head trauma. She was also stabbed numerous times. The police have arrested one person, another teen, in the assault, but they've been released on bail and are awaiting trial. The police chief, Mark Thompson, is due to give an update any minute now.

Ben Perez: Tessa, what an awful situation. Do the police have a motive for the attack?

Tessa Hopkins: Hold on, Ben. We're about to start.

Detective Mark Thompson: Hello, everyone. First, I want to thank the entire Castle Cove Police Department for their diligent work on this case. Anytime a child is in danger, it's tough on everyone, but this particular case hit home, as some of our own officers' children were at that dance. As you can imagine, with an event of that size, our investigation is going to take some time. There were upwards of one hundred and fifty people in attendance, and interviews are ongoing. One has been charged in connection with the attack, a minor who also attends Castle Cove High School. They were positively placed in the room with the victim through a witness statement. There were two weapons in the attack. One was an antique letter opener, which was used to stab the victim several times in the abdomen. Regarding the second weapon . . . an inventory was done of the room in which the attack took place, and an item is missing from that room. Analysis, forensics, and the dimensions of the victim's wounds lead us to believe that item was likely the other weapon used in the attack. We are actively looking for this weapon.

Reporter: Can you be more specific about the second weapon? How—

Detective Mark Thompson: At this time, I cannot.

Tessa Hopkins: Can you tell us what the possible motive is for the attack? There are rumors that Miss Kennedy and another teen at the dance were fighting prior to the attack. Is this the same teen that was charged? Do you have evidence pointing to them?

Detective Mark Thompson: We are in possession of a piece of evidence that leads us to believe Miss Kennedy may have been lured to the room. Prior to Miss Kennedy's attack, there was a fight between her and another teen. The state of the room where the attack took place also leads us to believe robbery may have been a motive, but again, I can't go into details.

Reporter: Do you have evidence linking the teen charged to the weapons used in the attack?

Detective Mark Thompson: We have positively identified fingerprints on the letter opener, yes.

Tessa Hopkins: But what was the motive for the attack?

Detective Mark Thompson: We're concentrating on the fact that the suspect in the attack was involved in a very public fight with the victim at the dance. This fight was filmed and distributed on social media.

Tessa Hopkins: If two weapons were used in the attack, and one is missing, are Castle Cove Police considering the possibility there may have been others involved in this attack?

Detective Mark Thompson: We're investigating all avenues.

Reporter: The suspect is charged with assault and battery. You said the victim may have been lured to the room, which would mean the attack was premeditated. If true, that would signifi—

Detective Mark Thompson: Yes, that would increase the charge because of the likelihood of premeditation. Look, at this point, we have a case of two teens, girls, who had a spat about hairdos and dresses at a dance. Did it get out of control or was there more to their relationship in the background? That's what we're trying to determine.

Tessa Hopkins: So Miss Kennedy's attacker was a girl?

Detective Mark Thompson: A female classmate, yes.

Reporter: Can you tell us what other items, in addition to the missing weapon, may be missing from the room? What in the room would be of interest to Miss Kennedy's attacker and do you think this points to the possibility of multiple people involved in the attack?

Detective Mark Thompson: As I said, some items in the room, and other rooms on that floor, were disturbed, which may point toward a possible attempt at robbery, but again, I can't give details.

Tessa Hopkins: Were there any other people at the dance who may have had a motive, Detective? Was Rebecca Kennedy dating anyone? Have you interviewed—

Detective Mark Thompson: We are still conducting interviews at this time.

Reporter: Can you tell us the condition of Rebecca Kennedy?

Detective Mark Thompson: This is Dr. Felicia Ramos, who is currently caring for Miss Kennedy.

Dr. Ramos: Good evening. Miss Kennedy has suffered a severe head trauma, swelling of the brain, blood loss, and internal injuries. She's in a medically induced coma to allow her body time to heal and to monitor the swelling in her brain. We plan to begin the process of bringing her out of the coma in the next four to five days.

Reporter: Will she have long-term brain damage? What is the prognosis?

Dr. Ramos: This is significant neurological trauma. Miss Kennedy is an otherwise healthy seventeen-year-old girl. However, we won't know the extent of the damage until she's conscious.

Tessa Hopkins: Is there a point at which charges against the suspect may increase? By that I mean, if Miss Kennedy's condition were to deteriorate—

Detective Mark Thompson: Let's just concentrate on getting this girl better, all right? I'm sure her family would appreciate any positivity.

Reporter: Detective, the victim is from a prominent Castle Cove family and the rumor is the suspect in the attack is, as well. Is there any possibility that animosity between the families might have played a part—

Detective Mark Thompson: Son, this isn't a television show. This is a very real and active case involving a vicious crime between two teen girls. You want to play armchair detective, be my guest, but I'd like to remind *everyone* in the room and *anyone* who might be watching that we are the unit investigating this case. Outside interference will not be tolerated and will be prosecuted to the fullest extent of the law. Speculation is not going to help here. It will only hinder. There is only one person who can tell us truthfully what happened in the room that night, and it's Miss Kennedy. God willing, she's awake soon and

can tell us everything we need to know. Thank you,
have a good night.

Tessa Hopkins: Well, there you have it, Ben.

Ben Perez: Just a very sad case all around, Tessa.
Teen girls fighting over hairstyles and outfits, and
now one of them is fighting for her life. Thank you,
Tessa. Folks, it's Valentine's Day and we've got you
covered for last-minute gifts for your sweetie. You
can head on down to—

Tessa Hopkins: It's obvious you've never been a teen
girl, Ben.

Ben Perez: I'm sorry, what's that, Tessa?

Tessa Hopkins: I said, Tessa Hopkins, reporting
live from the Castle Cove Police Department. Have a
pleasant evening.

CHAPTER TWENTY-THREE

IRIS
FEBRUARY 14
7:52 P.M.

> Oh, Linda. All I wanted was a nice card and some
> chocolates and maybe a kiss, and instead I got a
> whole lot of heartache.
>
> —MONA MOODY, *DOUBLE TROUBLE*, 1946

FOR A MINUTE, EVERYONE in the bar is silent, watching as Ben Perez and Tessa Hopkins smoothly segue into a segment about Valentine's Day. My mom changes the channel on the bar's television and motions to my plate of uneaten food. "You have to eat," she urges.

I'm sitting at the bar on my break, but there's no way I can concentrate on a burger and coleslaw now. I wait until my mom's stepped away to serve a customer to pull out my phone and text Raf.

Tell me what it is, I type. *The other weapon. I know you know.*

Hello to you, too, Iris. A candelabra.

I pause. *Wait, for real? That's so . . . old-timey.*

And heavy. There was a set on the mantel in the study. Gotta go.

I text Alice. *Did you see the news? Raf says the other weapon is a candelabra.*

Brenda just replayed it for me. Really? Those old ones are super heavy. Brooke had some in her house and we were playing with one once and it fell and broke two of her toes.

So, one is missing. Probably one of the people Park heard took it.

Yah. Alice replies.

I text back, *And ditched it somewhere or kept it. It would have evidence on it. Blood, skin, fragments.*

Gross. I chew my bottom lip, then add: *Was this a robbery gone bad? The detective said other stuff was taken. Maybe from those boxes that were torn open in the study? And Kennedy stumbled into the room and they panicked, like we talked about earlier.*

Right, Alice texts. *But if it was a robbery, what the hell were they looking for?*

I'm about to text her back when someone says my name, softly. I look up.

Spike.

"I thought I'd find you here," he says, sliding onto the stool next to me. His hair is damp.

"Is it raining?" I ask.

He scoops some wet hair behind his ear. "Nah, I showered. I wanted to look nice."

I look around the bar, where we're currently surrounded by humans in various stages of existential regret and dishevelment. "Nice for the Moon Landing?"

"It's Valentine's Day, Iris." His face reddens. He pulls out a box from the pocket of his coat and puts it in front of me on the bar.

It's a small, red, heart-shaped box of chocolates. The kind you get at the drugstore when you don't have a lot of money.

"Spike," I say slowly. My heart tightens and swells at the same time. How is that possible? No one's ever given me something on Valentine's Day before. I mean, except my mom, and that's usually a card.

"Don't get all weirded out. I was just sitting around, missing my mom, you know? She used to give me chocolate on Valentine's Day."

Spike's mom. I haven't thought about her in a long time. We were in third grade when she died. Spike wasn't the same for a long time after that. How could you be, I guess? But that's when Neil moved to Castle Cove, too, and somehow, his goofy self latched on to Spike and Spike became Spike again. Or at least, as much of the old Spike as he could be.

"So anyway," he says, looking me right in the eyes, "I wanted some chocolate and I wanted to share, and who better with than you? Things seem strange between us, and I don't want them to be. Okay?"

"Okay."

"Iris, what happened with Cole the night of the dance?" Spike asks.

I keep my eyes on my plate of food. Push the coleslaw with a fork. "He ripped his jacket. On a nail in the treehouse. He got really angry and I . . . freaked out."

"Oh, Iris." Spike's voice is soft. "I get it. And I'm sorry."

"Yeah," I say.

I bite my lip again and unwrap the red ribbon around the box and open it. There are just six chocolates inside. I hand one to Spike and take one for myself. We sit in silence, chocolate melting on our tongues.

My phone buzzes and I look down. Alice.

"You going to ignore her?" Spike asks.

"You answer her," I say, my mouth still swirling with chocolate. "Tell her we should all go to the Historical Society tomorrow with Neil to see his mom and check out those blueprints."

Spike takes my phone and taps away at it. "Done," he says, but doesn't set my phone back down. Instead, he squints at our messages. "Candelabra?"

"Yep," I say. "Let me tell you about it."

CHAPTER TWENTY-FOUR

ALICE
FEBRUARY 15
3:42 P.M.

"But I believe in luck—in destiny, if you will. It is your destiny to stand beside me and prevent me from committing the unforgivable error."
"What do you call the unforgivable error?"
"Overlooking the obvious!"
—AGATHA CHRISTIE, *THE A.B.C. MURDERS*

I HAVE LIVED IN Castle Cove, California, for the entirety of my seventeen years on this planet and I can say with assurance I have never *ever* set foot inside the Historical Society.

The only time I've come close was freshman year, when we were supposed to take a field trip (I use the term loosely—the place is two blocks from our high school) here for a unit on local history, but I ditched it and went down to the beach with Steve and Brooke and Gerber and Kennedy instead.

The museum is tiny, located in the center of town in a run-down single-story building with red clapboard siding.

The cool winter wind whips my hair into a miniature cyclone as Neil leads us up to the museum door after school. Winter in coastal central California is unpleasant, filled with chilly, damp, gray days, and I could really do without it right now, thank you very much. So could my hair.

We follow Neil into a small, dimly lit room lined with glass display cases. I pause in front of one that holds two broken wooden wagon wheels. A placard informs me they're from wagons that traveled to California via the Oregon Trail, which is sort of cool; maybe I should have gone on that field trip instead of to the beach.

"My mom's probably back in her office," Neil says. "This way." He motions for us to follow him to the rear of the museum.

"Wait," Iris grabs my arm as I pass her. She's leaning close to the glass of another display case, staring at a photo inside. "Did you see this?" She points to a grainy photo of a tall building under construction.

I squint down at it. "Is that . . . ?"

"Levy Castle," Iris finishes. "The information card says it took over twenty years to build. An amazing female architect designed the whole thing, too, which was almost unheard-of at the time. Levy moved in while the place was still being worked on, actually."

"Really?" I ask.

"Yeah, and—" Iris begins, but Neil pokes his head out of the doorway he and Spike and Zora had disappeared through and waves to us.

"You guys coming?"

"Yeah, sorry," Iris says, and I follow her into the back office.

We barely fit into the room, which is stuffed full of old things: model boats, taxidermied animals, frames filled with sheet music. Several vintage dresses hang from a garment rack. In the middle of the room is a round table with piles of papers stacked haphazardly on top. Next to it stands a bespectacled woman chatting with Neil and Zora. She's wearing a stylish three-piece suit similar to one my mother owns.

"Is that Neil's *mom*?" I ask Iris in a low whisper. She's . . . fashionable, which is not a word I ever thought I'd use in relation to Neil.

"Her? Yeah."

"Really?" I sound so surprised that Iris lets out a snort.

"Yes, Alice."

"You're joking, right?"

"I am indubitably not joking."

"I . . ." Huh. I blink, looking from Mrs. Neil back to Neil, realizing slowly that not only is Neil's mom a fashion icon, I also don't know Neil's last name. How have I spent so much time with him over the past few months without learning his last name? An odd feeling creeps up into my belly.

"Um, what's their last name?" I whisper to Iris, who bites her bottom lip, clearly trying not to laugh.

"It's Cetas."

"His last name?"

"Yeah. You know you should——"

"I know, I know. I should try harder."

She shrugs. "You said it, not me."

I purse my lips, but don't argue.

Mrs. Cetas walks over to us. "You must be Alice Ogilvie," she says, offering a hand. Her grip is firm and her glasses are vintage Chanel. This woman really has it together. "I'm Mrs. Cetas. I've heard a lot about you from my son."

"Mo-*om*," Neil says behind her, voice breaking on the word.

"Sorry, I think I'm embarrassing him," Mrs. Cetas says with a grin. I like this lady. "So. Neil filled me in a little. You're interested in taking a look at the Levy Castle floor plans? Is that right?"

Iris nods. "The originals, if you have them. Construction on the Castle finished in, what, 1938? So the blueprints from back then, please."

"It's good to see you, Iris," Mrs. Cetas says, grabbing a pair of cotton gloves from her desk and slipping them onto her hands. She walks over to a file cabinet. "Let me see what I can do." She opens a drawer and starts riffling through it.

"It's funny. There's been a real influx of people interested in the Castle recently. They're hosting a big retrospective on Mona Moody's career. Just the other week, I sent over a huge number of boxes filled with artifacts we collected on her life over the years. Old paperwork, diaries, newspaper clippings about her, items that the public has never seen. Unfortunately, I think the police have them now, since they were in the same room where that terrible incident happened."

"I think I saw those boxes the night of the school dance, when I went up there to help Kennedy," Iris says.

"Do you have anything still here?" I ask. I would literally die for the chance to look through Mona Moody's belongings, even if it's just one box of them. "I'm a huge fan of hers," I add. "I would *love* to see anything you have."

She frowns. "Unfortunately, everything was at the Castle the night of the dance." She turns away, carefully pulling out a roll of bluish papers and heading over to the round table with them as she continues to speak. "We can set this up over here. You know, it's funny: I didn't realize until very recently that Moody has so many fans in your generation."

"What do you mean?" I ask as we all gather around her.

"Be gentle with these, please. They've very old, and *very* fragile. No touching them directly. Neil, you know the drill." Mrs. Cetas says as she lays the blueprints flat. "Oh, just that there was another boy in here recently, about your age, asking after these blueprints."

"Another kid our age was here?" My heartbeat kicks up. "When was this?"

"Mmm-hmm," she says. "Must have been about a week ago?"

I glance at Iris, whose eyes widen. Someone our age was in here just before the dance, asking about the Castle plans? That could be the lead we've been looking for.

"Did you get his name?"

She shakes her head. "I don't remember it off the top of my head, but I have everyone sign in up front, so it's probably on there. We can look on your way out?"

"That would be great." I can barely contain my excitement but force myself to remain calm. First things first. The plans.

Neil is already bent over them, examining the pages carefully, his face a picture of concentration.

"This is the wing where the dance was held. . . . The ballroom is here." He points to a large rectangle at the bottom of the thin, blue paper.

"So down the hallway from the ballroom . . . here," I indicate to a square shape. "That must be the library. See behind it? There are—"

"The secret stairs!" Mrs. Cetas exclaims from across the table.

"All the secret passages Levy built are so much fun. Like something out of a mystery Agatha Christie might write."

My head jerks up at the mention of Agatha Christie. "Are you a Christie fan?"

"*Am* I—" she starts, but Neil groans.

"Mom, *god.* Can you two do your Agatha Christie thing later, please? We're trying to concentrate."

"Sorry," she says to him, and rolls her eyes a little so only I see it. I smile. We've known each other for ten minutes, and I already feel like I have more in common with her than with my own mother.

"The study is here, above the library," says Neil. His brow furrows. "Wait. This is the little closet you were in that night, Alice, but what's this room? It's right next to the study, but I don't remember seeing it the night we were there. Look, here." He points to a small rectangle next to the study.

"You're sure you didn't see that when you were looking around that night?" Iris asks.

"Looking around?" his mother asks with a frown.

Zora jumps in. "Mrs. Cetas, this is so random, but I was looking at this sheet music over there"—she points to a small glass case sitting on a desk on the far wall—"and I wondered if you might be able to answer a couple of questions about it for me?"

Mrs. Cetas looks between her and Neil, clearly aware something is up, but nods after a long moment. "All right. But, Neil, be *gentle* with those."

Neil rolls his eyes.

"I most definitely did not," he says quietly after they walk a few feet away. "There was only one door in the study besides the hidden entrance through the closet: the one that led into the hallway. And speaking of the hallway, we checked all the rooms off it, and I definitely did not see this one."

"Interesting," Iris murmurs.

"We need to go back there. Check it out," I say. "Rooms don't just disappear. There are tons of secret passages in the Castle; maybe there's another one in that room. Maybe it's how Kennedy's attackers escaped without being seen."

"You still have that dress you stole, right? The one you wore home?" Iris asks.

"Yeah, why?"

"Great. That can be our excuse, should anyone see us. You needed to return it. It is state property, after all"—she gives me a look, which I ignore—"and we came along as moral support."

Neil nudges us, clearing his throat. His mom is heading back in our direction with Zora on her tail. "Sorry to rush you out, but I have to get ready for a Zoom call. Did you all get what you needed from the blueprints? Is there anything else I can help you all with?"

"No, this was great," Iris says with a smile. "Thank you so much for taking the time to show these to us."

We all gather our book bags from the ground and then follow Mrs. Cetas as she leads us to the front of the building.

"So you mentioned a sign-in sheet?" I ask her, trying to keep my voice casual. No need to rouse her suspicions.

"Oh yes, thank you for reminding me, Alice." She reaches behind the front desk and picks up a clipboard, handing it to Iris. "Here you go. We don't get that much foot traffic anymore, sadly. It's mostly just a sprinkling of older people interested in learning more about their ancestors. . . ."

"Alice," Iris whispers to me as Neil's mom continues to speak. "Alice. *Look.*" She points to the list of names, then looks up at me with wide eyes. "There." Her finger is next to one at the bottom of the list.

Alɛx Schaɛfɛr.

My heart skips a beat. "The *e*'s! It's the same——"

"I know. *And* I remember that name from Raf's list of cater-waiters there that night." Iris scribbles our names onto the list and then hands it to Mrs. Cetas.

"Do you happen to remember if that's the person you mentioned earlier, who was here looking for the blueprints?" Iris points to the name.

Mrs. Cetas takes the clipboard from her, then tilts her head. "Alex Schaefer?"

"Yeah. He's my partner for this project," Spike jumps in. "And he's been totally slacking. If he was here working on it, it'd be a huge relief."

Mrs. Cetas smiles at Spike. "Ah, I understand. Group projects are so frustrating. I remember back in high school when I was assigned to work with this cute boy, Bobby Engelman. I thought that we'd hit it off, but——"

"Do you remember if that's the guy, Mom?" Neil interrupts his mother's musing, cheeks red.

"Yes. I'm happy to report that was him." She sets the clipboard back down on the top of the desk. "I hope this was helpful to you all."

"It was for sure. Thanks, Mom." Neil gives her a one-armed hug and ducks as she tries to kiss his head. "See you at dinner."

We step out of the building to find the sun has broken free of the clouds. The chill in the air has started to lift. A car drives by on the street, stuffed full of Castle Cove students, their shrieks of laughter a reminder that Kennedy might be lying in a coma, but for most of the kids at our school, life is continuing as normal.

"Um, what was that all about? Who is Alex Schaefer?" Zora asks as we walk down the path away from the museum.

"He's one of the cater-waiters from the dance. Whereabouts unknown during Kennedy's attack. His name is on the sign-in sheet, and it has those same strangely written *e*'s as on the piece of paper we found," Iris says excitedly. We veer left on the sidewalk, heading back in the direction of school. "The fact that he showed up at the Historical Society right before the night of the dance, looking for the blueprints of the Castle. . . . It sounds like he was casing the place."

Neil frowns. "But what was he looking for? What's his connection to Kennedy? His motive?"

I shake my head. "I'm not sure. It could just be a strange coincidence. But Agatha Christie said, 'It is the same motif three times repeated. That cannot be coincidence.' And we have three things now—Alex Schaefer MIA during the time frame of the attack, his handwriting on the sign-in sheet that matches the writing on the note you found, and the fact that he went to the Historical Society to look at the blueprints for the Castle."

Iris's eyes are lit with excitement.

"The only way we'll know is if we go find Alex Schaefer," she says.

CHAPTER TWENTY-FIVE

IRIS
FEBRUARY 15
4:45 P.M.

Some people are driven to be bad.
Others are just born that way.
—MONA MOODY, *THE HIDDEN TRUTH*, 1948

I LOOK IN THE rearview mirror. Neil, Spike, and Zora are crammed in the back seat of Alice's car, with Spike wedged in the middle.

"There was more room in Neil's van," Spike says, shifting uncomfortably.

"Thanks, but no thanks," Alice says. "I've seen your van, and from the looks of it, there are probably disgusting things living inside."

"Okay, but it's a perfect surveillance van," Neil says. "Lots of room for tech and recording stuff, a cooler full of food, which reminds me, I'm starving."

"Yes, Neil, we love your van, and also, when *aren't* you starving?" I ask.

"I burn a lot of energy," Neil says.

"Doing *what*?" Alice says testily. "You're buried in a screen twenty-four hours a day."

"I'm *thinking,* Alice. That requires energy." Neil cranes his neck. "Pull in here. Go through the drive-through. Wait, does anyone have any money?"

There's a seismic shift in the back seat as everyone scrounges around for wallets and money.

"I'll pay," Alice says, sighing heavily. "How exactly do these things work, anyway? Hello! Hello!"

I giggle as Alice continues to yell at the drive-through screen, everyone in the back seat shouting their food orders. My phone lights up. Cole. I sneak a look at Spike.

Hey, the text reads.

Hey, I type back.

> **The other night, the treehouse. That was**
> **weird. I didn't mean to make you scared.**

I get it. It's just me. It's my fault, I reply.

> **Nah, Iris, maybe we should talk soon, I have**
> **some stuff I should probably tell you**

I can feel Alice staring at me, so I type quickly.

> Can't talk right now. Sorry.

I shove my phone in my backpack.

Alice is frowning at me as she distributes bags to the back seat, the smell of burgers and fries permeating her car. She mouths, *Cole?* I nod.

She gently puts two coffees in the console cupholders between us and looks in the rearview. "If any of you drop one fry, one crumpled napkin, or so much as get a smear of ketchup on my car, you are cleaning it *by hand.*"

She turns to me, all business.

"What's the plan when we get there?" she asks.

"I don't know," I say. "I'll know what to do when we find him. I mean, we have the matching handwriting. And Neil's mom said those boxes we saw in the study? The ones that were all looked through? Those were Mona Moody's. Which makes me wonder, *was* Schaefer planning to rob the Castle, maybe? And Rebecca was a side job?"

Beside me, Alice's brow is furrowed. "But he wrote her that note to get her upstairs. So, it can't have been accidental."

I sigh. "Neil, have you done your due diligence?"

From the back seat comes a garbled voice. "He lives at The Waves motel down on Highway One. He's headed there right now."

Alice purses her lips. "And you know this how?"

Neil's mouth is full. He holds up his phone. "I Googled him. His address came up and his Twitter. He said he's leaving work to go home. See?" It sounds like *I googy huh addy up his teeter leef wuk see.*

I look back at his phone. Alex Schaefer's Twitter profile picture. A little fuzzy, but I can make out longish, curly blond hair, deep-set eyes.

My stomach tightens a little. "The Waves," I say. "That's . . . a not good place."

I haven't thought about The Waves in a long time.

"Maybe it's time to go to the police?" Spike says. "We could tell them about the matching writing. About our pieces of the note and Alex going to the Historical Society to maybe case the place out for a robbery. That seems like *enough.*"

Alice snorts and takes a sip of her coffee. "Right. Like they'd believe us," she says.

Spike jiggles the ice in his soda cup. "There was a shooting at The Waves a while ago, wasn't there? That doesn't bode well. I'm just saying."

"I'm not afraid," Zora says. "Are you, Alice? Iris?"

I swallow my coffee in a determined way. "Nope. We're just taking a drive, checking out Alex Schaefer. Not being unsafe. Not at all. We're just scoping things out, Spike."

"Okay," he says warily. "But I have to be home by eight. I have a lot of homework."

"Stakeouts do *not* have time limits, Spike!" Alice says.

We're on Highway 1 now, traveling at a good clip. I roll down the window, the sea breeze taking away some of the hot, salty grease smell of the car.

The Thing stayed at The Waves for a few months, that first time he left us. I remember visiting him there. Small room, stained bathtub, him laying out soggy sandwiches from the vending machine at the end of the motel's walkway for our dinner.

Out the passenger window, the ocean is roiling, crisp dark waves with frothy foam. On the other side, it's a lot of small, boarded-up houses and old, abandoned single-story motels. They're surrounded by fencing that says *Berayne Enterprises: Coming Soon, a Whole New Way of Life.*

"What's up with that?" Spike asks. "I haven't been out this way in a while, but that's . . . weird."

The fencing stretches forever, encompassing scrubland and wooded areas off the road.

"Well," Alice says matter-of-factly. "Sooner or later, someone was gonna come out here and develop this. I guess now it's happening."

"Berayne," Zora muses. "Sounds like a laxative or something."

"We're almost there," Alice says. The car gets very quiet. My stomach flips a little, but I don't mind. It actually feels good, which I know is *not* a good thing. I should not feel excited about confronting a possible—not murderer, because Kennedy isn't dead—but an obviously, possibly dangerous person. This could bring us close to getting Park off the hook and getting justice for Kennedy.

Alice pulls into the farthest part of the meager, potholed parking lot. The developer's fencing butts up right against the weedy lot of The Waves motel.

There are people outside their doors, sitting on lawn chairs, smoking. Little kids in shorts riding around on tricycles on grass in front of the motel, even though it's too chilly for that.

"Okay," Alice says. "We're here. What's the plan, Iris? Stakeout?"

A furious burst of adrenaline chugs through me and I grab my door handle.

"Screw a plan," I say, getting out. "I'm going to knock on every door and find out if he's around. That's it. No stakeout. Let's just have at it."

I shut the door and start walking across the parking lot. I hear a scramble of car doors opening and closing behind me. Alice catches up to me, along with Spike.

"Is this really a good idea?" Spike asks.

"Zora and Neil are in the car," Alice says. "Probably looks bad, all of us just . . . walking around here. Maybe."

The people on the lawn chairs are watching us with interest. There's a hint of nervousness in Alice's voice.

"What?" I ask Spike. "You want to sit in the car and just wait for him to appear? And then what do we do? Just watch him? We could follow him around in his car all day, but what would that help? Isn't this what detectives *do*? Scope out the situation? Just . . . talk to people and, like, see if they trip up?"

Spike nods slowly. I can tell he's a little worried, and that's okay. This is uncharted territory.

"We'll just suss him out," I say. "There are five of us. We'll be fine."

My voice cracks a little, though. I hope no one heard it.

There are fourteen units in The Waves, seven on each side of the parking lot, with a manager's office in between. I pull open the door to the office, the bell jingling above me, sending a little memory down my spine of my dad giving me money and directing me in here to pay the weekly rent. Behind the desk, a man is hunched over a magazine, the top of his bald head glistening under the ceiling light. I rap my knuckles on the desk to get his attention. He looks up slowly.

"Help you?" he asks matter-of-factly.

"I'm looking for Alex Schaefer. What room is he in, please?"

The man stands up and my heart—and I swear, Alice's and Spike's, too—knocks around in my chest. The man is tall, tall, tall, and as he looks down at us, his eyes turn a shade darker.

My brain stutters a little, looking at him. It's been years, and he's lost all his hair, but he was here. Back when I had to come in and slide the money across the counter and watch him count it.

Does he know it's me? Does he remember people?

Get it the f together, Iris, I tell myself.

164

"Who's asking?" he says.

"Me," I say. "I'm asking. You can tell me or not tell me, but I'm going to knock on every door if you don't, so you might as well tell me."

His eyes narrow. "You going to cause trouble? I don't do the trouble here. The kind with girls."

"Eww," Alice says. *"No."*

I think quickly. "We worked a catering job together and he never picked up his paycheck. I have it."

Behind him on the wall, a business license. *Nicholas Schaefer.* Alex's *dad?*

Suddenly, the man's face breaks open and he barks out a laugh. "Uh-huh. Right. He's in twelve. You cause a ruckus, you'll have to deal with me. Do you understand?"

"Yep, sure thing, no trouble, none," Spike says, hustling Alice and me out the door by our elbows.

Once outside, he says, "That was horrid and I just about peed myself."

I untangle his fingers from my arm and walk quickly across the lot, heading toward room twelve, Alice hot on my heels.

I rap three times, my heart pounding. I don't know what I'm going to say. What am I going to say? *Hi, did you stab a girl at Levy Castle, and by the way, was anyone with you? Was it Helen Park?*

The door opens. A veritable sea of beer-smell and clove cigarettes pours over us. Alice coughs delicately.

The bearded young guy at the door looks us all up and down. "Trey isn't here," he says. "Come back later." He starts to shut the door, but I shove my foot in the way.

"Whoa, hey now, girl," he says. "No need for that. He'll be back later!" There's laughter behind him.

"I'm not here for Trey. Where's Alex? Is he here?"

The guy looks back into the room. "Hey, anyone seen Alex? Alex, yo, you here, bro?"

Someone on the bed in the dimness says in a fake, prim, lady-like voice, "No, not here, come back too—mooorrroooww."

They are high as kites.

I push the door, and the guy, out of my way and look deeper in the room.

There are four people inside and none of them looks like the Alex Schaefer in the Twitter profile pic. The room is a mess, cans and dirty clothes everywhere, takeout containers on a lopsided table.

"I mean, you're welcome to stay and wait," the guy at the door says. "You and her. Not him." He gestures to Spike and then smiles in a way I don't like.

"Hey, now, that's not right—" Spike's voice is shaky, but firm.

The guy in the doorway takes a step out, toward Spike. I move so I'm standing in front of the guy again.

"I'm afraid that's an invitation we'll have to decline," Alice says firmly, nudging Spike out of the way.

"You tell him Iris Adams came by," I say. "I'll be back."

"Sure thing," he says. "You do that."

The door closes and Spike sputters, "You gave your *name*?"

"Whatever," I say. "I don't have anything to be afraid of. Maybe he'll come to me. To us."

Alice is leading me across the parking lot and I extricate my hand from hers. I'm not a *child*.

"That was not fruitful," Spike says, opening the car door. "That was, in fact, horrific. We should just go to Thompson. This place doesn't have great vibes."

I get in the car, Spike clambering over Zora and Neil to squeeze in the middle. "I'm not well," he says softly. "I need to go home."

"What *happened*?" Zora asks. "You're white as a sheet, Spike."

I'm sucking back cold coffee as Spike starts to answer her when a sharp rap on the glass of my car door makes me jump.

A tall, reedy guy with curly, sandy-blond hair tucked behind his ears is staring at me. He's wearing a *CC Subs* work shirt. Tiny silver rings in his ears.

"Oh god," Alice breathes.

I roll down the window slowly, blood thundering in my ears.

"I don't know what you want with me, but you better believe I will make you regret it," Alex Schaefer says.

I think sometimes there is nothing to say except the exact thing that needs saying. Maybe Miss Marple would be more smooth, or sweet, and gently lead her suspect into a trap, but I have no idea how to do that, and so I just . . . say it.

"Why did you stab Rebecca Kennedy at the Sadie Hawkins dance at Levy Castle?"

There's a flash of darkness on Alex Schaefer's face before it re-arranges itself into something like . . . amusement.

I don't know which is more dangerous, the darkness or the amusement.

"Listen, I don't know you, *Iris Adams,* but you have no idea what you're talking about. *I* don't know what you're talking about."

"You stabbed a girl named Rebecca Kennedy on the second floor of Levy Castle. And hit her over the head. Did you have help?"

He puts his hands on the lip of the car door, stretches back, like a cat, lean and relaxed.

"You know *nothing*," he says quietly, his eyes locked on mine. "And whatever you think you know, you're dead wrong."

The car is eerily quiet. I feel like none of us has taken a breath in years, but we've gone too far now.

"Why did you give Kennedy a note?" I say, pressing forward. "We know it's your writing. Were you going to rob the place and Kenn—"

He suddenly juts his face into the car, up close to mine, and it's then that I notice them.

Three deep scratches on the side of his neck, easily hidden by his longish hair.

The kind of scratches a person maybe gets when someone is fighting them, trying to get away.

Alice starts the car; it begins to purr.

"Maybe you should ask your friend Helen," he says. "Maybe she's not exactly who you thought she was. What's it to you?"

I try not to flinch; his face is so close. I can't break eye contact. I can't appear scared.

"Why did you go look for blueprints at the Historical Society, Alex?" I say. "Were you going to rob the Castle? Why did you go through the boxes of Mona—"

"Listen to me." His breath is hot on my cheek. Onions, oil, peppers. Deli lunch from CC Subs, where he works, and something sweet to wash it down, like Sprite. In the back seat, Zora whimpers.

"When people take things from you, get them back," Alex says. "And if you can't, do whatever else needs to be done."

"Alice!" Zora screams. *"Go."*

Alice doesn't need to be told twice. She hits the gas and Alex jumps back, his hands briefly catching against the doorframe.

"What the hell, what the hell," Spike keeps saying. "Not cool, Iris, not cool."

"Maybe not," I say. "But he didn't say he *didn't* do it, did he? And did you see his neck? Scratches."

"I saw," Alice says grimly, catching her breath.

"I would like to erase his face from my memory, thank you," Spike says.

His face. My brain pings. I grab my phone from my backpack and bring up the photos I took of Angelik's ballroom pictures, scrolling furiously, zooming in on each and every one, cursing myself for not studying them more carefully when we first got them, but I've been working so much at Moon Landing. Alex Schaefer's Twitter profile pic was tiny and somewhat out of focus, but this . . .

"Alice," I say urgently. "Alice!"

"What, what?"

"Look." I hold up the phone and she quickly glances over. Her eyes pop.

"Holy—" She inhales sharply.

"What?" A cry in unison from the back seat. I flip the phone toward them so they can see Alex Schaefer, curly-haired and slightly blurred, tucked in the middle of the ballroom floor, sur-rounded by Castle Cove High kids, time stamped *9:54 p.m.* and not wearing the white Splendid Spread Catering jacket.

Because it would have had blood on it.

And now we have two things to do: find that jacket and find that secret room at the Castle.

SUSPECT BOARD

Gerber

Teachers (McAllister, spite)

Alex Schaefer:

   - scratches on neck

   - handwriting matches note

   - combative

   - looked at Castle blueprints at museum

   - not wearing catering jacket in ballroom
     just after the attack

   - motive: robbery?? "when people take things
     from you, get them back"

Staff

Park—

   - no blood on clothes

Unknown

CHAPTER TWENTY-SIX

ALICE
FEBRUARY 16
6:42 A.M.

Never do anything yourself
that others can do for you.
—AGATHA CHRISTIE,
THE LABOURS OF HERCULES

Where the hell were you yesterday, ALICE?

MY ALARM HASN'T EVEN gone off this morning and Ashley Henderson is already texting me about our biology project. The incessant buzzing from her incoming texts woke me. The girl really needs to give it a break; I could not care less about genealogy or stupid DNA. All I've learned so far is that my great-grandfather was a farmer in Southern California, a fact I could have gone my entire life without knowing and been perfectly happy.

YOU BETTER SHOW UP TODAY. UR GRADE
AFFECTS MINE AND I WILL NOT FAIL

I throw my phone back onto the stack of Agatha Christie books sitting on my bedside table and flop over, eyes adjusting to the still-dark room. It's not *my* fault McAllister decided to tie our grades together for this project. Sure, I skipped class once or twice (or three times), but *Henderson* is the one who made that snide little comment about McAllister's biology-themed bow tie and pissed him off so much he forced us together as punishment.

It's the worst, because Henderson is a freak about school and her grades, and now she's taking out all her intensity on me. Plus, I've come to realize over the past few days that I might have to actually start trying in class so as not to fail bio. If I do, my parents might never leave.

I sigh and roll to my side to grab my phone.

> Good lord would you calm down it's not even 7am

Don't test me Alice

> Fine. I'll be there. Now leave me alone

There's a pause, three little dots appearing and disappearing on the screen.

You better be

God, she's annoying.

Biology is my last class, so by the time I arrive, I'm exhausted from an entire day spent pretending that I care about school. I should be researching Alex Schaefer—figuring out his connection to Kennedy and what he was looking for up in that room—not sitting here in *class*. But I have no choice, thanks to my parents.

To make everything even more annoying, McAllister gasps rudely as I enter his classroom, like he can't believe his eyes that I'm here. I skip a few classes and suddenly I'm some sort of truant? The guy needs to get over himself.

"Alice *Ogilvie*?" He rubs his eyes like he might be seeing things. "To what do we owe the pleasure?"

It takes all my willpower, but I manage to bite my tongue instead of snapping something at him that would surely get me sent to Principal Brown's office. If the only way to get my parents to leave is to be a model student and do my homework, you better believe I'll be doing just that. At least for a little while.

"Good, you're here," Henderson hisses through clenched teeth as I slide into the seat next to her. She's drumming her fingers against the top of the desk over and over and over again.

"Could you *please* stop doing that?" I say primly, gesturing to her hand. "I have a headache. Or, if it's easier"—I grab a scalpel from the bin of biology tools that sits in the middle of the table— "I could cut them off for you." I bat my lashes at her. She glares at me, but pulls her hand back. It disappears onto her lap.

"I should report you for that threat," she mutters. "And I would, except I need you for this stupid project. I can't fail this class. I have to get a good grade to get a scholarship for college next year."

Before I can reply, McAllister starts class. I spend the next forty-five minutes trying not to fall asleep. He talks on and on about DNA and genealogy and *blah blah blah,* who cares, how is this going to be relevant in my life in the future?

Next to me, Henderson types note after note, basically copying everything McAllister says verbatim into her computer, like she's the freaking class stenographer. After what seems like a lifetime, McAllister wraps up by telling a joke about a strand of DNA that asks a strand of RNA if it's still single and the RNA replies "*Always.*" I don't understand it, but who cares. At least class is over.

Ashley types a few more things on her computer, then turns to me.

"Do you think you got everything?" I say sweetly, which she ignores.

"About our project. I've done my half, as you know. But have you done yours? *No.* Have you even *started* yours?" She narrows her eyes. "Again, no. Unless there's something you haven't told me . . . ?"

"Sorry, but all this ancestry stuff is boring. I'll get around to it. *Probably,*" I tack on, because I know it'll piss her off.

Which it does. "*Dammit,* Alice! Get it together. It's just like you, messing up something important to me. I know you've gone off the deep end, hanging out with those weirdo stoner kids, but I will *not* let you bring me down with you. This project might not mean anything to you, but it's important to me. I will not allow you to be the reason I get a bad grade in this class!"

She slams her laptop shut, so hard I jump, and then leans in close to me. "Do your part by the deadline, or you will be very, *very* sorry."

With that, she grabs her stuff and storms out of the room.

Good lord, what has gotten into everyone lately? First Iris yesterday, acting all tough to that Alex kid, like she wasn't concerned that he might have *stabbed* someone, and now Henderson, threatening me about a dumb bio project? I know she cares about her grades, but the girl really needs to take a Xanax.

Iris meets me outside the classroom. It's the first time I've seen her today and dark shadows rim her eyes, like she barely slept last night.

"You okay?" I ask as we start down the hall. We're supposed to meet everyone outside and head to the Castle to see if we can find an entrance to the room next to the study and figure out if that's how the people Park claims to have heard escaped. We have a halfway decent excuse for being there, should we be questioned—like Iris said, I need to return the gown I . . . borrowed. Plus, my own dress is still there somewhere, and I should probably get it back.

"I'm fine," Iris says without looking at me. I wait for her to say something—anything—more, but she's quiet as we exit the building into the bright afternoon sun.

"Were you up late talking to Cole?"

"What?" Iris's cheeks redden. "No, Alice. God, not everything is about relationships." She spits the word out like it tastes bad.

"Okay, rude much?" But I decide not to push it.

We find Zora and Angelik sitting in front of the main building on a wooden bench, heads bent together, laughing at something on a phone.

As we approach, Zora looks up wearing a happy smile. I've never seen her so content. It's weird.

"Where are Spike and Neil?" Iris asks.

"Haven't seen them yet," Zora says. She kisses Angelik on the cheek and hops up. "I'll see you later, okay?"

Angelik nods, waving at Iris and me as we head off in search of the boys.

"Have you texted them?" Zora asks.

Iris shakes her head.

"Hang on. . . ." Zora types on her phone. "There. I told them to meet us at the car. We gotta get moving—I need to be home at five to babysit my little sister."

"Great," I say, hiking my bag farther up onto my shoulder. "Let's go."

We find Spike and Neil waiting by my car, and ten minutes later, we're pulling off the driveway to the Castle, into a small space between the shrubs and trees where my car will be hidden from anyone who might pass by.

"Remember," I say. "If anyone asks, I'm a dumb high school student"—Zora snorts from the back seat and I give her a dirty look—"who left my dress here the night of the dance. I had no idea the Castle was closed to the public and I dragged you guys along because I was too scared to come alone."

We exit the car. I snap the fanny pack that holds my forensics kit around my waist, then grab a small bag from the trunk that holds Mona Moody's dress. I pass Neil his Forensics Club duffel and he takes it, pulling three pairs of gloves from it. He passes them to Zora and Spike. Zora takes them and slips them on, but Spike just stares at Neil's outstretched hand.

"What?" Neil asks. "You okay?"

Spike shakes his head slowly. "I just realized . . . don't you think the Castle has a security system? How are we going to get around it?"

Neil smirks. "Worry not. First, chances are it's off right now, given the amount of law enforcement that's been roaming the place over the last few days, but even if it's not, I have it taken care of." He pats the bag he's swung up on his shoulder.

"Um, what exactly does that mean?" I ask. I'm down for many, many things, but I'm not sure if hacking state-owned property is on that list.

"The less you know, the better," Neil says. He shades his eyes with a hand and gazes up to the bright blue sky. "Though, alarm system or none, it's gonna be hard to sneak in there since it's still light outside. I know we had to come now because of Zora's baby-sitting and Iris having to work, but it does make it a little more complicated, so we need to cover our bases. Stay close to the tree line so we're out of sight."

I nod. "Agreed. We should head to the service entrance off the back side of the property, where the driveway dead-ends. Every-one ready?"

I look around at the other four and I'm reminded of last fall, the first time the five of us banded together to solve a mystery, when we did a sweep of the side of Highway 1 to figure out what happened to Brooke. Being here again, with these people, sends a little shiver of excitement down my spine. One by one everyone nods and I nod back.

"All right, let's go," I say.

We cut through the trees, through overgrown brush, until we reach the circular driveway where the foliage ends. There's no coverage between us and the Castle now, only open sky.

"Shit," Zora says, as we all realize the same thing at once. We're going to have to go the rest of the way exposed.

"I guess . . . I guess our only option is to haul ass over there as fast as we can?" Iris says, looking at me.

I nod. "Seems like our only option, yeah."

We all start running.

We stop at the back door, and Neil starts doing whatever he does on his phone. A moment later, there's a soft *beep* as the door unlocks.

CHAPTER TWENTY-SEVEN

IRIS
FEBRUARY 16
4:10 P.M.

Oh, gosh. I'm a very lucky girl, you know? I didn't
come from much and now I have a wonderful life
with so many comforts. It's like a dream.
—MONA MOODY, INTERVIEW, *SCREENLAND,* 1948

"SOMEONE NEEDS TO STAY behind," I whisper as Alice reaches
for the doorknob. "Just in case security comes around the grounds
or something. To text us a warning."

"I'll do it," Spike says, and before anyone can agree or object,
he disappears around the side of the Castle.

Alice pushes the door wide as we cluster behind her. There's a
foyer looking down a long hallway with an intricately tiled floor.
"This way," she whispers. "The kitchen is to the left, ballroom
down there, and here . . ."

We follow her quietly through the foyer when she suddenly
stops. Zora bumps into my back. Alice turns to us and puts a
finger to her lips, angling her head. I look to my left. Through
a partially open door, there's a man and a woman, both wearing
suits, sitting at a long table, fast-food bags and files spread around
them.

Alice takes a sharp right and suddenly we're in a darkened library, blinds drawn, with hundreds of old-looking books on the shelves. Only, there's a space between the shelves with crime-scene tape crisscrossed over the opening. "This is the staircase," Alice whispers.

"Damn, parting bookshelves," Zora whispers. "This is some real old-timey mystery stuff."

Alice ducks under the tape and through the opening and we do the same as she turns on the flashlight on her phone.

"Voilà," she says triumphantly.

In front of us, illuminated in her phone light, is a narrow staircase.

The stairs are musty-smelling and webby, the wood steps groan slightly as the four of us make our way up, trying not to trip. It's very twisty. When we reach the top, Alice pauses at another opening crisscrossed with police tape.

"This leads to the cedar closet," she whispers.

Beyond the opening, I can see tons of old gowns.

"This is where I was when I heard noises the night of the dance," she says, "and when I came out, that's when I saw Park standing over Kennedy."

One by one we duck under the tape and into the cedar closet. I reach out and feel some of the gowns. Silk, velvet, tulle. Lilian said they were Mona Moody's. If so, she was even tinier than she seems in photos. I guess it makes sense the gowns are still here. Where would they go after she died? She was an orphan in a foster home; she had no family. The wall behind the gowns in front of me is mirrored; I meet my own eyes between the gowns and then I jump at a shadow behind me. But when I turn, it's just a mannequin in an elegant fur evening cape.

The door from the cedar closet to the study is open. Alice slips in, followed by Neil and Zora.

I look through the opening into the study, my fingers still tracing the impossible softness of a gown. And then something occurs to me. I turn on the flashlight of my phone and shine it around the cedar closet.

"Alice," I whisper.

She looks through the doorway at me.

"Your dress isn't here," I say.

She frowns. "Well, we can't worry about that now."

She tosses me the bag with Mona Moody's dress and I carefully pull it out, smooth it, and hang it on one of the padded hangers.

I go into the study and look around. All over the large mahogany desk, on the mantel, on the carpet, are evidence pins with numbers. Where Kennedy's body was, a large portion of the carpet is missing.

"We need to be efficient and quick," Alice says. "We're looking for Alex's jacket and we need to find out how he, or *they*, got out of this room."

"And where they *went*," Zora adds. "Which might lead us to the jacket or something else."

Neil is looking at the windows, feeling around them with his gloved hands. "They don't open," he whispers. "No handles, nothing."

Alice moves to the paneled portion of the wall on the left-hand side of the room, where the blueprints indicated a door to a room on the other side should be, a black piano off to the side.

The three of us stare at the wall, thinking. Neil pats it in various places.

"Okay," I whisper. "Park said she heard loud voices, arguing,

180

then banging on the piano, then . . . nothing. So, if there were two other people besides Kennedy in here, and they've effectively left her for dead on the floor, what are they arguing about and how—"

"They're arguing about how to get out," Alice says. "Right? Because—"

"Because Alex saw the blueprints and said they could use this room, but now they're in here and . . . ," Zora says.

"He messed up," Neil says. "So they're mad. The windows don't work. There's no door here, they're probably freaking out and thinking someone's coming and they're . . . fighting? And . . . playing the piano?"

"Okay, but who plays a piano in the middle of an argument after attacking a random girl?" Zora's voice is frustrated.

"But they weren't *playing*," I hiss. "I told you that. Park says it was like a bang—"

Just then, Neil advances toward Alice. "You stupid fool! You said there was a door here—"

"Excuse me!" Alice whispers harshly. "Neil, what are you doing? Ew, out of my personal bubble, please!"

She tries to skirt around him, free, but he's backing her up against the piano. She stumbles, her hands flailing behind her to find balance, her palms smacking against the keys.

With an eerie, slow groan, the wall parts.

"Like that," Neil says triumphantly. "They argued, maybe it became a little physical, one of them hit the piano, and voilà. Levy must have rigged the piano somehow. Impressive."

We gape at the opening in the wall. It's a pocket door.

"Yes, but now you've made *a lot* of noise," Alice says nervously.

"Then let's go in and be quick about it," I say.

Inside the room, there's a four-poster bed, flowered wall-paper, and an immense portrait of Charles Levy, who, for some reason we haven't ascertained, felt the need to wall up the door to this room, so there was no way in or out unless you knew about the piano. What a puzzle of a man.

"If I'm Alex," I say, "I have blood on my jacket. I have to get out of here and get back to the party, to work, so everything's normal, right? Where do I ditch it and how do I get out?"

On the right side of the bedroom, there's a door. I walk over and open it, revealing a small bathroom with a window above a sink. I look back at Alice.

Zora starts opening the drawer of a giant dresser, rooting around. Neil dives under the bed, his sneakered feet sticking out.

Alice and I look around the room and then at each other. I can tell we're thinking the same thing.

"If Alex looked at the house plans, he saw this room, and he also thought there was a way in and a way out, because those plans were the originals; the door to this room hadn't been changed yet, and over there . . . he would see a door to the hallway and think that was an exit . . . but look, it's been walled over. So now he's in here and there's no way out because he can't go back into the study where Park is," Alice says. "So the only option is . . . ."

Just as she says that, the pocket door, the secret door, begins closing. Zora and I make a move for it, but it closes too quickly and Zora begins to feel around on the wall.

"Well," she says slowly. "That's not good. Also, if there's a secret way to get in here, um, why is there no way to get *out*? This is all sorts of creepy."

Neil looks out from under the bed. "Oh, that is a pickle," he murmurs. Then he ducks back under the bed.

Alice and I look at each other. I shrug. Nothing to be done now except what we came to do. I walk into the bathroom. There's a clawfoot tub, a sink, a toilet, a shelf on the wall, and a window above the sink. A window just slightly cracked open.

He washed his hands in the sink, I bet, or tried to with such limited time. "Alice, there would be fingerprints here, right? From him washing his hands, maybe? Wouldn't he do that? Do you have something fancy in your pack to check for prints?"

She unzips her forensics fanny pack and then pauses. "Look."

In the sink, faint traces of dried pink. "Bingo," I say.

Neil appears in the bathroom doorway. "Look what I found tucked in the bedsprings under the bed. Which seems like a weird place to put a photo, don't you think? You don't just go around tucking—"

Alice snatches the crinkled black-and-white photograph from him and peers at it. "What in the world?" she whispers. She holds it out to me.

Three people. Mona Moody, face gleaming and in a beautiful gown, her neck adorned with a jeweled necklace, sandwiched between Charles Levy and two other men, a theater marquee above them showing the movie *Angel in Exile,* a crowd of screaming people holding out pens and autograph books.

There's something familiar about her necklace, but I can't quite place why.

"Save it," I tell Alice and she zips it inside her forensics fanny pack.

I look back at the window above the sink. "There. It's the only way."

Outside the window is a sturdy, tall tree.

"Through the window, down the tree." Alice nods. "But the jacket?"

Zora squeezes in, looking around. She lifts the lid to the toilet tank. "No jacket. He could have stashed it anywhere, really. Maybe somewhere inside downstairs when he came back in? It was raining. He could have thrown it away and thought he could ask for another, say it got wet on his break? Also, again, how are we going to get out of this room? It's not like there's a piano on *this* side of the wall. Are we going through that window, Iris? Is that what you're telling me?"

"Maybe I can figure it out from this side," Neil says, and starts feeling around the closed wall.

Zora's phone buzzes.

I unwind the pull handle on the window and the window pops out more, a slow roll.

"He'd need two hands to get through this," I say. "He can't hold the jacket and—"

I climb onto the sides of the sink, trying not to disturb the faint blood traces in the basin, Alice steadying my back. My phone is pinging in my pocket but I ignore it. I'm trying to get a foothold on the sink. I'm much shorter than Alex, he's tall enough to maybe not have had to stand on the sink to get through the window, he could just angle and slide and grab the tree? The window was partially closed when we came in. He could have pushed the frame from the outside if he was in the tree because the tree is so close to the window. Police walking around outside the Castle investigating wouldn't necessarily notice a slightly open window because . . . well, they didn't believe Park when she said two people disappeared from this room, which is a room they don't know about, anyway. So they weren't looking for clues about that.

184

I'm halfway out the window, leaves from the tree in my hair.

"Oh god," Zora says, her voice tight. "Oh no."

I look down.

And what I see is Spike, his face pale, two scowling policemen behind him, staring up at me.

There's a clatter of noise and voices on the other side of the bedroom wall in the hallway and Alice is pulling me from the sink, but not before I get a glimpse of the bushes below the window, in front of Spike, and a flash of fabric.

"Open this . . . whatever this is. You open it right now. This is the Castle Cove Police Department."

My stomach sinks at the sound of Detective Thompson's voice. He starts pounding on the secret wall between the bedroom and the study. Neil backs away from it slowly and looks at me.

"My mother is going to kill me," Zora whispers.

"I came back to get my dress," Alice calls out. "I left it here the night of the dance. And then, because our friend is in trouble, we decided to do a little digging. Is that so wrong?"

It sounds like Thompson is pushing at the wall. He's ordering people around. Taps, thunks, and clunks sound against the wall.

"You need to check the bushes below this window!" I shout. "Alex Schaefer. Cater-waiter working the night of the dance. I think you'll find his catering jacket covered in Rebecca Kennedy's blood down there—"

"I don't want to hear one thing from you except how to open this door, Iris Adams. However you got in there, you will get out, and I do mean right now."

When I look at Zora, Alice, and Neil, everyone's face is very pale. I feel my stomach curdle. I nod to Zora.

Slowly, she approaches the wall and leans very close to it. Her voice shakes. "You have to hit the piano."

Silence.

"It's how we got in," Zora continues. "Just, like, bang on some keys. Try Middle C."

From the other side of the wall, Thompson barks, "Who the hell knows Middle C?"

A tiny voice says, "Nine years of piano, sir."

"Get to it, then!" Thompson says.

"Alex Schaefer was casing the Castle," Alice calls out. "He went to the Historical Society to check blue—"

Very carefully, someone is pressing piano keys. *Plink, plank, plunk,* like the book about bears and blueberries from when I was very little.

"Not like *that*!" Zora yells. "Harder."

"It wasn't Helen Park!" I shout. "She had no blood on her, correct? There had to be at least two people involved, and we don't think—"

And then very suddenly, and very loudly, an ear-splitting volley of notes, as though someone slammed a fist down on the keys.

The pocket door slides open, revealing Detective Thompson and three confused policemen.

He looks around at all of us.

"You kids seem to like games," he says. "I've got a really good one. Let's play, shall we? Eeny, meeny, miny, moe, catch an intruder by the . . . toe."

With that, his finger lands on me.

"Guess who's going to jail?" Detective Thompson asks. "It's you, Iris Adams."

TEXT CONVERSATION BETWEEN
ALICE OGILVIE AND PATSY ADAMS
FEBRUARY 16
5:54 P.M.

AO: Mrs. Adams?

PA: Yes. Who's this?

AO: Iris's friend alice?

MA: Of course, hi Alice

AO: Hi I don't know how to tell you this but Iris and I were looking for something at the Castle . . . it was legit I swear . . . but then the cops showed up and now she's been hauled down to the station and I think she might be in trouble

MA: Alice hold on. What are you saying?

AO: . . .

AO: . . .

AO: Iris is in jail

TEXT CONVERSATION BETWEEN
RAFAEL RAMIREZ AND ALICE OGILVIE
FEBRUARY 16
6:39 P.M.

RR: Why did I just see Iris at the station???

RR: Alice????

AO: Raf don't yell at me

RR: Alice.

AO: We were at the Castle and maybe we were trespassing and maybe Thompson caught us there and maybe he decided to make her a scapegoat bc he's a tool

RR: You were maybe trespassing at the Castle?

AO: Fine. We WERE trespassing at the Castle. Happy now?

RR: Not really

AO: We found something! All we could see was some fabric, but it might have been one of the jackets from the catering company you work for

RR: Hold on

AO: Fine

AO: Raf where tf are you

AO: Raf?

6:52 p.m.

RR: Sorry im at work

AO: Mmm

RR: So. Yes. It was a catering jacket

AO: I knew it. Are they talking about it at the station?

RR: Honestly im not sure I should tell you anything. Iris is in JAIL

AO: We're trying to help Park! Get on board, Raf. You aren't my parent

RR: Oh trust me I know that

RR: Fine. Since you won't quit no matter what I say. They were talking about finding a diary inside the jacket

AO: Hmmm. What sort of diary?

RR: I haven't seen it

AO: Whose diary is it? Kennedy's? Alex's? The mysterious person who was in the room with them that night?

RR: Alice, I don't know. They seem to think it's not important to the investigation so take that for what it's worth

AO: I don't care what they say. I need to know what's in it. I need you to help me get that diary

AO: RAF?

RR: I know I'm going to regret this, but fine.

RR: The things I do for you, Alice Ogilvie.

CHAPTER TWENTY-EIGHT

IRIS
FEBRUARY 16
9:45 P.M.

*Meet adorable Mona Moody, a plucky young starlet
on the rise! This cheeky gal is full of vigor—from an
orphanage to the silver screen, this gal doesn't give
up, with six movie roles this year! Read on for her
favorite chocolate cake recipe, romance advice,
and skin care tips!*
—*"MEET MONA MOODY," MOVIELAND, 1947*

DETECTIVE THOMPSON'S LITTLE GAME wasn't a fun one.

Alice yelled and pouted, but he didn't listen. I knew handcuffs would be tight, but I didn't think they'd be *so* tight.

I still have red circles on my wrists and I've been sitting in the same gray room for what seems like hours. They fingerprinted me and took my mug shot (*turn to the left*) and then put me in here. I had a brief glimpse of Raf down a hallway, staring at me in shock. They gave me an orange soda and took the cuffs off.

My mother is going to kill me.

Just when I think I might finally let the tears I've been holding in spill, the gray door to the room bangs open. Thompson comes in, paper cup of coffee in hand, pulls out a chair, and sits down across from me.

"You need to stop playing these games, Iris," he says quietly. "It's not funny. It's dangerous. This is a bad road to be on in life, do you understand? You'll get hurt. Think about your poor mother."

I will never let Thompson see me cry. I push it all down and let it sit in my stomach, a painful little ball.

The only thing I say is "You found Alex Schaefer's jacket, though, didn't you? We were right."

Detective Thompson sighs, takes a sip of his coffee, but his eyes flicker, and I know I'm right.

"His fingerprints will be all over that bathroom," I say. "You saw the blood in the sink? You know he did it. He did it with someone else, maybe, but not Helen Park. She's too small, she's too timid to be physical that way. She walked in, she picked up the letter opener, she panicked when Alice came in, and ran."

"I'm not going to discuss the details of an ongoing investigation with you, Iris."

"You should get him in here. He has defensive scratches on his neck."

He gives me a long look.

"You know I'm right," I say. "Alice and I are right."

"If a citizen feels they have information regarding a crime, they're welcome to share that with the police department," he tells me. "All leads will be followed. But you and Alice Ogilvie didn't do that. Just like before, you went full steam ahead on your own, and now look where you are."

"You wouldn't have believed us, just like before," I say. "And I'm right about that, too."

"And why wouldn't I believe you?" His voice is calm.

"I want to say it's because you think we're silly teenagers, just stupid girls," I answer slowly, rubbing my sore wrists. "But honestly, I think it's because you're just not . . . curious enough. You think by the book. There's no room for interpretation. And I think there's a lot more to this case, but I know you wouldn't believe me if I told you that, either."

"More to the case? Do tell, Iris." He folds his hands.

"Why were boxes from the Historical Society pawed through in the study? Those were Mona Moody's things. Who would want them, least of all a teenager like Alex Schaefer? If he wanted to rob the Castle, there was probably plenty downstairs, right? Why go upstairs? And why attack Rebecca Kennedy? There's a whole host of interesting things here and even if I can't quite put them all together right now—"

The sound of his laughter reverberates around the room.

"See," I say softly. "By the book. You have no imagination."

He's shaking his head, still chuckling, when the policewoman opens the door and in steps Ricky Randall, her hair in a disheveled ponytail, her suit jacket misbuttoned, her face sunburnt.

"Ahh, Mark," she says cheerily. "Are you interrogating my client without her lawyer present?"

"No," he says, getting up. "Just a friendly conversation. She's all yours now, Ricky."

At the door, he looks back at me. "Remember what I said, Iris. You could get very hurt, and I don't want that. I mean that sincerely."

The door closes behind him. Ricky sits in the chair he was just in and tilts her head at me.

"This is what I come home to?" she says. "After my well-deserved vacation? I have to step off the plane to numerous voice mails from your mother?"

I feel my mouth quiver. "I'm sorry," I say.

"I'd hug you, but that's not allowed," she says softly. "What is going on? Stabbings? Head injuries? A coma? The Castle? I can't wait to hear it all, kid."

"I think it was a cater-waiter named Alex Schaefer. Right? Did they find his missing jacket? Are they arresting him?"

Ricky sighs, taking a sip of my orange soda. It must be flat by now.

"I don't know yet. I pressed some of my contacts here for some info. Kid's got a juvenile record, which would be sealed. I don't know much."

She pauses. "You and Ogilvie just can't quit, can you?"

"I guess not," I say. "But Kennedy's in a coma and we don't think Park did it. Those seem like the right things to care about."

"Maybe so," Ricky answers. She runs her fingers around the rim of the soda can.

"Am I going to juvie?" I ask quietly. They couldn't put me in a cell here because this is the adult jail; that's why they stuck me in this room.

"You'll probably wish you were when your mom gets through with you," Ricky says. "I managed to talk Thompson down, get you a fine and community service for trespassing. But he's *pissed,* not gonna lie."

I can't help but crack a smile. "You're my lawyer now. I officially have a lawyer. That's kind of cool—"

"No," Ricky says. "*No,* it isn't. Your mom is *devastated.* This is . . . I'm sorry, Iris, but it's bringing up your dad, and all the times she had to bail him out for something, or call the police on him, and . . ."

I look down at the table, that hot little ball in my stomach twisting around.

"You can't do this to her," Ricky says. "You just can't."

I don't say anything, but in my head, a tiny little voice is whispering, *What if I am just like him?*

"Thompson has your phone, too, by the way, which he showed me briefly. You two have really been up to a lot, haven't you? I saw some of your texts, and what are you doing hanging out with that Cole Fielding kid? His family—"

"What?" I ask. "What about Cole's fam—"

She shakes her head. "Not now. But in the future, don't give up your phone so easily. Wait until they have a warrant to search it. California is tricky: If you give consent, they get to search. If you don't, they can't."

"Fine," I say.

Ricky sighs. "I have to go deal with paperwork and a judge who's not happy about working at this time of night."

"So, am I getting out soon?" I ask, my voice small.

She stands up, looking down at me. "Oh, god, no. Thompson would have let you go an hour ago, but your mom said you should sit in here and stew until morning. It's one thing to piss off the police chief, girl—it's a whole other thing to piss off your *mom*."

CHAPTER TWENTY-NINE

ALICE
FEBRUARY 17
7:32 A.M.

But surely for everything you love,
you have to pay some price.
—AGATHA CHRISTIE,
AGATHA CHRISTIE: AN AUTOBIOGRAPHY

I KNOCK ON IRIS'S apartment door early the next morning, bearing Dotty's Doughnuts and coffee as a peace offering to her mom. The morning is gray, low clouds hanging over the ocean behind Iris's building, and the cool humidity cuts through my thin sweater, making me shiver.

Iris's mom opens the door.

"I brought doughnuts," I say, holding the cardboard box up. "And some coffee."

She pauses for a moment, then waves me inside. She's dressed in blue jeans and a flannel button-down and is the polar opposite of my own mother, who I glimpsed in a Chanel suit on my way out the front door. Gotta be properly dressed for those Zoom meetings, I guess.

I set everything down on the kitchen table except my own coffee, which I continue to suck down like my life depends on it.

Mrs. Adams glances at the doughnut box but makes no move to open it. She does, however, pick up the coffee. "Alice," she says. "What are you doing here?"

"I . . ." I trail off. If I'm being honest, I thought maybe I'd show up and act as an intermediary between her and Iris. I know Mrs. Adams is pissed, and I thought maybe I could defuse the situation before they saw each other in person. In retrospect, that plan was sort of dumb.

"I wanted to make sure Iris was okay," I finish, which is true. I didn't sleep much; I feel responsible for Iris's foray into a life of crime. We all know who Thompson *should* have taken with him last night.

Me.

Her mom's mouth flattens into a thin line. "You kids . . . you have to get this under control, do you hear me? I know it's easy for you, Alice, with your parents' connections and your family's money. You'll be fine no matter what happens to you. But Iris?" She sweeps a hand around the apartment.

"This is where Iris is from. I wish I could say that if she got into serious trouble, I could make it all go away, but that's just not true. I think you know that, somewhere deep inside you. You two can pretend that you're the same all you want, but you're not. You're just . . . not."

She sinks into a chair, rubbing her forehead. I don't know what to say. I've never really thought about it, I guess, the fact that maybe Iris and I are not actually really the same, that things like this would be harder on her than they would be on me, and the guilt that's been nudging at the edges of my mind all night comes crashing in. I bite my bottom lip.

I shouldn't have let Thompson take her.

"I'm sorry," I say after what seems like an eternity. Iris's mom still hasn't moved, but she nods at my words.

"I'm sure you are. I'm sure Iris is, too. But sometimes sorry just doesn't cut it."

I hate to admit it, but I know she's right.

We head down to the station in Mrs. Adams's car, a newish Chevy Impala that Iris bought her with the reward money from Lilian. I thought briefly of offering to drive my BMW, but then thought better of it. That speech she gave back in her kitchen really shook me. I had a plan for when we got to the station, one Raf and I discussed last night, but it involves Iris . . . and now I'm not so sure it's a good idea. I pick up my phone, send a text, and then watch the town pass by my window.

"I'm glad they're letting her out," I say when I can't take the silence any longer.

Mrs. Adams takes a bite of the doughnut she grabbed before we left the apartment, sugar cascading down her chin. She swallows before she responds. "I'll let you in on a little secret. Thompson wanted to let her out yesterday. I asked them to hold her overnight."

"Why—"

"I thought she could do with a little shaking up," she says. "Like I said back at home, you two really need to realize that you're not in a TV show or an Agatha Christie novel. You're romping around like little teen detectives, but that isn't your job. Your job is to go to school, *graduate,* have opportunities. My daughter deserves that."

"I know she does," I say quietly, balling my hands into fists in my lap.

We reach the station a moment later, and she parks at the end of a row of cop cars.

"I have to go in and get her," she says, unbuckling her belt. "Wait here."

"I'm coming with you," I say. I have to. Raf is waiting.

"Alice——" she starts.

"Please," I say. I don't have to fake the quiver in my voice.

She lets out a long, tired sigh and then nods. "Fine. C'mon."

Inside, the waiting room is buzzing with activity. A man wearing a tracksuit, who I think I recognize from the lawn of The Waves motel, is arguing with the cop behind the front desk. He bangs his palm against the counter and yells something about *constitutional rights.*

Iris's mom points to the row of black metal folding chairs set against the far wall and says, "Wait there." She walks off without waiting for a reply, and I do as I was told.

I give it a few moments, then text *Here.*

All set? Raf responds immediately.

Yah

I hop back out of my chair and walk over to the front counter, where Iris's mom stands behind Tracksuit. She sees my approach and her mouth turns down in displeasure. I cringe internally— I like Iris's mom, and in just a moment, she's not going to be my biggest fan.

"Alice, what are you——"

I nudge by her, pushing past the man and up to the counter.

"Excuse me——" starts the man, but I talk loudly over him.

"Who do I need to speak to around here to get some service?"

The woman behind the counter glares at me. "What do you think you're doing?" She rises from her chair. She's much taller than she looked sitting down. At least six feet.

Focus, Alice.

"I think I'm trying to retrieve the dress—my dress—you all took into evidence at the Castle. A dress which, for your information, cost over one thousand dollars! Why exactly are you all holding on to it? Is it evidence? I don't think so. I think—"

"Miss, I'm going to have to ask you to calm down." The cop is growing steadily angrier as I rant, her face blooming into a dark red.

Behind me, Mrs. Adams says in a low voice, "Alice, what in god's name are you doing?"

I ignore her. "I will not calm down! My dress! Where is it? I demand to speak to Detective Thompson this very minute—"

"Alice Ogilvie." The door leading into the back of the station opens, and none other than Thompson appears, followed by a uniformed cop and then—thank god—Raf, his eyes trained on the floor. I'm going to have to speak with him about his poker face, because he looks guilty as hell right now.

"To what do I owe this displeasure? Coming to retrieve your friend, I assume?" asks Thompson.

"Yes, but I would also like my dress back," I say. "The one you took from the Castle for no reason, which is very expensive. My mother is going to kill me if I don't get it back; I went all the way to the Castle to find it but you'd stolen it—"

"I'm sorry, who do you think you're talking to, Miss Ogilvie?" says Thompson, his face darkening.

"Detective Thompson," Iris's mom interrupts, stepping between us. "I'm here to pick up my daughter."

Thompson's gaze swings between the two of us. "You two are together?"

"You could say that," Iris's mom admits reluctantly.

"My dress?" I say again.

Thompson rolls his eyes. "Yes, we have your dress, Ms. Ogilvie. You're welcome to it; we don't need anything extra clogging up the evidence room."

"I can get it!" Raf says to Thompson. "I mean, if that works on your end, sir."

Thompson shrugs. "If you want to, fine by me." He nods at the other cop, who hands Raf a key card. Raf disappears back into the depths of the station.

"Now." Thompson turns to Mrs. Adams. "Officer O'Hair will get Iris signed out as soon as she's finished with—" He frowns at the man in the tracksuit. "Mr. Lasagna. I see you're here. Again."

"Your name is Lasagna?" I say without thinking. The man turns on me with a frown and I stumble backward a step.

"Yeah. What of it?"

"Nothing, nothing." I really need to learn to keep my big mouth shut.

The man turns back to Thompson. "Your little lackey here is telling me I have no grounds to file a complaint, but I know my rights!"

Thompson addresses the cop beside him. "Soler, could you . . . deal with him, please?"

Soler grunts, but complies, taking Mr. Lasagna by the arm and leading him away from the reception desk.

Iris's mom completes the necessary paperwork, and Officer O'Hair hands her a clear bag crammed with Iris's things. "We'll have her out in a few minutes. Wait over there," she says, and gestures to the row of metal chairs.

As we settle on them, Iris's mom leans toward me. "What in the world were you doing, Alice, making a scene like that? About a silly dress? Do you think that was in your best interest? Or Iris's best interest?"

I grit my teeth. This feels even worse than I thought it would, Mrs. Adams's anger and disappointment. "Sorry," I say, digging my nails into the soft flesh of my palm. "I didn't—"

"I have the dress." Raf appears on the far side of the counter, handing both the key card and a large plastic baggie to the officer stationed there. "You just have to fill out a form to get it, Alice."

"All right," I say, hopping to my feet and over to the desk.

I'm most of the way done with my paperwork when Thompson appears from the rear of the station. Behind him, Iris, escorted by a uniformed officer.

"Iris!" Her mom rushes over, throwing her arms around her, loving even in her anger. The awful churning in my belly expands. I think about going over and hugging Iris, too, but can't get up the nerve. What if she blames me for all this?

"Hey, Alice," Iris says after her mom finally releases her. "What's that?"

I squeeze the dress in my hands, feeling its firm center, and shrug.

"Nothing much," I lie.

• • •

Once we're out of the station, Mrs. Adams and Iris head back to their apartment, and I start walking toward school, the dress gripped tight in my hands. I'm going to pick up my car later, after school, because I'm already on the verge of being late.

Halfway there, I stop, ducking behind a patch of bushes near the Castle Cove Public Library. Out of sight of anyone passing by, I take the dress out of its plastic bag and slowly unfold it. A moment later, I smile for the first time today.

Because stuck in the center of all the tulle and fabric is an old leather diary.

CHAPTER THIRTY

IRIS
FEBRUARY 17
8:04 A.M.

I believe you have to make the best of a bad
situation. This is a tough world, and a girl's gotta
have plenty of pluck and nerve.

—MONA MOODY, INTERVIEW, *SCREENLAND*, 1947

MY MOM'S VOICE ISN'T mad. It's sad. Which is way worse than mad.

"I hope spending the night in jail gave you some time to think, Iris. I didn't want to do it, but I had to."

I twist the hem of my hoodie in my fingers.

She keeps her eyes on the road. "I don't know what's going on with you," she continues, "but I wish you'd talk to me. I know what happened with your father was awful, and that it's weighing on you, but you have to believe me, he's not going to bother us again."

"You don't know that," I say dully, looking at the ocean outside my car window. "And it's not that, anyway."

"Then what *is* it? You're up until all hours of the night, you're tired and testy, your grades are slipping, and now *this*? Detective

Thompson could have placed charges on you. If it hadn't been for Ricky—"

"Well, he didn't," I interrupt. "And we're just trying to help Park and Kennedy."

I can feel my mom's eyes on the side of my face, but I don't turn to meet them.

"I thought maybe after Brooke in the fall, that that was just a lark for you and Alice. This isn't safe, what the two of you are doing. And I . . . I saw your closet."

Now I whip my head toward her. "You went through my private space? You always said my room was *mine.*"

"When Alice texted me, and then I had to call Ricky, I didn't know what to do. Was it drugs? Was it something else? I was looking for a reason that you'd so willfully put yourself in danger, that you'd deliberately break into a building. What else was I supposed to do? And why, Iris, *why* do you have all those pictures of that poor girl Remy Jackson?"

The tears that I tried so hard to keep down at the jail suddenly come bubbling up. I don't know how to explain to her why Remy matters to me, why Brooke mattered, why Park and Kennedy, two girls who have only been mean to me for years, suddenly matter. But they *do.*

"I . . ." I'm furiously wiping at my face. "I just . . . It isn't right. I don't know how to explain it. It just isn't right . . . girls getting hurt. It isn't right. And it seems like no one cares."

"Iris, honey," my mother pleads. "That isn't something you need to solve. That's for the police. You're seventeen. You should be studying and roller-skating and worried about romance or college or—"

"My life has never been that simple," I say flatly.

"I think maybe you and Alice need a break from each other," my mother says quietly.

"What? What are you . . . That's stupid. *No.*" I shake my head. A break from Alice? That's absurd. "You can't take her away from me. She's my *friend.*"

I have the Zoners, especially Spike, but . . . Alice is different. I've never had a close *girl* friend. Until Alice.

"Iris—"

Up ahead is Mercy General. Kennedy. In a hospital bed, drifting in some induced dream, her body trying to heal the wounds she's suffered.

"Can we stop there?" I say suddenly. "I can't go to school today. I just can't. But can we go there? Please. To see Kennedy. I just need to see her."

My voice is shaking, and maybe that unnerves my mother, because softly, perhaps from relief, she says, "Yes, Iris. Yes."

My mother is downstairs in the cafeteria. She told me I have fifteen minutes and then she'll take me with her to the Moon Landing. She doesn't want me home alone.

There's a behemoth of a security guard outside Kennedy's room, staring resolutely into space. I pinch my forearm, hard enough to bring tears.

"No visitors," he says gruffly.

"Please," I say. "She's my friend. I just want to check on her. *Please.*"

Tears are dripping onto my shirt. Maybe now they're a mixture of the pain and being tired from last night, but also my mom's comment about taking a break from Alice.

"Please," I whisper, feeling like I'm in *Oliver Twist* or something. "Please, sir. My friend, you know, Brooke Donovan, she was murdered last fall? You remember? And I just . . . I don't want to lose anyone else."

He sighs and looks both ways down the hall.

"Fine," he says. "Five minutes."

I push open the door to the room. I don't know what I expected. I mean, Kennedy *is* in a coma. She's got bandages wrapped around her head and her face is super puffed up, her eyes ringed with dark bruises. That might be from the brain swelling?

Tubes are everywhere. From her nose, her mouth, her arms. Machines hum all around her. It kind of takes my breath away.

"Oh god, it's you."

I turn toward the voice. In the corner of the room, a sullen girl of about thirteen is sitting curled in a chair, her phone in one hand, and a takeout coffee container in the other.

"Rayne," she says and nods to Kennedy. "I belong to her. Little sister. You're Alice Ogilvie's friend. I've heard about you. I suggest you leave now, before I tell Pop-up Cop outside to kick you out."

"I just wanted to see her," I say. "I'll only stay a minute."

I step closer to the bed.

"They're going to start waking her up tomorrow," Rayne says. "I'm sure she'll have a lot to say when she comes out. At least, I *hope* so."

"Me, too," I say.

Rayne gets up and stands next to me. "I don't like her, of course, because she's awful, but I still love her. You know?"

I look at her. I don't remember Kennedy or Alice ever mentioning a little sister before.

She smirks and flips her long brown hair over her shoulder. "I know what you're thinking. Becks never talks about me. I've been away at boarding school. I'm a problem child."

"Okay," I say slowly.

"You should probably go," she says. "My parents wouldn't be happy you're here and they'll be back any minute from the police station. I think there's a break in the case."

"Oh, yeah?" I ask, trying to keep my voice flat. I don't want her to see how interested I am in that.

"Maybe," she says. "Something about robbery. Becks's necklace is missing. My mom told her not to wear it; it's super valuable. But my sister never listens to anyone. I think they have new evidence, too, like, they think Park had an accomplice."

"Necklace?" I say. I'm so tired from last night, the word volleys around my brain.

"Yeah. Becks wore that thing to the dance and now it's gone."

I think back to the night of Sadie Hawkins. She was wearing that über-expensive-looking necklace; Park almost ripped it off her neck during their fight. I try to remember if it was on Rebecca when we were with her in the study, but how would I have noticed? She was hurt, and there was so much blood on her body and face.

Rayne sips her coffee and keeps talking. "I mean, if you ask me, there's no way Helen could pull this off. She's more of a pull-your-hair, text-behind-your-back girl, and I know what I'm talking about. I go to school with girls who would slit your throat for looking at them the wrong way, and that's not Helen Park."

I look at Rebecca, lying still in the bed. Did Alex Schaefer want the *necklace*? He did say if someone takes something from you, get it back. And if the police think there's an accomplice with Park, but Alice and I don't think Park was involved, then . . . who was working with Alex? Unless . . .

I'm so *tired.*

"How pleasant," I answer, shifting away from Rayne slightly toward the end of the bed, where Kennedy's medical chart is. "Do you mind?"

Rayne snorts. "You a doctor now? You can read that stuff?"

"Just taking a look," I say, picking up the chart and flipping through pages. I can't make heads or tails of it, really, but I snap some pictures anyway. Maybe they'll be useful later.

"What, you and Ogilvie gonna solve this one, too?" Rayne's eyes narrow. "You know something I don't?"

"No," I say. "Probably not. Did they find anything on Rebecca's phone?"

She giggles. "Nothing but nudes and stupid texts. Becks isn't exactly deep, you know."

"So, nothing interesting? Maybe she was texting someone named Alex Schaefer?"

"Just the regular stupid stuff." She pauses, thinking. "Did you say Schaefer?"

"Yeah."

She gives me a weird look. "I don't think my parents said anything about texts from an Alex, but . . . you know, the whole motel thing. The Waves. It's owned by a guy named Schaefer. My dad's been talking about him a lot. Because of the resort."

"The—the resort?" I stammer. My brain is like a pinball machine with all this new information. Missing necklace, accomplice, Alex Schaefer, resort.

"My dad's company. He's turning a bunch of land way out on Highway One into some sort of mega resort. That motel, that guy who owns it, he's holding out. He's the last one standing; everybody else who lived out there has already taken the money. You can't have a luxury resort next to a crappy motel, right? All I know is, you shouldn't mess with my dad. He wins every time."

That's right. When we drove out there to see Alex. And his dad was behind the counter.

Berayne Enterprises. Be . . . Rayne. Rebecca . . . Be . . . Rayne. Ahhh.

Did Alex Schaefer hurt Rebecca Kennedy as payback for threatening his family's motel?

But then, what else did he want in the study of the Castle so badly? Mona's boxes were torn through. Rebecca's necklace is missing.

"I have to go," I say quickly.

"Wait, why? What are you thinking? Don't hold out on me."

"I can't say." I look back at Kennedy and pangs of sympathy course through my body. She doesn't deserve this. No one does.

"Nice meeting you," I say. "I hope things get better at boarding school."

"Oh," Rayne says, settling back into her chair with her coffee and phone. "I'm not going back to that hellhole. I'm sticking around Castle Cove. Things are way more interesting here."

CHAPTER THIRTY-ONE

ALICE
FEBRUARY 17
12:30 P.M.

Our weapon is our knowledge.
But remember, it may be a knowledge
we may not know that we possess.
—AGATHA CHRISTIE, *THE A.B.C. MURDERS*

AS SOON AS THE lunch bell rings, I rush out of bio to the library.

The last time I sat in here was when Iris and I got into a spat last fall. She'd been planning to leave town, to move to Whispering Pines, and I, well, I got pretty annoyed that she hadn't even bothered to tell me, her alleged friend, about her plans.

Now, though, I regret not encouraging her to go. Maybe if I had, she'd be up the coast with her mom, still getting straight As, on a solid trajectory. Not getting picked up this morning from the local jail.

I take the carrel farthest from the librarian's desk, carefully removing the diary from my backpack. There wasn't much time earlier to get a proper peek at it; I had to get to school in time to turn in a paper in French class, then make an appearance in bio so Henderson wouldn't bite my head off.

The cover of the diary is leather, cracked and worn. It must be decades old. I turn it over in my hands, examining it, but there's no sign of who it belongs to from the outside.

I carefully open it, and realize the inside is in even worse condition than the outside. Its pages stick together—probably because of their age—and I'm reluctant to try to pull them apart. What if I rip them? The only writing I'm able to see is old-fashioned cursive, faded from age, and basically impossible for me to read.

Why the hell did Alex Schaefer end up with this thing in his pocket?

I drop my head into my hands. I'm tired. Today has not been my day from the moment I woke up, so I don't know what I expected. The diary to reveal everything to me? To prove Park's innocence in some straightforward manner or give me some clue about Alex's motivations?

My phone dings next to me on the desk. I could use a distraction right about now, so I pick it up.

It's the group message with the Zoners, again. It's been blowing up since last night when Iris got taken into the station, and now that she's out, they're all trying to get her to respond. I told them she's okay, that she's with her mom now, and in a whole lot of trouble, which is probably why she isn't responding, but they don't listen.

The latest message is from Neil. I read it with disinterest, and then turn back to the diary. Something nudges the corner of my mind as I struggle to make out the words on the page in front of me.

Neil's text . . . Neil . . . I sit up straight and grab my phone again. His mom had all those weird gadgets at the museum. I wonder . . .

Does your mom have anything at the museum that can help you read old things?? I text Neil separately.

He responds immediately: *What?*

> Idk something that like, might help you
> read faded ink?
>
> **Yeah. People bring her stuff like that all the
> time. Old letters. Receipts. Diaries. She uses
> a special UV light. Why?**

I ignore his question, slowly setting my phone back down on the desk. The bell rings above my head and low chatter starts behind me as everyone gathers up their stuff to go to class.

I head out, too, but not to class; I wait for a while in the bathroom outside the library until the halls have fallen quiet, then take off out the side exit of the school.

There's only one person inside when I enter the Historical Society, an older gentleman wearing oversized pants and a button-up shirt, examining the contents of a display case. Mrs. Cetas is nowhere to be seen.

I clear my throat, hoping to catch the man's attention— maybe he knows where she is—but he ignores me.

"Excuse me, do you know where Mrs. Cetas is?" I call to him, but he doesn't respond. *"Hello?"*

I'm about to walk over to him when Mrs. Cetas appears.

"Can I help you?" she asks. When she sees me, her eyebrows shoot up in surprise. "Alice?"

She glances at the clock on the wall and then back to me. "It's the middle of the school day. What are you doing here?"

I clear my throat. "Well, I'm actually here *because* of school. Has Neil mentioned the genealogy project our grade is doing in bio?"

She nods.

"So, because of it, I've gotten really into Castle Cove history. This museum is awesome, by the way; I've been telling Neil how I'd love to spend an entire day here sometime. Anyway, I found this old diary. I think it's possible that it might hold a connection to one of my relatives. I'm here for *educational* purposes." I give her my best smile.

She frowns. "An old diary?"

"Yes!" I drop my book bag to the ground and dig out the diary, handing it over to Mrs. Cetas. "Except it's mostly impossible to read; the ink is really faded and its pages are all stuck together. I think it's, like, a hundred years old."

Mrs. Cetas turns it over in her hands, then looks up at me with a curious expression. "Where did you find this?" she asks after a long moment. "Alice Ogilvie, I cannot believe you were wandering around school with this sitting in your backpack, exposed. My office, now."

Once there, she grabs a pair of white gloves and a pane of glass, placing the glass on the center table, and carefully laying the journal onto it. After a second, she seems to remember I'm here.

"Please sit," she says, adjusting the pane of glass over the diary.

I take a seat, watching in silence as she examines the book. After a moment, she stands and walks to the far side of the room, picking up a long, thin object and bringing it over. "First this . . . the light. And then . . ." She heads over to her desk and pulls out two pairs of goggles. "You need to put these on. UV light is bad for the eyes."

I pluck a pair from her outstretched hand. Not my ideal look, but I guess being a detective can't be all glamour and glory.

"We need it as dark as possible in here. Could you cut the lights?"

I nod and head over to the switch on the wall. The room plunges into black but a moment later a blue-green light snaps on, casting eerie shadows around the room.

Mrs. Cetas picks up the lamp and holds it out to me. "Could you hold this for me so I can have my hands free? Over the diary, like this."

"Okay." I take it from her.

"Give me just a minute, dear, and then you can see," she says, leaning over the diary. I carefully hold the light steady as she pages through it. ". . . lots of stuff in here about dress designers," she murmurs. Another long moment goes by, and then she looks over at me, her brow drawn into a V. "Alice, whose diary did you say this was?"

"Um . . . I'm not sure whose it is. . . ." I hesitate, considering how much I should tell her. I'm pretty sure she wouldn't be thrilled to know it came directly from the evidence room at the police station.

"Alice." Mrs. Cetas straightens, abruptly. "This is Mona Moody's diary." She narrows her eyes at me. "And the last time I saw it, it was being shipped over to the Castle in the boxes I packed for her retrospective. Which, I was told, the police have now. Where on earth did you get it?"

"Oh my god, that's *Mona Moody's* diary?"

"Yes. It is. Now please tell me, where did you get this?"

I swallow and decide to gamble on the fact that she's as cool as I think she is. "I had no idea it was Mona Moody's diary. I found it at the Castle the night of the dance before . . . you know, everything happened." I fudge that part a bit. "I forgot about it until last night, when I found it in the jacket I wore that night."

"You *found* it? Alice, this is state property. That's a crime."

I feign innocence. "It *is*?" I can tell she doesn't quite buy my act.

"And now you need me to tell you what it says inside because . . . ?"

"Like I said, it's for school."

After a long moment, during which I age approximately four years, she shakes her head. "I'm not going to press this anymore," she says. "But whatever information I give you better be used for the purposes of good, not evil, or you'll have a lot to answer for. Do you understand me?"

My throat has gone dry. "Yes."

"All right. I'll tell you up front that this diary has seen much better days, but I think I should be able to make out some of the passages, especially toward the latter part of the book. Those pages were better protected from the elements. Let's begin."

She clears her throat. "The first entry is dated December . . . I can't quite make out the date, but the year is 1947. '*I wore the most gorgeous Dior gown last night.*' The next line is too faded to read, I'll just read what I can: '*a gorgeous deep green,*' '*who's going to change my life,*' '*all night and then I had to leave with Charles,*' '*this morning I found it, tucked inside.*' Hmm, I wonder what she's referring to there. . . ."

She carefully turns the pages. "Here's another one I can make out, dated April twenty-third. Not sure of the year of this one. '*Truly be the kind of famous I've always wanted to be,*' '*shooting out in Palm Springs.*' I wonder if she's talking about *Boom Shakalaka!*—that was her first major studio role. *'I leave in a week and,' 'didn't realize he was going to be there, too,' 'It feels like fate, almost, but I can't write . . .'"*

"Who is *he*?" I ask, and Mrs. Cetas blinks up at me like she's forgotten I'm here. "In that entry," I say, "who do you think she's talking about?"

Mrs. Cetas frowns. "Well if she *is* referring to *Boom Shakalaka!*, it could have been her costar Clifford Hayes. By all accounts, they were great friends. But it's hard to say for sure, since the date is missing. The movie came out in early 1949, so they filmed sometime in 1948."

She carefully turns a few more pages. "Another entry. *'Ap'*— I think we can assume that means April—fourth. Again, the year is too faded to read. *'. . . warm today on the set of,' 'shooting ran long and he,' 'terrible pity.'* The next entry is from June, and we finally have a year: 1948. So she must be referring to *Boom Shakalaka!* I can't make much of this one out, just a few half sentences and words. *'. . . other hot,' 'desert,' 'coming for me,' 'this is what I've,' 'my entire life when I was . . .'"*

Mrs. Cetas straightens, hand on her lower back. "Just need a moment. . . . Okay, let's continue. *'June twenty-first, 1949.'* Finally, a full, legible date. This is the last one I see in here that's readable, but it's meatier than the rest. *'The last time I wrote was many months ago,' 'stuck in the Castle,' 'four walls of this room are closing in around me,' 'staring at the flowers on the wallpaper for months,' 'Dr. Gene is the only one,' 'comes and sits,' 'I don't want to take them but he says I must for the . . .'"*

Mrs. Cetas stops reading, frowning down at the page. "This is strange. I think . . ." She walks over to the bookshelf next to her desk and grabs a thick book titled *The History of Castle Cove.* "If I'm remembering correctly . . . Yes, here. Mona Moody, by all accounts, was out of Castle Cove in June of 1949 at the sanatorium where she was treated for tuberculosis."

She turns back to the diary. "But, here . . . no, I'm not misreading. This is clearly dated June. What does she mean, '*stuck in the Castle . . . staring at the flowers on the wallpaper for months*'? That seems to indicate she was here? In Castle Cove?"

Flowered wallpaper. Where have I seen flowered wallpaper recently? I think back, trying to place it, and then suddenly it snaps together. That small creepy room in the Castle. The one with no door. *That* room has flowered wallpaper.

What if . . . A chill runs up my spine.

Good lord, what I'm thinking is almost too horrible to consider.

"I have to say, I'm glad this isn't sitting in the evidence room at the Castle Cove Police station, improperly stored," Mrs. Cetas says. "It's invaluable. Honestly, we should have been more careful with it even here. Sending it over to the Castle in those boxes . . ." She shakes her head. "Not our best moment, I must say. Regardless of the Moody introspective, this diary should be handled with care, by the right people. Thank you for bringing it back to me, Alice."

My heart sinks. She's going to keep the diary. Of *course* she is; I should have expected that from the start. I guess, given that it's nearly impossible to read without this extremely fancy machine, it doesn't really matter.

"Is there any way of getting a few photos? Of the pages that we've read? For my project," I add quickly.

"Not as such," she says, "but if there's any information you want from it, you can write it down—I know, I'm so old—or I can scan the pages for you, if you'd prefer?"

I leave the museum a little while later, scanned notes from the diary securely stored in my bag, head spinning with questions.

What happened to Mona Moody in 1949? If she was at the Castle, and not sick in a sanatorium, why would they have lied about it? Was it because Mona was being held in that small doorless room in the Castle, a prisoner in her own home?

And, more relevant to the Park situation, why in the hell did Alex Schaefer and his accomplice go to all that trouble to steal an old diary the night of the dance?

Even though I know I should handle this on my own, that I should leave her out of it, I'm also starting to realize that there's something very, very strange about this case, and Park needs our help. So I shove all my guilt down deep into the pit of my belly and pull out my phone.

I need to talk to Iris.

CHAPTER THIRTY-TWO

IRIS
FEBRUARY 17
2:30 P.M.

Don't despair, angel. Fix your ponytail, wipe your
eyes, and straighten your skirt. We're going to figure
out this mess right quick, easy-peasy.
—MONA MOODY, *DOUBLE TROUBLE,* 1946

I HAVE MY CASEBOOK open on the table of a booth at the Moon
Landing, where my mother insisted I go after the hospital, because she didn't want me home alone. I'm taking notes from the
photos I took of Kennedy's chart. I don't *really* understand what
all the names and terms mean and will have to spend some time
Googling or, like, asking Neil, who is pretty much a human ver-
sion of Google, but frankly, it's all bad. There are body diagrams
with the locations of four stab wounds, a brain bleed, a fractured
skull, a punctured lung, and the wound on her head. I think this
is so whoever changes her bandages will know exactly where and
what to change, but who knows. That wound is an inch-deep,
four-inch-long chunk out of the middle of her head. Wherever
that candelabra is, it probably still has her flesh and hair on it. I
shudder.

"Fancy meeting you here."

I look up as Ricky Randall eases into the booth across from me, setting her drink on the table.

"Your mom make you come here?" she asks. "Keep an eye on you?"

"You got it," I say.

She turns my casebook around and grimaces. "Grisly stuff, what happened to that girl. You want to know a secret?"

"What?"

She leans across the table. "They've got somebody. Interrogating them right now."

My heart skips a beat. Rayne said the police thought Park had an accomplice and that her parents were at the station because of new information. "Is it Alex Schaefer?"

"I can neither confirm nor deny. I'm not supposed to be encouraging you, you know."

It *has* to be Alex. So the cops *did* do something right for once.

She takes a long sip of her drink. "I guess that's a wrap, then, on what happened."

I look back down at my casebook.

"Or am I wrong?" Ricky says. "What are you and Moneybags up to this time? Speaking of, where is your lesser half? You two are usually joined at the hip."

"I don't know. Mom doesn't want us to hang out so much anymore. But listen," I say, leaning forward. "There's a lot we can't connect yet. Like, Alex, if he *is* in fact the person the police have right now, was looking at Castle blueprints last week at the Historical Society. Maybe to check out rooms to steal from? But if that's the case, how does Kennedy fit in to that? Did he steal her necklace? It's missing."

"Mmm-hmm," Ricky answers. "It sounds like an interrupted

robbery to me. Maybe he and Park cooked something up. Kennedy happened upon them—"

"That doesn't explain the note."

"Note?" Ricky asks.

"There was a note that asked someone, maybe Rebecca, to meet in the study. That's what the police have on Park. Well, that and holding the letter opener in her hand when Alice found her. And the fight she and Kennedy had in plain view of everyone."

"Maybe he knew she'd be wearing the necklace before the dance? Somehow? Did they know each other?" Ricky asks.

"Sort of?" I say, sipping my Coke. "Rebecca's dad wants to develop the land Alex's dad's motel is on for a fancy resort. The Schaefers don't want to sell and it sounds kind of ugly, so maybe . . ."

"You think Alex attacked her for that."

"Maybe? But if he had an accomplice, and we think he did, because Park said she heard two voices that weren't Rebecca's in the study arguing before she went in, that's where it gets sticky, because . . . who is that person? Person X? And what did *they* want?"

Ricky twists a silver ring on her finger, thinking. It's making me nervous, so I plunge on.

"The thing is, if Alex wanted revenge on Kennedy, he could have done that anytime, anywhere, right? So, why the dance? This is where Person X must come in, don't you think? There were boxes of Mona Moody's things in the study that were looked through. Did Person X want them and figured the night of the dance with tons of people around would be the perfect time? And who *is* Person X? Did *they* want the necklace—"

"Calm down, Iris," Ricky says, taking my hand. "Look at you. You're in a tizzy."

I take some deep breaths. "Sorry."

"It's all a puzzle," Ricky says calmly. "But you need to take things one step at a time. The police are handling it. I want to tell you to relax and be patient and see what comes of that, but the lawyer and mystery fan in me can see that you have the thirst now."

"The what?" I ask. My mom is glancing at me from the bar. She can't be mad, though—I'm only talking to Ricky. My phone pings. I glance down as Ricky continues talking.

"You cracked one case. Well, one and a half, because you uncovered the Coach thing, but that's unresolved, and now you have *the thirst*. To crack another. But watch out, okay? Stuff like this . . . it can take a toll. You're already carrying around enough, don't you think?"

It's Alice. Something about a diary—

"Iris?"

A diary? Mona Moody being kept in the secret bedroom for months . . .

"I'm sorry, what? I'm just—"

I look up, blinking, barely listening to Ricky. She finishes her drink, sighs, and gives me a resigned smile. "Nothing. Nothing at all."

TEXT CONVERSATION BETWEEN
ALICE OGILVIE AND IRIS ADAMS
FEBRUARY 17
2:40 P.M.

AO: I wasn't going to tell you because of everything that happened last night but now I HAVE to tell you because I'm freaking out. Raf told me that there was a diary in the jacket we found at the Castle, but the cops didn't think it was important . . . sooooo

IA: You weren't going to tell me?? WTF Alice?

AO: Your mom was so mad Iris I don't want to get you into more trouble

IA: I'm a big girl. I don't need you to make those decisions for me

AO: I know

AO: Im sorry

IA: Don't keep things from me

AO: I wont

AO: I promise

IA: Good. Now . . . what happened with this diary?

AO: Ok well I made Raf steal if from the evidence room

IA: Maybe I don't want to know this after all

AO: It's fine. They weren't going to do anything w it anyway! So he gave it to me and GUESS WHAT?? It's Mona Moody's diary

IA: Mona Moody?? Why would Alex steal that?

AO: I have no idea. He might not have even known it was hers maybe? It's ancient and I had to have Mrs. Cetas help me read it

IA: Mrs. Cetas? You've certainly been busy without me

AO: I know I said I was sorry! But listen. I think she was being held in that creepy secret room in the Castle for some reason

IA: WHAT?

AO: Yes. I'll tell you more in person can you meet? I need to get my car from your apartment anyway.

IA: Im at the bar

AO: Ok tomorrow then

IA: Wait I have new info too. I saw Rayne

AO: Kennedy's sister??

IA: Yuh I went by the hospital and she was there and she told me that Rebecca's necklace was stolen the night of the dance

AO: I think I remember seeing it. It looked extremely expensive

IA: Yeah . . . which could be one of our motives for Alex. He wanted the necklace. Or . . . Person X, his accomplice, did

IA: I gtg sry my mom is watching me but we'll talk tomorrow

AO: Ok. Tomorrow.

TRANSCRIPT OF INTERVIEW BETWEEN
DETECTIVE MARK THOMPSON, ALEX SCHAEFER
FEBRUARY 17
3:04 P.M.

Thompson: This is Detective Mark Thompson. Before we begin, Mr. Schaefer, I want to make you aware that this conversation is being recorded.

Thompson: Can you confirm for the record that you have been read your rights?

Schaefer: Yes.

Thompson: Thank you. Can you state your name and age, please?

Schaefer: Alexander Schaefer, 18.

Thompson: You were present the night of February 11, 2023, at Levy Castle, working as a cater-waiter for Splendid Spread at a dance, is that correct?

Schaefer: Yeah.

Thompson: Do you recognize this?

Schaefer: It's the sign-in sheet for my shift. We sign in when we get to an event, sign out. Take breaks. That crap.

Thompson: Do you have to sign for your jacket, too, for each shift?

Schaefer: Yeah. They make us pay for it if it gets damaged or we lose it.

Thompson: There's a number inside each jacket. Yours was 31?

Schaefer: I dunno. I guess.

Thompson: You signed in at 5:30 p.m. and checked out for a break at 8:50 p.m. Where did you go?

Schaefer: Nowhere. In the kitchen, mostly. Around.

Detective Thompson: Did you go upstairs to the second floor?

Schaefer: Maybe. Yeah. I was bored. Couldn't go outside, it was raining too hard. Didn't want to hang around the kitchen.

Thompson: You were in juvenile detention for several months for petty theft and assault. Did you go

upstairs to, you know, look around? Maybe nick
something? Is that when you ran into Rebecca Kennedy?

Schaefer: Who? I don't know who that is. What's this
all about, man? You already talked to me once at the
Castle. Do I have to repeat it? Are you dumb? Yeah,
took a break. I went upstairs. I didn't take anything.
And then I came back down and everything went crazy.

Thompson: You never signed back in. You didn't return
the jacket. In fact, you quit your job the next day.
Why?

Schaefer: I just told you what happened. Everything
went crazy and I took off. I quit 'cause I hated it.
I have another job, anyway. Big deal.

Thompson: Let me cut to the chase. Your signature on
the time sheet shows you checking out jacket number
31, which was never returned. Jacket number 31 was
located at the base of Levy Castle not too long ago,
with significant bloodstains that match the blood
of Rebecca Kennedy, who is currently in a coma at
Mercy General. The fingerprints from your juvenile
file match fingerprints not only on the desk in the
library but on the letter opener used to stab Ms.
Kennedy, on the sink in a bathroom at Levy Castle,
and on this note. Was this note for Ms. Kennedy? Did
you have a prior relationship with Ms. Kennedy?

Schaefer: I never met that girl before in my life, man. And maybe I was in that room. I don't know. I went into a couple of rooms. Picked up some stuff. Thought about stealing, but I didn't. Might of picked up that . . . opener thing. Who knows. You pick up stuff and put it back down all the time.

Thompson: How did your fingerprints get in the bathroom?

Schaefer: I don't know. Maybe I went in there to take a leak.

Thompson: How?

Schaefer: What do you mean, how? I need to tell you how to take a leak? You gotta lot of problems if you need me to teach you that.

Thompson: The door to the bedroom, where the bathroom, and the sink, is located, is opened in a special way, but you knew how to open it. How?

Schaefer: Man, whatever. Special doors, what is this? That door was open when I got to the room. Maybe that Kennedy chick opened it. I don't know.

Detective Thompson: One thing that bugs me. How do you explain the blood on the jacket that was checked out in your name and we found on Castle grounds?

Schaefer: Beats me. I hung the jacket up downstairs in the kitchen when I went on break and when I got back it was gone. Maybe somebody took it. Maybe you should look at them. Maybe they hurt that girl.

Thompson: Do you recognize this photo?

Schaefer: No.

Thompson: Is that you?

Schaefer: It looks like me.

Thompson: And who's that?

Schaefer: Don't know.

Thompson: You don't know.

Schaefer: Nope.

Thompson: Let me refresh your memory. That is Helen Park. And that? That's you. With your arm around her and, well, kissing her neck. In the selfie photo booth, on the night in question.

Schaefer: I don't know her.

Thompson: We're supposed to believe that? You were caught in a very public act of PDA with her here, in this photo.

Schaefer: You know how this stuff goes. Parties. Everyone's popping in and out of the booths, taking weird pics. It's a whole thing.

Thompson: Do you realize, son, that we have your jacket? Your catering jacket? The one you lost that night? I just want to make that clear. You don't seem to be understanding.

Thompson: Were you and Helen Park dating? She roped you in—a kid from the wrong side of the tracks, a kid willing to go the distance for his richy-rich girlfriend—and you got in too deep? Is that what happened? Is Helen Park the one you passed the note to, to meet you upstairs? Or was that for Rebecca, so you and Helen could attack her and, oh gosh, let me think . . . steal a necklace worth hundreds of thousands of dollars?

Schaefer: [silence]

Thompson: Did you steal Rebecca Kennedy's necklace? Maybe to give to Helen Park? Or to sell.

Schaefer: I don't know what you're talking about.

Thompson: Was it you or Helen Park who hit Rebecca Kennedy with the candelabra?

Schaefer: The what now? I don't even know what that is.

Thompson: Son, your fingerprints are everywhere upstairs. They're on one of the weapons used in the attack. We've got your catering jacket with the victim's blood on it.

Schaefer: [Chuckling.] You guys are so stupid.

Thompson: Is that so?

Schaefer: You got no idea.

Thompson: This is the end of the line, here, Alex. It's time.

Schaefer: Is that right.

Thompson: It is. I'm trying to give you a chance here, to explain what happened. I'll find out one way or another, but this is your moment, son. I'd take it, because we've got you, anyway. The only question is, who are you bringing down with you? If you tell us, that might work in your favor.

Schaefer: Fine. Yes. It was me. And . . . what's her name. Helen Park. That girl, she made me do it. All of it. She planned it all out. Told me to slip her a note when I was ready for her upstairs. I thought we were just gonna steal some stuff, but she had other plans about that girl. She went crazy in there, stabbing her friend, hitting her over the head, it

was nuts, I've never seen anything like it. I tried
to stop her, but it was too late and she was fighting
me and I hit the piano. That's how the wall opened
up. I don't know. That shit was weird. Ask that Helen
girl about the necklace. I never touched it.

Thompson: Alex Schaefer, you are hereby under arrest
on the charges of breaking and entering, robbery,
and the conspiracy to commit the murder of Rebecca
Kennedy. You have the right to remain silent. . . .

CHAPTER THIRTY-THREE

ALICE
FEBRUARY 18
8:33 A.M.

I've never met a murderer who wasn't vain. . . . It's
their vanity that leads to their undoing, nine times
out of ten.
—AGATHA CHRISTIE, *CROOKED HOUSE*

I'M UP IN MY room reading Sherlock Holmes for English class when my phone buzzes against my leg.

There's one new message, and my stomach jumps when I see who it's from.

They arrested Schaefer yesterday, says the text from Raf.

I smile. We did it. We got him. We—

Another message buzzes in, interrupting my silent celebration.

> He claims the second person in the room
> was Helen Park. There's a photo from earlier
> that evening with the two of them looking
> real cozy. Plus, a note that he says Park told
> him to give to Kennedy when he was ready
> to meet

My hand tightens around the phone as I stare at the message in shock. That note was to *Park*?

> Why do they think that??
> **Alex told them it was**
> **Park is now going to be charged**
> **formally . . .**

I don't even think. I simply stand up, swing my bag over my shoulder, and head out my bedroom door and down the stairs. My heart is beating so loud in my ears that I don't hear my mother calling after me until I'm already out the door.

I've sent Iris approximately fifty SOS texts in the past fifteen minutes. She's the only person I want to talk to. The only person who will understand.

> IRIS ADAMS GET YOUR ASS OUT OF
> BED RIGHT NOW & MEET ME IN THE
> PARKING LOT
> Did you talk to Raf??
> ALEX PINNED IT ON PARK!!!!
> SOS
> SOS
> SOS
> Iris what the hell is so important that
> you're ignoring me???
> SLEEP CAN WAIT!

I'm outside her apartment building in my car, nervously tapping on my steering wheel when she finally replies.

ALICE CHILL OUT I AM COMING.

HURRY UP!!!!!!!! I write back, fingers shaky.

Finally, the car door swings open to reveal an irritated Iris. She's furiously typing away on her phone and holds up a hand when I begin to speak.

"Hold on," she says without bothering to greet me. She slides into her seat.

After several long seconds, she drops her arm down by her side and finally meets my eyes.

"Who was that?" I ask, pointing to her phone.

"Raf," she says. "He told me—"

I nod. "Yeah. Me too. Did he tell you—"

"That they were in a photo together earlier that night looking cozy? Yeah. Has Park been lying to us this whole time?"

"I have no idea," I say. "It seems unlikely, given what we know about Schaefer. Park's dad would not be on board with her hanging out with someone who has a record. Did Raf mention the other thing to you?"

"About the note? Yeah." She starts scrolling on her phone. "Raf sent me a photo of the pieces of the note the cops have." She examines the screen and then sucks in a breath. "Oh no."

"What? What?" I'm peering over her shoulder, trying to get a look at the image.

"Look." She hands me the phone. On the screen is a photo of a small piece of paper that's clearly been ripped apart and then taped back together, with jagged holes in its middle. There's writing on either side of the hole.

"The parts of the note we have say *'meet me . . . study . . . nine-thirty,'*" says Iris. "It looks like they fit right into those holes. So the note in its entirety would read *'R meet me in the study at nine-thirty—H.'*" She looks at me in horror.

"Good lord," I say, my heart sinking. "H. For Helen. Helen Park. But that note was in *Alex's* handwriting. What the hell is going on?"

Iris shakes her head. "I don't know, but I think we need to pay her a little visit."

Twenty minutes later, we're pulling up to Park's front gate.

"Hello?" a gruff voice says through the intercom. It's Mr. Park. I've never heard him answer the front gate before. Things must be dire in the Park household right about now.

"Hello, Mr. Park," I say, "It's Alice Ogilvie and Iris Adams. We need . . ."

Before I even finish my sentence, there's a loud beep and the gate begins to slowly swing open.

At the top of the drive, we're greeted by Frances, who waves us inside.

"They're in Mr. Park's office," she says. She leads us through the foyer, past the kitchen, and into the west wing of the house. I've never really been over here before—it's where all of Park's parents' rooms are located and was always off-limits when we were younger.

Halfway down the long hall, Frances stops in front of a closed door. Loud voices bleed through it. Loud, *angry* voices.

"I should warn you," Frances whispers, leaning close to me and Iris, "Mr. Park is in . . . quite a mood."

She knocks before I can respond.

"What?" a voice yells.

Frances cracks open the door. "Sir? I have . . ."

"Well, what are you waiting for? Bring them in."

CHAPTER THIRTY-FOUR

IRIS
FEBRUARY 18
9:22 A.M.

We all live two lives. The one we show the world,
and the one we live in secret, in the shadows.
—MONA MOODY, *DARK WHISPERS*, 1948

HELEN PARK SITS BEFORE us, her eyes red-rimmed and fierce. She's not quite as timid as she was before, or frightened-seeming, but maybe that's because she knows she's been caught in a lie.

Beside her, her father's face is grim. I have to admit, he makes me very nervous. He still wouldn't acknowledge me when Alice and I came in. I have no idea what's going on with that, but Alice and I have a job to do, so I'm going to have to tuck that away for right now.

"Exhibit A," I say firmly. I hold up my phone, displaying a copy of one of the photos Raf texted to me. Photos from the selfie booth at the Sadie Hawkins dance. This photo is Helen Park and Alex Schaefer deep in Makeout-land, with one of his hands firmly on her butt, his mouth plastered to her neck, sparkly stars on the backdrop behind them. He's wearing the Splendid Spread catering jacket.

Helen's mouth quivers. Her father makes a sound that makes my stomach tighten. Alice shifts uncomfortably beside me.

"There are more of these," I say. "But you get the idea."

"Helen, when we spoke before, you didn't mention that you spent some time playing tongue hockey with a boy in the selfie booth before going upstairs," Alice says gravely. "A boy who's just confessed to assaulting Rebecca Kennedy."

"A boy who says you helped," I add.

Helen is silent, as is her father.

"Exhibit B," I say, holding up my phone, which displays screenshots of the note pieces Alice and I have and the screenshot of the note pieces the police have.

"This note is in Alex's handwriting, Park. It asks Rebecca, the 'R,' to 'meet me in the study at nine-thirty.' It's signed 'H.' Which would be you. Alex says you told him to write it to get her up to the study so you both could attack her."

"I've never seen that note before in my life," Helen says, her voice shaking, but firm.

"It says *H,* Helen," Alice says. "That's *you.* And of course Rebecca would go up there, thinking it was from you. She likes nothing more than a fight."

"I've never seen that before! I swear," Helen says, her voice trembling. "It's a *lie.*"

"I think there are a lot of lies going around," Alice answers roughly.

I try to stay calm. "When you were in the selfie booth with Alex, did he mention Rebecca Kennedy to you? Did you mention her to him?"

Helen shakes her head. *"No."*

"What did you two talk about?" Alice asks.

"I told you, nothing, really. I was in there, he barged in, he was cute, it was just weird and kind of spontaneous. He kissed me, said I was cute, we started making out, it was *fun*. I didn't even know his name until all of this, to be honest."

"I don't believe you," Alice says, exasperated. "We can't figure this out unless you tell us the truth, and right now, it feels like it's just lie after lie after—"

Helen begins to cry. Mr. Park stands up.

"This is going nowhere. I'll not have my daughter treated this way. Helen, come with me."

"She's going to be treated much worse on a witness stand," I say to him. "Or in jail."

"Yes, I suppose you have firsthand knowledge of *that,* Ms. Adams. Come, Helen." He reaches down to take Helen's arm.

"Fine," I say, standing up, stinging from his comment. "Let's go, Alice."

"Iris, wait. Come on," she says.

I grab her book bag from the floor. But my hands are shaking and I lose my grip, and the bag falls across the coffee table, spilling the contents all over.

"Great," I mutter, and try to gather tampons, pens, folders, and lipsticks together.

"Stop," Helen says suddenly, prying her arm from her father's grip. "What is that? Why is that lady wearing Kennedy's necklace?"

"Excuse me?" Alice says.

Helen jerks her arm away from her father and pokes at the pile of things on the table. "This. Here. That's Rebecca's necklace. *Here.* Why do you have a picture of it and who *is* this? You know the police think I stole this thing, right? I . . . don't even know what to say."

She pulls the photo of Mona Moody at the movie premiere from the pile.

Alice and I look at each other. Rebecca Kennedy has . . . Mona Moody's *necklace*?

"Did he mention Mona Moody to you?" I ask.

"The dead lady from the Castle? No. This is her?" Helen asks, studying the photograph. "Wow, she was gorgeous. But this is Rebecca's necklace. See the teardrop shapes? God, she went on about wearing it to the dance. Bragged to everybody she was going to wear a special surprise. Said it was a family heirloom or something, and ultra-expensive."

She rolls her eyes.

"Don't you remember, Alice? Like a few years ago when we slept over at her house and she brought it out and let Brooke and Ashley try it on and then her mom walked in and flipped out?"

Alice grimaces. "I do not. Perhaps I wasn't invited to that particular soiree."

"Alex didn't say anything about Mona Moody, or the necklace, Helen?" I ask, ignoring Alice.

"No," she says emphatically. "I *told* you."

"You've lied to us before, Helen," Alice says. "Before, you said you went upstairs to confront Rebecca. But you conveniently left out the part where you were making out with the person who now says you helped him attack her. I don't know how we square that."

"I didn't lie," Helen answers. "I just didn't tell you, because my dad . . . would get mad. We made out in the booth and then he asked me to meet him upstairs later, that's—"

"Oh my god!" Alice cries. "Another detail you conveniently left out!"

"That's lying by omission," I point out. "We asked you to tell us everything, every detail, because we needed those details to help us figure out what really happened. We——"

Mr. Park cuts me off. He angles his head toward his daughter, but doesn't look at her.

"I'm very disappointed in you, Helen." He shakes his head slowly. "I'm very disappointed."

"There!" She suddenly cries, the photo slipping from her hand back onto the table. "That's why I didn't say anything! Because of you! Because I can never do anything. *Anything.* I can't date anyone, I can't get anything less than an A, I can't wear this, I can't wear that. Do you have any idea what it's like to live that way, Daddy?"

Helen begins to sob. "It's a horrible weight over me, all the time. *Disappointing* you. I'm not even a person. I'm just another thing you want to do *well.* So, I'm sorry I lied. I wanted to kiss a boy. But I did not touch Rebecca Kennedy in that study and I did not tell anyone to write that . . . that *note.*"

Alice glances at me and bites her lip. I take a deep breath, ready to continue, but Mr. Park speaks again.

"I'm not disappointed in you because you kissed a boy. I'm disappointed in you because you had the choice to tell the utter truth right from the beginning and you chose not to. We are not a family of liars. And now a girl's life is at stake."

Helen chokes back a sob, looking at him.

"Helen," I say quietly, because the room is now thick with tension and pain. "I'm going to ask you one more time. Did you and Alex Schaefer attack Rebecca Kennedy together? It's a simple yes or no question."

Helen Park swipes at her face. "I made out with Alex. He never gave me a note. After the selfie booth, I went to the restroom to fix my makeup. I came out, I passed by a room where Reed Gerber was yelling and some guidance counselor was trying to coax him out. Then I went upstairs to find Alex. I just wanted to hook up again. He was cute. It was fun. And after I got upstairs, everything happened just like I told you. There were two voices coming from that room, and neither one was Rebecca Kennedy's."

She stands up. "I did not touch one hair on Rebecca Kennedy's head and I have never seen that note, ever."

She runs out of the room. It's then that I notice the monitor on her ankle, a bulky thing under the hem of her leggings.

Mr. Park looks at Alice. What is up with this man? I can feel my stomach starting to boil.

"This is an awful moment," he says. "The lawyers I've hired, they want to do a plea deal. My daughter will go to jail, at least for a little bit. Unless the other girl dies, and then . . ."

His voice wavers, but he collects himself. "I believe my daughter, and I hope you still do, too."

"We do," I say, looking at him intently. Mr. Park still won't look back at me, though.

"I'd like to pay you," he says to Alice. "If you can do anything, if you have any bit of information that might help Helen, I can compensate you generously."

"We—" Alice begins to say.

"No," I say, standing up. "I don't want your money. You can't even look at me. I don't know why you find me so . . . distasteful."

"Iris!" Alice exclaims.

"We'll do this because we want justice for Rebecca, and to prove your daughter's innocence, but I won't take money from someone who thinks I'm less than nothing. You wouldn't even shake my hand. Why would I accept your money?"

With that, just like Helen, I leave the room, and Alice, behind.

CHAPTER THIRTY-FIVE

ALICE
FEBRUARY 18
10:42 A.M.

What good is money if it can't buy happiness?

—AGATHA CHRISTIE, *THE MAN IN THE BROWN SUIT*

THE DOOR SLAMS BEHIND Iris and I'm left staring at a thoroughly irritated Mr. Park.

"Your friend is very stubborn," he says to me after a long moment. "But if she insists on doing this work for free, who am I to stop her?"

"About that," I begin. I glance over at the door to the room. "Iris . . . she sometimes doesn't think about the big picture."

He raises a brow. "And?"

"And, if you're willing to compensate us for our work, I don't see any reason to say no. As you know, I don't need the money, but Iris does. She's—"

"I know who she is," Mr. Park says with distaste, and for a moment I wonder whether I'm making a mistake. Maybe Iris is right, maybe this man really isn't someone we should be doing business with.

If he were any other person, I'd make it clear that he best watch how he speaks about my friend, but Mr. Park is imposing at the best of times. And right now, annoyed and disgruntled by the situation at hand, he's sort of terrifying.

So instead, I force myself to be polite. "May I ask, what is it, exactly, that you have against my friend, Mr. Park?"

His lips pinch together, and for a moment I worry I've gone too far.

"I think you know, Ms. Ogilvie," he says at last.

I shake my head. "No. I don't. Iris is one of the smartest, most loyal people I know. I have no idea what you have against her."

"You're aware who her family is?" he asks me. "Her father?"

At the mention of Iris's father, dread washes over me. I remind myself that he's behind bars, in jail, locked away where he can't get to her or us.

I swallow and manage to respond without my voice shaking. "I know who her father is, yes. But you can't choose your parents. She didn't ask to be related to that man."

"That might be, but he's still a criminal. I've dealt with him in the past. And, although I'm fine with you two trying to help my daughter, I prefer to keep my distance from anyone related to him."

My nostrils flare. Every molecule of my being wants to tell him off, but I take a breath. I can't mess this up for Iris. I'm here to help Park, sure, but Iris and her mom need money, for her college tuition, for *life,* and the money Mr. Park is offering could really help them.

"I think we need to discuss a price," I say, changing course.

"How much do you think is reasonable?" he asks. "Twenty thousand if you can get my daughter out of this mess? My one stipulation is that *you* take lead on the investigation, not the Adams girl."

Twenty thousand might seem like a lot to most people, but I have a little insider knowledge of just how much this man is worth, so I shake my head.

"Thirty thousand and you have yourself a deal." There's no way I'm going to tell Iris that I'm taking the lead, because that's not how we operate, but he doesn't have to know that. And Iris doesn't need to know about this little agreement, not until after the fact, at least. She's being stubborn right now, but once I have the money in hand, money that she *needs,* I know she'll appreciate what I've done for her. Mrs. Adams will, too. Maybe it'll make up for me getting Iris into so much trouble.

In the meantime, Mr. Park can believe what he wants. When we get Park out of this mess, he won't care how we did it, only that it's done.

He smiles. "I see you learned something about negotiation from your father. All right, I respect a person who won't take the first offer they're given. Thirty thousand it is."

He rises to his feet, holding out a hand.

"Great." I stand and we cement our deal with a shake.

CHAPTER THIRTY-SIX

IRIS
FEBRUARY 18
4:30 P.M.

Filming on *Jane Eyre*, with Mona Moody in her
first major starring role, has been put on hold.
Miss Moody has been sent to a sanatorium at an
undisclosed location for treatment of tuberculosis.
We're sure all Miss Moody's fans wish her a speedy
recovery! In the meantime, Mona and Clifford Hayes
are heating up the big screen in *Boom Shakalaka!*
—"JANE EYRE PRODUCTION HALTS,"
HOLLYWOOD GAZETTE, 1949

ALICE IS PACING MY tiny kitchen while I get my laptop going.
We're at my apartment because I'm grounded for the time being
and I have to play nice with my mom. I assured Alice my mom
wouldn't be home until late, since she's working a double today.

"Does she even know how to do this?" Alice frets. "She is, no
offense, like a billion years old."

"Yes," I say. "She knows. She's the head of a multimillion-
dollar corporation, Alice. She knows how to Zoom. And she's the
only one I can think of who might know about how a necklace
possibly got from Mona Moody to Rebecca Kennedy, seventy-four

years later. I mean, Mona was her dad's girlfriend. Lilian's got to have *some* clue."

I look at the screen. It's just me staring back at myself as I wait for Lilian to join the Zoom. There are circles under my eyes and my hair looks zanier than usual. I try to focus.

With a tiny bloop, Lilian's face appears on my laptop. She's wearing her bright red glasses and squinting. Her assistant delicately places headphones on Lilian's head and disappears from the frame.

"Hello, my dears," she says.

Alice scrapes a chair over to sit next to me.

"Hello, Lilian," she says.

"Well, as I live and breathe. Alice Ogilvie, you get more beautiful every day."

Beside me, I feel Alice perk up a little.

"Now, to what do I owe the pleasure?" Lilian says gleefully.

"This photo," I say, cutting to the chase. I hold it up close to the laptop camera. "What can you tell us?"

Lilian leans way forward, giving me an alarming view of her nostrils.

"Oh, well, now. That is an old one. I remember that. Or those days, I should say. What are you doing with that ancient thing?"

Suddenly she doesn't sound so gleeful. Her voice shakes the tiniest bit.

"Do you remember these people?" I ask. "I mean, I see your dad, and Mona, but do you remember the other two? We found it. In the Castle. We're working, like, a little on Mona Moody."

Alice is impatient. "That necklace, Lilian. Do you know anything about it? We need to know."

Lilian fingers the cord on her headphones, a filmy look passing across her eyes. "That was a strange time. I know all of them, of course. Oh, my father. Look at *him*. They were at the Castle all the time. Parties. Premieres. The little man on the left there, that's Eugene Kennedy, you know he treated Mona Moody? She was always ill with something or other. But when she wasn't, she was lovely to me. My mother passed after I was born and Mona had no family. She and Mrs. Pinsky were really my only friends at the Castle."

"Wait just a minute," barks Alice. "Full stop here, Lilian. Did you say *Kennedy*? And he treated Mona Moody?"

Alice grabs my casebook and scribbles *In her diary Mona says a person named Gene is giving her pills!!!!*

"Yes," Lilian says softly. "Dr. Eugene Kennedy. He treated all the actresses back then. He was always at the Castle."

"Kennedy," I say, leaning forward. "As in . . . related to Rebecca Kennedy?"

Lilian scrunches her forehead. "I suppose so, yes. Let me think. . . . Yes, her great-grandfather. Though I've no idea how on earth that necklace came to be in *his* hands."

She shakes her head. "I don't remember much. My father gave that necklace to Mona to celebrate starting *Jane Eyre,* a role she dearly wanted. She was so excited; it was to be her first starring role after so many B movies and bit parts. I can't even tell you how much it was worth then or now, but it was one of a kind. Cartier, a string of baroque emeralds, shaped like teardrops. I remember when we lost the Castle in the 1950s and they were doing inventory. You know, the banks and whatnot. They want to know every little thing you have of value so they can swipe that away, too. The necklace was missing. I remember that. My father didn't seem bothered, but I was. I loved that necklace."

She lifts her chin. "The other man, the good-looking one, he was a minor movie idol, so handsome, *swoony,* we used to say. Clifford Hayes. He came around the Castle all the time when my father was away, to visit with Mona. She was living with us by then. She and Cliff were in a movie together, I believe, and then . . . well, she became ill and they sent her away to a spa. TB."

"They had to send her away for that?" I ask.

"It was common back then for tuberculosis. She was gone for months," Lilian said. "I was so very young, so I can only remember fragments—"

"Are you positively sure they sent her away?" Alice asks.

Lilian frowns. "I think I would know, Alice. She was gone from the Castle and that's what my father told me. Why would you ask such a thing?"

I glance at Alice. We have to be careful, because . . . it's possible Lilian doesn't know about the secret room. She was little. You believe what you're told when you're little.

"Lilian," I say slowly. "Around that time that Mona went away, what . . . was it like in the Castle?"

"Oh," Lilian answers. "We all missed her, of course. I wrote her letters every day and my father would mail them and then Mona would write back. But Castle life was a bit frenetic. My father was renovating the second floor and it took months. I wasn't allowed in that wing. My bedroom was moved to the east wing."

Lilian didn't know. Alice gives me a look, but I'm not going to say anything, not right now, to Lilian. How could you possibly phrase "Your father made a secret room and kept his girlfriend in it"?

Lilian is musing. "I was overjoyed when she returned, though she was very weak, still. Run-down. She was different, quieter. Illness does that to people. And then just a few weeks later, she was gone.

"It was a frightening time for me. One thing after another. Press everywhere. There had been a drowning at the dock, too, just before she fell."

Alice leans forward. "Dock? Drowning?"

"Yes. I remember tiny bits. I was on my father's yacht with Mrs. Pinsky and Mona. They were good friends. My father often had Mrs. Pinsky accompany me to things like parties, to babysit. It was after a large party. She'd put me to bed in a cabin on the yacht, but I woke up because I heard thunder. I woke and walked to the deck. A great storm had started. I remember Mona on the dock, sobbing, sopping wet. I caught glimpses of something floating in the water before Mrs. Pinsky hustled me away. Later I found out that was Clifford."

Lilian is blinking quickly. "I used to have nightmares about it. That night on the dock. Everyone screaming. I drew pictures of it all the time. Hid them in my treehouse. I put some of the letters Mona wrote me in there, too. She was so fun; sometimes she'd write to me in invisible ink."

She laughs lightly and adjusts her headphones. "These are not comfortable at all."

"Back to the necklace," I say. "How on earth could it get to Kennedy? When was the last time Mona wore it?"

"Well, Iris, I'm no detective, but I would assume Eugene stole it, wouldn't you? Though I put nothing past the Kennedys. They didn't come into their real money until later, but they were always strivers. They're a foul family—" Lilian says dryly.

"Lil—" I say.

"I must go," Lilian says. "But I've been following the news. That girl, Rebecca, what a mess. Poor thing. Though as I told you before, the Kennedys have many enemies. I'm just sorry whoever is behind this hurt a child."

"They've arrested someone," I say. "And they're charging another, but we don't think the second person was involved. It's someone else and we can't figure it out."

Lilian's eyes glimmer. "Oh, you will. I bet you're closer than you think."

"Listen, Lilian," Alice says. She's finally lost her patience. "If you know something, tell us. Don't just 'old lady' yourself around this."

"You're such a pill, Alice," Lilian says firmly. "If I had the secret to the assault of a child, do you really think I would keep that to myself? That's abhorrent."

Alice blushes. "Sorry."

"I'm simply saying," Lilian continues, "as it appears the two of you are on some sort of quest, that nothing is off the table. People are never who they appear to be. Grudges can last generations. Necklaces end up in strange hands. Lives are altered by the merest of connections. I'm off."

The Zoom session blips away.

Alice smacks her hand on the table. "This is a veritable goose chase, Iris. I feel like we're running in circles, here. We've spent all this time trying to find evidence, trying to figure out who could have done it if not Park, only to find out she *lied* to us. And one of the worst things is, that note, that *H,* and the selfie-booth photos, and her fight with Rebecca, they *all* point to her and I don't think we have enough to disprove that."

There are tears in the corners of her eyes. She takes a deep breath. "And everyone's going to think it's my fault, *again*."

"What do you mean?" I ask softly.

"Like last year. How it was my fault Brooke ran off from the party. Because I showed up and made things horrible. If she'd never run off, she'd still be alive. And it's me who's going to have to get up on a stand and positively identify Helen Park as standing over Rebecca's body and holding the weapon used to stab her. And then there's *you*."

I stiffen. "Me? What about me?"

She blinks rapidly. "This is all bad for you, Iris. You were in *jail*. I don't . . . I don't want . . . My parents might suck, but they could bail me out of anything. But all of this could ruin your whole future and—"

I hold up a hand to get her to shut up. "You're not the boss of me. I'm going to be fine. You don't have to protect me. I can take care of myself, thank you very much."

"Can you? Have you looked at yourself lately? You're tired all the time. Grumpy. You work so much. And I just wish I could help somehow." Alice pauses for a second, then adds, "There's something I should—"

I interrupt her before she can finish. "You know what, Alice? I'm a big girl. I'll be fine." I stand up, clearing a space on the table. "I appreciate you wanting to help me. I do. You know how you can help me right now? By focusing on *this*. Yeah, we're running in circles, and we need to sit here and figure some things out. So put on your big-girl panties, wipe your eyes, and *focus*."

I grab some large sheets of drawing paper from my art supplies in the corner. They won't be as swanky as Alice's whiteboard in her conservatory, but they'll have to do.

"A starlet and a mogul, a great Hollywood love story, and then the starlet falls to her death at the Castle. Seventy-four years later a girl goes to a dance at that Castle wearing the starlet's necklace and gets attacked. Why?"

I toss her a pencil.

"Think, Alice. *Think.*"

CHAPTER THIRTY-SEVEN

IRIS
FEBRUARY 18
5:15 P.M.

To make sense of anything,
you've gotta start at the beginning.
You can't bake a cake without butter, Ruth!
—MONA MOODY, *MATCHED SET*, 1947

WE BEGIN AT THE beginning. With Mona Moody. Born 1929, died October 10, 1949. Location, Castle Cove. Stated cause: accidental death from fall off Levy Castle balcony. And somewhere in the middle, a love story splashed across movie magazines and newspapers. A pretty young girl, an orphan, works her way from soda counter to starlet, and goes to live at a fairy-tale mansion owned by a powerful, handsome, rich widower. But she gets sick, and she's sent away to a sanatorium, and when she returns, she's weakened from her illness and tumbles to her death from the balcony. The rich widower falls into despair and begins embezzling from his own company. He dies years later in prison.

"Only," Alice says, chewing her pencil, "that's not entirely what happened, is it?"

"No," I say. "Because the dates in her diary, where she mentions being in a flower-wallpapered room for months, are the same dates she was supposed to be in a sanatorium. And the room, the secret room, at Levy Castle has flowered wallpaper."

Alice is scribbling on the large sheet of paper. She pauses and looks up at me. "Why would Charles Levy put her in that room? Because that's what we're both thinking, right?"

"Yes," I say. I get up and rummage in the cabinet and return to the table with a bag of potato chips. I nibble one, and Alice takes one, too. We look at each other. I'm glad she's not teary anymore.

"What was Levy, like, fifteen years older than her?" I ask.

"Something like that," Alice says. "I mean, that happened back then. Still happens, I know."

"But they weren't . . ." I don't know what I'm trying to say. "Equal? I mean, she came from nothing, as far as I can tell. Abandoned at birth, orphanage, minimal schooling. He was from a very wealthy family. And Lilian said he was often away. Maybe that was lonely for her?"

I flick my eyes to the photograph between us. Mona, flanked by three men, one of them very young and very handsome. Clifford Hayes.

Alice looks at it, too. "Lilian said he came over a lot when Charles was away."

"Mmm," I say, chewing a chip.

"You don't think . . . I mean . . . that Charles Levy would purposefully wall off a room and keep her prisoner, do you? Because in her diary she mentions being stuck in the room, but do you think he deliberately did that if she—"

"Fell in love with someone else?" I shrug. "Who knows why people do what they do. Maybe he snapped. Jealousy, as we learned from Westmacott, kind of makes you do awful things."

"Okay," Alice says. "But he obviously let her out at some

point, because Lilian says she was at that party where Clifford drowned. So what changed?"

She scribbles that down.

"Where Clifford drowned," I repeat, thinking. "And soon after, Mona fell and died, and Lilian was sent away to school, and her father went haywire. And years later we find this particular photograph in a strange place: tucked in the bedsprings of the secret room. That seems like an odd place to store a photograph, and just one, at that. And it wasn't just on the floor: it was tucked inside the springs on the underside of the mattress."

Alice writes down *Clifford Hayes* and *Eugene Kennedy,* then she clears her throat.

"Who is Clifford Hayes?" she asks her phone.

The strangely endearing, robotic woman's voice says, "Clifford Hayes was a film actor in the 1940s. He starred in such films as *Song of Santa Fe* and *The Farrington Incident.* He drowned in Castle Cove, California, on October fifth, 1949. Clifford Hayes was born Reginald Kennedy on April thirteenth, 1927, in—"

"Whoa, Nelly!" I say. "Hold on there. Excuse me? Reginald Kennedy?"

Alice frowns, unzipping her backpack. "Lilian said Eugene Kennedy was a doctor to the stars, and to Mona, too. Wait—"

"Were they brothers?" I sputter. I look at the photograph again. Eugene Kennedy is small and plain-faced. Clifford Hayes— Reginald Kennedy?—is the proverbial tall, dark, and handsome.

Alice is flipping through the photocopies of Mona's diary. "Here, look. Mona mentions a Dr. Gene visiting her in the room, bringing her pills to help her sleep. So, he knew. He was in on the room. He was helping keep her there."

"That's disgusting," I say.

"Uh, yes," Alice says. "This is all getting very gross."

We look at each other.

"This is nice," I say tentatively. "I feel like you and I haven't really been together, just us, in a while. We're always . . ."

"I know," Alice says, brushing strands of hair from her cheek. "I like Spike and Neil and, well, even Zora, but . . . sometimes it's a lot of noise."

"I'm sorry," I say quietly. "That your family is back and it's . . . weird for you. But maybe it's also nice?"

Alice looks down at our sheet of paper. "All they ever want to talk about is my 'future.' And I'm not sure what I picture is what they picture."

"Let me guess," I say. "College, money, success, upstanding Alice enters the world?"

"Yeah," she answers. "And I don't . . . I mean . . . I guess I picture those things, too, but my picture is different. My picture is this. I like this."

She gestures at the paper. I nod.

"Did Rebecca ever talk about them? Like, that she was related to a dead movie star and a doctor to famous people?" I ask, switching back to the topic at hand.

"Not really," Alice says. "She was a little sketchy about it. Like Lilian said, the Kennedys got rich all of a sudden. They weren't old money, like the Levys. They're a little flashy. I think I remember my parents kind of joking about them at some point, like they can buy whatever they want, but the one thing they can't is respect."

I shift the sheet of paper away from her and start a new column.

ALEX SCHAEFER, I write at the top.

"Lilian said the Kennedys have lots of enemies. The Schaefer family would be one. They were trying to buy out The Waves, a crappy motel that serves as a home for a lot of poor people, to build a luxury resort for rich people, who of course don't want to be near poor people. The Waves is prime property, right across the road from the beach."

"Why wouldn't the Schaefers just sell?" Alice asks. "I mean, that has to be a ton of money."

"Maybe sometimes what you have, even if it's small, is worth more than money to you," I answer. "Rayne said her dad always wins. Maybe he's using some horrible tactics or threatening them, but the Schaefers are stronger than Mr. Kennedy thought, at least for as long as they can be. I'd assume at some point, since this will bring in money for Castle Cove for tourism, the city will make them sell?"

"I wouldn't rule out hating the Kennedys as a motive for Alex," Alice says. "Especially if you know you're probably going to lose anyway. Fight till the death, right?"

I nod.

Alice continues. "Alex went to the Historical Society to look for blueprints of the Castle. Robbery, right?"

"I think so," I say.

"But then he attacks Kennedy. Viciously. But he wouldn't know she would wear the necklace to the party, right? How could he?"

She pauses. In capital letters, I write, *PERSON X.*

"Park said that Kennedy bragged to everybody that she was going to wear it to the dance."

Alice nods. "Person X might have known. But still, if he

wanted to hurt Kennedy, he could have done it at any time, right?"

I chew my lip. "I think it was Person X who wanted Mona's things, and the necklace, and Alex agreed to help for half the necklace, if they were going to sell it, and the fact that Kennedy was involved was a good lure, too, because Kennedy is personal to Alex."

Alice tilts her head at me.

"Icing on a revenge cake," I explain. "He agrees to help commit a robbery and it turns out the person who's ruining his whole life is there. A rich, spoiled girl who gets everything she wants, including his home."

"But . . . Park," Alice says quietly, shaking her head. "Everything she says seems logical, though she did lie about Alex and . . ." She sighs. "Iris, Park told us about the necklace earlier today. About knowing Kennedy would be wearing that necklace to the dance. You think Person X might have known that beforehand. There are an awful lot of arrows pointing to Park right now. The *H* on the note, the connection to Alex, being in the room, the letter opener . . ."

The H *on the note.* I blink, thinking. Alice just called Helen *Park* and . . .

"Alice," I say.

"What?" She's downcast, looking over the notes we've made.

"The *H* on the note. That doesn't make sense, does it? Because you—I mean, the Mains—you don't use first names."

Alice glances up. It's dawning on her.

"Park would have signed it *P,*" she says slowly. "And addressed it to *K.*"

"Yeah," I say. "Alex wrote the note, pretending to be Park, but he couldn't have known about the last-name thing. And the police wouldn't, either."

Alice closes her eyes. "Why are we so stupid?"

"Not stupid," I answer. "It's just . . . a very complicated case, is all."

"It's literally breaking my brain," Alice murmurs.

"Well, pop an aspirin because there's more," I say. "When I went to the hospital I took some pictures of Kennedy's medical charts. They were at the end of her bed. I printed them out. Look."

I pull a folder from my backpack and spread the papers over our investigation sheet.

"See," I tell Alice, pointing at the figure on the paper. "People have to come in and check her wounds. Different staff, different shifts, but everyone needs to know where the dressings are, et cetera. Kennedy is a good five inches taller than Park and heavier—"

"Don't let Kennedy hear that," Alice murmurs.

"For one, I don't think Park could overtake Kennedy. She's just a little thing, not to mention we don't think this matches her usual devious ways. Kennedy would have been able to fight back pretty easily, I'm sure."

"Park could have been the one to hit her on the head, though, and then Alex stabbed her. Or he hit her and Park stabbed her."

I shake my head. "Whoever hit her on the head did so from behind. The wound is here." I point to the drawing of the skull on the paper, where an X is smack in the middle of the skull.

"If Park hit her with a candelabra from behind, she's not that tall, the wound would probably be lower down the back of the skull. Whoever hit her on the head was as tall, if not taller, and really whacked her. And what I think, at least I *think* I think, is that Kennedy probably started to scream, or shout, when she realized whatever was happening was happening, and to shut her up, Person X thwacked her from behind and she fell toward Alex, who was probably holding the letter opener, and he stabbed her, and then pushed her away from him, and she fell."

Alice studies the figure on the medical paper. "Because if Park was holding the letter opener, and Kennedy fell toward her, the stab wounds would be lower on the body?"

"I think so," I say. "But Park had no blood on her. Alex's jacket has Kennedy's blood on it because she fell against him as he continued to stab her. Then he pushed her and she fell backward onto her back, which is how Park, and you, found her."

"So you think Person X would have blood on their clothes."

"Maybe not," I say. "A clean hit on the head probably doesn't cause as much blood splatter as stabbing. I'm not sure. I'm not an expert, I'm just theorizing."

"It still doesn't explain the note," Alice says. "The note is killing me. Let's talk it through."

"I'm listening."

Alice grabs a potato chip and chews thoughtfully. "Okay. I'm Person X and I want that necklace, and I've also seen a girl named Helen fighting with Kennedy earlier in the evening. And maybe I tell my friend Alex to go mack on Helen in the selfie booth, because she's an easy mark—"

"And I have Alex write a note that makes it look like Helen tried to get Kennedy upstairs for more fighting—"

"So we can try to frame her. And lucky for us, poor Helen Park picks up the letter opener," Alice finishes.

"Right," I say slowly. "But Alex went into the booth with Helen. That leaves photo evidence. How stupid could he be to do that? Because obviously, even if he frames Helen, that's still him in the photo with her."

"Maybe he just didn't care," Alice says, "He's not going to win this fight against Mr. Kennedy. He's going to lose that motel, no matter what. Rich people, and cities, always win when the possibility of money is involved. What else did he have? He was not a pleasant person, Iris. He was actually quite scary. Maybe literally all he wanted was to steal what he could and kill Rebecca Kennedy and that was enough for him. I mean, he had ample time to go back and get that bloody jacket and he didn't even *try.*"

We're quiet.

Finally, Alice says, "I don't even know if we're any closer, truthfully, Iris."

The light outside the kitchen window is fading, just like Alice's spirit.

"No," I say. "We are closer. We know that whoever Person X is, they have a connection to Mona Moody and this necklace."

Alice's phone pings. "Merde," she says softly. "I have to go. It's Brenda. I need to get back for dinner. Do you want to come over and we can keep working?"

I hesitate. "I don't think I should."

Alice's face falls. "Because of your mom? She doesn't want us hanging out so much, right?"

I nod. "She'll get over it. I mean, I'm dying to meet your parents and all, but I have to play nice with the one I have, you know?"

Alice collects her things. "I get it. Text me later, okay?"

She starts to walk toward the door, her shoulders slack.

"Alice," I call after her. "We *are* getting closer. I know we are."

"I know," she says, opening the front door. "I just want it all to be worth it."

I lock the door behind her and sit for a long time after she leaves, thinking of what Lilian said. *People are never who they appear to be. Lives are altered by the merest of connections.* I know we can figure this out. I know that, somehow, we can draw a line from Mona Moody to what happened to Rebecca Kennedy.

CHAPTER THIRTY-EIGHT

ALICE
FEBRUARY 18
5:49 P.M.

How true is the saying that man
was forced to invent work in order to
escape the strain of having to think.
—AGATHA CHRISTIE, *DEATH ON THE NILE*

I CATCH HIM IN the headlights of my car as I approach the house: my dad, standing by the trunk of his Tesla, heaving a suitcase.

Guess he's on his way out again. After all, it *has* been six days; I'm surprised he managed to stick around this long.

"Alice," he says as I step out of my car. He slams his trunk shut.

The house behind us is mostly dark, save for a few lights on upstairs in Brenda's rooms. She's probably watching her stories, waiting for me to get home. Hoping that I don't get into any more trouble than I already have.

"Dad," I reply, voice flat. "Taking off?" I kick the gravel under my feet, not quite meeting his eyes.

He nods. "I have a big meeting in Tokyo later next week, so—"

"Yeah." I cut him off. It's not like I expected him to stick around. "Great. See ya."

I start toward the house.

"Alice—" The sound of my name stops me. I turn partway back to him.

"What?"

He hesitates. Something flashes across his face, but it can't be what I think it is—guilt—and it disappears before I can figure it out.

"Remember what we talked about. Your future. It's important you do your work, that you make sure you—"

I interrupt him. I can't take this, yet again. "Yeah. Okay. Right. Bye."

I hurry up to the big, dark house before he can respond.

In my bedroom, I drop my bag onto the floor with a thunk and flop across the width of my bed, burying my head in my pillow for a long moment.

My mind is swirling. Park, Lilian, the fact that Mona Moody was, by public accounts, in a sanatorium exactly when her diary says she was trapped in that creepy wallpapered room. The hidden photo of Kennedy's ancestors. Alex and Person X stealing the diary of an old film star and the necklace from Kennedy. The note that the cops think was from Park, which was actually written by Alex who, along with Person X, was trying to frame Park.

I think back to what we talked about with Lilian earlier. It can't be a coincidence, how the names that keep popping up in her stories are the same ones we're talking about today. I know it's all connected, but I feel like we're missing that final piece, that *thing* that would tie it all together. The central piece of this puzzle.

I wonder what's in the drawings Lilian mentioned, the ones she drew after that night on the dock.

I pick up my phone and text Iris.

> I think I should go to the treehouse. Find
> Lilian's drawings and Mona Moody's
> letters. Maybe there's something in them
> that will help us tie the past to the present

Iris's response is immediate.

> **Not without me.**
>
> No way. You cannot come. Your mom
> would kill you
>
> **I'll sneak out. You cannot go without me**

I pause. I wouldn't want to miss this, either, so I can't blame her.

> Fine. Be ready in 15
>
> **I'm ready now**

Iris and I make our way through the wooded area surrounding the Castle and then into the brush, heading to the backyard where the treehouse is. Clouds cover the moon and the night is dark, an inky black that sucks away my breath, unpunctured by the lights from Castle Cove's small downtown.

"Maybe we should have waited till morning," I mutter as I trip over yet another stick.

"Alice, I swear to god, you better buck up," Iris says through gritted teeth. "Look, at least we're not trying to get inside this time, right? Could you imagine going in there right now?"

We stop at the edge of the brush, staring at the Castle for a long moment. From this vantage point, I see the bushes where the police found Alex's jacket, now sectioned off with police tape, and next to them, a huge old tree. My eyes travel up its trunk to the Castle's second floor, the dark bathroom window Alex and Person X escaped through that night.

I grab Iris's arm. "Wait. Wait. Iris. Look." I point to the window, the tree. "That's got to be where Alex came down that night, right?"

"Yes, that's how he got down."

"Do you think the tree was there back in the day? It looks old. But if it was, why didn't Mona climb down it, if she was being kept in that walled-off room?"

"Maybe she was afraid of heights?"

"Maybe . . ." I stare at the tree for a moment longer. In the distance, a dog lets out a loud bark, sending prickles of anxiety down my spine. "Okay, let's get out of this open area. You know where the treehouse is, right?"

She nods. "This way."

I follow her, both of us doing our best to stay out of sight, ducking behind bushes and large trees.

"It's over here." Iris points a few hundred feet in front of us. I shine my light up ahead and spot a small wooden structure tucked up into the branches of a tree. It must be ancient if it was here when Lilian was little.

We stop at the bottom of a crooked ladder. "Is this thing safe?" Iris shrugs. "Held me and Cole."

"Gross." I grab one of the rungs. "So. We're going up there?" There's a crackling sound above me and I jump, about to sprint back to the car until I realize it's just a squirrel.

"Here, I'll go first." Iris pushes me aside and starts up the ladder without so much as a glance back. After a moment, I follow close behind.

CHAPTER THIRTY-NINE

IRIS
FEBRUARY 18
8:00 P.M.

A touching centerpiece of the magnificent Levy
grounds is this treehouse, lovingly built by
Levy himself for his cherished daughter, Lilian.
"Little girls need their secret places," he explains.
"Places of wonder and imagination. I sure did
get a lot of splinters, though."
—*CASTLE COVE GAZETTE*, 1946

MOONLIGHT STREAMS THROUGH THE windowpane in the treehouse, catching spiderwebs in its light.

Alice pinches my leg and I howl, then clap a hand across my mouth.

"Help me," she whispers. "We probably don't have much time. If we get caught, we're definitely getting charged this time and your mom will never forgive me."

I hoist her up the final rung of the ladder and onto the widow's walk.

I look around the inside of the treehouse. It still smells damp, even a few days after the storm. The floorboards feel soft under my feet, springy. I walk gingerly.

If I was a kid, where would I hide things in a treehouse? Alice is feeling the walls carefully, pressing her hands over them, as though there might be a secret door up here, too, just like in the Castle. I look up.

I would hide something where I hoped no one would see it. But if I'm a kid, I'm small, so I can't reach the ceiling of the treehouse. I can only go where I can go, which is . . . down.

I drop to my knees and pat around, feeling for loose boards. Maybe Lilian tucked things under here, in the floorboards.

Above me, Alice is still feeling the walls. "I'm not appreciating all this dust," she whispers.

Beneath my hands, a board shifts. I slide my fingers beneath one end, try to pry it up. There's an odd creak and something that sounds suspiciously like cracking, but I keep trying. The nails are old and soft, but it won't quite give.

"Here," Alice says. "Let me help."

But just as she starts to kneel, something dark and fluttery shoots through the treehouse. Alice shrieks and waves her hands, tumbling very hard butt-first onto the soft wood of the floor, which lets out a series of snaps and cracks. Alice is swatting at something that's alive and in her hair.

The board I'm pulling suddenly pops up from the floor, smacking me in the chin. I fall backward.

And then I keep falling backward.

When I open my eyes, the breath has been knocked out of me, every bone hurts, and Alice is a few feet from me, with a bloody lip and feathers in her hair. Splinters of wood litter the lawn around us. We look up at the same time, at the gaping wound that used to be the floor of the treehouse.

"Holy . . . ," Alice says shakily.

I put a finger to my lips.

All around us, cracked wood, rusty nails, but also . . . things. Through my blurred vision, I peer closer.

A flat box and what looks like a small jewelry box? A ledger. Pencils. A child's book. Hair ribbons. A tiny wooden monkey.

Suddenly the lawn is bathed in light. The floodlights outside the Castle have popped on.

"Grab it," I say to Alice as I scramble up. "Grab it all and haul ass."

Alice and I grab everything and run, back toward the darkness of the woods off the Castle lawn, as we hear the crisp clack of security guard walkie-talkies far behind us.

Alice . . . is not a good runner.

She's panting, the feathers of whatever flew into the treehouse still in her hair.

Glancing behind me, I see the shapes of two guards walking the grounds, looking around. Suddenly a beam of light blinds me and a voice yells, "Stop!"

I take a U-turn, grabbing Alice's hand, veering us through a block of bushes. I pant.

Alice and I wait, listening. The crackle of the walkies is getting closer.

I try to adjust my eyes after the blindness of the guard's flashlight. I blink, and gradually realize we're in a row of hedges with a long path that veers suddenly at one end.

"Um, Iris," Alice whispers. "What in the world . . ."

"Shh," I say. "We're in the maze."

"Oh, well, okay, that's just spectacular. How are we going to get out? And what if they come in?"

"I'm thinking," I snap. We can't go back out where we came in, because I think that's where they are. We have to keep moving.

"First rule," Alice suddenly whispers. "I read it somewhere. The right hand rule. Walk with your right hand on the row where you started and it will eventually lead you out."

We begin creeping forward quickly, Alice leading the way, right hand brushing the hedge wall, and me holding on to the back of her jacket.

"Alice," I say, glancing over the wall at the Castle. I can see the window to the bathroom of the secret room she pointed out earlier. The tree outside the window is definitely old and sturdy, perfect for climbing down, as Alex Schaefer proved, though not without possibility of peril.

"Alice, maybe Mona didn't try to escape out the window because of the drugs Dr. Gene was giving her. Maybe they made her sluggish, and she was afraid."

"Maybe," Alice whispers back. "But then why didn't she run away or tell anyone what had happened to her once they let her out?"

We turn a corner. I hear the crunching of footsteps across another row. Alice looks back at me. I can feel us both holding our breath. My cheeks are cold.

"Who's there?" a voice calls. "You're trespassing on state property."

"Damn kids," says another voice. "Probably high. I don't get paid enough for this."

Alice picks up the pace. I tighten my grip on her jacket, holding the loot tight against me with my other hand. If we get caught here, this is probably the last straw with my mom. My chest tightens.

Alice is still following the hedge with her hand, turning left again, then right. I'm starting to get dizzy. Alice suddenly turns again and then we're out, the woods before us. We take off running back to the lot where we parked. Alice shoves everything into my hands and aims her car key at her car. There's a *meep meep* and the doors unlock.

We peel out of the lot with the lights off until we hit Highway 1.

On the road, safely away from the security guards, Alice checks her bloody lip in the rearview.

"I'm hideous," she moans.

I look through the stuff in my lap. The ledgers are filled with drawings, just like the ones a child makes. Suns, the moon, birds, cats, mountain landscapes. But mixed in, other, more interesting drawings.

Wavy line drawings, people with pop-eyes, distorted bodies. The pages are so old and damaged I turn them carefully, because I'm afraid they might crack. The pencil is faded, but you can make out stuff in several of them. I turn on my phone flashlight and peer closer at one.

There are three men on a dock. Moon in the sky. Rippling water. One of the men has odd, large fingers, very much like something a small child would draw. Seven fingers on one hand, angled in a crooked manner.

"Oh, Lilian. An artist you were not," I say, holding up the ledger to Alice.

Alice glances quickly at it, then turns the car off the road, into the parking lot of Dotty's Doughnuts.

"Sheesh," she says. "Those are some strange fingers. Which one do you think that is? Levy, Hayes, or Dr. Gene?"

"Do you have that photo still in your bag?" I ask.

Alice leans into the back seat and grabs her backpack and rummages through it. She pulls out the photo and holds it next to Lilian's drawing.

There are three men in the drawing, in an awkward circle, one man with his back to the edge of the dock, crudely drawn waves of water behind him, slashes of pencil marks that I take to be rain cutting through the whole drawing. His hair has been blackened, just like the black hair Clifford Hayes sports in the movie premiere photo.

Alice points to a short man wearing glasses in the drawing. "Dr. Gene."

We look at each other and back at the photo and the drawing. All of the men are scowling.

"So, if Clifford Hayes drowned and then a week or so later Mona died, that seems kind of close, doesn't it?" I say.

Alice is quiet for a minute. Then she says, "Do you think Hayes's death . . . Do you think it wasn't an accident?"

"And that Mona's fall wasn't so accidental?" I say. It's all so confusing. "Possibly. I mean, she was locked in a room. Dr. Gene was giving her pills, right? Then her maybe lover suddenly drowns and then . . ."

"Merde," Alice murmurs.

She sifts through the rest of the pile on my lap, opening the lid to the flat box and pulling out what look like cassette tapes? No, they're too big and round.

"Reel-to-reel tapes," I say. I open the jewelry box. Inside, the letters Lilian said Mona wrote to her when she was supposedly away.

"Alice," I say. "One, it looks like we have two deaths to figure out, on top of trying to help Park. Two, we need to listen to this reel-to-reel, and there are only two people in the world who probably know how to do that."

GROUP MESSAGE

ALICE OGILVIE, IRIS ADAMS, ZORA JOHNSON, SPIKE FLICK, NEIL CETAS, ANGELIK PATTERSON

FEBRUARY 18

9:32 P.M.

AO: EMERGENCY!!! Where are you guys?? We need to meet, stat

IA: Here.

AP: who is this

SF: I'm not going to like this am I

ZJ: Here . . . I can't meet tonight tho I'm babysitting. Speaking of my bratty little sister just bit me hold on

NC: Present

AO: You guys are not going to believe what we found tonight!!

NC: What happened??

AO: Ok so you know how we texted you all earlier to bring you up to speed on our call with Lilian and how she mentioned hiding some stuff in her old treehouse behind the Castle? So Iris and I decided to go there and check it out . . . and we found this old reel to reel tape thingy, and we think it might be Mona Moody's

IA: We'll fill you in more in person but in short we need help w/ reel to reels

NC: Can do. School's open tomorrow, even tho it's Sunday. Club meetings and that sort of thing.

AJ: Yah we can get into the newspaper office, no problem. I think the AV club at school has a bunch of old equipment in storage. I'll pull it out.

AO: Tomorrow, AV room. 7:30 a.m. Don't be late.

TEXT CONVERSATION BETWEEN
IRIS ADAMS AND RAFAEL RAMIREZ
FEBRUARY 18
11:02 P.M.

IA: You there?

RR: You know, some people enjoy sleeping, Iris

IA: What wonderful lives they lead

RR: I'd like to be one of them

IA: Moving on. Mona Moody died on October 10, 1949. I found some articles, but they all say she fell from the balcony at The Castle from complications of TB.

RR: Just tell me what you need. I'm tired.

IA: I have a source who says there was a death at the Yacht Club on October 5, 1949. Clifford Hayes. Police would have been called, right?

RR: Sure. Routine investigation. How did he die?

IA: *Castle Cove Gazette* archives say accidental drowning.

RR: Let me guess. You don't think that really happened.

IA: I think two people who were possibly lovers dying accidental deaths within a few days of each other is a little weird, don't you?

RR: Um, I don't even know what to say about that.

IA: I'm just trying all avenues here.

RR: Ok. What is it you want?

IA: Can you look up at the PD, like in old files or something, were police called to the docks that night? Is there a report on the drowning?

RR: Ok. The old files aren't digitized. Might take a bit.

IA: Cool. Thanks.

RR: Iris?

IA: What?

RR: You didn't look so good. At the jail

IA: Because I was in jail, Raf.

RR: Just . . . take it easy, ok? I'm worried
about you

IA: Gotta go.

CHAPTER FORTY

ALICE
FEBRUARY 19
7:31 A.M.

Now, there is no murder without a motive.

—AGATHA CHRISTIE,

THE MYSTERIOUS AFFAIR AT STYLES

"WHERE IS IT? THE machine thingy we need?"

"Good morning, Alice, it's *so* nice to see you. How did you sleep?" Zora says, turning slightly in her chair to make a face at me. Angelik puts a hand on her arm. They're sitting at one of the center tables in the newspaper room, in front of an ancient-looking machine.

I ignore Zora. "Where's Iris? Where's Neil and Spike? Is that it? The reel player?"

"We haven't seen them yet," Angelik says. "And yes, this is the machine. These knobs are what control how fast it goes." She points at something on the machine.

I make a displeased noise—how dare everyone be late?—and set my bag down on an empty spot on the table, carefully taking out the long box that holds the reels.

"Hey, guys. Sorry I'm late." Iris enters the room, breathless, her cheeks red like she ran part of the way here. She stops next to me and drags in a breath. "Where's Neil and Spike?"

"Seems to be the question of the hour," Angelik says.

"Oh wow, is that the reel-to-reel?" Iris hurries over to Angelik and Zora, gaping at the machine in awe. "That's so cool. It looks like something out of a black-and-white film. Do you know how to use it?"

"I think we figured out part of it," Angelik says.

I walk over and set the box next to the machine, getting a full view of it for the first time.

"So we put the tapes on those?" Iris asks, pointing to the two black circles near its top. "And then it'll play them for us?"

Angelik nods. "That's definitely where the tapes go. We're trying to figure out all these buttons. Like how to get the tapes to play and . . ."

"We need to be careful with it," I grab the box, cradling it. "We only have one set. If we mess them up . . ."

"Have no fear, Neil is here!" Neil enters the room, singing.

"Oh my *god,* no singing, Neil!" Zora barks at him. "We have had this conversation multiple times. You are banned from singing. Forever."

He rolls his eyes. "I'm in a good mood this morning, Z. Why you gotta rain on my parade?

"What do we have here?" Neil walks over to the machine, petting it like it's a cat. "She's a beaut. CCHS had this just wasting away in storage?"

Angelik nods. "I doubt it's been used in decades."

"A shame. People have no regard for history anymore. Do you mind?" He motions to Angelik, who slides her chair over. He squats in front of the machine and pokes around for a minute, then asks, "Who has the tapes?"

"Me." I'm hugging the box against my body. "You're sure you know what you're doing? These are super old and fragile and if they get ruined . . ."

Neil shakes his head, his expression serious. "I'll be careful. I've used reel-to-reels a bunch of times. My mom taught me how. I know what I'm doing, I promise."

I take a breath. I trust Mrs. Cetas; I just wish she were here to help. After a moment, I hand him the box. "All right, but if anything happens to them . . ."

"You'll have my head, I know, I know." Neil grins, turning back to the machine and opening the box. "Okay, so we—"

He's cut off by a voice in the doorway. "Sorry, sorry! I'm only . . . well, I guess I'm ten minutes late, sorry." Spike rushes into the room, talking the whole time. "On my way here, I got stuck behind a city bus that I swear stopped at every possible driveway between my house and school. I don't understand why this town only has one-lane roads."

"It's okay," Iris says, smiling at Spike in a way that makes me pause. I make a mental note to question her about it later, when I have the brain space to think about it.

"Anyway," I turn back to Neil. "Can we get to it, please? The tapes."

During Spike's dramatic entrance, Neil managed to get the tapes hooked up to the machine. He's still tinkering with something, but after a moment he sits back on his haunches.

"I think we're good. Shall I?" he asks me and Iris and we nod.

"Cool." He presses a black button, and the tapes start to roll.

At first, there's nothing. Just unintelligible murmurs, the hissing sound of static. A full minute goes by where those are the only sounds, and my heart sinks. Maybe our excitement was for nothing. Maybe the tapes are too old and too damaged to be of any use.

My thoughts are interrupted by a loud *crunch.* "What was that?"

Iris grabs my arm. "Did you hear that voice?"

"A *voice?*" I step closer to Neil, cupping my hand around my ear and leaning toward the machine's speakers. "I can't—"

And then I hear it. It's faint, almost eaten by background noise, but it's there.

"Is there a way to mess with the levels of the recording?" Iris asks Neil.

"Hmm . . . let me see . . ." He plays with the knobs on the machine, and after a moment the static lowers in volume.

From the machine we hear: ". . . (static) . . . the docks . . . (static) . . . I saw everything." It's a woman's voice, high and shaky, speaking in a loud whisper. "He didn't drown . . . (static) . . . my love. I'm . . . (static) . . . scared."

"Did they just say *scared?*" Zora whispers. "Whose voice is that?"

"Shhh." I strain to make out the words from the tape, my ear so close to the speaker it's almost pressed against it.

". . . if you find (static) . . . something terrible happened." For a moment, the voice grows clear and strong. "I think . . . I think he's trying to—"

A burst of static explodes from the speakers and I jump away, knocking into Neil. As we watch in horror, the brittle old tape of the reel-to-reel snaps apart.

CHAPTER FORTY-ONE

IRIS
FEBRUARY 19
7:50 A.M.

I don't like silly little games. I never have. And I
don't like the people who play them, either. They're
always hiding something.
—MONA MOODY, *DARK WHISPERS*, 1948

I TRIED TO CONVINCE Alice to hang out in the library with me
and work on her homework, since we're at school anyway, but
she hightailed it out of the AV room after the tape broke. She
is seriously going to fail this semester if she's not careful. I think
she's mostly doing just enough to remain viable, grade-wise, but
she's definitely going to flunk McAllister's class if she doesn't get
cracking on that ancestry project. Working with Henderson is
probably killing her, to be honest. I didn't mind my own project in his class. It's an interesting scavenger hunt, trying to ferret
out distant and long-dead relatives from passenger logs on ships,
the loose hints from other people's complicated trees, an address
used for voter registration that belongs to an apartment above
a butcher shop that, when Googled, doesn't exist anymore, replaced by tony condos and quaint eateries.

I got pretty far with my mom's relatives, but I didn't do much with my dad's side. McAllister accepted it half-finished, really. He's a jerk in general, but I know teachers talk, and I know he knows about what happened with the Thing in the fall. There's no way I want to know where that guy came from. Not right now, anyway.

Ms. Shelby's book club is meeting a few tables away. I wish I'd joined that. I'd like to get lost in a book right about now to take my mind off things.

I just wish that reel-to-reel hadn't been so scratchy. Hadn't broken. What would Mona Moody have told us? What's in her diary that we can't decipher?

Mona Moody, I type into the search bar of my iPad.

Images of her pop up instantly. Creamy skin. Luxurious hair tumbling over her shoulders. Early bit parts in big movies, bigger billing in B movies, a girl at the edge of the crowd in a scene, face shining. Dressed in a modest swimsuit, pink-cheeked, healthy and vibrant, lounging in the sand. Studio portraits, starkly lit, eyebrows expertly molded with brown pencil, eyelashes thick and dark, her mouth a bright, dark plum in black and white.

After a deep dive on YouTube, I find old film footage of her on Levy's arm, a white mink snug on her bare shoulders, as they make their way through press at a movie premiere. I put my earbuds in, plug them into the laptop, turn up the sound. A reporter is right in her face, pencil and pad in hand.

Are you happy to be here tonight, Mona? What can you tell us about your dress?

She giggles. *This old thing? Oh, I'm just joshing, silly. This was made just for me by Miss Edith Head! Isn't it dreamy? This whole night is dreamy. I can't believe—*

I turn up the volume as high as it can go.

He's a wonderful actor. We had such a wonderful time on set. I'm a lucky girl.

That's her. That was her on the tape. Here, she sounds rehearsed, like she was given a script, and maybe she was. But the voices are the same: throaty, a lushness. It's just that the one I'm listening to right now isn't . . . scared.

I pull out the scans of her diaries that Alice gave me. Even scanned, the cursive is light and difficult to read. Mona Moody isn't giving us any clues.

My phone buzzes. Raf.

> **So that drowning you asked me about. The**
> **one at the docks in 1949?**
>> Yeah?
> **It's weird. I found one police call listed for**
> **a death in Castle Cove on that date and it's**
> **a car accident on Guadalupe. Nothing for**
> **a drowning and nothing at the Yacht Club**
> **docks.**

Oh, I type, dejected.

> **The weird thing is that the guy? Clifford**
> **Hayes? He has a medical examiner's report**
> **that says it was an accidental death by**
> **drowning but it's signed by Dr. Eugene**
> **Kennedy and there was no autopsy. And**
> **Hayes's real name according to the report is**
> **Reginald Kennedy.**
>> They were brothers . . .

**Iris even back then you'd call police for a
suspected drowning, just to rule out foul play
or something and you almost always had an
autopsy. I'm also pretty sure that immediate
family members, even if they were doctors,
would not be the ones signing off on the
death report. It's fishy as hell. To me, anyway.**

I stare at his text.

Thanks, Raf, I quickly text back.

I sneak a look up at Ms. Shelby. She's busy at her desk on her laptop.

Alice, I type. *Eugene Kennedy signed off on his brother's death report. No autopsy. Raf says police should have been called for suspected drowning, but there's no report.*

What??

I think the only way to figure out why Person X wanted that necklace and who Person X IS is to find Eugene Kennedy. I mean how did HE come to have the necklace unless he stole it? If he's even still alive, I type.

I think about that. Damn, how old would he even be?

He cannot possibly still be alive, I type to Alice.

**Oh, I think he very much is, Iris. I just found
his address.**

CHAPTER FORTY-TWO

ALICE
FEBRUARY 19
9:03 A.M.

Murder, I have often noticed,
is a great matchmaker.
—AGATHA CHRISTIE, *THE A.B.C. MURDERS*

I WALK INTO THE kitchen carrying my overnight bag to find Brenda sitting at the counter, a mug of coffee cupped in her hands. Her brows dart up in surprise when she sees me.

"Alice?" She puts a hand over her heart. "It's barely nine a.m. You do know today is Sunday, right? Are you feeling okay? Are you carrying . . . is that *luggage*?"

I purse my lips, dropping the bag to the ground with a thud. "Yes, I am aware of the day of the week, thank you very much. Iris and I are taking a little road trip."

She's quiet, watching me as I pour myself a to-go cup of coffee from the pot, and then says, "Does your mother know about this?"

My freaking mother is, for some ungodly reason, still here in this house. I thought she'd be long gone by now, taking off soon after my father, but no. She's still here, working from her home office and making horribly awkward attempts at conversation when we run into each other in the hall.

I frown. "Why would she?"

"Alice . . ." Brenda sighs. "You know she's trying, right? That's why she's still here. She wants to make sure you're okay. After last year, after Brooke—"

I snort. "Great way to show that you care, showing up four months after the fact to lecture me about schoolwork. What, does she expect me to be grateful? She's—" I cut myself off, biting the insides of my cheeks. I don't care. I do not care. I think of Hercule Poirot, how he always retains control of his emotions, regardless of the situation at hand. I simply will not allow my mother to get to me, not anymore.

"It doesn't matter. This is important, Brenda. We have to go speak to a man about . . . about a school project." There, that should make my mom happy.

"We're doing a genealogy thing at school and Iris found a lead, down in LA. Someone who might be able to connect her with . . . with one of her dad's relatives, who she's lost touch with because of"—I wave a hand—"you know. That whole situation. With her dad. The project is due next week, so we have to go, now. Today. To talk to them. It's *important*. It's a three-day weekend, because of President's Day, so it's the perfect time to go."

Who knew this stupid genealogy project would come in so handy as an excuse? Maybe school is useful for something, after all.

Brenda's eyes have grown moist as I've been talking. "Oh, poor Iris. She's so lovely, and I'm sure this has been difficult for

her. You're a good friend, for going with her. I'm proud of you."
She smiles at me and something twinges in my midsection, something sharp and hard. Guilt? "I'll let your mom know where you went, but please text her, too. She'd appreciate it."

"Mmm . . . sure," I say, my momentary guilt over lying to Brenda erased by yet another mention of my mother. I give Brenda a sideways hug and leave without so much as a backward glance.

After three hours of winding our way down Highway 1, we finally hit the 101 and I take the opportunity to really test out the horsepower on my car. I never get to, not in our boring town where the speed limit maxes out at twenty-five, lest someone, you know, drive themselves over the cliffs and into the sea. Which happens more frequently than you might think.

I press my foot hard on the gas, and the car lurches forward.

Iris shoots me a dirty look. She's been reading something on her phone for the last thirty minutes, so sorry if I got bored.

"I'm an excellent driver, Iris," I say, rolling my eyes. "I spent time in Tuscany—"

"Yeah, yeah, I know, you spent time in Tuscany and had a moped and those hills are rolling, et cetera, et cetera. I *know*. That's all well and good, but when the cops pull us over, I don't think they're going to care about how handy you are on a scooter. I think they're going to care that you're going"—she peeks over my arm—"Alice, you're going thirty miles over the speed limit. *Slow down*."

She's such a party pooper.

"Fine." I jerk us out of the left lane, saying a silent goodbye to the Tesla in front of us that I've been following for the past thirty minutes. "Is that better, Grandma?"

Iris nods.

"By the way," I ask, careful to keep my voice neutral. "What did you tell your mom? About where you were going?"

Her mouth presses into a flat line. "I don't want to talk about my mom."

Irritation flames in my belly. "Fine."

We fall quiet as I twist the wheel and we lurch into the right lane.

"Look at that sign!" Iris bounces in her seat excitedly. "Ten miles to Sunset Boulevard! That's, like, *Hollywood.* Right in the center of LA! Oh my god!"

"Yeah," I say quietly, thinking about the last time I was here. It was a few months before Steve broke up with me—we took an overnight trip with Brooke and Kennedy. I thought we were all friends, at the time, that Steve and Brooke got along so well because they both loved *me,* not because they were starting to fall in love with each other. I would never have guessed how different things would be a year later.

"I booked us into the Sunset Spire, which is pretty close to Dr. Kennedy's house in Hancock Park. We can stop there first, check in, and then—"

"I can't wait to see it!" she squeals. Iris is bouncing out of her seat. "I can't believe stars like Marlon Brando used to stay there! Do you think anyone famous will be there right now? Zora would like this. She likes that singer Courtney Ray. And . . . *Sean Powell.* She loves him. She and Neil still talk about his Nickelodeon show."

"I loved that show," I say, thinking back. "Brooke and I used to watch it together all the time."

Iris is quiet for a moment and then clears her throat. "You know . . . if you ever want to talk about her . . ."

I'm considering how to respond when my phone buzzes with a text. "Can you check that for me?" I ask, nodding to it in the center console.

Iris picks it up and reads: "*Brenda told me you went to LA. I hope you are all caught up on your schoolwork, as we discussed. Please be home tomorrow at a reasonable hour.* From your mom," she adds unnecessarily.

"Yeah," I say.

"She's still home?"

"Yeah." I merge into the right-hand lane as traffic slows.

"So, like I was saying—" Iris starts, and this time it's my turn to cut her off.

"Which exit do we take?"

She pauses, reading the directions on her phone. "Exit fourteen. Laurel Canyon Boulevard. That's where all the musicians lived back in the 1970s. So cool."

"So, this Kennedy doctor guy is old, right? Like, *really* old. He has to be, what, at least ninety?"

Iris's mouth quirks up. "Um, Alice, you do realize it's 2023 and Mona Moody died when she was twenty, in 1949, right? That means *she* would be . . ." She waits for me to fill in the blank.

"I'm sorry. Math isn't my strong suit."

"She would be ninety-four. That means Eugene Kennedy is a hundred and one. He would have been twenty-nine in 1949."

Something occurs to me. "Wait, twenty-nine? How the hell was he a practicing doctor? I thought it takes literally forever to get through medical school. Aren't most doctors, like, in their thirties?"

"Yes! Okay, so after our conversation last night, I wondered the same thing. I did some Googling and apparently during the war, so many doctors were overseas that there was a shortage in the States. The government offered incentives to medical schools to accelerate programs to just two and three years. That's what Dr. Kennedy did. He was a general practitioner, which meant he did a little bit of everything back then. Which apparently meant ministering to Hollywood stars, as well."

"Huh." I'm impressed that Iris even noticed that, because I definitely had not put it all together. I knew he was old, but I didn't realize he was ancient. "Well, if he's a hundred and one, he can't live alone, right? There will probably be someone else there, at least a nurse or something? Ah, here's the exit."

I turn onto the ramp leading off the 101 and into Los Angeles. Soon, we'll pass by the Hollywood Bowl and into Hollywood proper, the streets where people like Mona Moody left their handprints in the pavement.

Iris nods. "I would assume so."

"Well," I say as I slam on the brakes at a red light. "We should make a plan. Perhaps we should pull a Poirot? Like in *Murder on the Orient Express,* where no one takes him seriously because they think he's just a 'ridiculous-looking little man'? I think we could pull that off. We're down here, just trying to find answers for our silly little genealogy project, we have no idea what we're doing. Not really. We're two bumbling teenage girls."

Iris smiles. "And as everyone knows, teenage girls don't know *anything*."

I laugh as we sail down Cahuenga Boulevard into town. "Yeah. We know nothing. Nothing at all."

CHAPTER FORTY-THREE

IRIS
FEBRUARY 19
12:45 P.M.

> This is really quite a complicated pickle, isn't it?
> I don't know if we'll ever make
> heads or tails of it, Betty.
> —MONA MOODY, *SHIP TO SHORE!*, 1947

HOLLYWOOD. MOVIE STUDIOS AND famous restaurants and nightclubs. I wonder where the Mocambo is, where Levy met Mona when she worked as a coat-check girl. I should look up the Los Angeles Orphans Home Society. That's where she was put as a baby after her parents couldn't take care of her. But she went out on her own at sixteen and moved into a boardinghouse. I'm trying to search for the boardinghouse on my phone, but Alice is driving like a maniac again and I can't concentrate.

I have my phone on silent but I see it flash.

Cole. *Hey, I'm really sorry. Can we talk sometime? About what happened?*

Alice sees it and makes a small *tsk*. I turn it over in my lap.

"So tell me, Iris! Cole. There must have been a lot of kissing in that treehouse. Is this why you look so tired all the time lately? Late nights with Cole?"

She laughs a little, but it sounds thin and forced.

Her words needle at me in an uncomfortable way. "There wasn't any kissing, Alice. There wasn't anything. And there probably never will be," I say. "Happy now?"

Alice frowns. "I didn't mean—"

"What do you have against him, anyway? He's done literally nothing to you."

She snorts. "Well, he's certainly done quite a bit to *other* people."

"Who cares?" I ask. "If I hooked up with a lot of people, would you call me a slut?"

"No!" she says, glancing at me, surprised. "Because . . . well, you wouldn't *do* that, and plus—"

"Plus, what? I didn't see him taking advantage of anyone, Alice. If anything, all those girls? They used *him*. He was in love with Brooke, and she wanted nothing of the sort."

Alice is staring straight ahead at the road. She tries to make her voice lighter. "Plus, I feel like you and Spike . . . I mean, he's a little dorky, but I can see it."

"Alice. Spike isn't dorky unless you call kindness dorky." I know I'm being mean, but sometimes Alice's words sting.

"I don't know why you're being so rude, Iris," she says flatly. "Whatever. Let's just do this, okay?"

She pulls the car to the curb and turns off the ignition abruptly.

"Here," she says. She flings off her seat belt.

Out the window the streets of Hancock Park are grassy and tree-filled, with lovely, gorgeous old homes lined up one by one. I check the address to make sure we're in the right place.

Alice grabs her bag and gets out of the car, and I climb out after her.

On the sidewalk, the air between us is heavy.

"Alice," I start to say, but she cuts me off.

"You have to put your tantrum to the side, Iris, so we can do our work."

I bury a snide retort and follow her up the front walk of the address. It's lined with fragrant and colorful flowers.

The front door is dark and heavy-looking, arched. Alice reaches out for the door knocker, but before she can clack it, the door opens.

"Oh," says the man in the doorway. "I was just getting my mail. Can I help you? You look a little old to be selling cookies."

He chuckles and scratches his belly. He's wearing a stained T-shirt and jeans. His face is shadowed and unshaven. Clumpy hair under a backward baseball cap, thick-framed glasses. He's not old-old, maybe thirties or forties. It's hard to tell with anyone over twenty, really.

"Hi," I say. "Does Dr. Eugene Kennedy live here? We'd like to speak to him about his time in Castle Cove."

The guy looks from me to Alice, who smiles brightly. "Alice Osterman," she lies. "Nice to meet you. I'm doing a genealogy report for my class? And, oh, it's been a whirlwind of discovery, which has led me here. To you. And you are?"

His eyes narrow slightly. "I'm Theo. Theo Kennedy. The doctor is my grandfather. There are plenty of Kennedys up in Castle Cove. Haven't you already talked to them? They could probably tell you everything you need to know."

"Yes!" Alice says eagerly. "And that led me here. I think we might be related. Distantly! It's so nice to meet you!" She smiles bright, holding out her hand.

He takes it hesitantly and then looks beyond us to the neighborhood. "Maybe you should come inside. Not really a good look for me to be standing outside with two young girls, if you know what I mean."

As we're walking inside, he gives a small laugh. "You aren't setting me and my grandfather up to be robbed, are you? Knock me out and steal all our valuables?"

"Ha," I say. "Like those girls up in Auburn with the old lady?"

"Exactly!" he says. "Asked for a glass of water and then went in and . . ."

Beside me, Alice blanches.

He chuckles. "Sorry. Don't mind me. My brain's always going nutty with scenarios. I'm a screenwriter."

"Oh, how lovely," Alice murmurs.

Inside, the house is comfortably cluttered. Books everywhere, art, lots of overstuffed couches.

Theo scratches his neck. "So, you did, like, that 23andMe thing, or . . ."

"Ancestry. The website? And a lot of sleuthing," Alice says. "And I came upon your grandfather's name and discovered he was still alive. His story is so fascinating! The Hollywood stuff, especially. I think I might be a cousin of yours, in fact, and I just wanted to ask him a few things for my project. You know, give it some flair."

Theo thinks for a moment, then says, "I've never heard of any Ostermans in our family. Where—"

"She's failing the class," I blurt, to distract him. "She really needs a good grade. So, could we, you know, talk to him? We're harmless, I swear!"

"I guess that would be okay. You should know, though, he's . . . he goes in and out. He's been in homes, but he keeps getting out and wandering around. Says he needs to go back to the water, for some reason. It's probably better for him here, with me, then at a home, anyway. I take him to the ocean, but he gets upset, says it's not the same water he needs to see. Old people, you know?"

Alice and I look at each other. We're thinking the same thing. *Not the same water he needs to see.* The docks. He wants to see the ocean in Castle Cove. Where his brother supposedly drowned and perhaps Eugene Kennedy covered it up.

Theo leads us down a long, narrow hallway, the walls lined with beautifully framed photos that I desperately want to stop and look at, because they're all old, mostly in black and white. Dr. Kennedy with Elizabeth Taylor. Dr. Kennedy with Jane Russell. A signed photo of Cary Grant. Nothing with Mona Moody, which seems strange. None of his brother, Clifford, born Reginald Kennedy and then remade into a strong-jawed romantic lead. A few photos of a younger Rebecca Kennedy and two very good-looking people who must be her parents.

Theo raps on a door at the end of the hallway. "Gene? Grandad? You have some visitors." He pushes the door open slowly.

Tucked into a plump brown leather chair is a tiny old man, dressed in a crisp white buttoned shirt with a deep blue-and-pink-dotted bow tie and a cinnamon-colored cardigan. His face gleams in the sunlight pouring through the window next to him. He smiles as he turns to us.

"Oh," he says softly. "How lovely. You've come back."

You've come back? I look at Alice. She mouths *Old people* and sits daintily on the edge of a four-poster bed, which is much too large for the room. The room is filled with boxes, some half-opened, and there are file folders on the bed.

Theo shakes his head. "He's been going through his things,

looking for something. Sorry about the mess. Like I said, he's in and out. I'll be back in a bit. Just working toward a deadline. If you need anything, I'll be across the hall."

"Hello, Dr. Kennedy. My name is Alice," Alice begins, "and this is my friend Iris."

He holds out a wavering hand and we each take it in turn. His skin is papery thin and dry.

"We . . ." I look around for a place to sit, but the only place is a small spot next to Alice on the bed. I sit carefully next to her. A jumble of prescription bottles and creams clutter the bedside table. "We were hoping to ask you some questions. Alice . . . *we're* from Castle Cove. Alice is doing a family tree for her school project."

Dr. Kennedy's watery eyes blink rapidly and he murmurs, "Castle Cove." It's not a question, it's a statement.

"Yes," Alice says. "You're in my tree? Have you heard of it? Ancestry? It's a website. The internet? You start a tree with family you know and then you get hints from census records or recorder's offices and sometimes other people's trees? If they might have links to you and . . ."

Dr. Kennedy looks away from Alice to the window. I think he might be a little too old for all this internet talk. I nudge Alice.

She clears her throat. "Anyway, I ran across your name in my research, but beyond that, really, I'm just so fascinated by the life you've led."

He looks back at her, his forehead wrinkling in confusion. "I told you all I know the last time," he says. "I don't remember everything . . . all the time. Bits and pieces."

"I . . ." Alice glances at me. "I haven't been here before, Dr. Kennedy."

"You were," he says gently. "You were so upset. I gave you a candy. But you didn't like them."

He gestures to a bowl of butterscotch candies on the windowsill.

"You were upset I couldn't remember everything," he continues. "But I'm an old man. I don't know why I've lived this long when others haven't. Life isn't fair. I should have . . ." His voice dies out. He looks at the window again, lost in thought.

Alice gives me a *what now* look.

"Who was here?" I say firmly.

He turns back to us. "Her."

He raises a finger in Alice's direction.

"When?" I say.

He tilts his head. "It feels like yesterday, but I'm not very good with days, I'm afraid. Perhaps it was much longer? I'm sorry you were upset."

"Me, too," Alice offers, straightening her shoulders, trying a different tack. "I needed you to tell me the truth about the necklace and you didn't. Maybe you can now."

I like this Alice. Playing along. Being Poirot.

Dr. Kennedy folds his hands in his lap and drops his eyes. "I don't know what the truth is."

"Mona had a beautiful necklace, Dr. Kennedy." I try to make my voice firm, but gentle. "What happened to it?"

He looks at his hands. They're shaking. Old age or . . . fear?

"I'd never held such a beautiful thing before," he murmurs. "I deserved to have it. For all I did. For how I helped him."

The necklace? Alice mouths at me. I half nod, unsure.

"It slipped right off her," he murmurs. "We spoke of this before, do you remember? She was so upset. She was going to tell.

It would have ruined us all. And when she fell, it . . . came right off in my hands."

My heart stills. Fell? Mona Moody? Was she wearing the necklace on a balcony of the Castle and he . . . pushed her? And the necklace came off in his hands?

"Did you keep it? For your family?" Alice asks, her voice trembling.

He doesn't answer, just knots his fingers together in his lap.

I look around at the file folders on the bed, at the boxes with their tops open, for something to do, because . . . are we sitting here with a murderer?

"Your grandson said you were looking for something, Dr. Kennedy. What are you looking for?"

He looks up at me. "A secret. A silver secret. From my brother."

"I'll help you look," I say. "Can I help you?"

"Yes," he says softly.

Alice switches gears. "Your brother gave you something? I'm sorry he passed. That must be lonely."

I'm pawing through the boxes, which are filled with old books, bow ties, wooden boxes that when I open them are filled with old matchbooks, cuff links, spare buttons.

When he speaks again, the doctor's voice is hoarse and hard, startling me.

"There's nothing I could do but go on, do you understand?" he says. "What was done was done. I'd hated him my whole life. So handsome. Everyone loved him. I was a sickly child, an inconvenience."

"Reginald?" I say quietly, pausing over a box. "Your brother, Reginald? Are you talking about him? What happened at the docks, Dr. Eugene?"

Dr. Kennedy lifts his eyes to Alice and they're filled with tears. "I told you what I know about your family, the little things I've kept. But people have died. It's so far in the past, it can't help you now. Sometimes things just need to be . . . swept under the rug, after so much time."

Why would he say "your" family to Alice instead of "our family" if she told him she was here because she thought she was related to him?

He's staring at Alice. She's staring back.

"Dr. Kennedy, what happened to your brother the night on the dock at the Yacht Club?" I ask again. I start looking through the boxes faster, looking for the "silver secret," whatever that is. I can hear Theo across the hall on the phone, saying he needs to go soon.

"Let it go," Alice says quietly. "No one can hurt you now. Like you said, it's been so long."

Dr. Kennedy's shoulders shudder. He drops his head again, and when he speaks, his voice is muffled. "Why do you want to open the past? It's gone. They're gone. I . . . shouldn't have done what I did, but I hated them so . . . and he was weak. I wish you wouldn't come here anymore. Didn't you find what you needed last time?"

Tears are splashing onto his hands.

"Poor Mona. But she would have ruined us all."

"How?" I say gently. "How would she have ruined you, Dr. Kennedy?"

"When was I here last, Dr. Kennedy?" Alice asks. "Did you give me anything?"

His head is shaking as he looks at her. "I can't remember. But it was you. You were sad. I said you could have a look around, but what would it matter? The answers aren't here."

Alice reaches out and touches one of his damp hands. Very carefully, he curls a finger around one of hers like a small child sleepy at bedtime.

"She was going mad, they were all going mad. I was the only one who knew what to do. I am always the one who fixes things. And Leitha, she was a good woman. Loyal."

Who is *Leitha*? Alice shoots me a glance.

His finger is still curled in Alice's. "We had to send the child away. It was the only way. It broke her heart."

I frown. "Lilian? To boarding school? But Mona was . . . dead already. What do you—"

"I'm so sorry," he weeps. "I'm so very sorry. I'm . . . not feeling well. May I rest now? I need . . . Where is Theo? Please don't come back. I've told you what I know. I've said everything. I have. Please. Let me be."

"Who was here? What happened on the dock?" Alice presses.

"Alice," I whisper. "He's already crying."

Old movie magazines, *Harper's,* scarves, postcards. My god, this man has a lot of stuff.

"Iris," Alice says. "We need the truth."

Dr. Kennedy reaches out and takes a butterscotch from the dish on the window. He has trouble unwrapping it, so Alice helps him. He holds the candy in his mouth, sucking gently.

"I'd like to die in the water, like Reggie. Wouldn't that be right? Mona always told me I deserved to die for what I'd done."

Theo's voice rings out from the doorway. "Oh, geez. I thought this might happen. It usually does around this time. He's fading out."

My heart jumps. I jam my hand down inside a box and hit something hard wrapped in fabric. A yellowed wedding veil? I peel it apart to discover a silver box and shove it inside my peacoat just as Theo comes into the room.

He kneels down next to Dr. Kennedy and rubs his shoulder. "You should probably go now. He doesn't like to talk about family. I haven't the heart to tell him about Rebecca. Poor kid."

"Yes," Alice says. "It's so sad. I think, though I can't be certain, that she's my second cousin. I'm so sorry about what happened to her."

I motion for Alice to get up.

"Thank you," she says, standing. "I'm sorry we troubled you."

Theo gets up. "I'm going to get his medication ready," he says. "You can show yourselves out?"

"Yes," Alice says. "But one thing. He said I was here before. I wasn't, though. Who was it?"

Theo shrugs and sighs. "Sometimes I have to leave him for an hour or so, for business. He answers the door. I really need to get some in-home help. I'm not sure what he's saying. Could be real, could be in his head."

Alice nods and goes through the doorway to the hall.

"The closer you get to the truth, the further away it is," Dr. Kennedy says to me. He beckons me to him and I lean my head down. I can smell the sweetness of butterscotch on his breath.

"The secret," he whispers, "is in the pines."

Check Out Receipt

BPL- East Boston Branch Library
617-569-0271
http://www.bpl.org/branches/eastboston.htm

Thursday, July 27, 2023 4:49:43 PM

Item: 39999104539653
Title: Betrayal by the book
Material: Book
Due: 8/17/2023

Item: 39999104645252
Title: When the vibe is right
Material: Book
Due: 8/17/2023

Total items: 2

Thank You!

CHAPTER FORTY-FOUR

ALICE
FEBRUARY 19
1:45 P.M.

*The truth must be quite plain, if one
could just clear away the litter.*
—AGATHA CHRISTIE, *A CARIBBEAN MYSTERY*

"I TOOK SOMETHING," SAYS Iris in a low voice once we're almost back to the car.

I start to glance back over my shoulder to the front door, but she stops me. "We need to go. Don't act suspicious."

We scramble into the car and I take off, twisting and turning through Hancock Park's back roads until we're far enough from Dr. Kennedy's house that it seems safe to stop. I screech to the curb.

"Excuse me, now. You *took* something?" I ask.

Iris pulls a silver box out of her peacoat and holds it in front of her, inspecting it. "I did. I took this. It looks . . . important, don't you think?" She tugs at its lock, frowning. "Except it's locked."

"I have a crowbar in my trunk. Let's get that thing open." I whip off my seat belt and push open my door. Iris follows.

I pop open the trunk and pull out the crowbar.

"Try not to ruin the box itself," Iris says. "It's very nice."

I roll my eyes. "I think we have bigger things to worry about right now." I set it on the ground and take a step back. I take a few practice aims at the lock, trying to get the angle right so I don't smash the thing to smithereens. Then I lift the crowbar over my head and bring it down, hard.

The box splinters and its lock pops open.

Iris bends down and flicks broken bits of wood away, opening the mangled clasp.

The first thing I see is a sealed envelope. I slip it out and peel it open.

Iris dumps out the rest of the box's contents onto the ground. A few yellowed documents, some postcards, and an object wrapped in a piece of cloth. She starts unfolding the cloth but stops at my gasp.

In my hands is an ancient birth certificate and a small black-and-white photo of a newborn baby wrapped in a white blanket with a little white cap on its head.

"It's a baby," I say. "A *baby.*" I read the birth certificate out loud. *"Certified Copy of Birth Record. Name of Child: Jane Kennedy. Maiden name of mother: Doris Monahan. Name of father: Reginald Kennedy."* My stomach flips. "Oh my god. Doris Monahan is Mona Moody's birth name."

"And Reginald Kennedy is Clifford Hayes. Alice . . . do you think . . ."

"That Charles Levy locked Mona Moody in that creepy, horrible hidden room while she was pregnant with another man's baby?"

Iris nods. "And that's why she couldn't climb down that tree, the one Alex and Person X went down the night of the dance. She didn't want to hurt her baby." Her voice wobbles and I glance over at her. There are tears at the corners of her eyes. "That's horrible."

I shudder, trying to get the mental image out of my head. "Jesus. That's even more twisted than I expected. What else is in here?" I grab a stack of aged documents, unfolding them carefully. They're so old the paper crinkles between my fingers.

I read the heading on the first one and then skim the contents of the page. "It looks like these are adoption papers for Mona's baby. She was given up for adoption only a few days after she was born . . . to Frederick and Leitha Pinsky. Renamed Susan Pinsky."

"Wait, did you say Pinsky?" Iris asks. "Leitha? Dr. Kennedy mentioned her and . . . Can I see those?"

"Sure." I hand them over to Iris, who skims the pages, frowning.

When she finishes, she looks up at me. "Lilian mentioned a Pinsky, do you remember that? She said Mrs. Pinsky worked in the kitchen. That she couldn't have children of her own? Jesus, Alice, did Levy give Mona Moody's baby to his cook?" As she talks, she absentmindedly tugs at the folded white cloth, and it falls away.

We're staring at a tiny silver pistol.

I suck in a breath. "Is that . . ."

Iris jumps up and runs to the car. She grabs her pack and hauls out the ledger of Lilian's drawings, flipping the pages maniacally as she walks back to me. She stops next to me, pointing at the drawing, to one of the men on the dock.

"Not seven fingers crudely drawn by a little kid, Alice. Five fingers, plus two, like this."

She holds out her forefinger and thumb, like a pistol.

"Hayes didn't drown. He was shot. By Charles Levy."

"Because he fathered a baby with Levy's girlfriend."

"I'd assume so, yes."

"Jesus." I push a hand against my forehead. My brain is spinning. "This is nuts. So, we have an affair, a pregnancy, a baby, a hidden room, an adoption, a murder, and then . . ."

"And then Mona Moody died, falling off that balcony. Which was potentially not an accident, from the sounds of it," Iris finishes.

"Yeah, no kidding. For that creepy doctor to have grabbed that necklace off Mona's neck when she 'fell,' he would have had to have been super, *super* close to her. It's more than a little suspicious, if you ask me."

Iris nods. "Agreed. So he ends up with that necklace, which he passes down to his great-granddaughter Rebecca Kennedy . . . who wears it to the Sadie Hawkins dance."

I nod. "But how the hell does this relate to what happened that night? To Kennedy being stabbed? To Park?"

Iris shakes her head. "I don't know. But I feel like we need to find the Pinskys somehow. Talk to them about all of this."

I sigh. "I don't know how that's going to help Park."

"At the very least, if we talk to them, we might get answers about one of the cases we've been circling. I think it would be nice to get closure on *something,* don't you?" Iris digs into the box. "One of the other papers in here might tell us where they are. Some old photos . . . a postcard from San Francisco . . . Wait, what's this?" She takes out a piece of paper that's in much better condition than the other ones we found and unfolds it. After a second, she grabs my arm. *"The secret is in the pines."*

I groan. "Iris. No more riddles, please."

She grins. "No more riddles. Look at this." She shoves the paper into my hands.

Whispering Pines Ledger

JANUARY 15, 1997

Frederick Pinsky, 72 years old, died Monday, January 13, 1997. "Fred" was born in 1925 in Castle Cove, California. As a boy, he loved the ocean and following the adventures of *Gasoline Alley* and *The Katzenjammer Kids* in the Sunday papers. Frederick met his beloved wife, Leitha, when he began working at Levy Castle in the mid-1940s, where he was employed as a groundskeeper. Leitha was a cook's assistant. Fred and Leitha moved to Whispering Pines in 1949, where they became the proprietors of Camp Moonglow, a summer camp for children.

Frederick was preceded in death by his wife, Leitha (1986), and his dear daughter, Susan (1992) Miller (Jonathan). He is survived by a great-niece (Helen Hahn, Whispering Pines) and great-nephew (Louis Hahn, Albany, New York) and many other family and friends. Frederick will be remembered for his excellent sense of humor, singing voice, and his many tales of meeting movie stars while working at Levy Castle.

Visitation is Wednesday, January 15, at 5 p.m. at the Hofstadt Family Mortuary in Whispering Pines, 1 Starry Sky Lane. In lieu of flowers, donations may be made to Camp Moonglow to aid in repairs and restoration of this wonderful respite for children.

CHAPTER FORTY-FIVE

ALICE
FEBRUARY 19
5:30 P.M.

*They have a genius, young ladies, for getting into
various kinds of trouble and difficulty.*

—AGATHA CHRISTIE, *THIRD GIRL*

WE'RE THREE HOURS FROM Whispering Pines when Iris lets out
a small scream from the passenger seat.

I almost drive off the road. "What? What happened?"

"Oh my god," she says. I cut my eyes to her and see that she's
staring at her phone in horror.

"Iris. What?"

"So I set up a Google alert yesterday for Eugene Kennedy, just
to see if anything new popped up about him that would be useful
and . . ." Her voice wobbles.

"What!"

"Apparently he died, Alice. He freaking died after we left his
house. And they're looking for us."

"He died? And who's looking for us? What are you talking
about?" I slam on the brakes and the car behind me honks angrily.

Iris grabs my arm. "Alice, be careful!"

I drag in a breath and manage to get us over to the breakdown lane. I stop the car, breathless from panic. "Okay, please tell me what the hell you're talking about."

"Look at this." She holds out her phone and I take it. On the screen is a video of Kennedy's grandson, hysterically talking to a reporter. "And the one girl, the shorter one, she specifically mentioned a real murder where two girls murder an old woman in her house. They seemed harmless enough at the time. . . ."

The headline of the post is *Two Teens Wanted for Questioning in Death of Elderly Doctor,* and below it, some very crude drawings that are supposed to be me and Iris. "Gross. I look hideous in this."

"They say he fell off his chair," Iris says. "His grandson went out to grab dinner and came back and Eugene was on the floor, surrounded by all those pill bottles that were on his nightstand."

I frown. "So, what? They think we went back there and force-fed him pills? Maybe he took the wrong ones. We didn't kill him."

"I know. But they don't know that."

I drop my head to the steering wheel and let out a scream that echoes the one Iris let out. "Jesus. We're wanted criminals, Iris."

"I know."

"What are we going to do?"

"I don't know. We're four hours out from LA now, at least. We need to figure out this case so the cops realize we didn't go to see him for nefarious reasons."

"You're right." I pull my head up. "We need to figure this out."

"Yeah, and Alice?"

"What?"

"You have to drive more carefully. They're looking for us, plus we have a gun in the car. If we get pulled over by the cops . . ."

My stomach drops. "Oh god. They'll lock us up for life."

I pull back onto the road as carefully as possible, and, keeping in the right lane, we continue our journey to Whispering Pines.

Whispering Pines is barely anything, or so it seems at first glance. Tucked in a foresty valley with a main street that's mostly a bar, a general store, and a few shops, there's very little traffic and hardly anyone walking around. I see a lopsided sign up ahead, its ink faded, that says *Camp Moonglow.* An arrow points to a dilapidated road that disappears into the woods. Far off, the husk of what looks like a formerly grand hotel stretches up behind the trees.

I roll down the window. It's eerily quiet outside. Where are the people?

"There," Iris says. "We have to turn right there." She Googled Helen Hahn's address as we were heading into town.

I'm seized by a sudden fear. "What if she's not here?"

Iris shrugs. "There wasn't a phone number listed for Helen Hahn, just an address, so . . . I guess, we wait?"

I frown. "There's nothing out here. Why would a person *live* here?"

"It's a good place to disappear," Iris says. "I'd assume Levy thought that made it the perfect place for his horrible little secret to go."

There's one house in the distance, a small, cabin-like thing with a porch and gray car out front. We fall into silence as we drive toward it and I pull up next to another car.

I take a deep breath. "Here goes nothing."

On the porch is a neat stack of firewood, a blue metal chair, and a broom.

Iris knocks on the screen door.

After a moment, the door opens, revealing a woman who can't be much older than Ricky. She's wearing a flannel shirt and a frown.

She squints out at us. "What do you want? Who are you?" she says, and I realize what we must look like, exhausted after nearly twelve hours straight in the car. I plaster on my best smile. "We've just been to see Eugene Kennedy," I answer. "We're here to talk to you about Mona Moody."

CHAPTER FORTY-SIX

IRIS
FEBRUARY 19
8:49 P.M.

*You can't bury the truth. It has a way of biding its
time and then poking through the dirt.*
—MONA MOODY, *DARK WHISPERS*, 1948

THE WOMAN GIVES ALICE a quick, intent look, and then shakes
her head.

"A lot of people seem very interested in Mona Moody these
days," she mutters. "You can come in, but I don't know what I
can tell you."

"You are Helen Hahn, right?" I say quickly. "Frederick Pinsky's
great-niece?"

She opens the screen door for us. "Actually, that's my mom,
the one you want, but she's passed away. I'm Rachel."

"So, you don't know anything?" Alice asks, her voice dejected.

The woman looks at us for a moment, then sighs. "I'm making tea. I suppose I should offer you some to make this friendly,
but do kids your age even drink tea? I don't have anything else,
except water or whiskey," she says and turns around and walks
toward a kitchen area.

"I myself would love some tea," Alice says, following her in. "And then I think we should get down to business, if you can be of any help."

The inside of the house is dark, with only one lamp lit. There's a crackling fire in the fireplace. The windows are covered; thick curtains, heavy shades. Newspapers and magazines are in piles everywhere and a calico cat nests on top of a crocheted blanket on a couch propped up with bricks.

"You?" Rachel says begrudgingly, looking me up and down. "You want some, too? You both are an odd pair, aren't you?"

Alice and I glance at each other.

"I'll take some," I say. It seems like I should. It seems like a very Miss Marple thing to do, after all. She drank an awful lot of tea in *A Pocket Full of Rye,* which is the last Christie book I read. Then I remember that Rex Fortescue dies after drinking his morning tea, and Adele gets a healthy dose of cyanide in hers, and I keep an eye on this Rachel person as she pours the tea into dainty cups. Who *is* she?

She motions for me to help her bring the cups to the coffee table in front of the couch. Alice nestles in an easy chair across from us, takes a delicate sip of tea, sets the cup back on the saucer. "This is for a genealogy project at school."

"Right," Rachel says. "That's what the other person said, too. 'Family tree.' I didn't believe her, either."

"Other person?" I ask.

"Yep. A few weeks ago.

Alice looks at me, frustrated. I get it. Is this person the "Other Alice"? What is going *on*?

The calico cat stretches and climbs into Alice's lap, nestling. She frowns.

"Be nice if I knew some names, here," Rachel says, leaning back into a pillow on the couch. "Just for fun."

"I'm sorry," I say. "I'm Iris and this is Alice. And you're right. There is no project. I mean, there *is,* but . . . A girl down in Castle Cove was assaulted and it's a long story, but another girl is being framed for it, and frankly, it connects to Mona Moody."

Rachel folds her hands in her lap. "You mean Doris Monahan. That seems like a leap."

"Stranger things have happened," Alice says. "We're just looking for answers. For a friend who might go to jail for something she didn't do."

Rachel looks at both of us and then shakes her head. "I don't know what I could tell you that would possibly help your friend. I only know bits and pieces and it's all handed down. My mom, she was working on something, using what she was told, trying to get everything down before she passed, but a lot is just hearsay, you know?"

I reach into my backpack and pull out the silver box, placing it on the couch between us.

"Open it," I say. "There's some proof in here."

"But be careful," Alice says. "There's a gun in there."

Rachel smiles. "I'm not afraid of guns."

She angles her head to a rifle propped in the corner.

My stomach squeezes a little. A house in the remote woods? A person we know nothing about? I try to push it out of my mind while Rachel lifts the lid of the dented silver box. She pulls out the birth certificate and the adoption papers and looks them over. She leaves the pistol in the box.

When she's done looking at the papers, she folds them up carefully and puts them back in the box, closing the lid softly.

"Rich people . . . ," she says slowly. "They live different lives. I mean, really, *really* rich people, like Charles Levy. You know? Leitha and Frederick loved Susan. You should know that. I've got photos and letters in a storage unit. They couldn't have a baby of their own. Leitha tried. And she loved that other little girl, too, although I'm blanking on her name right now."

"Lilian?" I offer.

"That's it." Rachel nods. "You should know that for a very long time, everyone was sworn to secrecy. That's what my mom said. Frederick and Leitha were very afraid of the Levy guy and they were afraid of that other one, too . . . the doctor?"

"Eugene Kennedy," Alice says.

"My mom learned most of it from Frederick when he was dying. She took care of him. He had a lot to get off his chest, and my mom started writing some of it down. I guess he figured after such a long time, with everyone so old and even Susan gone, what did it matter anymore?"

Alice leans forward and sets her teacup down with a clank, upending the cat, who tumbles to the floor and yowls at her.

"This is all very well and good," she says. "And I'm enjoying it, to be honest. But we're in a bit of a time crunch and we need to know . . . Iris, what *is* it exactly we need to know?"

They both look at me. "Well, I guess I just thought . . . What exactly happened to Mona on the night she died? What happened on the docks at the Yacht Club? Do you know about that, Rachel?"

Rachel takes a breath. "Frederick and Leitha took the baby. Mona signed the adoption papers, or at least I hope that's her signature. The rest I only know from what my mom took down from Frederick. They were here by then; Charles had given them

321

a lot of money, and a house—it's not far from here—and the camp. But they still kept in touch with people who worked at the Castle—I still can't believe it's called that, by the way—"

"It's quite a structure," Alice says.

"I gather," Rachel says. "And from what I understand, Doris—Mona—changed her mind. She wanted Susan—or Jane, as she named her—back. She was threatening Charles that she'd tell the police, I think. The doctor was keeping her pretty medicated."

"They kept her locked in a room for the pregnancy," I say. "Did you know that? Leitha and Frederick would have known."

Rachel looks sad. "I didn't know that. That's awful. Frederick heard from one of the other workers at the Castle that Mona had sent a telegram to Clifford Hayes—he was shooting a movie overseas—and told him, finally, about her pregnancy and the baby. I think one of the staff at the Castle felt sorry for her and sent it. I'm not sure. He came back immediately, of course, and that's"—she looks down at the box—"when I suppose this pistol was used. He confronted Charles on the dock and Charles shot him."

"Dr. Kennedy covered it up," I said. "His own brother's murder."

Rachel nods. "I suppose so."

Alice shakes her head. "If workers at the Castle knew, why didn't they say anything?"

"Fear, probably," Rachel says. "Money. Maybe they were paid off. They were scared. Their boss had just murdered someone, after all. Anyway, Mona went downhill from there. Frederick's friend said she was weak from the drugs, talking wild, saying she was going to tell about the baby, about what had happened to

Clifford, and she and the doctor got into a struggle and he pushed her from the balcony."

"So he *did* push her," I say to Alice. I think back to when he said *it slipped right off her.*

"Do you know anything about a necklace?" I ask Rachel.

"You, too, with the necklace?" Rachel sighs. "That's what the other one was on about, too."

Alice and I look at each other. Alice frowns.

"That other one? The one who was messaging me," Rachel says. "Wow, I did not like her. Just a very bad vibe. That was what she was really concerned with. A necklace. Went on and on about it. Family legacy, stolen from her. She wanted family documents, the whole deal. Made me sorry I'd ever answered her first message, to be honest."

"Wait," I say. "That has to be Person X! That's the person we think hurt our friend in Castle Cove!"

Rachel looks confused. "If you say so. Listen, the whole thing started when my mom became sick. I wanted to know, you know, family stuff, where we were from, who we were, that sort of thing. So I started an Ancestry account. You know, that thing onli—"

"I'm familiar, thank you," Alice says dryly.

"My mom gave me names, she told me what Frederick had told her, I typed it up for her. It was a little hazy, but I got some details. Enough to start a tree. It was fun. You get these great hints from other people's information, right? They ping you! If you have an open account, they can email you. I found some cousins in Pola—"

"What is her name?" Alice pleads.

"Easy, girl," Rachel says. "I'm sorry to say, I don't know. She had a private account, but mine is open so she could see

323

everything, and I'm pretty sure, at least after the fact, she contacted me from a fake account when I got her message on the site. But she had some details that made it seem like it was legit and she wanted to come up and see me and learn more. That was kind of a red flag for me, so I refused. It's one thing to want to connect families, but a whole other thing when people start pestering you about *things,* like necklaces. I made my account private after that."

"What . . . name did she use for the fake account?" I ask.

"Brooke Donovan."

Alice guffaws and puts her head in her hands.

"What? What did I say?" Rachel asks.

"Brooke Donovan was a girl who died last year in Castle Cove," I explain. "Alice's best friend."

"Oh god, I'm really sorry," Rachel says. "Well, whoever Mystery Girl is, she couldn't care less about finding family and linking histories. Just wanted to know about the Kennedys and the Levys and that necklace and did I have a certificate of authenticity for it and lord knows what else. I don't know. I didn't care for her, so I went private."

Alice suddenly stands up. "You know what? I am tired. I've been driving for what seems like a day and a half straight and I need to go to bed. This entire thing was a bust, Iris. Let's find a motel."

"You're welcome to stay here," Rachel says. "I have a spare room. It's not fancy or anything. Double bed. You probably shouldn't drive, anyway. Seeing as how the police are looking for both of you."

She smiles.

Alice's mouth drops open. "You . . ."

Rachel pulls her phone from her shirt pocket and wiggles it. "I love crime alerts, don't you?"

"Listen," I say desperately. "We did *not*—"

"Kill that old doctor," Alice finishes.

"I'm thinking that this is not where you'd stop on the lam from a murder, so I believe you," Rachel says evenly. "Why don't you pull your car around back to be on the safe side and I'll get you some towels and sheets."

Alice picks up her car keys and heads outside.

Rachel and I look at each other.

"Thank you," I say. "I know Alice doesn't think it helped, but it does. It's a sad and horrible story."

"No one would believe it," Rachel says. "I hope you can help your friends down in Castle Cove."

"Did you say you typed up what your mom told you?"

She shrugs. "I did. I originally wrote it all down. Yellow legal pads, and I had some typed up on my laptop, but I had a break-in a couple of days ago—I'm wondering if that was Mystery Girl making a little trip up here, maybe—and a lot of my papers and things were stolen. I think she was looking for that certificate or maybe even just information about the family and what happened? I can't be sure. And do I even care? I know what I know, but does it matter? It's a wild and sad story. That poor girl. Mona Moody. I've seen some of her movies."

"She deserved better," I say. "I think people *would* care." I reach into my backpack and pull a card out. "Take this."

I hand it to Rachel. "This person, they might want to hear the story you have to tell."

GROUP MESSAGE
IRIS ADAMS, ALICE OGILVIE, SPIKE FLICK,
NEIL CETAS, ZORA JOHNSON,
AND ANGELIK PATTERSON
FEBRUARY 20
11:47 A.M.

ZJ: Did you guys hear??

SF: Hear about what?

ZJ: KENNEDY

SF: No! Is she ok?

AP: Very much. According to my sources they have started bringing her out of her medically induced coma

NC: Oh that's very good news

ZJ: YES. Plus, now she can finally tell us who did it. Apparently she could be awake by tonight

ZJ: Unless of course Alice and Iris have figured it out? They're on that mission down south.

SF: Excuse me? I went over to her apartment and her mom said she was staying with you tonight.

ZJ: Oops. Shut up, Spike. You know nothing.

NC: Uh, Iris lied to her mom?

ZJ: You know nothing, Neil. NOTHING. DO YOU HEAR ME.

SF: I have a really bad feeling about this, Z.

CHAPTER FORTY-SEVEN

ALICE
FEBRUARY 20
12:02 P.M.

There is a proverb my grandmother used to repeat:
Old sins have long shadows.
—AGATHA CHRISTIE, *ELEPHANTS CAN REMEMBER*

WE CRASHED AT RACHEL'S for the night. She was kind enough to offer up her spare room after I had a meltdown at the thought of getting back in the car. I barely slept, tossing and turning thinking about the case, about Park going to jail if we don't figure this out, about the fact Iris and I are wanted in connection with Eugene's death.

Since leaving Whispering Pines two hours ago, Iris and I have barely spoken. I'm exhausted and frustrated—more than frustrated, really. This whole thing is a mess. We went to see Eugene, and then the next thing you know, he's dead and the cops want to talk to us. Sure, we got answers to our questions about Mona Moody, about that creepy room and her relationship with Reginald Kennedy/Clifford Hayes, but it didn't get us any closer to helping Park. Plus, who is this person who contacted Rachel through the Ancestry website and who visited Dr. Kennedy? I really wish Rachel had seen them in the flesh, because I'm not about to rely on the memory of an old, confused man who died shortly after we talked to him.

I sigh loudly.

Out of the corner of my eye, I see Iris look at me. Dark circles ring her eyes; she looks just about as tired as I feel.

"You okay?" she asks.

"No! This is just—" I grit my teeth. "It's like I'm having this dark night of the soul or something. Like everything I thought we were heading for just crashed down around us. I thought . . . I thought maybe we'd figure something out in Whispering Pines, that maybe we'd magically figure out a way to help Park up there, but instead, we're no closer to getting her off than we were when we left Castle Cove."

Iris nods. "Look, I've been thinking about it. Rachel put up the info on the Ancestry site, right? To try to right the wrongs of the past. Soon after, someone with an anonymous account contacts her on the website, asking questions about Mona Moody and the necklace and the Kennedys' connection to it all. Do you think . . ."

"What?" I steer the car onto the off-ramp of the freeway, following signs for the nearest gas station. I need to pee.

"Well, we're doing that project in bio, you know. The ancestry one. Do you think maybe they're related? Like maybe one of our classmates was doing their project, and *bam,* all of a sudden they realize they're related to freaking *Mona Moody,* of all people? It seems like quite a coincidence, doesn't it?"

"Good lord." I pull into the gas station parking lot and throw the car into park. "It does. But . . . who?"

She presses her lips together. "I'm not sure. The doctor said they looked like you."

I sigh heavily. "Yeah. But I don't know if we can trust him, do you? I'll be right back and we can discuss."

"Okay."

Without another word, I grab my phone and head into the gas station. I haven't had a chance to check it since leaving Rachel's, and I have a slew of unread messages from the Zoners group message.

My stomach seizes as I read through them in the bathroom. Iris's mom thought she was with *Zora* this weekend? What, now she has to lie to her mother about hanging out with me?

I guess I knew that her mom probably wouldn't be thrilled that we were taking off for LA in search of information, but it was easier for me to just not think about it.

If her mom finds out about this, she's going to hate me even more than she already does.

But clearly Iris doesn't care about that.

Walking back toward the car, I'm mad. Not only that Iris lied to her mom, but that she *had* to lie to her mom, that she had to lie to her mom specifically about me, that I'm that friend again, the one who parents think is trouble. It's too much, on top of everything else.

I climb into the car and slam the door behind me.

"What's up, Alice?" Iris says.

"Nothing," I say curtly, jabbing the ignition button. We're silent as I steer us back onto the freeway.

"What the hell?" she says, confusion climbing onto her face. "You were fine when you went to the bathroom. What's up?"

"Nothing."

We fall into silence.

After twenty minutes of me stewing, Iris finally speaks. "Alice, I'm way too tired for this. If you have something to say, could you just spit it out, please?"

I exhale hard. "*Fine.* I'll tell you. I know you lied to your mom about me."

"Lied about you?"

"Yeah. About where we were going. About hanging out with me."

"You think my mom would have been thrilled to learn I was leaving town to chase info on the same case that just landed me in jail?"

"Then why didn't you tell her that you were hanging out with me, at my house? Instead, you told her you were going to Zora's." The sign up ahead says *Castle Cove 10 miles,* and we cannot get there fast enough. I press my foot on the accelerator and we lurch forward.

She splutters. "Yeah, well . . ."

"Your mom doesn't want you hanging out with me anymore," I say flatly.

She's silent for a moment. "That's not—"

I interrupt her. "I know it's true, don't bother. She gave me a long lecture on why. And it made sense, really, what she said." I jerk the wheel to the left to pass a particularly slow car in front of us.

"You're being ridiculous. I lied to her because I . . . because she told me I had to stop doing all of this. I lied to her *for* you, for this case. For us. Sometimes it seems like you don't see anything or anyone around you unless they do exactly what you want them to do, how you want them to do it. Unless they fit your exact goals in the moment. Like with school. You're going to fail out if you're not careful—your parents came home to try to talk some sense into you and—"

"My parents? Are you defending my *parents*?" I feel like my heart has stopped beating. "You've got to be kidding me. You know how they are; they have no right to walk back into my life trying to tell me what to do. I can't believe you—"

"So, what? You're going to fail out just to annoy your parents? Talk about cutting off your nose to spite your face."

I make a face. "What the hell does that mean?"

She sighs. "Nothing. Forget it."

"No, I'm not going to forget it."

"It means that if you think failing out of school to be a detective is a smart thing to do, you are even more naive than I thought."

"Naive?" I bark a laugh. "*I'm* naive? I'm not the one who tried to turn down Mr. Park's money because of *pride.*" I spit the word out.

Iris is quiet for a second, then says slowly, "Did you just say *tried*?"

"What?" I exit the freeway, heading into Castle Cove proper.

"You just said I *tried* to turn down Mr. Park's money. I didn't *try* to turn it down, Alice; I *did* turn it down. Unless—"

God, I'm so over her high-and-mighty act. "Yeah, you tried to, but luckily I was there. I stepped in, as I *always* do, and fixed the problem. You need that money, Iris, you know you do, and when we solve the case, thirty thousand dollars is going to—"

"*Thirty thousand dollars?* Did you agree to take that man's money? He wouldn't even shake my hand."

"He told me that it's not you, it's your dad, and—" I cut myself off. As soon as the word *dad* comes out of my mouth, I know it's the wrong thing to say. Iris's face slams shut.

After a long moment, she speaks. "You know what? You can just drop me off here."

I look around. We're on the edge of downtown, still far enough from Iris's apartment that if she gets out here, she'll have a hike ahead of her.

"Here?"

"Yes, here. Pull over!" Iris yells, and something inside me snaps.

"Fine." I screech the car to a halt on the side of the road. "You want to walk home? Go for it."

"Great. I will." Iris grabs her bag out of the back seat and slams the door behind her.

She hauls the bag over her shoulder and starts walking. I hesitate for a split second, but clearly she doesn't want anything more to do with me. It's not like we're in the middle of nowhere; town is just up ahead, less than a half mile away. She'll be fine.

I pull the car back onto the road and drive away without looking back.

CHAPTER FORTY-EIGHT

IRIS

FEBRUARY 20

1 2:55 P.M.

Everyone needs a best girlfriend. If you don't have
someone to tell all your hopes and dreams to, then
do you really have anything?
—MONA MOODY, *MATCHED SET*, 1947

I WILL FORGIVE ALICE Ogilvie. *I will forgive Alice Ogilvie. She's having
a hard time right now. Grief. Brooke. Kennedy. Her parents. School. Me. I will
forgive Alice Ogilvie.*

I keep repeating this inside my head like some sort of medita-
tion as I stomp down the street, adjusting my backpack. Which
contains not only excerpts from a mind-blowing memoir but,
uh, a gun. I look around at my surroundings. It's going to take
forever to walk to my apartment.

I will forgive Alice Ogilvie. Even for the taking-money-from-
Park's-dad thing. I mean, I'm not her charity case, and I'm pretty
angry she'd lie about that, and no, I don't want his money, but
how could I not forgive her? We're friends. And partners. Like
Ricky Randall said to me, never leave your partner behind. But
it's more than that. Alice and I are joined at the hip now.

Maybe she's mad because we can't connect these cases. But at least we've solved *something*. I mean, I don't know what we can do with it, exactly. Helen Hahn is dead and her memoir is gone. Dr. Kennedy is dead and we're suspects. What, are they going to exhume Clifford Hayes's body to check for a bullet wound? And she was so busy being mad in the car, when we should have been discussing the fact that Person X is somehow related to Mona Moody and that's what caused all this, some sort of years-old unbridled revenge, right? But no . . . And—

Lilian. My heart sinks. Am I going to have to tell Lilian her father was a murderer?

My phone rings. It's Zora. But why would she call and not text?

I hit accept and say, "Hello?"

A pause. "I just want to say I'm really sorry, Iris. I tried, I really did. I told her you went to the store for chips, but she insisted on waiting and then my little sister—"

"*What* are you talking about, Zora?"

"Your mom. She came over with pizza earlier. To see how things were going. And . . ."

Oh. My. God.

My body floods with cold.

"She's—"

I hang up on Zora. My mother went over there. My mother knows. My mother knows and she didn't even text me. Or call me, angry, while I was in the car with Alice. That means things are going to be bad.

A little sound comes out of my throat that I don't like. A car zips past me, too fast. I flinch.

I suddenly feel very, very tired. Everything was for nothing. We aren't going to be able to help Helen Park. Or Rebecca Kennedy.

I bite my lip. I can't avoid it. I call my mom.

"You lied to me," she says. Her voice is even, clear.

"I'm sorry. I wanted to—"

"You lied to me. I don't know what's happening with you, Iris. I put my trust in you. What if something happened to you and Alice? Do you think this is a game and you can't get hurt? Zora was going on and on about a murder? That is not *safe*, Iris. There are people in the world who—"

"I'm sorry." It's all I can think to say.

"I won't be home until midnight. Clara is out sick. I'm very angry. I never wanted to be this angry at my daughter, or disappointed, but I am. Things are going to have to change. There's a dynamic between you and Alice that seems to—"

"She's my *friend*," I interrupt.

There's a pause. "We'll talk when I get home," she says calmly. "You aren't to go anywhere, do you hear me?"

She hangs up and I slide my phone into my coat pocket, my stomach tightening. I'm hungry and tired and mad and sad all at once. And I'm not home.

I keep walking. I wanted to help Helen Park, and Rebecca, but why, exactly? Would they help me if the situation were reversed? Probably not. But still: they were girls who were hurt. I'm not sorry for what Alice and I tried to do. You can't just write people off or throw them away, even if you don't like them as people.

My mind drifts to Remy Jackson, another thrown-away girl. Someone saw her that day. Someone *had* to. Was she pulled into a car? What happened then? How did she get into the dumpster?

Something happened between her walking on the sidewalk, turning in to the alley, and then being put in the dumpster. In the notes Raf and I cobbled together, four girls on the softball team saw her leave the field.

Is the real and most horrible truth that sometimes bad people just do bad things? Like Alex Schaefer? He could have taken his half of the necklace money, if that's what the necklace was stolen for, and bought his dad a place to live. But instead, he helped hurt a girl. And why do I seem to care so much about bad people who have nothing to do with me? Like Eugene Kennedy? Or Person X?

The Pinskys kept a secret for years and years because they were frightened someone would find out and they'd get in trouble. Someone is keeping a secret about Remy. *Someone* knows something. If anything, the Mona Moody case has taught me that's always true. I make a mental note to meet with Raf soon to talk.

Alice should be pleased: we found out what happened on the dock that night. *How* Mona Moody came to tumble off that balcony at the Castle. We discovered those answers. We found out the truth about what happened to at least *one* young woman. Shouldn't that matter?

Up ahead, the hospital's sign is neon red. My stomach grumbles. My cheeks are freezing in this wind and the sky is getting dark with coming rain. Maybe I can stop and get something from the vending machine. Maybe I can call Spike to come get me and give me a ride home.

Something prods my brain as I walk, thinking about that word: *home.* Mona had none. She had the orphanage, then the boardinghouse, then the Castle. She had no people, really, until Charles and Lilian and Leitha and Clifford and then . . . her baby.

I have my mom. And the Zoners. And Alice. That's a lot.

That's family. Helen Park has her dad, who would do anything for her, including hiring us. I don't want his money, but I do want to help Helen Park. We have to finish what we started.

I text Alice, though I know she won't answer. *We aren't done. When you're through being mad, let me know. We need to find Person X. The Other Alice. This case isn't over.*

I forgot my gloves and my fingers are getting numb. Maybe I'll call Spike and we can get a hot chocolate at Dotty's after he picks me up. Maybe tomorrow I should go to Seaside Skate and finally talk to Cole about what happened the night of the dance, why I was so frightened when he got angry. But how do you explain that? People are allowed to get angry, but am I always going to wonder if when they do, they'll hit me?

I feel very heavy all of a sudden. I'm never going to get past my father.

I'm going to lose Alice, and probably Spike, and Zora, and Neil, and here I am lying to my mother again. What is *wrong* with me?

Up ahead, Mercy General looms. Kennedy. She's supposed to be coming out of her coma soon, according to the group text message I didn't respond to, since Alice and I were fighting in her car.

Has anyone been to see her besides her family, and me that one time? I wonder what, if anything, she knows about her own family and the hand they played in so many people's lives. The history of the necklace she wore so proudly to the Sadie Hawkins dance.

I jerk to the right and head down the hospital driveway, walk into the bright downstairs lobby of the hospital. She's on the fourth floor. It's not a huge hospital, but it seems awfully quiet, even for a Monday afternoon.

When I come out of the elevator, it's pandemonium. Nurses and doctors and staff running in one direction down the hall and lights are flashing. Is it Kennedy? I run with the crowd.

But they pass right by her room and turn right at the end of the hallway. There's no pop-up security guard outside anymore. I push open the door slowly and quietly.

The lights are dim and I blink. There's a nurse standing by Kennedy's bed, her back to me, her blond hair loose. Shouldn't she have that pinned up or something? Seems a little unsanitary.

Something sparkles on the floor and I bend down and pick it up. It's jewel-encrusted and gaudy. It looks familiar.

Rayne's phone?

There's a muffled sound from the bathroom at the end of the room.

The nurse doesn't seem to notice, her shoulders hunched in concentration over Kennedy.

Just then I notice Kennedy's feet. Shaking. Like, her toes out of the blanket, curled and strained, trembling.

All the hairs on my neck prickle.

"Hey, what are you—"

The nurse turns around, a pillow clenched in one fist.

Only it's not a nurse.

"Iris Adams," she says in voice that sends a chill down my spine. "I should have known you'd show up."

CHAPTER FORTY-NINE

ALICE
FEBRUARY 20
1:06 P.M.

*One can never go back, that one should not ever try
to go back—that the essence of life is going forward.
Life is really a One Way Street.*
—AGATHA CHRISTIE, *AT BERTRAM'S HOTEL*

I'M IN THE KITCHEN making myself a snack when she finds me.

"Did you just get home, Alice?" She stands in the doorway, arms folded, watching me as I slice cheese. *A Caribbean Mystery,* the Miss Marple first edition my mom bought for me in Vancouver, is in front of me, and I quickly close it and shove it under a dish towel.

"Yes." I don't bother turning to meet her eyes. I'm too tired for this. Everything has been spinning in my head since I got home—the potential connection the case has to our stupid biology class, the look on the old doctor's face when he talked about his brother, Iris lying to her mom about me. I've been trying to clear my head so I can focus, so I can think about which of our classmates might have climbed to the top of the list of prime suspects, and my mother's presence is not helping.

"It's Monday. You have school tomorrow. Have you finished your homework?"

I'm murdering this block of cheese with my knife.

"Yes," I lie.

"Okay, good. You know how important school is, and that your father and I are concerned. I don't know if Brenda already told you, but I have to head out tomorrow morning. I have a meeting on set in Vancouver.

"You know"—she continues as I stab the wedge—"you're growing up with every privilege in the world, Alice, and it would behoove you to understand that shouldn't be taken for granted. Your grades at the end of this semester are important, not just for college but to show me and your father that you're trying. We discussed it, and certain privileges will be taken from you if you don't pull your GPA up to an acceptable level."

I drop the knife on the counter with a clatter. I am so sick of people telling me what I should do and how I should act and how I should feel. Everyone badgering me about school. I debate saying something to her, telling her off, but I'm too tired, and what's the point? It would be wasted breath, wasted words.

Instead, I grab my book and walk out of the room, leaving her and the cheese and the knife behind. I head up to my room for some peace and quiet, flopping down on my bed, but carefully, so I don't harm the book even though it's from my mother. It *is* a Christie, after all.

I'm toward the end, and the facedown body of the hotel manager's wife has just washed up on the beach of the Caribbean hotel where Miss Marple is staying. Everyone is predictably distraught, until Miss Marple notices something and they turn the body over.

I let out a small gasp. It wasn't the manager's wife at all—it was another woman, with hair just like hers.

I pause. They were mistaken for each other because of their hair.

An idea starts to crystalize in my mind. Maybe the old doctor wasn't so batty after all.

In the front hall, I pick up my keys and my bag and head for the door. I might be grasping at straws, to think that an Agatha Christie book might hold the key to this entire mess, but at least I'm doing something.

Even if I'm wrong, at least it will take my mind off the dissolution of my friendship with Iris Adams.

Ten minutes later, I'm knocking on a familiar door.

I turn my back to the house, watching dark clouds roll into town as I try to keep myself calm.

The door opens behind me. "Ashley?" a man's voice says.

I turn.

"Oh," Mr. Henderson says, pressing his hand against his heart. He's a tall, thin man with a long beaky nose—the same nose Henderson had up until last year, when she forced her parents to pay for a nose job. Her mom was totally on board, her mom has been the driving force behind Henderson's not-so-burgeoning acting career since we were little, but I wonder now what her dad thought about it all. The Hendersons have never had as much money as the rest of my friends, and nose jobs are expensive.

"Sorry, Alice. I thought you were—" He shakes his head. "Has anyone ever told you that you and Ashley could pass for twins from the back?"

My heart jumps. I hold up my bag and interrupt him. "I'm here to work on a school project. With Ashley?"

He frowns at me. "Did she know you were coming? She left about twenty minutes ago. She was going to go to the hospital to visit Rebecca, and then she and her mother are heading out of town for the night, down to LA. Again. Third time this month." He sounds tired.

"Oh." I think fast. I need to get into her room, to check out my theory. When in doubt, lie. "Do you know when she'll be back? Will she be in school tomorrow? We really need to get this project done and . . . she told me to come over. This afternoon."

"Ah, well, I'm sorry to disappoint," he says, starting to shut the door. I stick out my foot to block it.

"Can I just go up to her room for a minute? Take a peek at her work?"

He scratches his head. "I'm not sure . . ." He glances back into the small empty foyer, which tells me he might be close to breaking.

"*Please?* It'll only take a few minutes. I'll be out of here before you know it. It'll be our little secret." I bat my lashes at him and step into the house, forcing him to move back a little into the hall.

"I suppose. . . . I'm not sure if you can get into her computer, though; I think she has a passcode on it."

I wave my fingers in the air. "That's okay. I'll figure it out." Without waiting for a response, I push past him and head up the stairs to Henderson's room.

Her bedroom walls are covered with movie posters and black-and-white photos of Old Hollywood actors and actresses. Tacked above her desk is an image I recognize: Mona Moody and Charles W. Levy at the premiere of Mona's last movie.

And around Mona Moody's neck is a teardrop necklace. The same one Kennedy was wearing the night of the dance.

343

Ashley, with hair enough like mine to confuse her own father, who's always wanted to be an actress, who's always claimed it was in her *blood,* has *this* picture of Mona Moody prominently displayed in her room.

Her desk is clean. No laptop. Maybe she took it with her?

I stop in the center of the room, trying to gather my thoughts. If what I'm thinking is true, then Ashley Henderson is the person who visited Dr. Kennedy and was in touch with Rachel. The person who found out recently, through our stupid bio project, that she's related to Mona Moody.

I pull out the drawers of her desk. In one I find a few folders filled with old tests, but nothing more. I slam it shut, rummage in the next. School papers, tests marked with As, and then my fingers land on a smaller piece of paper. A receipt from a pawnshop up in the tiny mountain town of Matlock, a place I know from my five-day disappearance last year. It's not the sort of place you go to on vacation, or at all if you can help it. Why was Henderson there?

I read it over.

One minute later, I'm running down Henderson's steps and out the front door, ignoring her dad's questions, and head straight to my car.

CHAPTER FIFTY

IRIS
FEBRUARY 20
1:24 P.M.

I wouldn't touch that woman with a ten-foot pole.
She's pure evil and she delights in it.
—MONA MOODY, *THE LONELY LIFE,* 1947

ASHLEY HENDERSON IS STANDING in front of me wearing scrubs and clutching a pillow, her face eerily cold, and yet . . . serene.

On the bed behind her, Rebecca Kennedy's toes have gone slack. There's a whimper. She must be conscious? But no one is here to see. They're all somewhere else, where the commotion is.

Ashley stares at me, a smile creeping across her face. She takes a step in my direction and it's then that I can see Rebecca Kennedy's face, hair fanned across the pillow, her mouth struggling to form words, to breathe, her eyes blinking rapidly, filled with fear.

"Oh my god," I say. "You."

Ashley drops the pillow on the floor.

My brain is like a domino run, one tile falling into another, a series of clicks as facts get closer and closer to locking into place, but—

Surely, someone will come soon. From the bathroom, sounds

of scraping and hoarse screaming. Rayne? I could scream. I should scream. I will—

Ashley puts a finger to her lips. "Shhh. You're a smart girl, Iris. Aren't you? You don't want to get hurt, do you? I know how much you don't want to get hurt. We all know about your *dad*. Be a good girl, now."

Be a good girl. A crack widens in my brain, spilling out a long-ago memory, that first time he hurt me. Arm out of the socket. Pain flaring through my body. Whispering to me in the ER before the doctor came in. *Don't tell. You fell. Be a good girl.*

Here. Here in this very hospital. All the lies from then on piling up inside me.

"Iris." Ashley's face is sympathetic as she advances toward me, pulling something from the pocket of her scrubs. Rope? Zip ties?

Behind her, a whimper from Kennedy. *Please.*

With every ounce of speed and strength I can muster from my trembling body, I attack Ashley. Fistful of hair, knee to the groin. Her perfect nails dig down my face in a long and painful groove as she moans in pain. I grab hold of her neck in my hands, try to force her down, but she's strong, swearing, and cuts one of my legs from under me with her foot and I hit the ground with a smack, my head cracking against the floor, spots like stars in front of my eyes.

Ashley is scrambling next to me for something under the hospital bed. A bag. Rooting inside, desperate. I grab at her shirt, nauseous from the fall. Try to kick, but she kicks back and then I sink away, can't breathe, close my eyes, head throbbing.

I open my eyes, gasping for breath, because Ashley is sitting astride me, all her weight on my chest, a candelabra bottom-up in her hands above her head. A candelabra. A candelabra.

"I told you to be good," she mutters. "And you didn't listen."

CHAPTER FIFTY-ONE

ALICE
FEBRUARY 20
1:54 P.M.

> For in the long run, either through a lie,
> or through truth, people were bound
> to give themselves away. . . .
> —AGATHA CHRISTIE, *AFTER THE FUNERAL*

I SCREECH INTO THE parking lot of the hospital, earning me a very dirty look from an old woman in a giant boat of a car, who I realize on second glance is none other than Dotty, of Dotty's Doughnuts. I can only hope Henderson is still here, that she wasn't lying to her dad about where she was going. I can't let her leave town.

"Move it! This is an emergency!" I yell out my window at Dotty. She sticks up her middle finger, which seems uncalled for.

I'm about to give her a piece of my mind when something catches my eye across the lot, driving toward the exit. An obnoxious bright blue Nissan Cube, a car I'd recognize anywhere, because it's such a total eyesore.

Ashley Henderson.

And she's getting away.

I jam my car into reverse and lurch backward, turning to

make sure I don't mistakenly slam into Dotty's station wagon, because honestly, her coffee is really good and I don't want to be banned from the doughnut shop. She lays on her horn, shouting something at me that I don't quite catch but sounds like it contains some very choice words.

"I'm sorry!" I yell. I doubt she hears me, but no matter. I have more important things to deal with right now.

Once past her, I make a tight U and skid back onto Highway 1 without slowing. Up ahead is Henderson's monstrosity of a vehicle.

A billion questions skitter through the edges of my mind: *If Henderson was at the hospital, is Kennedy okay? If Henderson is Mona Moody's great-granddaughter, and Mona Moody had an affair with a Kennedy, are Henderson and Kennedy, like . . . related? Did Henderson steal that necklace off of Kennedy after trying to kill her? Did it all go down the night of the dance because Kennedy just had to wear that necklace to show off how rich she is to everyone? And did Henderson really have to choose* such an ugly color for her car?

I tail her from a distance, sending a silent prayer into the universe that she hasn't spotted me yet. Traffic is light right now; it's a holiday, so Castle Cove is sleepy, and there's nothing between the two of us but empty space.

I've always known Henderson was a scumbag. Brooke and I used to argue about inviting her places; Brooke, always too nice, would tell me I wasn't giving her enough of a chance. That underneath all her cattiness, the bragging she would do about stupid Hollywood events she wormed her way into, her obsession with being an actress, she had a decent heart.

Sorry, Brookie, wrong again.

After several long minutes, her left turn signal blinks on and her car slows. She's headed into the Yacht Club. Strange, considering that during the winter season, it's closed during the week.

I debate what to do as I approach the entrance in my car. The parking lot is empty apart from Henderson's car, so if I turn in there I risk scaring her away. Instead, I drive past it and pull over to the side of Highway 1. It's starting to rain.

As I sneak through the manicured shrubbery that edges the perimeter of the club, I pull my phone out of my back pocket. To hell with our fight: Iris needs to know what's going on.

At Yacht Club, I type. *IT'S HENDERSON!!!!! COME ASAP.*

I watch the screen for a beat, and then two, but there's no response. Fine. If Iris wants to stay mad, so be it. I shove my phone down into my back pocket.

I can handle this on my own.

CHAPTER FIFTY-TWO

IRIS
FEBRUARY 20
2:03 P.M.

Well, the pumpkin hit me square in the head and
knocked me out cold, and when I woke up, there he
was, smiling down at me, and gosh, I've never been
so grateful for a pumpkin in my life.
—MONA MOODY, *THE GIRLS IN 3B*, 1947

I'M IN A TUNNEL and I can't get out. I fight, kick out my arms and legs, but they go nowhere. I can't breathe. Someone is whispering my name. *Eye-ris. Eye-ris.* Cole? That's always so nice, the way he draws out my name: *Eeeeyyyris* . . . Maybe we can talk now.

Something wet over my face, my eyes. Am I in the water? Am I drowning? But how could that be? I was just with Ashley, in the hospital room.

Alice. Alice needs to know. She needs to know about Ashley. I try to move again, but I'm so heavy, and it's so dark.

I need help, we need help here, please. Eye-ris, can you hear me?

Cole. He came for me. He must have known something was happening, something was wrong. I wish I could get up, hold him, kiss him. I don't want to die before I get a chance to kiss someone.

There's a squeak of rubber on tile, many people running, and I can't see much yet. It's like a veil being lifted from my face, a very wet, dark veil, and the heavy is lifting off me. I can breathe.

Eye-ris, oh my god. I thought—

It's not Cole.

It's Spike, kneeling next to me, holding my hand, smoothing my wet forehead. Nurses and doctors crash around him, moving quickly to help Kennedy, who is hoarsely whispering, "Her, her, it was her. Ash. Ash."

The stern face of a nurse swings into my view. She jams something into my arm that pinches, wipes my head, squints, says very many things very quickly, and suddenly I hear tremendous shuffling and clacking and there are wheels next to me. The floor is a cold, cold place.

"Spike," I say, my words coming out in gasps of breath. "What—"

He shakes his head. "I don't know. It's loony tunes here right now. I came to see my grandma. Something happened to a bunch of patients and I thought I might say hi to Kennedy, you know? And here you were. Holy nutballs, Iris, what *happened?*"

I'm being lifted up, placed on a gurney. The nurse murmurs *CT, X-rays,* and *mother* to Spike.

"It's Ashley," I say, every word hurting. Sparks fly in front of my eyes. I lift a shaking hand and wipe them; my hands come back bloody. "She . . . tried to smother Kennedy. We fought. I tried to stop her. She hit me with the . . . Find the candelabra, Spike. It's gotta be the same as . . . when she hit Kennedy. In the Castle. Not Park. Ashley. She took it. It's here. It has to still be here, but—"

I look around wildly. Spike puts a hand on my shoulder.

"Where is she?" I'm panicking.

"She . . . I don't know," Spike says. "It was just you and Kennedy when I came in."

"Call her! Call Alice. Tell her it's Ashley. Please, Spike, I know she'll know what to do. Please, Spike, don't let her—"

"I'll call, I'll call. I will."

Just then a screech from the bathroom. "Can somebody please get me *the freak out* of here?"

The screeching hurts my ears. The bathroom door is jostled, then yanked open by a particularly burly-looking nurse.

Rayne appears in the doorway, hands zip-tied, a scrunched-up rag tied around her neck. She must have been gagged and finally worked it from her mouth. A nurse quickly cuts the ties.

"I'm going to kill her, literally. Like, with my bare freaking—"

"Hello, brat." Kennedy's voice is soft.

Rayne stops when she sees Kennedy. "Oh my god. Oh my god."

She runs to the bed, puts her head on her sister's shoulder. Kennedy pets her hair gently.

"Damn, Iris." Spike reaches out, touches my cheek. "Ashley messed you up good."

Right. Ashley's expensive manicure digging down my face.

His hands feel nice on my cheek. He brought me chocolate on Valentine's Day.

"I got in some good ones, Spike," I say. I'd smile, but it would probably hurt. I think I might have a loose tooth, too. "I clocked her a couple of times."

Spike's face breaks into a grin. "Noooiiiiice."

CHAPTER FIFTY-THREE

ALICE
FEBRUARY 20
2:06 P.M.

The past is the father of the present.
—AGATHA CHRISTIE,
HALLOWE'EN PARTY

THE CLUB IS DARK inside. As I approached the building, I saw Henderson slip through a side door, and I followed, watching that I didn't get too close to her. I'm not sure how she managed to get in so easily, but if I had to wager a guess, I'd say she stole a key from the Kennedys, who have full access.

At this point, I'd put nothing past her.

Up ahead I hear a crash, followed by a muttered string of curse words. From the sound of it, she's toward the back of the building, in the restaurant where Kennedy hosted her sixteenth birthday party last year. Henderson was there, of course, and Brooke, and Park.

It was one of the last times we were all together, those brief few weeks after Steve broke up with me but before he and Brooke started dating, when things had really started to crack between the five of us.

I run my fingers along the wall, feeling my way forward in the dark. The hallway is windowless, and I don't want to turn on my phone's flashlight in case it alerts Henderson. I need the element of surprise on my side.

My fingers run over the photos hanging on the walls, pictures of members present and past, generations of Kennedys. I'm trying to remember the story of the club, a story I was subjected to far too many times over the years by Rebecca Kennedy. The thing is, I always zoned her out. There's nothing more boring than someone who can't stop talking about their own importance.

What I do remember is, once Charles W. Levy went off to prison for embezzlement, Lilian left town and Kennedy's great-grandfather took over as the heir apparent. Now Kennedy's dad unofficially runs the club, along with everything else he has a hand in in this town. I shiver. What else have the Kennedys done over the years to the people of Castle Cove?

I reach the entryway to the restaurant, realizing a moment too late that it's much brighter than the hallway. The far wall is one long pane of glass, polished within an inch of its life so Yacht Club members aren't subjected to the horror of fingerprint smudges. Through it, I can see that the rain has picked up. Henderson stands by the windows with her back to me, gazing out toward the sea.

Crap. I stumble back toward the shadows of the hallway, but instead crash into the side of a doorway to the room.

Henderson whirls around.

"*Who's*— Oh. Alice Ogilvie." She sounds enormously displeased. "I should have known it was you. Who else would be annoying enough to follow me here?"

I'm going to have a major bruise on my side from that stupid wall, but I ignore it.

"I know it was you."

She snorts. "*What* was me?"

"The person who assaulted Kennedy. Who tried to freaking murder her!" I jab a finger in the air. "I bet you didn't think I'd figure it out by reading an Agatha Christie novel—"

Her eyebrow arches. "A what-Christie novel? Are you feeling okay, Alice?"

I ignore this. "And, Iris and I went to LA . . . and to Whispering Pines. I cannot believe you. Did you set up Park to go down for all this? What kind of friend are you, anyway?"

She lets out a loud bark of laughter. "What kind of friend am *I*? You're one to talk."

"What's that supposed to mean?"

"Please," she scoffs. "Everyone knows Brooke wouldn't have died that night if it hadn't been for you. Interfering at that party, driving a wedge between her and Steve so she took off, alone. Talk about being a *bad friend.*"

I grit my teeth. I will not let her get to me. "Is all of this because of Mona Moody? You're related to her, aren't you? You found out doing that dumb bio project. Being your partner actually turned out moderately useful, too, since I showed up at your house pretending that we needed to work on it and your dad mistook me for you—"

"My dad ruins everything," grumbles Henderson.

I ignore her. "Old man Kennedy mistook me for you over and over again when we were at his house, too. I thought he was just confused at first, but he wasn't, was he? Then there's the picture of Mona Moody taped up on your bedroom wall, the one where she's wearing that necklace that was stolen off of Rebecca the night of the dance. So, the baby Mona Moody had, the one with . . ."

"Clifford Hayes," Henderson finishes for me.

"Yeah, otherwise known as Reginald Kennedy. The baby Charles Levy made her give away to his employees. Who no one even knew existed for almost a century? That was your grandmother, wasn't it?"

Her face darkens. "Charles Levy was a horrible, horrid man. Yes, that was my mom's mom, Susan Miller. We knew she was adopted, but no one knew who her birth parents were. Charles Levy thought he could control everything, but I bet he didn't bet on ancestry research to become so popular and easy."

She scowls. "Yeah. Imagine my surprise when Mona Moody's birth name was listed as one of my ancestors. I really owe that Rachel woman one. It was about time *someone* finally righted the wrongs of the past."

I start slowly scooting forward, hoping she's too distracted by her story to notice my approach. I have to keep her talking.

"The part I don't get is, who the hell is Alex? You know he's in jail taking the fall, right? Why would he do that?"

Her eyebrow arches. "Alex? They already had enough evidence to put him away, no matter what he said. This way, at least the Kennedys will remember the face of the person who tried to kill their precious daughter. Alex hates that family—Kennedy's dad wants to develop the land his dad's motel is on, but his dad won't sell. It's getting ugly, with lawyers involved. I know you don't think about that stuff, sitting in your mansion on the coast, but there are real people living in this town—hardworking people—who don't deserve to lose their livelihood at the whim of some rich guy. We met in line at CC Subs and figured out pretty quickly that we had a common interest."

"So, you two broke into Levy's study to try to kill Kennedy and, I gather, to steal her necklace?"

She glares at me. I freeze, crossing my fingers she doesn't notice I'm now a whole table length closer to her than I was before.

"Yeah, and what of it? I was just taking back what's mine. If the Kennedys hadn't mucked things up all those years ago for me, it would have been in *my* family. It's worth a fortune, and I'm owed that, for what they did to my great-grandma.

"When Kennedy got up to that room, she started jabbering on about how she'd expected Helen Park to be up there, *blah blah blah*. You know how she is. She never shuts up. So, yeah. I slammed her over the head with that candle thingy. And then, well, Alex already had the letter opener ready, and he just . . . you know. Stabbed her. Kennedy is a bitch. I bet you would have stabbed her, too, given the right opportunity."

Henderson sniffs. She clearly planned to be gone by morning. Is she meeting someone here? If she is, I need to stall her.

"What about Park?" I ask loudly, drawing Henderson's attention back away from the window.

"Park?" She smiles. "How *is* she doing? I assume you've seen her recently?"

"She was going to go to jail for what you did, you know. I thought you two were friends."

"Oh, get off your high horse, Ogilvie. Park's the worst. Always whining to her daddy to solve all her problems. Did you know back in fifth grade, I was supposed to have the lead role in the production of *Our Town* we put on in theater class, but Park got all upset because she thought *she* should have gotten it, so her dad called the school and complained, and just like that, I lost the part?" Her face grows dark.

"She deserved to go down for this. Her embarrassing little fight with Kennedy earlier that night? It was the perfect motive. I couldn't pass up the opportunity to involve her, now, could I? Now, if you'll excuse me, Ogilvie, I must be on my way."

And with that, she turns and starts toward the far side of the room.

If she thinks I'm just going to let her leave, she has another thing coming. I dart forward, closing the last hundred yards between us, and leap onto her back.

"What the hell?" she screeches, arms flailing in a vain attempt to dislodge me. I clutch at her shoulders, wrapping my legs around her waist. I imagined as soon as I made contact, we would topple to the floor, and then I would subdue her and tie her up like I did with Ms. Westmacott last fall, but somehow she's still standing.

She flings her body to the side, throwing me off-balance. My grip loosens, and she plants an elbow into my ribs.

"Ow!" I drop off her to my knees, clutching my stomach with one hand. "That hurt! Why are you so strong?" I shrink back as she plants her foot on my chest.

"Because unlike *your* sad self, I know that being in peak physical condition is a requirement when entering into a life of crime." She presses her heel into me, hard, forcing me to the floor.

She glowers down at me, and I can't help but let out a snort. She's so ridiculous, always making these dramatic declarations, like she thinks her entire life is an audition for some crappy soap opera. Makes sense, considering she's wanted to be an actress for as long as I've known her.

Wait.

"Is that why?" I manage around the pressure mounting against my chest.

She tilts her head. "Is *what* why?"

I cough. "The reason you were so pissed when you learned that Mona Moody was really your great-grandmother. Is it because you think what happened all those years ago ruined your chances of being an actress?"

Her eyes narrow, and the pressure on my chest subsides. I take advantage of it, grabbing her ankle and twisting as hard as I can.

"Ow!" She wrenches back and I lose my grip, but she's backed off me enough that I'm able to struggle up onto my elbows.

"You've got to be kidding me. You think that if Mona Moody had kept her baby and your grandmother had grown up as Hollywood royalty, you would be famous?"

"I—" she splutters, taking a step backward, face red. "*Yes.* But I'm not wrong. Have you ever studied the entertainment industry? All those actors and actresses who only get parts because of who their parents are? It's incestuous. I've been telling my dad for years that he needs to step it up, try to produce or direct or do *something* interesting, but he claims he loves being a key grip. He has no desire to do anything else. Do you really think that if my mother had known her grandmother was a freaking film star, she would have ended up married to such a . . . such a loser? No! And then *I* would have had all the opportunities in the world. I would be on every billboard in LA! I would be—"

I have heard just about enough of this nonsense. "Did you

ever think that maybe what ruined your chances of acting profes-
sionally is that *you just aren't good at it?*" I reach out and grab her legs,
tugging at them as hard as I possibly can, and send her toppling
to the floor.

"You really tried to murder one of your oldest friends because
of your *acting* career? Of all the stupid things I've heard in my life,
I swear to god." I crawl over to her and plant myself on her chest.
"You are—"

Before I even know what's happening, Ashley has managed to
twist out from under me. She crawls to her feet and looms over
me, wearing a very nasty expression on her face.

"You are such a weakling," she says, before sending a hard
kick into my already sore side. "You think you're so smart, Alice
Ogilvie. You think you can learn how to play detective from a
bunch of old books? Please. Everyone knows books are over. No
one reads anymo—"

How *dare* she.

Ignoring the tearing pain in my midsection, I force myself
sideways and kick my legs out as hard as I can. I connect with her
shin, and she yelps in pain.

"Don't you dare be rude about Agatha Christie!" I yell up at
her. "I solved this case because of her!"

"Oh my god, Alice, get a life," she says, sighing. "Ever since
Steve broke up with you, you've gotten so weir— *Ow!*" I connect
with her shin again. She glares down at me.

"You just don't know when to quit, do you? I'll see you, Alice.
My ride is waiting."

She sends another hard kick into my stomach. Black dots explode into my field of vision and I squeeze my eyes shut against
the pain.

RR: Alice where are you? Are you ok?

RR: Iris is hurt. Are you at the Yacht Club?

RR: Are you ok?? Pls text back ASAP.

RR: I'm on my way.

CHAPTER FIFTY-FOUR

ALICE
FEBRUARY 20
2:29 P.M.

People with a grudge against the world
are always dangerous. They seem to think
life owes them something.
—AGATHA CHRISTIE, *A MURDER IS ANNOUNCED*

SEVERAL LONG MINUTES LATER, my head stops pounding enough
for me to crack open my eyes.

Ashley's gone. The room is quiet, like she was never even here.

I force myself to my feet and over to the wall of windows just
in time to see a figure with long blond hair running out of the
building toward the docks.

Ashley.

Dragging myself through the restaurant, I make my way into
the kitchen. There must be a door that leads out to the docks in
here.

I find it and fling my body against it, tumbling out into the
rainy afternoon.

Ashley's at the end of the dock, untying a rope that connects
a small boat to a nearby pile. She's getting away.

Where the hell is Iris?

"Stop!" I yell. At the sound of my voice, Ashley glances over her shoulder and then starts unwinding the line even faster.

Holding my throbbing stomach, I lurch forward as fast as I can make my aching body go, off the deck, down a small grassy hill, and out onto the long wooden dock.

"Stay back!" Ashley calls, holding an object up in the air. She waves it above her head, and I gasp.

"Is that a *gun*?" She really *has* lost it.

She glances up at it and then back to me. "No, dummy. It's a *flare* gun."

I take a slow step forward. "Um, like there's a difference?"

"Actually, there is a huge——" She cuts herself off. "Never mind, I don't have time for this. Just stay back, will you?"

She waves the gun at me again, and I freeze. She might claim there's a difference between it and a gun with bullets, but I personally have no desire to find out if that's true.

"Now, stay there."

She places the gun on the top of one of the wooden piles, and tugs the rest of the rope free of the boat. I take the opportunity to dart farther down the dock toward her. She notices me coming and grabs the gun, wiping away her wet hair from her eyes.

"I *said, stay back.* Are you trying to make me kill you?" Fury winds itself through her words, and I realize she'd actually do it. She'd shoot me.

"God, you and Kennedy, it's like you two don't know when to quit. You're both so similar in the worst ways; I have no idea how Brooke put up with you for so long." She steps into the boat. "Whatever. I'm done with this whole crappy little town and all you losers. I'm off to better things. I'll be seeing you, Ogilvie."

And with that, she revs the boat's small engine and starts puttering away.

Really slowly.

For all her talk about preparing for a life of crime, she clearly didn't consider that she might need a faster getaway vehicle.

I run down to the slip, but it's too late. She's off, heading toward the open ocean. Where the hell does she think she's going in that tiny boat? She's not even going to make it down to LA in that thing; it'll run out of gas long before she gets there.

I can't let her get away. I twist around, frantically looking for something I can follow her in.

My gaze lands on a little shed in the middle of the dock. Inside are extra keys to all the boats moored here, a fact I remember from summer breaks when we'd take Kennedy's dad's yacht out to sea.

I run over to it, tugging on the door, but it's locked. Luckily, I have my forensics kit. I rummage through my fanny pack, pull out my lockpick, and get to work. After a brief moment, the lock pops.

Inside the shed are sets of keys hanging from numbered hooks. From what I remember, each number corresponds to that boat's individual slip, so I grab a few and head back outside.

Ashley has all but disappeared. If I hope to have any chance of catching her, I have to hurry.

The first set of keys are to a tiny sailboat, which looks like it's made for a literal child. Thank you, but no. The second option is better, a small dinghy with a motor attached to its rear. I debate whether to check the third set but decide against it. There's no time.

I hop into the dinghy, revving the engine, and start maneuvering out from the dock's piles. The waves rock the boat precariously, but I manage to make it out in one piece. I'm about to press down the throttle when I hear my name.

"Alice! What the *hell* are you doing?"

I turn. Raf's standing on the dock's edge, frantically waving at me as he shields his face from the rain.

"Where are you going?" he yells.

"I have to follow Ashley!"

"Why are you in a boat?"

"I'm—Raf, I can't explain right now. I'll be back soon." With that, I press down the throttle, and the boat heaves forward.

Raf screams something else, but it's swallowed under the roar of the engine and the smack of waves against the sides of the boat. The wind whips my hair, twisting it up into the sky and then down into my face. I wipe it out of my eyes.

I'm heading in the direction where Henderson disappeared, but as the mainland fades out of sight, I begin to grow concerned.

Where the hell did she go?

For that matter, where *am* I?

A sick ache twists through my midsection.

What am I doing? Is everyone right about me? Iris, Kennedy, my parents? Am I totally incapable of being a real detective without Iris next to me, leading me in the right direction? Am I useless on my own?

Tears pinch at the corners of my eyes, and I wipe at them furiously. *Dammit, Alice, get yourself together. What would Agatha Christie do?* I ask myself, but the question doesn't focus me like it usually does.

I pull my phone out of my fanny pack. On the screen are

approximately one thousand notifications, texts, and missed calls. Whoops. I'm about to send Raf an SOS when something catches my attention.

A flash of white a few hundred yards up ahead.

I shove the phone back into my pocket and set my jaw. That's her. It must be.

The smudge grows larger, sharpens, forming a boat. A yacht, really. And it's *nice.* The kind celebs rent out when they vacation off the coast of the Mediterranean.

My heart sinks. It's not Ashley. She's gone—

Wait.

Off to the left, I see it: Henderson's small dinghy, now floating loose in the water. Then: Henderson climbing up the metal ladder of the yacht, a flash of blond hair as someone on the deck bends down to help her up the rest of the way.

I squint, trying to make the person out from this distance.

Good lord, is that Mrs. Henderson? Are she and Ashley running away together? Leaving poor Mr. Henderson and his key-grip work behind?

Ashley *did* say her mom would never have married him had she known who her grandmother was. They must have used the money from the pawned necklace to buy that yacht and plan their escape.

I idle my boat, scrambling to figure out what to do next. There's no way I can chase down that giant yacht, not in this crappy little dinghy. A crack of thunder overhead sounds its agreement.

Mrs. Henderson falls back out of sight, but Henderson turns and grips the boat's guardrail, catching sight of me watching her from a distance in my little boat.

Even from a distance, I can see her grin.

"Too late, Ogilvie!" she calls out. She raises a hand over her head, waving once, and then, I swear to god, she gives me the finger.

With that, she turns and disappears inside.

A moment later, the yacht roars to life and starts moving, my tiny boat bobbing in its wake.

I yank my engine back on, making a wide U to try to get out of the waves, and realize that I'm not alone.

There's a boat approaching fast, a speedboat, with a very, very irritated-looking boy behind the wheel. It pulls up a few hundred yards away from me and its engine cuts off.

Raf.

And he does not look happy.

"Alice Ogilvie," he calls across the expanse of sea between us. "I swear to god you are going to be the death of me."

CHAPTER FIFTY-FIVE

IRIS

FEBRUARY 20

6:45 P.M.

*Well, we've done it, Hodges! We cracked the case. We
figured out who did it, when, and why. Now what?*

MONA MOODY,

THE HOUSE AT THE END OF THE STREET, 1946

I'M NOT IN PAIN anymore. In fact, everything is completely fine.
I'm floating around in some weird and wonderful haze of drugs as
a very handsome doctor is carefully stitching up my face.

"You'll probably want to think about some reconstruction at
some point," he murmurs. "This is a bad one. A girl doesn't want
to move through life with a scar like this, that's for sure."

I'm so pleasantly high that I can't even think of a snappy retort to that obviously sexist remark.

"Where's my mother? And my friend?" I can't quite remember what happened to Spike. And I briefly remember my mother
arriving and hovering over me, her face crinkled with fear. Good
god, these drugs are *insane.*

"Your mom went to get coffee and your friend is outside with
the police. They want to talk to you. You're a popular girl. It's

not every day we get real-life crime-solvers in here. Or, at least, crime-*stoppers,* anyway."

Spike. But where is Alice?

I hear the tiny snip-snipping of sutures. "Mmm-hmm," says the doctor. "As soon as I'm done, the police want to talk to you. I can hold them off, but frankly, I'd like to know what the hell happened here, too. We had four patients go into seizures almost simultaneously, and one almost smothered with a pillow, if I'm to believe your skinny friend outside. And then there's you, in a knock-down, drag-out with a girl pretending to be a nurse. Who *are* you, anyway?"

"Nobody," I say softly. "I'm no one."

"Oh, I think you should give yourself more credit than that, Iris Adams." The singsong voice is strangely familiar.

Oh god, Tessa Hopkins. Standing next to my hospital bed in a velour tracksuit, holding a cup of coffee, her television makeup exquisite, as always.

"Hello, friend," she says cheerily. "I got a call earlier from a very interesting young woman who lives in the woods, claiming to have some sort of unfinished memoir? She had some *very* fascinating stories to tell about Charles Levy and Mona Moody and murder. We're meeting soon to talk. I . . . have a feeling that what she has to say might be connected to what happened here tonight? Care to enlighten me beforehand? I'm going to do a little spot on it tomorrow after I chat with her."

My heart sinks. "No, no, Tessa. Please don't. You can't. Not yet. I have to talk to Lil——"

I stop. Tessa's face lights up.

"Lilian Levy? I left her a message. I wonder what she knows

about her father being a murderer and baby stealer? She must have a lot of thoughts about that."

My heart sinks. Lilian can't find out this way. It will break her. I need to tell her everything first, before it's splattered all over the news.

Tessa's phone beeps. She looks at it, frowning, and then to me.

"You wouldn't happen to know anything about a stolen boat down at the Yacht Club, would you, Iris? Looks like your friend Alice Ogilvie is in a spot of trouble."

Yacht Club? Alice? A stolen boat?

Snip, snip, on my face.

The door to the hospital room opens again. From behind Tessa and the doctor emerge my mom and Ricky Randall. Ricky grimaces when she sees Tessa.

"I think you can go now, Tessa," she says firmly. "Iris needs to rest."

Tessa shrugs. "Suit yourself. Hey, Ricky, you got any info on that perp who busted into Dotty's and stole all the jelly doughnuts? I need some filler for tomorrow's six o'clock."

"Ah! Sweet Tooth is my favorite client, but do your own legwork, sister. *Out.*"

Tessa pats my hand and I move it away. "Talk soon, Iris?" she says, but she's not expecting an answer. She flashes me a smile and then slips out of the room as Mom sits in the chair by the bed.

"I don't know what I'm going to do with you, Iris," she says, touching my matted hair. "I was worried something like this would happen."

Her eyes are filled with sadness.

"I'm sorry," I say softly. "But we had to know. I had to . . ."

Ricky leans down close to me, peering at the stitches on my face.

"I like it," she says softly. "That doctor does good work, but you're still going to have a scar here. It'll add some mystery to you."

"*Where* is Alice?" I say, exhausted. "What's happening with Ashley Henderson? It wasn't Park. It was Henderson. The candelabra—"

Ricky makes a *tut-tut* sound. "Spike gave it to the cops. They've reviewed security-camera footage already and, whoo, girl, that Ashley is some piece of work. You know she tried to off four people at once just to create a diversion? Impressive. Last thing they caught was her hightailing it out of the parking lot with what I *think* was Alice's car hot on her heels."

"Tessa said Alice stole a boat at the Yacht Club," I say. "It was Ashley all along. With Alex. She was Person X. There was a baby, an old man in LA, and Lilian's dad shot someone, and Mona was pushed—"

"Hush," my mother says. "You're rambling. You're tired and hurt. What is all this? This sounds *crazy*. A baby? A shooting? You need rest, and quiet."

"I don't need rest, and I don't need quiet. I *need* Alice." I push my mother's hands away from my hair and try to sit up, but a flare of pain punches through the drugs and leaves me gasping.

"Yeah," Ricky says, nodding. "That'd be your broken rib. You might want to sit this one out, Iris. You've done your twelve rounds."

I flop back onto the pillow and close my eyes.

When I open them, Spike is there, a hot chocolate in his hand. He holds it out to me.

CHAPTER FIFTY-SIX

ALICE
FEBRUARY 20
9:23 P.M.

Ah! Madame, I reserve the explanations
for the last chapter.
—AGATHA CHRISTIE, *EVIL UNDER THE SUN*

"I CANNOT BELIEVE I'M being subjected to this nonsense *again*," I tell Thompson, who's sitting across the table from me wearing a stained white button-up. A smug smile plays on his lips. Mounted high in the corner of the room is a camera, recording our conversation.

After Raf led me to land, we were met by a cadre of officers. Apparently, Raf had called them on his way to the club.

To my great dismay, they included Thompson, who immediately shoved me into the back of his sedan and drove me down to the station. They put me in an interrogation room with uncomfortable metal chairs, gave me a cup of steaming hot water, a bag of crappy tea, and then left me here to rot for two hours.

And, to make matters worse, they took my phone.

It's incredibly rude: I solved their case for them—again—and they have the audacity to hold me here because I borrowed a boat? It wasn't even a nice boat, for god's sake.

"Alice, you're here because you stole Dan Gerber's boat and took it for a joyride," Thompson says. "He called it in to the department after getting an alert from his security company that—"

I've heard enough. "Good lord. I was chasing after—"

He holds up a hand, stopping me. "Please let me finish. As you know, when Dan—er, Mr. Gerber—called, we were already on our way to the Yacht Club because Rafael Ramirez had called to let us know what was going down there. We'd been to Mercy General Hospital, and according to hospital security footage, Ms. Henderson tampered with several patients' medication in what appears to be a distraction technique so she could get to Rebecca Kennedy without notice. Unfortunately for Ms. Henderson, Iris Adams walked in before she could finish the job, and she attacked Ms. Adams instead—"

"Iris was attacked?" I push back from the table. "Why is this the first I'm hearing about it? Where is she?"

"Please sit down, Ms. Ogilvie." He gestures to my chair, and after a long moment, I comply. "Your friend is okay. She's at the hospital, being monitored, but from what I understand, her condition is stable.

"When we arrived at the scene"—Thompson consults his notebook—"Spike Flick handed over a candelabra, which I gather was the weapon used in the Kennedy assault. It is with forensics now, and I think we'll be able to connect it to both Ms. Kennedy and Ms. Henderson without much issue."

"Wait. Wait, back up," I say, struggling to take in all this info.

"You found the candelabra? Why did Spike have it?" Apparently I missed a few things while at sea.

"Mr. . . . er, Spike, was visiting a relative when he heard the commotion down the hall. He walked into Ms. Kennedy's room and found Ms. Adams unconscious and the candelabra beside her. We think Ms. Henderson left it when she ran.

"We are thankful," he continues, without actually sounding thankful at all, "you and your friend Iris Adams were able to . . . help us figure out." A pained expression flickers across his face. "That Ms. Henderson had . . . a hand in what happened to Rebecca Kennedy.

"But this leads me to my last point. It's becoming apparent to me that, between the Brooke Donovan case and this one, you two think you're some sort of crime-solving duo, but I hope Iris's injury serves as a reminder to you both that you are not, in fact, detectives. You are teenagers, inexperienced teenagers, and you need to leave the investigative work to the professionals. You—"

"You have to be kidding me." I interrupt, leaning back in my chair. "We just solved another case for you people, and all you can say is don't do it again? I know it must be embarrassing for you, being shown up by teenagers. Girls, at that," I add. "But it's not our fault that you suck at your jobs. Hercule Poirot would be ashamed that you call yourselves detectives."

"Hercule—" He shakes his head. "I'll remind you that you are speaking to an officer of the law right now, Ms. Ogilvie. I ask that you watch your tone."

There's a knock on the door, and Thompson stands. "Excuse me."

He walks over and opens the door, conversing with the person on the other side quietly before turning back to me.

"It appears your ride is here," he says without trying to disguise his displeasure. "But, before I can let you go, I do need a rundown of what happened at the Yacht Club tonight."

Ah. Finally. My ride can wait.

"Well," I start, folding my arms across my chest, "to tell you that, I'll have to start at the beginning. . . ."

Forty-five minutes and one very irritated Thompson later, I leave the interrogation room. I suppose I didn't *really* have to give him the minute-by-minute replay of how Iris and I solved this case, but he deserved to hear it, particularly after his little speech about us being *inexperienced teenagers*.

An officer leads me to the front of the station, where I'm met by another cop, who hands me a small bag of my personal items, including my phone. I take it out immediately. I have to make sure Iris is okay.

I'm so engrossed by my screen that I don't notice the person waiting in the lobby of the station until I'm almost upon them.

"Alice," she says. It's not Brenda or Raf.

"Hi, Mom," I reply.

We head out to the car in silence, me typing furiously on my phone, my mom just plain furious.

What happened to you?? I text Iris, who responds in seconds.

Youre ok. Thank god

I'm okay but are YOU okay??

Yes. Well, I mean, I got hit over the head and apparently I'm going to have a scar, but I'm told it'll give me character.

> I cannot believe Ashley did all of this

Including poisoning a bunch of people at the
hospital!!! Shes nuts

> No kidding

Im glad youre ok

> I'm glad YOU are ok

I should be out of the hospital soon. ill call
you when I am

"Alice," my mom says as we reach the car. "We need to talk."

I think briefly about turning and running down the street away from her instead of getting into the car, but honestly, I'm not sure how far I'd get. My legs are tired. I swear to god, I'm going to start working out immediately. Ashley might be nuts, but she was probably right that if I plan to continue a life as a detective, I need to work on my cardiovascular strength.

"What now?" I say as I climb into the passenger seat of my mom's Mercedes.

She gets in the car, but doesn't turn it on, instead wrapping her hands around the steering wheel. She stares out the front windshield, quiet. It's unsettling. I'm used to being lectured by my parents, but this silence thing is new.

"Um, hello?" I say.

She shakes her head and drops her hands to her lap. "I canceled my trip. Ever since Brooke's death, you've been struggling, and your father and I agree that it's best if one of us is here for the time being."

I suck on my teeth. "You don't have to cancel your trip. I'm fine. I've *been* fine. Brenda is here."

"I just picked you up from the police station."

"Yes, thank you, I realize that," I say, crossing my arms tight against my chest.

She sighs. "And you don't see that as a problem? You ignore your schoolwork, your grades are . . . well, let's just be honest. They're terrible. We thought your tutor last semester would help, but I've come to learn all she's been *helping* you with is committing misdemeanors. I know you think you're going to be young forever, Alice, but trust me that it doesn't last for as long as you think it does. You have to think about your future and—"

"Did you ever think that maybe this *is* my future?" I explode. "I'm so tired of everyone acting like I'm some dumb girl just trying to stir up trouble. I'm *good* at this stuff. I like it. I like reading Agatha Christie, thinking about her plots, the twists and motives, how they might apply to real life. Remember when we went to Egypt? But you worked the whole time and I basically hung out in the hotel?"

She has the decency to wince. "I know you like Christie, Alice, but—"

"Can I please finish?" I say it quietly, without venom, and she nods. "Well, I read the full collection from the hotel library. Then, last year, after . . . after Brooke died," I force myself to say it, finally. "I didn't think Steve had done it. I was *sure* he hadn't, and I thought if the cops won't listen to us because they think we're just dumb teenagers, well, we might as well take matters into our own hands. Miss Marple does it all the time. And no one ever gave her credit, either. But she still solved crimes, just like Iris and me." I look at her. "You do realize, this is the *second* one we've solved in less than six months?"

She furrows her brow. "That might be so, but—"

"What about all the young actresses you work with, who

figured out early what they wanted to do with their lives? Would you tell *them* to go to class? Doubt it."

"Alice, being an actress isn't as dangerous as—"

I scoff. "Being a child actor is plenty dangerous, *Mom,* and you know it."

She purses her lips. "Well, those kids also have on-set tutors. It's not like they just drop out of school."

"Well, get me another tutor, then!"

She shakes her head. "That's not going to happen."

"That's—" I start, but she interrupts.

"Give me a minute to think, okay? Before you start attacking me." She falls quiet for a long moment before clearing her throat.

"I don't know if you realize this, but I grew up reading Agatha Christie, too. I love her books. So, I get it. And it's becoming clear that the police department in this town needs a serious overhaul. But that doesn't mean I think you and your friends should be tromping all over, getting yourselves hurt . . . or worse. I can't condone that."

"Mom—"

"But, you've found a passion for something, and I don't want to drive you away from it. You're right, I wouldn't do that with one of the actresses I work with, so I shouldn't do it to my own daughter. That said, school is important."

I start to protest, but she continues. "Let me finish, please. School *is* important, no matter what you might think right now, Alice. You have a long life ahead of you, and college needs to be part of that. I would bet money on the fact that your Hercule Poirot would agree with me. You have a talent for this, so think bigger. Think of what you could accomplish if you start taking school more seriously. Someday, you might even have a career in the FBI."

The hair on the back of my neck stands up. "The FBI?" It's something I've never considered, but it sounds *amazing*.

"Absolutely, but you need schooling." She types something on her phone and hands it to me. "Read this. FBI agents need bachelor's degrees. It's helpful for them to know at least two languages. These are all things you can do, Alice, but you need to focus. You're seventeen, you're still a child. Think long-term."

I read the screen over and over again, my excitement building. The FBI. It sounds amazing. After a long moment, I say, "You're right."

Her eyebrows jump. "I don't think I've ever heard you say that before."

"Don't get used to it," I say, but I smile so she knows I'm mostly kidding. "But, Mom, if I'm going to do this . . ." I swallow, trying to keep the quiver of hope out of my voice. This is the best conversation my mom and I have had in years, but still. I can't believe I'm about to say this. "I need something from you." I wipe my suddenly sweaty palms against my pant legs.

"What's that?"

"Could you . . . maybe try to work from home a little more often? I love Brenda, but . . ." I trail off. I steel myself against what I'm sure will be a dismissive response, but she's quiet.

I'm about to take it back, to tell her I was just kidding, that I don't care, when she finally speaks.

"Yes, Alice. I think I can do that. By the way, this came for you." She leans over to her purse, which is resting on the floor by my feet, and pulls out a thick manila envelope with the words *Park Industries* embossed on its front.

She raises a brow. "What exactly is that, Alice? I didn't look inside, because I respect your privacy, but I need to tell you, Mr. Park is . . . not a man you want to do business with."

I flush, remembering the fight I had with Iris. "I know. I thought . . . I thought I was doing something good for a friend by making a deal with Mr. Park, but I think it was maybe the wrong thing to do?"

She considers me for a long moment. "I'm proud of you, Alice. And, if you'd like, we can drop that back off at the Parks' residence on our way home?"

"Okay," I say, biting the inside of my cheeks to stop the tears that have sprung into the edges of my eyes. "That sounds good."

She squeezes my hand and then starts the car. She's about to pull out of the space when she pauses and looks over at me.

"And, Alice? Before I forget: Did we somehow acquire a cat?"

KWB, CHANNEL 10

Breaking News

February 21

11:02 a.m.

Tessa Hopkins: This is Tessa Hopkins, reporting
live from the Castle Cove Police Department, where
Detective Mark Thompson is scheduled to give an
update on the Rebecca Kennedy assault at Levy Castle.
If you've been following along, Kennedy was the
young woman attacked at the Castle just last week.
She's been in a medically induced coma and regained
consciousness last night. Alex Schaefer, a local
youth, was arrested and confessed to the attack and
has been charged with attempted murder. He, in turn,
implicated another teen, Helen Park. But in a series
of twists that are sure to rock Castle Cove, the
story has taken yet *another* turn. Could this case
be related to not one but *two* deaths that occurred
years ago in our quaint town? Stay tuned. Detective
Thompson is beginning the press conference now.

Detective Mark Thompson: Good morning. Late last
night, after new evidence was discovered concerning
the assault at Levy Castle, all charges against
Helen Park were dropped. We are currently seeking

information about the whereabouts of seventeen-year-old Ashley Henderson, a citizen of Castle Cove, in relation to the assault at Levy Castle. Ms. Henderson was last seen on a yacht, leaving from the Castle Cove Yacht Club. It's believed that she's being aided by her mother, Jennifer Henderson. Any information as to their whereabouts should be relayed directly to us. Based on the evidence we have so far, Ms. Henderson has not only been implicated in the attempted murder of Rebecca Kennedy but also in four poisonings at Mercy General last night, and another brutal attack at that same hospital. Ms. Henderson and her mother should be considered armed and dangerous. They are now the subject of an international manhunt.

Ashley Henderson's alleged accomplice in the Castle attack, Alex Schaefer, remains in jail awaiting trial. While I can't comment on specifics concerning the case at this time, please rest assured that we are doing all we can. This case is extremely complicated and may be connected to two deaths that occurred in our fair city in 1949. Please, hold your questions until the press conference is over. I'd like to thank my detectives and police force for the tremendous amount of care and work they put into this case. A vicious crime was committed against a young girl, and that should never be allowed to stand. Please respect her privacy at this time, and again, if you have any information on Ashley Henderson or Jennifer Henderson's whereabouts, contact us or the FBI.

Reporter: Is it true that the assault is connected to the Clifford Hayes drowning in 1949 at the Yacht Club?

Detective Mark Thompson: I have limited details at the moment on that issue. That's a long time ago, buddy, you know?

Reporter: Did you consider Ashley Henderson a suspect at the start of the investigation? Was she ever questioned? How does her mother play a role?

Detective Mark Thompson: All guests of the party at the Castle on the night of the attack were—

Tessa Hopkins: There are rumors that Ashley Henderson is a descendant of Mona Moody and Clifford Hayes. What can you tell us about that connection, Detective Thompson, and did it play a role in the Rebecca Kennedy assault? Was Ashley Henderson's mother involved all along?

Detective Mark Thompson: Again, this is a very complicated case and I can't give specifics. We're talking about things that happened long ago—

Tessa Hopkins: Were death certificates falsified in the Mona Moody and Clifford Hayes deaths? Will you exhume Clifford Hayes's body? Was Mona's fall from the Levy Castle balcony really accidental? I have sources—

Detective Mark Thompson: Ma'am, with all due respect, let's not turn this conference into a circus, just for the moment, all right?

Tessa Hopkins: Have you spoken to Robert Kennedy about his family's possible role in those deaths? Will he give a statement?

Reporter: There are several posts on social media accounts claiming this case was cracked by two teens in Castle Cove, and not the police department. Can you—

Detective Mark Thompson: Everyone is a citizen detective these days, aren't they? But I'd like to remind John Q. Public that these things are real, and they are dangerous, and to stick your nose where it doesn't belong can get you very seriously injured.

Tessa Hopkins: How will the fact that members of the public had to take a hand in this case affect the ongoing investigation into practices at the police depart—

Detective Mark Thompson: Thank you. That's all we have time for today.

EPILOGUE

IRIS
FEBRUARY 22
5:30 P.M.

Does anything really ever end?
Sometimes it feels like the past is a
fast horse I'll never be able to outrun.
—MONA MOODY, *THE LONELY LIFE,* 1947

SEASIDE SKATE IS A familiar and soothing aroma of popcorn, nachos, too-sugary fountain soda, and sweat. Even though it hurts when I bend to tie my laces because of my still-healing rib, I'm glad to be here. Next to me, Alice is begrudgingly lacing her skates.

"I do not like this," she mutters.

"You never do."

"You'd think Thompson would thank us," she says.

I shrug. "He never will. But do we need it? We know what we did."

Zora, Angelik, and Neil flop down on benches across from us and start putting on their skates.

"I still don't get the Alex thing, though," Neil says. "So, he was in on it with Ashley?"

"They discovered they had a common interest: Rebecca

Kennedy's family had screwed them both, so why not team up?" Alice says.

"But he's in jail and she's off . . . somewhere," Zora points out. "Why did they even frame Park?"

"She was convenient," I say. "But I truly think Alex did not care whether he went to jail or not. He just wanted to hurt Rebecca because her family was hurting his. Also, it might just be in his nature, if you'll recall how, uh, scary he was when we saw him at The Waves."

I finish tying my skates. "The Kennedys won, anyway. It seems like they always do, somehow."

It was in the papers. Alex's dad finally sold The Waves. A strange fire destroyed three units. Legal fees. Too much pressure. Alex in jail. Now what was once a home for people who really needed it will be gone, and people who don't will someday sip champagne while cucumbers are placed on their eyes, the sea rippling not far from them, and they won't know a thing about the lives that used to be lived there.

"People do strange things for love or revenge, that's for sure," Neil says. "Not that I would know, personally. But I watch television, and that seems to be the case."

"Children." It's Ricky Randall, slouching over to us with a cup of beer in her hand. "Ashley totally played him. Tale as old as time. Seduce a guy, he'll do anything for you, like help you root around in a castle looking for clues and stealing a necklace and then, you know, helping you clock somebody into a coma. Maybe he'll even take the fall for it if you promise that when he gets out, you're all his."

"I don't like it," Alice says bitterly. "I don't like that Ashley

Henderson *got away*. And with her mother. I never did trust that woman."

"Sometimes the bad guys get away. That's the name of the game," Ricky murmurs.

Zora sighs. "So, the note was for Kennedy or Park?"

I scoop my hair behind my ear. "Alex wrote it so it looked like it was from Park to get Kennedy up to the study so they could steal the necklace. He cozied up to Park and got her all hot and bothered and told her to meet him upstairs in the study. So that when all was said and done, it would look like it was Park all along. But one, Alex's handwriting is obviously not Park's, once you figure the strange *e*'s. And two, Alex addressed the note to 'R' and signed it 'H,' which——"

"Ah," Zora says. "The Mains and their irritating habit of using last names. Good way to frame Helen, but you'd think Ashley would have looked at the note beforehand to make sure it was to 'K' and from 'P.' And did Rebecca not notice that, either?"

"Well," I answer. "She has some memory loss from the assault. She says she doesn't remember much after the fight with Park in the ballroom, and honestly? Even if the note had raised an alarm bell, I think she still would have gone upstairs to find out what was what. And sadly, I'm not sure that if and when she can remember anything, she'll speak up. We've basically tainted her family for life."

"Doesn't matter," Ricky says. "They'll always be fine. The kind of money they have? Her life is one big bouquet of roses."

"Okay," Zora says. "Because I'm kind of a doofus, let me get this straight: Ashley Henderson found some information while doing McAllister's genealogy project that made her think she was related to Mona Moody? And went sniffing around looking for information about that, and stumbled upon the baby-who-was-given-away and then kind of went batty? And her mom is her getaway wingman?"

Alice nods. "Basically, yes."

I'm watching Spike roll around the rink by himself, hands in his pockets. He's such a smooth skater.

"Well," I say, "the Mona Moody and Clifford Hayes thing? We did solve *that*. And Park is free, although everyone will probably always wonder if she's truly innocent."

"Have you . . . heard from Lilian?" Alice asks gently.

I wince. I've texted Lilian and left voice mails, but she hasn't answered. Tessa Hopkins aired the first in a series of sit-downs with Rachel yesterday. Bits of it went national, and I know Lilian heard about them or saw them. Pieces are popping up in newspapers about her dad's actions on the Yacht Club dock. I gave Thompson the pistol, but what fingerprints are left? Raf says they might exhume Clifford Hayes's body to see if the bullet wound matches a bullet that would have been used in the pistol. And while Alice and I are convinced Ashley is responsible for murdering Eugene Kennedy, I have no idea if the cops think so, too.

"No," I say. "I don't know what to do about that, either. That's kind of a tremendous blow, finding out your dad is a murderer."

"She's a big girl," Ricky says. "She's not an innocent. She can handle it. This is what happens when you start messing around with history. The bones begin to rattle."

I stand up, and Alice, Neil, and Zora follow suit.

"You coming, Ricky?" I ask.

"God, no," she says. "I don't drink and roll. That's dangerous."

She gets up and heads over to the arcade, and everyone else starts skating out to the rink. My phone vibrates in my pocket. Raf.

> **Sorry I can't be there. Studying for a test. Tell everyone I say hello.**
> Cool.
> **How are you feeling?**

Good, I text, although that's not altogether true. The wound on my face itches, and sometimes if I stand up too quickly, I get dizzy. And ah, yes, the broken rib. And the fact that Cole Fielding won't look at me every time I glance over at the skate counter. I guess that's what I get for blowing him off one too many times. I do wonder, though, about what Ricky told me when I was in the interrogation room at the jail; that little bit about steering clear of Cole because of his family. It's the same thing Mr. Park thinks about me. But we're not responsible for where we came from, right? It's not our choice. Isn't that what the whole ancestry project taught us?

I look down. Raf is on a tear, texting up a storm.

> **Excellent. Because I have some new leads on Remy. I think we've got some great new leads. There's a woman who used to work in the dry cleaners on Guadalupe who claimed—**

I shove my phone back in my pocket, because Spike has rolled up to me, the pretty colored lights of the rink swimming across his face. Everyone else is on the floor, Alice wobbling along.

Spike sees me looking at her.

"Did you tell her yet?"

"No," I say. "I will. And, just so you know, I blame you."

He shrugs, lifting his hands. "What can I say? I needed a job for the summer, your mom ran into my dad, he was still upset about the Castle break-in, and here we are."

I haven't told Alice yet that I'll be spending the summer in Whispering Pines, sweating it out on canoes and sleeping in a bag in the forest at Camp Moonglow, the very same camp that Charles Levy gifted to the Pinskys. Nowadays, it's a camp for kids who have "issues," whatever that means. I mean, *I* have issues. I guess I'll fit right in. But my mother says Alice and I need a break from each other and I need to make it up to her. Though I'm totally taking my Remy files.

"At least we'll be together," Spike says.

"That'll be nice."

My face flushes with warmth. *Calm* down, *Adams.*

And then . . . I don't.

"Spike, do you want to go to the movies with me?" I blurt out. "Maybe that Mona Moody retrospective or something?"

"Oh, sure, Iris," he says. "You know I do. I'll tell Neil and Zo—"

"No," I say. "Just, like . . . us."

Something shifts in his eyes. In a good way.

"Just me?"

"Yeah. Just you."

He nods, thinking. "Absolutely. Okay. Yes."

He grins.

"Noice," I say.

I'm just about to glide out onto the rink with Spike when I hear a soft voice behind me say my name.

"Iris?"

I turn around. It's Lilian Levy, blinking under the whirling lights.

"Dear god, child, help me."

It's then that I notice she's wearing roller skates.

"Lilian, what in the hell?" I rush to her side, taking her elbow.

"I couldn't stand it anymore. Holing up in my apartment in New York. Phone off the hook. Press outside. Afraid to talk to anyone because who knows who will turn around and sell what I say to the highest bidder? Honestly, Iris, what am I to do?"

Her eyes behind her red glasses are shiny and distraught.

"My life is a lie," she says sadly.

"No," I say.

"Yes," she says firmly. "It is. So many things have come back to me, things I don't even know how to talk about. That man was so loving to me and yet . . . how could he do what he did?"

I shake my head. "I don't know, Lilian. I truly don't know."

"I was right, though, wasn't I?" she says. "The Kennedy chickens came home to roost."

"You were."

"They took everything from me, those people, that *man,*" she says bitterly. "There's a thorough accounting going on now, through my father's old accounts. It appears Eugene Kennedy was blackmailing him. That's where the money went, I bet. My father took from the company to pay a terrible man to keep his terrible secrets."

"I . . ." This is all very complicated, and I'm not sure I'm up for any more complications tonight.

"Well, here I am," Lilian says. "Here I am. In these skates. I'll probably fall and break the hips I got replaced last fall and wouldn't that be a hoot, I suppose? Help me, Iris. I just want to have some fun. Your mother said you were here."

Carefully and slowly, I lead her to the edge of the rink. "Are you sure?" I ask, before I pull her onto it.

"I suppose if I have to die, it might as well be doing something as patently insane as this, at my age."

She gingerly steps a skate onto the rink. Alice clomps up, weaving back and forth, and grabs Lilian's arm.

"Come on, old woman," she says. "If I can do it, you can do it."

I take Lilian's other elbow and together, the three of us slowly, very slowly, begin to wind our way around the rink, people steering *very* clear of us.

"This isn't so bad," Lilian says.

"Nope," I say. "You just need to get the hang of it. Right, Alice?"

"Speak for yourself, Iris." Alice bends her head close to Lilian's and says, "I'm here because it's the only time I can see Iris. Her mom lets her go to school, here, and the Historical Society now, where she's stuck, what, looking through old boxes? We barely see each other."

"It's interesting, Alice," I say. "I like it. If you'd just pipe down—"

"Don't quibble," Lilian says sternly. "You can make it through life without a girlfriend or a boyfriend and even your parents, sad as that is, but you can't make it without a friend. You both are, for better or worse, my friends. And if that means stumbling around a fetid roller rink and risking death, so be it."

Which is exactly what we do, holding on to each other for dear life.

WHERE TO GET HELP

Though *The Night in Question* is, at heart, a fun book about two teen detectives, there are some very serious issues within this book.

Iris Adams is a child victim of domestic abuse. Her story might be your story, or it might be the story of someone you know. If you or someone you know is living with domestic abuse, or you suspect they might be, here are some resources to help:

CHILDHELP NATIONAL ABUSE HOTLINE
childhelp.org/hotline

THE NATIONAL DOMESTIC VIOLENCE HOTLINE
thehotline.org

No one deserves to experience abuse of any sort for any reason. Domestic violence and relationship violence warning signs are not always evident in the early moments of a relationship. This is the case with Mona Moody and Charles W. Levy. If you feel unsafe in your relationship, please check the National Domestic Violence Hotline for warning signs and resources for help.

TEEN DATING VIOLENCE
teendvmonth.org

If you need to talk to someone, anytime, anywhere, about anything, confidentially:

CRISIS TEXT LINE
crisistextline.org/text-us

ACKNOWLEDGMENTS

Kathleen: Well, Liz, here we are again. Agathas 2.

Liz: Hello, Kathleen. I'm so glad we got to write a second book together!

Kathleen: First, I would like to acknowledge that since Liz and I are across the country from each other, we have to write these books via Facetime and she has now seen me without makeup more times than anyone in my life, and yet she is still my friend and cowriter. Thank you, Liz, for not rejecting my morning face!

Liz: Kathleen, you are *beautiful,* with or without makeup. Thank you for writing with me again. And thank you to all the readers of book 1 for loving our girls so much and sending us messages about how excited you are about a second book!

Kathleen: (Technically, Liz is getting paid to tell me I'm beautiful, but I'll take it.) *Yes,* we were so lucky to be able to write *The Night in Question* and to take Alice and Iris into yet another mystery, and that's thanks to the readers of *The Agathas* and also, you know, the fine folks at our publishing house, like—

Liz: —our illustrious editors, Krista Marino and Lydia Gregovic, who helped us enormously with this tricky book and are so supportive, always. We also want to thank our publisher, Beverly Horowitz, who offered endless encouragement, and the whole publicity and marketing team, including Mary McCue, Kelly McGauley, and Jenn Inzetta, whose excitement about the series has been thrilling; Barbara Marcus; Casey Moses; Tamar Schwartz; Colleen Fellingham; and Ken Crossland.

Kathleen: We can write books, but it takes a whole team to shape them, dress them, feed them, and send them out into the world, and we're lucky to have great people behind Alice and Iris. Now let's talk about our fights. Because that's what people really want to know about. *The hot goss.*

Liz: I could never fight with you, Kathleen! [Proceeds to have Alice throw a phone at Iris's head on the page.]

Kathleen: LET'S NOT FORGET THE POST-IT NOTE INCIDENT, LIZ (iykyk).

Liz: Well, Kathleen, you managed to get back at me by almost MURDERING ALICE. (Jkjk but she did fall out of a treehouse, which . . . as Alice would say, RUDE.)

Kathleen: I think it's important to work out real-life issues in fiction. It's kind of my thing.

Liz: Oh, I know. Which leads me to our next round of thanks—to our wonderful agents. Andrea, thank you for always being there to talk me down when I'm getting super stressed about whatever-it-might-be in publishing, and for being so patient and level-headed. I'm so lucky to have you on my team!

Kathleen: Andrea is awesome! I'm lucky to have Julie Stevenson, who makes me laugh and always tells it to me like it is. She's a gem, I tell you.

Kathleen: Also, Liz, what a joy to write another Agathas mystery with you. We started cooking this up two years ago, combining our love for mystery, crime, and Old Hollywood into one magnificent, glamorous, complicated cake. Mona Moody!

Liz: I love Mona Moody. I'm so glad we got to delve into her life a little bit.

Kathleen: I have so many biographies of Old Hollywood stars, like Marilyn Monroe and Jean Harlow (I used to have a six-foot-tall poster of Marilyn in my room as a teen), and wow, did I love sketching out and researching Mona with you.

Liz: Oh, yes, we definitely had a great time figuring out everything Mona Moody related (except, maybe, figuring out the math behind the dates. I am not, and will never be, a math person). *The Night in Question* is, without a doubt, the most complicated book I've ever written, so I also want to thank my husband and child for putting up with all my hair-pulling while we were drafting it. I love you both very much.

Kathleen: Math is hard! When you have characters trying to solve two mysteries seventy-four years apart, and there are many, shall we say, elderly suspects still alive, math happens. I'm sorry. My kids wanted nothing to do with me while I was writing this book, but I love them anyway. They're my heroes.

Liz: Spending more time with Alice Ogilvie is something I'll always be grateful for. Her growth from a spoiled, self-centered (shall I say it?) brat at the beginning of book 1 to someone who actually cares about others was a joy to write. Her parents appear on the page more in *The Night in Question,* and developing her relationship with them (for better or worse) made me love her character even more.

Kathleen: Alice has evolved! Iris, not so much, heh. I still love their dynamic of good detective, bad detective and that they play off each other's personalities. It's my favorite part of writing these books with you, because friendships get rocky sometimes. It's not always smooth sailing. Speaking of friendships, one of the people we consulted for both books about medical issues passed away this summer. My friend Dr. Justin Cetas, neurosurgeon extraordinaire and fabulous soul, always had time to answer our questions about blunt force trauma and medical comas, and even at one point suggested we change one weapon from a (redacted) to a (redacted) because it seemed more "old-timey mystery," and he was right. I miss him, and I think he would have gotten a real kick out of us naming Mrs. Cetas, the Castle Cove historian, after him.

Liz: I love that Neil and his mom have that name. Thank you also (and again) to Amy Salley, for your invaluable knowledge of the legal system and all the help you've given us through the course of these books (we have to know what these people would be charged with in real life!).

Kathleen: Law, like math, is hard. Glad other people can sort it out for us.

Liz: Indeed it is. Also, thanks to our writer friends (JEFF BISHOP—there, are you happy??), who always are there when we want to moan and complain about how hard it is to write a book (it's SO HARD, trust me). And to my family, for everything.

Kathleen: I have a sturdy and witty group of people who talk writing and movies and books with me on a regular basis and keep me on track, like Jeff Giles, Karen McManus, Erin Hahn, Lygia Day Penaflor, and Holly Vanderhaar. Also the person who walks by my house every day and sees me watering my lawn and always says, "Shouldn't you be writing your book, bro?" You know who you are! Thank you, sidewalk person.

Liz: Is it my turn? Sorry, I was making a TikTok . . .

Kathleen: Never change, Liz. Never change.

Liz: If anyone wants to follow me on TikTok, my name is @LzLwsn—just saying. And now for the most important acknowledgment: thank you to my cats. You inspired us to add Alice's new cat, who she obviously secretly loves.

Kathleen: LIZ, YOU FORGOT TO NAME ALICE'S CAT.

Liz: Clearly, its (her?) name is Jane. After Miss Marple. Alice would approve.

Kathleen: Save it for book 3, Liz.

Liz: To end: as Agatha Christie once said, "Nothing turns out quite in the way that you thought it would when you are sketching out notes for the first chapter, or walking about muttering to yourself and seeing a story unroll." That is true for this book, and I'm so glad we spent the time working on this story and figured out what it really needed. We hope readers everywhere love it as much as we do.

ABOUT THE AUTHORS

Kathleen Glasgow is the #1 *New York Times* bestselling author of *Girl in Pieces, How to Make Friends with the Dark,* and *You'd Be Home Now,* as well as the *New York Times* bestseller *The Agathas* and its sequel, *The Night in Question,* cowritten with Liz Lawson. She lives and writes in Tucson, Arizona.

kathleenglasgowbooks.com

Liz Lawson is the *New York Times* bestselling author of *The Agathas* (with Kathleen Glasgow) and *The Lucky Ones.* Liz lives with her family and two *very* bratty cats.

lizlawsonauthor.com

WITHDRAWN

No longer the property of the
Boston Public Library.
Sale of this material benefits the Library